ABENI'S SONG

MORE BY P. DJÈLÍ CLARK
FROM TOR PUBLISHING GROUP

BOOKS FOR ADULTS

NOVELS

A Master of Djinn

NOVELLAS

Ring Shout
The Haunting of Tram Car 015
The Black God's Drums

ABENI'S SONG

P. DJÈLÍ CLARK

STARSCAPE

TOR PUBLISHING GROUP
NEW YORK

ABENI'S SONG

A Starscape Book
Published by Tom Doherty Associates / Tor Publishing Group
120 Broadway
New York, NY 10271

www.tor-forge.com

Tor® is a registered trademark of Macmillan Publishing Group, LLC.

Library of Congress Cataloging-in-Publication Data

Names: Clark, P. Djèlí, author.
Title: Abeni's song / P. Djèlí Clark.
Description: First edition. | New York : Starscape. Tor Publishing Group, 2023. | Series: Abeni's song ; 1 |
Identifiers: LCCN 2023007716 (print) | LCCN 2023007717 (ebook) | ISBN 9781250825827 (hardcover) | ISBN 9781250825834 (ebook)
Subjects: CYAC: Fantasy. | Magic—Fiction. | Adventure and adventurers—Fiction. | LCGFT: Fantasy fiction. | Action and adventure fiction. | Novels.
Classification: LCC PZ7.1.C577 Ab 2023 (print) | LCC PZ7.1.C577 (ebook) | DDC [Fic]—dc23
LC record available at https://lccn.loc.gov/2023007716
LC ebook record available at https://lccn.loc.gov/2023007717

Our books may be purchased in bulk for promotional, educational, or business use. Please contact your local bookseller or the Macmillan Corporate and Premium Sales Department at 1-800-221-7945, extension 5442, or by email at MacmillanSpecialMarkets@macmillan.com.

First Edition: 2023

Printed in the United States of America

0 9 8 7 6 5 4 3 2 1

For Nia & Nya, who have always liked my stories

PART I

CHAPTER ONE

THE SONG

Damju awoke to the song.

It was a *beautiful* song.

It danced in her head—coming from everywhere, all at once. She sat up, opening her eyes to a familiar world of light and shapes. It was the way she saw, which had always been different from others. It was still night. Night was dull. Not like daytime that glowed. And there were night's sounds that lulled her to sleep—chirping crickets, night birds, and howling animals that shared their small valley.

She tilted her head to listen. Only there wasn't any of that now. There was only quiet—like someone had told the world to hush. There was just the song. Beautiful and strange, filling up her thoughts.

But where was it coming from? Who would be playing music so late? Standing, she ran fingers along the cracked mud walls of her home, careful not to stumble over her mother—who lay sleeping. She reached down to put a hand to where her two brothers should have been, but there was only emptiness.

Not long ago Damju could walk easily under calabash bottles hanging from their ceiling. But she'd seen almost twelve harvests now and the bottles grazed her hair as she moved to the door. She pushed through it and outside.

The night air was warm and still strangely quiet. But she wasn't alone. She could just make out the shapes of people moving along narrow moonlit streets. Some were small. Others her height. All children, she realized in surprise. She frowned. What could they be doing? She reached out, catching someone's arm.

"Wait! What's happening?"

A breathless reply came. "The song, Damju! Can't you hear it? Can't you see—Oh! I'm sorry!"

Damju recognized the voice. Ewa, who always seemed to forget Damju saw differently. "I hear it. But what do you see?" How did you see a song?

Ewa fumbled. Her voice was strange—like someone still half asleep. "I can't explain. But the song shows you things. Beautiful things!"

Damju was confused. A song that showed you things?

"Where are all of you going?"

"To find the song, of course," Ewa answered. "Just like you."

"What? I'm not—" She stopped, realizing her feet were moving! But when had she started walking? The song! She could feel it pulling at her, urging her on. Ewa shrugged away, leaving Damju between other children, all marching forward like a flowing river.

Fighting, she made her feet stop, planting them firm in the middle of the street as others pushed past. "Kambo! Dawda!" she called to her brothers. They had to be out here. But how long ago had they left home? How far might they have gone? The thought made her panic, and she shouted their names over and over into the night.

"Damju!" Someone grabbed her. Her brother! She clutched on to him.

"Kambo! Where's Dawda?"

"Right here," her other brother answered.

Damju breathed in relief. "I thought you were gone."

"We almost were," Dawda snickered. "Came back when we heard you calling after us like a loud goat!"

Dawda was always the one to make jokes. For once, Damju didn't laugh.

"This song, it isn't right! We have to—"

"It's okay, Damju," Kambo said.

"The song's showed us what's out there," Dawda added.

"What? What did it show you?"

"Baba!" Kambo said. "He's waiting for us!"

Damju stared up at the shape of her brother's face, too stunned to answer. Other children passed by, and they were now the only ones just standing. Baba? Their father was gone. He'd died when she was small. Her brothers remembered him better than she did, but he was gone all the same. Did ghosts walk this night?

"I know how it sounds," Dawda said. "But we saw him, Damju. Calling us."

Something Ewa said came back. The song showed you things—beautiful things.

She shook her head. "No! It's not real! The song! It's showing you what you want to see. It must want you to—!"

"It's fine, Damju," Kambo assured her, his voice like Ewa's now—half asleep. "We'll come back, with baba."

"No, don't go!" But they were already gone, and her hands clutched at other children who pushed forward. One by one, they marched past the village's low stone walls, chasing what the song showed them, the things Damju couldn't see.

Somewhere in the valley came another curious sound. A woman's voice. Damju thought the woman might be crying, and she fought to hear the words above the song.

The children. He has taken the children. Taken them from me. The children, the Children of Night . . .

When everyone had gone, she stood alone, until the song and the voice faded away.

CHAPTER TWO

FESTIVAL

Somewhere very far away, Abeni woke up with a wide-mouthed yawn.

She'd been dreaming. Of a song, of all things.

But the dream was already getting fuzzy, the way dreams did. And the song and odd voice became distant echoes. Soon she couldn't remember what they sounded like at all. Then she forgot entirely.

Today is my birthday.

Abeni smiled, taking a long stretch and wriggling her toes. Sunlight crept into her home through slight spaces in the straw roof, bringing the heat of the day to come with it. It was early, but already she could hear the familiar sounds of morning.

Chok-a-chok-chok-a-chok.

Her mother pounding yam outside. That meant her aunts were here. And that she'd overslept! Sitting up abruptly from her sleeping mat, she kissed the back of her teeth and shook her herself fully awake—so that her plaited hair swung from side to side. How could she oversleep on *today* of all days!

"Abeni!" her mother called from outside. "Are you really still sleeping?"

"Um, no!" she croaked. Swallowing, she found her voice. "I mean, no, mama!"

Her mother kissed the back of her teeth, the way she did when she didn't quite believe you. "Well, I hope you're dressed! It's almost time to go!"

Dressed? Abeni looked down to her plain brown tunic and

made a face. This wouldn't do, not for today. She glanced at a pile of her clothes scattered in a corner. They wouldn't do either. She jumped up, meaning to run, then slipped on her sleeping mat, and landed with a thud.

"Abeni?" her mother called. "What's all that noise? What's going on in there?"

"Nothing, mama!" she called back, hopping on one foot while nursing a stubbed toe—and glaring at the sleeping mat. This wasn't how this morning was supposed to go!

Hurrying, she ran from her room. Her father had built their house before she was born, making it older than her. It had one long circular wall that was smooth to the touch and smelled of old earth. Smaller walls divided the house into separate parts. She passed through the cooking chamber where her mother's planting tools hung beside her father's hunting weapons. Reaching her parents' chamber, she found a bundle of neatly folded cloths with colorful prints. Her mother's best wrap skirts—which she was *not* supposed to touch. But she needed something nice for today. Rifling through them, she settled on a bright gold one, with spirals like little red snakes.

"Abeni!" Her mother's voice had *that* tone in it now. "Do I have to come in there and get you?"

"No, mama! Just a moment!"

Finding a large jug of water, she checked her reflection. She'd thought that today, her twelfth birthday, her face would seem different—more grown. But it looked the same as the day before, and the one before that. Brown eyes and a dark brown face, with a fleshy nose above lips people claimed made it look like she was pouting. Her tight coils of black hair had been parted down the middle and plaited into thin hanging braids that she could swing back and forth. That had taken her aunts *hours* to finish yesterday. They hadn't done it too tight, but it still hurt a bit if she raised her eyebrows.

Opening her mouth, she examined her teeth to see if they'd grown. Nope. Still the same size, even the same overbite. Altogether, she looked very much . . . the same. But it *was* her birthday. She *was* older. That was all that mattered.

"Abeni! Did you fall back asleep, girl?"

She broke away from her reflection. "I'm awake!" No time for a long bath. Wriggling out of her tunic, she scrubbed and dried quickly, wrapping the gold cloth about her. She tucked it in here and there—just right to make it stay on. She wasn't any taller than any other girl her age in the village, but her mother and aunts fretted at her skinniness. Her father teased he'd have to tie rocks to her feet to make sure a strong breeze didn't carry her away. She didn't find that funny.

She looked down with a smile. The cloth was nice as a skirt on her mother, but as a dress it looked *wonderful* on her. Still, it was missing something. Rifling through more of her mother's things, she found a set of necklaces—settling on one with sparkling green and red stones and snatching up the matching pieces nearby.

As she fitted on the jewelry her eyes caught sight of a small soapstone jar carved like a frog—where her mother kept her sweet oils. Opening the jar, she scooped out a handful and rubbed it everywhere. Satisfied, she slipped into her favorite red-brown sandals and stopped to admire herself. Or tried to.

"ABENI! If you're not out here by the time I count to—!"

She was out the door before her mother even finished the sentence.

Her village was alive. Everywhere were other rounded houses like her own, their brown straw roofs today decorated with colorful flowers and strips of bright cloth. People moved about in the streets, some with arms full, others holding clay jars atop their heads—their voices louder than usual in the early morning.

"Eh! Look here. The princess has awakened to greet us!"

Abeni looked to see her father smiling at her. He wore a white kilt that fell to his feet, alongside strips of leather with black and red designs that hung from his waist. His shoulders and chest were bare, except for fresh spirals of white chalk.

"Akanyo, I didn't know you were hosting the daughter of a chief," the man who painted her father's skin added.

"That must be it," her father said as if surprised. "The daughter of a chief!"

The two men stopped to give her a deep bow.

Abeni rolled her eyes but smiled. Her Uncle Tawayo and her father loved to joke. The two were the strongest men in the village, and everyone respected them as great hunters. Today they were dressed almost exactly alike. Even their hair was the same, shaved on all sides except for a flat patch at the top.

"What do you say, Afayo?" Her father nudged her brother. "Doesn't your sister look like a chief's daughter?"

Her brother looked up from where he sat, decorating a long spear with bits of rope and beads. He wore his hair just like the two men, though he still looked like a boy. He gazed lazily at her dress before turning back with a shrug. "She looks okay."

Abeni frowned. Okay? She simply looked *okay*? Her brother had three more harvests than her, but they'd always been close. Now he was all puffed up with himself, keeping to other older boys who soon would be counted as men. Well not today!

She ran over and tackled him, seeking the tickle spots she knew all too well. He cried out but it was too late. Between his protests, he laughed, until finally managing to twist away.

"Ayiee! You crazy little monster! Okay! Okay! You look nice!"

"How nice?" she asked, wriggling her fingers in threat.

"Very nice! Very nice!" He held up hands to ward her off. Pausing, he sniffed the air and wrinkled his nose, smelling the sweet oil. "But the chief's daughter stinks!"

She stuck out her tongue. He made a face back.

"It certainly took the chief's daughter long enough to come out here! And it seems the two of us have the same tastes."

Abeni turned at her mother's voice. She was using a long wooden pestle-stick to pound the contents of a wide wooden bowl. A green skirt with leaf patterns stretched to her ankles and a bright white fabric wrapped about her chest. At the moment, she eyed her daughter's dress with interest.

"I thought you might like it?" Abeni asked sheepishly.

Her mother raised an eyebrow, never stopping her pounding. It was hard to tell what she was thinking when she made that face. It always made Abeni squirm. She had tried to perfect it herself, but never seemed to get it quite right.

"Let the girl be, Yayawi," a short plump woman beside her mother chided. "How can the branch of a tree not resemble its roots?"

"Eh yes, Yayawi," another chimed in. "She's growing more into your face each day. Might as well grow into some of your clothes too."

Both women laughed. Her mother's older sisters—Aunt Awami and Aunt Awomi. They were twins. Not only did they look alike, down to their round moon faces and dimples, they thought alike and sometimes finished each other's sentences. They were her favorite aunts. They each gave her knowing winks, and she returned them back.

Everyone claimed she looked just like her mother—the same nose, high cheeks, round eyes, and those lips made for pouting. But where Abeni was gangly her mother was solid, with strong arms and legs. Not as stout as her sisters, whose wide hips swayed when they walked. But she certainly wasn't in danger of being carried away by a strong wind.

"Well can she help her mother pound yam? I was calling you awake to get you to help us. Or is the princess too good for that?"

Abeni beamed, matching her mother's growing smile. She bounded over to the large bowl that stood to her waist, peering down at the orange half mashed bits.

"Here, have mine." Her Aunt Awami handed over a pestle, showing Abeni how to grasp the long wooden stick properly. She'd often watched her mother pound yam, but they'd never asked her to take part. "Hold it with both hands, strong."

Abeni nodded, excited. When her mother brought down her

pestle, she waited to hear her Aunt Awomi's fall before letting her own drop in rhythm.

Chok-a-chok-a-chok.

Behind her, Aunt Awami sang about a woman who stole her neighbor's yam. Only it was magic and would jump when she struck it. Aunt Awami called out, and they answered like the frustrated woman, "Yam stop jumping in my bowl! Yam stop jumping in my bowl!" When they finished, the yams were an orangey mush. Abeni let out a breath. Her arms were tired!

"Wearing my clothes and now pounding yam," her mother remarked. "My little rain bringer is soon going to outgrow me." There was a sadness in her voice, though Abeni couldn't imagine why.

"Eh!" her mother cried, wrinkling her nose. "Abeni! Did you take a swim in my sweet oil?" Her brother barked a laugh. Abeni quickly changed subjects.

"Today is my birthday!" she reminded.

Her mother frowned, but her voice softened. "Yes, it is. Have I ever told you about the day you were born?"

Abeni groaned. Just about a hundred times.

"Don't be like that. It used to be your favorite story."

When she was little. She was twelve now!

"I'd like to hear it!" her brother called with a grin.

Abeni turned and crossed her eyes at him. He made a sillier face back.

"Yes," her mother murmured, as if just remembering. "It had been a very dry season right before you were born, and the village saw little rain."

"I remember that time," Uncle Tawayo added. "There were fires in the forest because it was so hot. All the animals ran off and we had little to hunt. Even the river began to dry up."

"The whole village worried," Aunt Awami said, scooping mashed yam out of the pounding bowl and into a large clay pot. "Every day we asked the spirits for rain."

"And you were in my belly," her mother added, smiling.

"That is because you knew how hot it was!" her father said. Everyone laughed and Abeni winced. *Please* let this story be over.

"Your mother's belly was big like a melon with you," Aunt Awomi said, helping scoop yam. "We took her to the healer to see if he could find a way to make you come out. But he didn't know what to do, so he sent your father to see *the old woman*."

She said the last words almost as a whisper. The old woman. Abeni didn't know her real name because that was all anyone called her. The other children said she was a witch, and grown-ups whispered the same. Whoever she was, she lived by herself in the forest and hadn't come to the village since before Abeni was born.

"What was it the old woman told you to do, Akanyo?" Uncle Tawayo teased.

Her father made a face behind his beard. "Beat a drum and dance around Yayawi at night." Uncle Tawayo bellowed with laughter.

"Your father beat that drum and danced very well," her mother said, giving him a teasing wink. Uncle Tawayo laughed even harder. "And it must have worked because that night two things happened—it rained, and you decided it was time to be born."

"You were almost as big a talk around the village as the rains," Aunt Awami said.

"And that's how I got my name," Abeni finished so they could get to the end.

"Yes," her mother said. "Abeni, 'we asked for her, and behold she came.' When the first harvest of those rains came, the village decided that day would be your true birthday, for what your luck brought us. And that is why at every Harvest Festival everyone calls you little rain bringer."

Abeni smiled despite herself. Okay, so she did like *that* part of the story.

"And how many harvests has it been now, Yayawi?" Aunt Awomi asked.

"Twelve," her mother answered.

"So many?" Aunt Awami exclaimed. She came over to pinch Abeni's cheeks. "Just one more and you'll be ready to take your first rites at Festival."

"I'll be a woman!" Abeni proclaimed. Maybe then she could just be *rain bringer*, and they could leave out the *little*. Also, they'd stop pinching her cheeks! The three women burst into laughter, and she frowned. What was so funny?

Her mother smiled. "You won't be quite a woman, little rain bringer. There are more rites to follow and you've got some growing to do yet. But you'll be on your way."

"Not if I can help it!" Her father bent down, bringing his forehead to touch hers, and they both smiled wide at each other. Everyone said she had her father's smile, so big and bright that it made others do the same. "Don't try to grow so fast, little rain bringer. Or I'll take out my hunting spear and chase away any little man with a boy's face who comes asking to marry you!"

Her brother snickered. And Abeni felt her face grow hot. Why were they so intent on embarrassing her?

"Going to have to fatten her up some before then, Akanyo," Aunt Awami taunted, patting her hips. "Those young men are going to want something more to hold on to."

Please, Abeni thought, *make them stop!* She was saved by the sound of someone approaching. She turned to see a girl her age running up and waving excitedly.

"Fomi!" Abeni called.

Fomi was her best friend, though in some ways the two couldn't be more different. Where Abeni was gangly, Fomi was stout—and stronger than some boys their age. Where Abeni was quiet, Fomi could be loud—very, very loud. And where Abeni tried to avoid trouble—most of the time—Fomi loved getting into mischief. That was probably why they were such good friends. Fomi made her life more exciting. Abeni made hers a little less reckless. And today, they had plans.

"Good morning, Fomi," her mother greeted her. "How are your sisters coming with that pepper soup?" Fomi's father had three wives, and between them she counted at least ten sisters! Whenever there was a Festival, they cooked up the biggest pot of soup for everyone to share.

"Good morning, Auntie Yayawi," Fomi answered with a deep bow. "They're almost finished."

"And you aren't helping?"

Fomi screwed up her face. "I scaled and cut fish all yesterday and this morning. I've helped enough!" The girl hated anything to do with fish, which was odd, since her family were the best fishers in the village. "I was hoping Abeni and I could look around before Festival?"

"Oh yes! Can I go, mama?"

"But you always help me bring the food to Festival," her mother said.

"Yes. But I could do something different this time. Maybe?"

Her mother opened her mouth to say something else, but Aunt Awami spoke first. "Oh, let the child be, Yayawi. We'll help you bring the food."

"That's right," Aunt Awomi joined in. "You can't expect her to keep clutching at your skirts. She's not a little girl anymore."

Whatever her mother had been about to say seemed to evaporate on her lips. "I suppose she isn't. Well, the two of you go on then." Her eyes narrowed. "And you won't be off getting into any trouble."

The two girls exchanged a hurried glance.

"Oh no, Auntie Yayawi," Fomi assured.

"Definitely not," Abeni added.

"No way," they both said together.

◎　◎　◎

"Did your mother get you that dress for your birthday?" Fomi asked as they walked.

Abeni smirked, showing off the skirt. "Sort of . . ."

"You're so lucky! On my birthday, there's no Harvest Festival. Even with three mothers, all I get are smelly, scaly fish! Blech! I wish someone had gone to see a witch before I was born."

"She's just an old woman," Abeni said.

Fomi shook her head. "Pretty certain she's a witch. Ever gone to see her?"

"No!" Abeni replied in alarm. "Why would I do that?"

Fomi put on a croaking witch voice. "One day, little rain bringer, I'll come back to take the one that got away!" Abeni pretended to shriek and the two laughed, making their way through the bustling village, where the sounds of drums and songs were beginning to fill the morning air. With Fomi taking the lead, they stuck greedy fingers into cooking pots, snuck away with small fruits, sweetened porridge, and other treats. They even harassed some practicing stilt walkers. A few people threatened to tell their families. But neither girl paid them much attention. It was Festival; no one was getting punished today.

"There it is!" Fomi pointed, as they finished off some fried yam they'd snatched off a plate. The two girls stopped at a walled enclosure painted in colorful symbols. From the other side they could hear people chanting and calling out. This was their destination.

"How are we going to get in?" Fomi whispered, eyeing two big women who stood guard at a doorway.

Not that way, for sure. Abeni motioned to a space near the back of the enclosure. "There. We can peek over the wall."

Fomi shielded her eyes from the sun, glancing up as they approached. "We can't climb that." True. The wall was smooth all around. There was nothing to hold on to.

"One of us can just get on the other's shoulders," Abeni offered.

Fomi stared flatly. "You mean *you* can get on my shoulders."

Abeni shrugged. "You're the strong one. I'll be quick. Promise."

Fomi sighed, motioning for her to hop up. "Surprised you came up with this idea." She grunted as Abeni climbed onto her back. "Usually that's what I do!"

"This is important," Abeni said, balancing on her friend's shoulders, then added hastily, "Not that what you do isn't. Just, well . . . this one I wanted to do." It was why she'd arranged for Fomi to arrive, to get her away from being her mother's helper, as she usually was each Festival. She had to lift up on her toes, but she managed to get the top of her head just over the wall's edge to see inside the enclosure.

It was a big wide empty space. This was where the village wrestlers and warriors practiced—trampling the earthen ground. But today, it was filled with women. And girls. One woman stood out, wearing a long blue and yellow dress. Her face was painted in similar colors and covered in white dots, while a matching cloth wrapped her hair. She danced and sang, holding a bushy tree branch over her head with leaves painted gold. A circle of girls knelt before her, each dressed much the same, as she touched the bushy branch across their shoulders.

Abeni's eyes rounded as she took it in. This was what they had come to see. These girls were completing their first rites on the path to womanhood. Here they would be tested, learn secrets, and be given new names. They would even start wearing their hair different. When it was done, they would be presented to the village. Next harvest it would be her and Fomi in the enclosure. There were all sorts of stories of the things they would have to do and endure. She wanted to see for herself. So, when it was their turn, they'd be ready!

"What are you seeing?" Fomi whispered. "What's happening?"

"All kinds of stuff!" Abeni whispered back.

"What kind of stuff? I want to see stuff! Oh! Ewowo!"

Abeni frowned. "Did you just say Ewowo?"

"No! I said *Ekwolo*! Coming this way!"

Ekwolo! Abeni spun her head around. Sure enough, walking towards them was a group of boys. Two were Adwe and Danwe, sons of the village's blacksmith. But the one Fomi was talking about, the one who caught her eyes, was Ekwolo.

Ekwolo was only a short season older than her. But he was already a well-known name in the village. Fast for his age, he bested all the other boys in games. By the next harvest season, he would be completing his first rites too. Abeni had known him most of her life and they'd played together since they were young. So she wasn't certain when the sight of him had started making her stomach flutter and her mouth go dry. It was an odd sensation that made her excited and nervous all at once.

"Abeni," he called out, jogging over. She lifted a hand to wave, forgetting that it was helping her balance. Her feet went out from under her, and she tumbled down atop Fomi, who let out a yelp! The two managed to scramble to their feet, with Abeni's face burning. Her eyes met Ekwolo, who laughed lightly as he reached them.

"Trying to see some first rites?" he asked, winking.

Abeni opened her mouth to deny it, but he only smiled. "We were just trying to do the same thing." He turned to his companions. "Should have thought about hopping on your shoulders, Danwe!" His attention fixed back on her. "I like your dress. You look nice."

Abeni blushed at the compliment. "Thank you. So do you. Your clothes, I mean . . . not your dress." *Be quiet now!* a voice in her head said. Fomi rolled her eyes, shaking her head. This wasn't the first time Abeni had embarrassed herself like this.

"Enjoying your birthday?" Ekwolo asked.

"So far," she said. He actually remembered! "Are you? The Harvest Festival, I mean, not my birthday." *Be quiet!* the voice in her head warned again. But her mouth seemed to have a mind of its own. "I don't expect you to enjoy my birthday. I mean, you have your own birthday." *Be quiet! Be quiet! Be quiet!* The voice was pleading now. Clamping her mouth shut she did just that, her cheeks heating as Ekwolo smiled wider. She must have sounded crazier than the village's timekeeper, who lived out near the spirit rocks and claimed he could talk to birds.

"The morning sun has your tongue doing fits, Abeni," Danwe teased.

Before she could respond, Fomi was doing so for her.

"You be quiet, stork-legs! No one's talking to you!"

Danwe scowled, rounding on the shorter girl. He did have thin legs that looked too long for his body. People said he'd grow into them, but he hated any reminder.

"I thought I smelled fish," he sneered. "Shouldn't you be off scaling some?"

"It would take a big old *stork* to smell some fish, wouldn't it?" Fomi barked back.

Abeni snorted. Fomi was always ready to catch her when she stumbled. Ekwolo laughed, patting his friend on the shoulder.

"Easy, Danwe, easy," he said. "Quiet down before someone comes back and sees us, eh?" His eyes returned to Abeni. "We're heading to watch your father and uncle practice the warrior dance!" At the mention the other boys began chattering eagerly.

Her father and uncle were not only the village's best hunters; they were also its best warriors. Ekwolo and his friends could spend whole mornings watching the two spar with swords or practice with shields and spears. She'd seen her father and uncle practice lots of times. And while it was impressive, she didn't understand the fascination. The closest thing to a battle she'd ever heard of had been between some goat herders and those from a nearby village. Only old people with no teeth even remembered it. From what she understood the battle mostly consisted of men and boys beating each other with herding sticks. It all ended when their fed-up goats began scattering away. And the herders had to go off chasing them. Since the Great Goat War there'd been nothing similar. Nothing much happened here in the Jembe forest. Her village was one of maybe a dozen that she knew of that called the forest home. Life here was pretty uneventful. People traded. Sometimes they argued over hunting grounds or water. But they didn't fight.

Before she could say anything else a cry rang out.

They all jumped, and for a moment Abeni feared they'd been caught. But no one was coming for them. Instead, there was chanting. They all walked hurriedly to the front of the enclosure to see what the matter was, just as the doors began to open. The woman in the long blue and yellow dress came out chanting and dancing while holding the bushy tree branch with gold leaves over her head. Behind her trailed the girls in pairs of twos, each copying her dance. Everyone stopped to watch them pass and Abeni felt a pang of envy. Next Festival, this would be them.

"Abeni!"

The call took her by surprise. It came from one of the dancing girls. Breaking from her companions, she ran over, beaming. With her painted face, it took Abeni a moment to recognize her. But when she did, she grimaced.

"Sowoke," she said, forcing a smile.

Sowoke was the daughter of the village's most prosperous trader. She had seen one more harvest than either Abeni or Fomi, and never missed the chance to remind them.

"I've completed my first ritual!" she exclaimed.

"That's good, Sowoke," Abeni replied. "I'm happy for you."

"Thank you," she said, looking Abeni over. "Such a pretty dress! For your birthday? I think my mother has a skirt just like it."

Abeni's smile tightened.

"Do you like mine?" Sowoke asked. She lifted the sides of her deep blue dress for Abeni to see. Of course, it was beautiful—with intricate gold patterns. "And these?" She pointed to a matching silver necklace and wrist pieces. "Father brought them from a trader who says they came from far outside the forest. The people who make them live in a dry hot place, with no trees or bushes or rivers at all. Can you believe that? He says it's called a 'desert' and—"

"I don't believe it," Fomi broke in.

Sowoke stopped and made a face as if she'd eaten some sour fruit. In her eyes Fomi's family of fishers barely needed to be acknowledged or spoken to.

"Don't believe what?" she asked, irritated at being cut off.

"In that 'desert' or whatever," Fomi answered. "There's no such place."

Sowoke's eyes narrowed. "Are you calling my father a liar, fisher girl?"

Fomi only shrugged. "Either that or someone who easily believes stories. That stuff probably came from some village right here in the forest." She looked the older girl up and down and sniffed. "I hope he didn't trade away too much for it."

Sowoke was scowling now. She stood her full height and seemed on the verge of telling Fomi off when suddenly she stopped and let out a long breath. "Believe whatever you want. I don't have time to play children's games. I'm on my way to being a woman now. One day, you'll understand." She took to smoothing down her dress and held her head up high.

Before either Abeni or Fomi could respond, she turned to the boys.

"Adwe, Danwe," she said sweetly. "The two of you look like young warriors!"

The brothers beamed brightly, stumbling over each other to return the compliment. Fomi made a face as if she were going to be sick.

"Ekwolo. You haven't said anything about my dress."

"It looks very nice, Sowoke," he replied calmly.

Abeni bit back a smile. Sowoke was pretty. That was true. But Ekwolo would never make a fool of himself over her, which was more than could be said for his friends. But the girl behaved as if he had showered her with praise.

"Thank you, Ekwolo! You will be there to see me dance at Festival, won't you?"

"Of course. But we have to get going if we want to see the warriors practice." Turning to go, he smiled at Abeni. "I'll see you there, then." With that he and his friends trotted off. Abeni watched them go, disappointed they didn't get to talk longer.

"I think that Ekwolo likes me," Sowoke commented.

The words snapped Abeni's neck sideways. "What makes you say that?"

"Didn't you see the way he was looking at me? And going on about my dress?"

Abeni exchanged a glance with Fomi, who pretended to strangle herself.

"I didn't see that," Abeni said. Her tone was more snappish than she intended, and Sowoke's eyes narrowed, studying Abeni before rounding again.

"You like Ekwolo!" she blurted out, genuine surprise in her voice.

Abeni felt like someone had just slapped her. She opened her mouth to say otherwise but something in Sowoke's gaze saw right through her. *Stupid, stupid!* the voice in her head whispered.

"Oh, that's wonderful!" Sowoke clapped. She leaned close, excited. "Does he know? Are you going to tell him?"

Abeni's face flushed under the questioning.

"Let it alone, Sowoke," Fomi warned.

The older girl flashed Fomi a cold look before smiling at Abeni.

"I didn't mean to upset you. Don't worry. Your secret's safe with me. After all, we're friends." She let out a breath. "Well, I have to get back. See you at Festival!" Then she was gone, leaving Abeni to stare after her.

"That Sowoke," Fomi fumed. "You just wait, we'll get itching root and smear it on all her fancy clothes, or dip her sandals in fish guts . . ." She listed off several more pranks—each more daring than the next. But Abeni shook her head.

"No," she said. Fomi looked ready to protest. But Abeni continued. "It's my birthday. And it's Harvest Festival. Why worry about silly old Sowoke?" She tried to push thoughts of the girl whispering into Ekwolo's ear out of her head. "Besides, next year it'll be our turn to go through first rites—and she won't be able to tell us a thing."

"Fine," Fomi muttered, crossing her arms. "You're right. No pranks on her today. But there's always tomorrow. And I know where to get *lots* of fish guts!"

Abeni laughed and Fomi smiled deviously.

"Now come on. I also know where we can get some sweet

cakes!" With that, her friend broke into a run. Abeni followed, the thought of the cakes dismissing worries from her mind. It was, after all, her birthday. And nothing was going to ruin it.

◉ ◎ ◎

Abeni and Fomi cried out as a dancer in a painted mask of wood and iron reared up in front of them. His face was menacing, with fiery eyes, a scowling down-turned mouth, and sharp teeth. His body swayed to beating drums and clapping chants from the crowd, making the ornaments he wore rattle and shake.

He was a spirit meant to frighten disobedient children and he demanded payment in sweets—his favorite meal. This was the last Harvest Festival he'd be able to go after Abeni and Fomi—before they completed their first rite. And he seemed intent on re-minding the two that they weren't big enough to escape him yet! They quickly answered his demands, throwing morsels into his open bag. Satisfied, he danced away, moving off to harass others.

Abeni and Fomi laughed, watching him go. But he didn't hold their attention long. Harvest Festival was filled with too many sights and sounds to linger in any one place. There were men on stilts who wrapped their bodies in long flowing fabrics, making them appear as giants. Others were covered in straw, strips of bright cloth, or bushy leaves that jumped and shook as they went. There were figures in alligator masks, long-billed birds, and even giant yams! Some had friendly faces; others were horrid and spit fire from their mouths. They were spirits—animal spirits, bush spirits, river spirits, sky spirits, even spirits of what was planted and grown. And they were all here to celebrate the harvest.

Of course, Abeni knew these were just people from her village. But with their masks and costumes, for a short while they *be-came* the spirits. She and Fomi called out to the friendly ones and clutched each other at the sight of the frightening ones. Earlier she had seen her father and uncle, leading the warrior spirits—their faces covered in veils of stringed domed white shells as they jabbed their spears to ward away other bad spirits. During these magical moments, the village became a place where spirits jumped, and sang and danced.

It was well into the day and the sun beat down on them all from above in a clear blue sky. But there was too much excitement for anyone to complain. And so much food! The village's harvest was laid out on a large straw mat that seemed to stretch on forever. Families had prepared their best meals to share pepper soup and smoked fish, yam porridge and moin-moin, spicy red rice and boiled quail eggs, goat meat stew and chicken stew, mashed plantain and grated coconut wrapped in steaming banana leaves, and so much more. She and Fomi stuffed their mouths until their bellies were near bursting. And things were far from over. When the sun set, masked dancers swathed in colors that glowed in the dark would perform in front of raging fires. All the houses had been painted with symbols and patterns that would shine just as bright. It would make their village truly look like the land of spirits!

Abeni was licking the gooey bits of a sweet yellow fruit from her fingers, when Fomi grabbed her and pointed with a gasp at the appearance of new figures. The deep boom of drums announced their arrival, as they moved in a slow dance. All of them were women, dressed in streams of white cloth while their faces were hidden behind red veils with white shells. Atop each of their heads was a wooden carving of snakes, all twisted into each other.

It was the secret women's society, which people claimed had been around since the village's founding. The snakes on their heads represented wisdom, and their faces were hidden like their secrets. Everyone knew it was them who advised the men's council that helped run the village. Abeni watched them quietly as they passed, feeling a tingle of fear and awe. Both her mother and her aunts were members of the society. Someday, hopefully, she would be too.

When one of the veiled women came directly towards her, she backed away hurriedly with the rest of the crowd. Everyone knew they were now filled with powerful magic and not to be touched! But as the woman paused for a moment to dance right before her

Abeni caught a familiar scent—sweet oil, just like what she wore. *Mama*, she thought silently, smiling in recognition. And for the briefest moment beneath that veil, she thought she saw her smile back.

She was so taken by her mother's presence that she didn't notice the drums falter. It was only when the women stopped dancing that she realized something was wrong. There was no more clapping, no more singing or even laughing. Everyone had gone still, looking off in one direction.

Abeni tried her best to get a view. But with all the grown-ups now standing and crowding around, she couldn't see a thing. There was a nudge from Fomi, who pointed to some abandoned stools. Hurrying, the two girls scrambled atop them, standing up on their toes and craning their necks. What Abeni saw sent her eyes wide.

It was a woman. A very old woman.

She leaned on a long piece of twisted and knotted wood she used as a staff. Her shoulders were wrapped in colorful shawls that sat over a long brown dress, while a thick bundle of beads hung from her neck. She had skin dark and brown like the color of earth, making it look as if she'd been plucked right out of the ground. Only her hair stood out: thick and long white locs that fell to her back. She stood there for a long time, the village staring at her while she glowered back from behind piercing dark eyes.

It was Fomi who spoke, her voice a breathless whisper.

"Witch!"

Abeni nodded numbly. It was the witch indeed.

CHAPTER THREE

WITCH

Abeni waited for the odd standoff between her village and the old woman to end. But the two only continued to stare, each seeming to wait for the other to blink. She thought she might yell if no one spoke soon.

But just as she had begun the face-off, the old woman ended it. Her eyes gave one last sweep across the village before making a loud *humph!* Without another word, she hiked up her long dress and started walking forward. No one got in her way—everyone moving quickly to let her pass. It wasn't hard to tell where she was going, because her eyes were fixed on the large round building ahead.

The great meetinghouse—where the grown-ups and leaders of the village met to discuss important things. The old woman stalked right towards it, never slowing, and walked inside to disappear from sight. For a long moment, everyone stood staring, uncertain what to do.

The Chief Elder of the village was the first to move. A small man, he was wrapped in red and gold cloth with a loop of ivory and blue stones on his balding head. The old woman hadn't said a word to him, or even looked at him. And he was a chief! But he was hurrying now, moving as fast as his legs could take him. The Chief Elder's attendant, a tall younger man named Abo, scurried behind. A low murmuring picked up among the crowd as people began coming out of their masks, revealing lots of worried faces. They all moved towards the meetinghouse, telling older children to head home and to look after their siblings.

Abeni watched it all in confusion. What was happening? Was Harvest Festival over? And what was that old woman doing here anyway? She looked to Fomi, who shrugged and shook her head. Soon the village's streets were cleared of grown-ups, leaving the children standing about. The more obedient scooped up the younger ones, heading back to their homes.

Abeni and Fomi stayed. So did some other children their age. Even that silly Sowoke. Ekwolo was there too, talking with a group of boys. At catching sight of Abeni, he hurried over, the other boys in tow. She moved to meet him, and everyone followed. The small group quickly convened, all speaking at once:

"The witch!"

"Here on Harvest Festival!"

"She looks angry!"

"Do you think she's come to dance?"

"Witches don't dance!"

"Witches dance all the time!"

"Have you ever seen a witch dance?"

"Abeni, do you know anything about the witch?"

Abeni blinked at the question from an older boy. "What? No. Why would—"

"You're little rain bringer," a girl said. "Everyone knows about you and the witch."

There was quiet, as every eye fell on her, waiting. Abeni shifted uncomfortably. "I wasn't born then. We never met."

Someone else started to comment, but Ekwolo broke in. "If she says she doesn't know, she doesn't know. This isn't getting us anywhere."

Abeni gave him a thankful smile. She looked to the meeting-house. The grown-ups who couldn't fit inside stood by the open door, pressed together and listening.

"I wonder what they're saying in there?" she asked aloud, and everyone turned to the meetinghouse. "Wish we could find out."

"Don't be ridiculous," a boy said. "Only grown-ups are allowed in there."

"Not so ridiculous," Ekwolo mused. "I know a place where we can listen."

The other boy gasped. "We'd get in so much trouble if we were caught!"

Ekwolo winked at Abeni and she bit her lip to hide the silly grin on her face. "Better not get caught then."

In a swift turn he was gone, leaving the small group to either stand or catch up. Abeni was already running after him, pulling Fomi along. Most of the others did the same. They skirted between some homes, approaching the meetinghouse from the back where there was no door. A large tree grew up against its mudbrick wall, towering just over the bushy straw roof.

"Up there." Ekwolo pointed. "We get on the roof and there's a place there where you can see in."

"How do you know?" another boy asked doubtfully.

Ekwolo smiled. "Last time it rained, it leaked from there. My brothers are supposed to fix it but haven't yet."

With that he grabbed hold of the tree and began climbing. Three other boys soon followed. When they reached the roof they scrambled atop, inching forward flat on their bellies to look down. There was a brief pause before Ekwolo turned back to them and nodded.

That was all Abeni was waiting for. She was making towards the tree eagerly with Fomi when one of the boys, Danwe, looked down and shook his head.

"This is for men," he declared. "Girls should wait down there."

"Then what are *you* doing up there, you big stork?" Fomi fumed.

Danwe looked ready to shout back but Ekwolo silenced him, motioning them up.

Abeni had grabbed hold of the tree when someone else tugged her arm. Sowoke. She'd almost forgotten the girl was there.

"Are you really climbing that tree like some silly boy?" she scolded.

"I sure am," Abeni retorted, pulling her arm away. "What's wrong? Scared?"

Sowoke frowned. "Don't be childish. I'm supposed to be set-ting a good example for you two. Besides, I don't want to mess up my dress. Father brought it all the way from—"

Abeni didn't hear the rest because she was already scaling the tree. Who had time to listen to that? When she reached the roof, she waited to help Fomi up, and the two of them crawled forward on their bellies to join the four boys. There was some elbowing to get Danwe to make room, but they found a comfortable spot. Somehow, she ended up right next to Ekwolo, and followed his gaze down. The hole in the straw roof was just big enough to make out the entire inside of the meetinghouse.

The round room was crowded. It hardly seemed possible that the entire village—all the grown-ups, anyway—could fit in there at once. The only open space was near the front. There, on a stool, sat the Chief Elder, holding a long wooden staff crowned by a golden bird. Beside him stood the Chief Attendant, Abo, in yel-low robes with a matching cap like a floppy cone.

Between them and everyone else was the old woman.

She sat on a stool too small for her tall body. As she spoke, Abeni leaned in closer.

". . . you were warned," she was saying. "All of you were warned to leave this place. Three times I gave warning. Once to your leader. Once to your holy men. Then again to all of you, in your dreams." She glared out at the crowd. "But none of you listened. You are all still here!"

There was another lengthy silence, the grown-ups reminding Abeni of scolded children.

"What warning could that witch be talking about?" Fomi whispered. "In dreams?"

Abeni shook her head. She'd never heard any warning.

"All I dreamed of last night was some stupid song," Danwe muttered.

Fomi jerked her head to him, and for once wasn't on the verge of scolding. "I think I dreamt about a song last night," she said.

The two were staring at each other in confusion when Ekwolo

broke in. "I had a dream about a song too." He turned to the other boys. "How about you?" They nodded quickly, their eyes going wide. Ekwolo's questioning gaze fell on Abeni.

"I . . . think so," she answered. She'd had strange dreams last night, but until now had forgotten about the song. "Though I can't remember how it went."

"I don't either." Ekwolo frowned. "I couldn't even sing it back to you."

Abeni nodded. It was more like having a memory of a song than the song itself.

"I remember it being beautiful," Fomi murmured. "The most beautiful thing I'd ever heard. It made me feel warm and happy. And that if I didn't stay close to it, I'd be cold. And alone. Forever." The others all nodded, as if trying to conjure the song back up. Abeni did too, remembering the warmth that had filled her up and how badly she'd wanted to follow it.

"It felt real," she said. "Like the song was playing for someone else."

"Where was that place?" Fomi asked. "It didn't *feel* like our village."

"No," Ekwolo agreed. "It felt and looked different. Like someplace far away."

"What about the crying woman?" Danwe asked uncertainly. His eyes darted between them. "Did any of you hear that too?"

Ekwolo nodded slowly. "Something about children. Lost children."

"He has taken the children," Abeni said. "Taken them from me. The Children of Night." She finished to find everyone staring at her. She'd completely forgotten about the crying voice. But now she could hear it clearly, echoing in her head.

"Whoever she was," Fomi whispered, "she sounded so sad. As if she'd lost the most precious thing in the world."

"What's happening?" Danwe asked, his face filled with worry and fear. "How can we all have the same dream? About a place we've never been? Do you think the witch—?"

But he was shushed by Fomi as the grown-ups below started up again.

It was the Chief Elder who broke the quiet. "Asha," he began, putting on a smile that looked painted on. So that was her name, Abeni thought—Asha. "We listened to your warnings and discussed it among ourselves, with great seriousness. We are always grateful for your wisdom—"

"But not now," the old woman cut in. "You come to me when your crops die, when there is sickness you cannot heal, when there is some question to be answered or thing that you need. Yet when I give you this warning, you ignore it!"

"What would you have us do?" the Chief Elder asked, frustrated. "You ask us to abandon our village? We have held this land for generations. Our ancestors founded this village, the mother and father of my mother and father and those that came before them."

The old woman leaned forward, seeming to tower over everyone.

"Do you forget who I am? I knew you before there was a hint of white on your head. I knew your mother and father, *their* mother and father, and those before them. I was here when this village was founded. And in all that time, your ancestors knew well to follow my wisdom. I do not give idle warnings!"

Abeni and Fomi exchanged startled glances. How old exactly was she?

The old woman sat back, her anger dying away. A long sigh passed through her lips and Abeni couldn't help but think she just looked tired. When she spoke again, her voice was calm, but filled with the weariness on her face.

"None of you know the happenings outside this forest. How can you? When I have protected you for so long? The world is not at peace. There is war and all the troubles and misery that war brings. I have hidden you away from these dangers. But I can do so no longer."

The Chief Elder frowned. But his attendant spoke for him.

"All this talk of troubles in the larger world," Abo said. He gave a quick laugh that didn't sound real. "What do we care for such happenings? We are a small village. We deal little with those beyond this forest. Their concerns are not ours."

The old woman gave the attendant such a grim look that his smile crept away.

"If only it were so," she said. "The dangers of the larger world are closer than all of you think. In fact, the danger is here . . . now."

At her words, there was a clap of thunder, so loud and sudden it shook the room. On the rooftop, the group of children jumped at the booming. The old woman turned her eyes upward, as if she could see right through to the sky above. Abeni followed her gaze.

There was a storm brewing.

Puffy dark clouds were beginning to spread across the blue sky, swallowing up the sun. In a moment, the day was plunged into darkness. Abeni shivered as a strong wind picked up. It whipped against her, howling through the village. She had seen storms before. They came with smells, like stone and earth. This one had no smell. It didn't even have rain. There were just clouds, thick and dark like smoke. They rumbled noisily, giving off flashes of white lightning.

And from somewhere inside, there was a shadow.

Abeni gasped at the sight. It wasn't easy to make out. But she could see it if she tried hard enough—an unnatural black in the already dark sky. It had wings like some giant bird or bat. And where it passed, the clouds grew darker still and a chilling cold crept over her. She shivered as she watched the shadow sweep across the sky before disappearing again.

"Did you see that?" she stammered.

Ekwolo followed her gaze. "See what?"

"The shadow! It was just there!"

Ekwolo squinted but shook his head.

"All I see is a storm," Fomi said.

Abeni wanted to tell them they were wrong. That there was something out there in the clouds, something that was circling their village, watching them. But the others had turned their attention back to the meetinghouse.

The grown-ups were shouting and speaking all at once—pleading with the old woman. They were afraid, Abeni realized in shock.

"I can no longer protect you!" the old woman yelled back. The strength of her voice brought quiet and she returned calm. "The day is too late. I've only come for what is owed me. I have watched over this village, never demanding as much as even a kernel of grain. All I've ever asked is that on the day of my choosing, I receive one of your children in payment. And I have come to collect."

On the rooftop, Abeni and the others all inhaled sharply. There was stunned silence from the grown-ups at the request. No one seemed to know how to respond. It was the Chief Elder who finally spoke. His face was furious as he rose to his feet, glaring at the old woman.

"You want payment?" he asked, voice trembling in anger. "You abandon us in our time of need? You leave us to ruin? And you expect us to hand over our children?"

"One child," the old woman corrected, lifting a finger. "One child and no more."

"You would not be given one goat!" the Chief Elder roared, striking the ground hard with his staff. "We will not give you one fowl! Not one yam! Not a single speck of grain!" He paused to catch his breath. "You . . . witch!"

The old woman said nothing, her face as calm as undisturbed water.

"The Chief Elder is right!" Abo added, shooting to his feet. He eyed the old woman sourly. "We will not hand over any child to you. We don't need your feeble witch ways. We can protect ourselves." Turning, he called to Abeni's father. "Akanyo! Gather the warriors to defend the village!"

Abeni looked to her father, who had stood quietly all this time. Like everyone else he was still dressed for the Festival, his mask in hand. He looked past Abo, to the Chief Elder. Only when the older man nodded did he unfold his arms and call to his brother.

Her Uncle Tawayo's voice came loud, barking orders. "Your swords! Your spears and shields! Gather them now!" Men snapped to attention, rushing from the meetinghouse to gather weapons. The room erupted into new excitement as talk turned to preparing for war.

Abeni watched her mother grab hold of her father before he could leave. The two of them were speaking, but she couldn't make out anything in all the noise and confusion. The two embraced tightly, then, turning abruptly, her father left—her uncle and the warriors following.

Atop the roof, Abeni found she was the only one still lying down. Everyone around her had become as frantic as the people below. The boys were all scrambling down the tree, crying out that the village was at war. Even Ekwolo flashed an excited smile at her before leaving.

Abeni stared at them all, confounded. War? War with who? Why would anyone want to fight her little village? And what was all that about the grown-ups agreeing to give that old woman one of their children? She put out a hand to Fomi, who was preparing to go.

"What are you doing?"

"Going home!" her friend said. "You should too! There's going to be a war!"

Abeni watched Fomi make her way down the tree and then turned to look out across the darkened village. People were running in every direction: going into houses and out of them again and shouting at each other.

"I just don't understand," she muttered.

Turning back to the meetinghouse, she looked down. The room had emptied, except for two figures. The old woman, who remained seated on her stool, her face unchanged despite all the commotion. The other person stood in the doorway, looking out and up at the stormy sky. When that person turned around, Abeni gasped. It was her mother!

She hurried to the old woman and the two began speaking, saying things that couldn't be heard. Then, to Abeni's surprise, her mother fell to her knees. Now she spoke loud enough so that bits and pieces filtered up to the rooftop.

". . . we need your protection!"

The old woman shook her head.

". . . no longer able . . . only come for what is due."

". . . my son, my daughter . . ."

Once more the old woman shook her head.

"Only one . . . choose one."

Abeni's heart beat fast as she watched the exchange. What was happening? Her mother's face looked anguished, her eyes filled with tears. She'd never known anything could so sadden her mother. And it frightened her. A long roll of thunder sounded before Yayawi finally answered.

"Abeni." She choked back a sob. "Let it be my Abeni."

The old woman looked at Abeni's mother hard for a moment. Then, placing a hand on her shoulder, she gave a deep nod.

Abeni lay on the roof, stunned. It felt like someone had punched her in her stomach. Had her mother just given her to this old woman? A woman people called a witch? How could this be happening? Her head swam, trying to make sense of the insensible.

Her mother stood up, turning and fleeing from the meeting-house. Abeni was still reeling in confusion when the old woman suddenly looked up, dark eyes fixed directly on her. She pulled away quickly, rolling onto her back out of sight.

Somewhere out in the village she could hear her mother calling her name, searching for her. But she didn't answer. She wouldn't just be given away to this old woman. She would find her father, or maybe her aunts. No, she would go and stay with Fomi. That's it! She'd hide there until she could figure this out!

And then the chanting began.

Eee-ya-ya! Ah-yo-yo! Eee-ya-ya! Ah-yo-yo!

The hair on Abeni's arms stood up on end. It sounded like many voices speaking at once, saying words she didn't understand. It came not from any one place but from all around, from the forest itself. Everyone else heard it too. All through the village people stopped what they were doing and went quiet to listen. The chanting grew louder—closer.

Abeni came to her feet, staring out. From atop the roof, she could see what others could not. All around their village a thick gloom was forming on the ground, dark like the clouds above. It crept forward like a living thing, hiding the forest from view and surrounding the village on all sides.

She shivered. She'd never seen mist behave like that before, as unnatural as this storm. The terrible chanting came from inside it, pounding in her ears like a drum. People were beginning to take notice of the encroaching darkness. They pointed and clutched each other while the warriors came forward, led by her father and uncle. They stood facing the gloom, spears at the ready. Then, quite abruptly, it all stopped.

Abeni listened close. The chanting had ended, leaving a terrible quiet. The gloom had stopped as well. It sat there on the edge of the village, a great hulking thing that churned. Like everyone else she stood waiting, heart pounding and breath held—knowing and feeling that something else was going to happen. Nightmares formed in her head: things with endless arms and great big mouths that would come from that darkness to swallow them up.

So, she was a little surprised when what stepped out of the gloom was no monster at all—but a woman.

CHAPTER FOUR

STORM WOMEN

Abeni blinked, wondering if her eyes were playing tricks. No, there was a woman there—quite possibly the most baffling woman she'd ever seen.

She wore a short skirt made from strips of scarlet and leather, while her torso was wrapped in green and yellow cloth. Her head was shaved on both sides, leaving a thick strip of hair in the center studded with white shells. White painted patterns covered the dark skin of her arms and legs, so that it looked as if she glowed. Even her face was decorated in swaths of red with white dots. The strange woman might have been mistaken for someone at Festival. But the weapons she wore said otherwise.

Abeni had never seen a woman dressed as a warrior before. But that's what she had to be. There was a sword strapped to her back, while knives and other sharp things covered her body and hung from her waist. Even the thick loops of iron bracelets encircling her neck and arms looked more like armor than jewelry. Her eyes stood out most of all. They were two bits of light that burned. Abeni stared, amazed and frightened all at once. Was this truly a woman at all, or some demon carried in by the storm?

The storm woman stood there for a moment. Her burning eyes swept across the village, looking the houses and other structures over. Then, almost as an afterthought, she turned to the people. Her head tilted to the side—and she smiled. Abeni rubbed her arms as a shiver ran through her. That smile was the most chilling she'd ever seen: the way a jackal might show its teeth before snapping you up.

There was a sudden shout as someone in the crowd stepped forward. Abeni recognized him. A young farmer who was one of the village warriors. He shook a spear at the fierce woman and his words came out in an angry rush.

"Demon! Monster! This is our village! Leave from here! Go back where you came from!" With a cry, he broke from the other warriors before they could stop him and launched at the strange woman with his spear. But he never touched her.

The storm woman moved in a blur. One moment she was standing still, the next she was grabbing his spear, sending him off-balance. As he fell, she struck him with her free hand in the chest. The sound of the blow made Abeni wince. He went down, hitting the ground so hard he was left gasping for air.

As he lay there, something new came out of the gloom from behind the storm woman. Abeni squinted, struggling to make it out. Were those snakes? No, ropes! Two thick lengths of knotted and frayed black rope that moved as if alive! They wrapped around his legs, creeping up to hold him fast. He screamed as they tightened and Abeni clenched her teeth, trying not to scream as well. She watched as the ropes wound themselves around his chest, reaching up to encircle his neck until he was choking. There was a sharp tug, and he was pulled away into the waiting gloom— disappearing from sight. All that could be heard were his cries coming from the darkness.

The storm woman glared at the stunned villagers. Bringing the captured spear down across her knee, she snapped it in two and tossed the pieces away. A hand went to the sword at her back, and she pulled the blade free to lift it high: a thing of dark metal with jagged edges like teeth. She swung the strange blade in a circle above her head while crying out unknown words. In answer to her call, new shadows stepped forward. Abeni's breath caught in her throat. There were more of them!

An army of storm women was emerging from the gloom. There were so many she couldn't keep count. They appeared from the darkness as if they were made from it. Each was as terrible looking as the next, with painted faces and bodies fitted with frightful weapons. They moved to encircle the village, drawing their swords as they made a slow march forward. As they came, they took up that frightening chant, beating the flat of their blades on the metal bracelets covering their arms:

Eee-ya-ya! Ah-yo-yo! Eee-ya-ya! Ah-yo-yo!

Behind them the black ropes slithered from the gloom like hungry serpents.

Everything after that seemed to happen at once.

Abeni saw her Uncle Tawayo give a cry. It was picked up by the village's warriors as they ran to meet the approaching women. Soon spears and shields and swords crashed against each other, making terrible sounds! She wanted to shut her ears so she couldn't hear, close her eyes so she didn't have to see. But she couldn't stop herself from looking. Her uncle and the warriors of her village were brave. But the storm women were too many, too fast, and too strong. She saw one pick up a big man as if he weighed nothing, throwing him to the ground. Another fought two men at once, her sword moving so swift it was all they could do to keep up.

One by one, Abeni watched in horror as the warriors of her village fell. And when they did, the black ropes were waiting, wrapping about arms and legs, dragging them away into the gloom. Soon only her uncle and two more of the warriors were left standing. With almost no one to block their path, the storm women surged into the village like an unstoppable river.

They laughed wildly as they came, pushing through everything in their path. Stools and masks that had been brought out for Festival were broken. Decorated clay pots were smashed. Food prepared with care to celebrate the harvest was overturned and trampled. The rampaging women lit torches and threw them atop straw roofs, setting houses on fire. Abeni watched in dismay as the village—*her* village—began to burn. Thick smoke rose to blanket the already darkened sky. Soon the sounds of choking coughs were added to screams and shouts. The storm women now ran through the streets unopposed, yelling their terrible war cries.

And the black ropes came with them.

The things moved like the tentacles of some unseen monster, searching out prey. Anyone they caught was snatched away, pulled into the gloom where only their unanswered pleas could be heard. The ropes took mothers clutching onto infants. They crept into homes to drag out old men. Whole families were carried off. No one was spared. The storm women worked with the ropes, burning houses to force people out and knocking others to the ground—where the ropes were always waiting.

As Abeni watched it all she slowly realized with horror what was happening. These storm women hadn't come to steal their harvest or their things. They had come to steal the people. They had come to steal her whole village away!

She saw the Chief Elder's attendant, Abo, fighting off a length of rope that had wrapped about the older man's staff. The ropes quickly circled him, pulling with such force he flew through the air before being swallowed up by the gloom. The Chief Elder quickly let his staff be taken and fled. Then the cries of someone familiar came to her ears. She turned about, searching through the mayhem.

Fomi!

Her friend was running, amid the tangle of fleeing people. She was yelling, calling for someone. Abeni's heart caught. Fomi was calling for her! She yelled back. But in all the noise, the girl couldn't hear. Then the rope came.

Abeni watched as the black tendril grabbed onto Fomi to drag her away. Suddenly someone else was there, hacking at the rope with a small axe. Sowoke! The girl cut and tore at the rope until Fomi was free, helping her to her feet. Abeni wanted to cry out with joy at the rescue. But their victory was short. New ropes replaced the last, tripping both girls to the ground as they ran. The two cried, holding on to each other as they were pulled into the gloom—and were gone.

Abeni stared after them. She had fallen to her knees, feeling sick. She couldn't watch this. She wanted to go home. She wanted to be with her family again. She wanted to be anywhere but up here, having to see everyone she cared for stolen away.

Get off this roof, a voice in her head said. *You need to get off this roof!*

It took all the courage she could muster, but she willed herself to leave. Maybe she could get to her house. A voice in her head warned that didn't make sense. Her house wouldn't be any safer than anyone else's. But it was all she could think of. *Get home, just get home.* She'd figure out the rest after that. Climbing down the tree, she landed on the ground behind the meetinghouse and hugged its surface, daring to peek around the corner. She yanked her head back just as one of the black ropes streaked by. It caught someone—a herder running with his goat. He fell as the rope wrapped around him and pulled him away. *At least his goat got free.* It was an odd thought, but she couldn't help but feel a pang of jealousy watching the animal trot off. Pressing flat against the meetinghouse she peeked around the corner again and saw the most wonderful thing ever.

Her father.

He was the last warrior of the village standing. He held a spear in one hand and a sword in the other as he fought four of the storm women at once. His eyes were as hard and cold as theirs were hot. And his face had a look she had never seen. Grim but determined, and strong. The storm women circled him like a hyena pack around a lion. Each time they came at him he pushed them back, swinging his sword and thrusting with his spear. His feet danced, and he spun so they could never surprise him.

Abeni had never sat long enough to watch her father practice with his weapons. It had always seemed so pointless. Even boring. But as she stared at him now, still in the dress of the warrior spirit, she tingled with the awe she imagined others did. And she swelled with pride at being his daughter.

It was as he was lifting his spear to fend off a storm woman that one of the black ropes latched onto his arm. He slashed at it with his sword and it broke apart, shrinking away as if wounded.

Abeni felt a cheer well up inside her. She wanted to see her father beat those cursed ropes! Send these monstrous women back into the forest. But before she could even speak more of the black ropes appeared. They grabbed at her father's legs and crept up, trying to wrap around him. He cut and hacked at them, tearing many to bits. But more came to take their place. In the end they were too many, swarming over him in a wave.

In despair, she watched her father struggle against the black mass. He tried to remain standing, planting his feet firm. But the ropes pulled harder, driving him to his knees. Somehow, he gathered enough strength to shoot up to his feet, moving so fast the ropes almost lost their grip. Abeni dared to hope! She wanted to shout out to him! Tell him to keep standing! Keep moving! But the ropes pulled him back down, tying his limbs so that he dropped his weapons. As he knelt, straining to break free, one of the storm women walked up, smiling. She bent down until she was face-to-face with him. He met her gaze, unblinking—until she struck him hard in the temple with the pommel of her sword. The blow sent him sprawling and a shroud of ropes fast swallowed him up, dragging him away.

Abeni shouted out in defiance as she watched them take her father. Whatever fear she held vanished, and she rushed forward from her hiding place. She would not let them take him! She would not! Her feet had barely moved when there was a sharp pull on her arm. She squealed, thinking it was one of the black ropes. But instead . . .

"Afayo!" she cried out at seeing her brother. "Father! We have to help!"

"No!" Her brother pulled her back, his voice almost breaking. "There's nothing we can do!" She glared at him, shocked and angry at the defeat on his face and in his voice. She tried to break free, but he held her fast.

"Abeni, listen to me! Listen!" His eyes filled with tears as they looked to their father, watching him disappear into the gloom. "It's too late! He's gone!" For a while the two remained there, everything around them seeming to go quiet as they tried to accept what they had just seen. Then it all came rushing back—the smoke, the cries, the fear—all too loud and very real.

"We can't stay here!" her brother said. "We have to run!"

Abeni looked at him. Run? Run where? With their father gone, home no longer seemed to matter. There was nowhere to go. The gloom surrounded the entire village. The storm women and those black ropes were everywhere. Where were they supposed to run? But she didn't say any of that. Because the truth was, she couldn't think of anything better. So, she took his hand and together they ran.

It was a hectic dash, skirting through the wreckage of their village. Smoke lay heavy in the air and Abeni could taste the embers on her tongue. Her nose filled with the scent of burning as her eyes watered. She blinked through the tears, trying to make sense of where they were running. Places she had known and seen every day were now scenes of horror. The black ropes left no one untouched. She saw small children huddled under a tree. As they passed, she wondered if they should stop and take them. But by the time she looked back, the children were gone—stolen away.

A sudden stop sent Abeni tumbling. She pushed back up on hands and knees, hearing someone crying out. Her brother. At first, she thought he'd tripped and hurt himself and wondered how bad it was. But then she saw the black rope wrapped about his leg. And her stomach went hollow.

"Help!" he yelled, trying to pull the slithering thing away.

Abeni scrambled to her feet, running to him. She was so terrified she didn't know what to do. He clenched his teeth in pain as the rope tightened. "It hurts! Cut it! Please cut it!" She searched around frantically, looking for something sharp. Her eyes fell on a bit of metal. A broken spearhead! She ran to snatch it up before returning to her brother, who was kicking desperately at the rope creeping up his leg.

"Cut it, Abeni!"

Her hands were trembling, but she moved quick, sawing at the rope as fast as she could with the broken spearhead. It was thicker than she'd thought—made up of bits of knotted fiber with frayed edges. It took all her strength and—there! The fibers broke apart. She expected them to fall away. But instead, right before her eyes, the rope began mending itself! She watched in disbelief as the broken strands twisted back together, creating an even more tangled knot.

Her brother's painful shouts sent her to cutting again. But each time she did, the rope fixed itself—and it was still moving. It had wrapped about both his legs now and was working its way around his waist. Then without warning, it pulled him—hard.

Abeni shouted in alarm, dropping the spearhead to grab her brother's hands. He looked up at her, his eyes round and filled with fright.

"Abeni! Don't let go! Please don't let go!"

She tried to hold on, but it felt like ten people were pulling on the other end. And his fingers began to slip.

"Abeni! Don't let it take me! Please!"

She clutched his hand harder, crying out for help. But none was coming. There was a final pull so hard it tore her brother away and sent her tumbling back. Her shrieks mingled with his as he was lost to the gloom.

She sat there dazed. Her brother was gone. The ropes had taken him. He was gone. She didn't know what to do. She didn't know if she could move. She just had to sit here. Just for a moment. Sit here and—something took hold of her. She jumped, flailing at it, kicking and slapping. The ropes! It was the ropes! They had her! They . . . But no, these were arms holding her. Someone was lifting her to her feet, telling her that she had to stand up. She lifted her head and looked.

"Mama?" Her voice came in a slow whisper. "Afayo. Father. The ropes took—"

"I know, Abeni!" her mother wailed, hugging her close. "I know!"

Abeni clung to her. Whatever anger she'd held earlier was

gone now. She couldn't even remember why she'd been upset. She buried her head and closed her eyes, wanting to remain there forever. But her mother was shouting something.

"Abeni! We have to run! Can you run?"

Abeni nodded slowly. *Run. Yes.*

Her mother grabbed her hand and they turned to run—then stopped. Someone was blocking their path. Abeni's insides went cold. A storm woman.

She was tall, even taller than Abeni's mother. Her lean body had muscles that Abeni thought only grew on men. Fine blue dots surrounded her eyes, continuing down the bridge of a flat nose on a face painted in swaths of red. A dark crimson cloth wrapped about her chest, while a short skirt covered in strips of green and gold with white shells on dark leather and bits of colorful stone hung to just above her knees. Thick bands of gold circled her biceps, along with endless bracelets of silver, copper, and polished bone covering her forearms. Like her sisters, she carried frightening weapons, including the sword she now held. But what Abeni stared at more than anything was the storm woman's skin.

It was pale, as if the color had been rubbed away. It reminded her of goat's milk and showed wherever she was not painted. Even her hair was different: thick, but the color of straw, it had been braided into rows that ran down to her shoulders. Whatever the woman was, Abeni found she couldn't pull her eyes away.

The storm woman with no color glared back, running her gaze across mother and daughter. Her eyes were dark circles ringed by fire—actual fire! Abeni shuddered as she looked into them. She may have been right the first time. These weren't women at all, but demons!

"And where are you going, pretty?" the storm woman asked.

Abeni gasped. She could understand the woman!

"So, you monsters can speak!" her mother said.

The storm woman twisted her full lips into a smile. "Our master has blessed us with many gifts, pretty."

Master? Abeni wondered who these fierce women could possibly call master?

"Let us pass," her mother demanded. There was a warning edge in her voice.

A rumbling laugh came from the storm woman's throat as she gazed at them with hunger in those fiery eyes. "And if I don't? What will pretty do? Fall to your knees like these others and beg your weak spirits to save you?"

Her mother's answer was swift. She stepped forward and lifted a sword. Abeni gaped. She hadn't even noticed her mother was carrying a sword. She didn't even know her mother knew *how* to hold a sword! But as she watched, her mother took up a fighting stance, much as she had seen her father do, and stared with eyes as hard as the steel blade.

The storm woman grinned back wickedly. She brought her own sword up, playing with it between her hands—then lunged for them.

Abeni was pushed away as her mother moved to meet the attack. The sound of metal striking metal clanged loud in her ears, and she watched with her jaw hanging. Her mother was fighting! With a sword! And she was . . . good! A whooshing slash almost cut the storm woman, and when she pulled away her mother used her free hand to send a balled fist crashing into her chin.

Abeni almost clapped as the storm woman's head snapped back, sending her stumbling! Her mother stood, breathing heavy, with a look on her face that was deadly serious. The storm woman staggered, holding her jaw where she'd been struck. Pulling her hand away she looked at the blood on her fingers. Then she did something unexpected. She barked out a laugh, loud and long, showing a set of red-stained teeth.

That sound made Abeni's insides quiver. The fires behind the storm woman's eyes seemed to grow brighter, as if she was thrilled by the fight. She reached for something at her waist and brought it up—a dark curving knife. At a word, the blade burst into flames the color of blood! And she came for them again.

This time she wielded both sword and flaming knife, moving easily with one in each hand. Her mother blocked and defended. But the storm woman fought wildly, laughing as if there was some joke only she could hear. Abeni's breath caught as the knife came close to slicing a fiery burn across her mother's face, but she backed away just in time. The next swing of the woman's jagged-edged sword, however, proved too much. When the two weapons met there was a sharp crack—and her mother's sword broke in two! The storm woman took the chance to repay the previous blow, jabbing a fist hard into her opponent's side.

Her mother fell to one knee, panting for breath and clutching where she'd been struck. Abeni watched in dismay that quickly turned to alarm as long dark shapes slithered from behind. The ropes! She cried out a warning and her mother turned, bringing up the bit of sword she still held to slash the black ropes. She cut them down once, then again. But more kept coming, as if they could sense weakened prey. The frayed and knotted black fibers wrapped about her mother's waist and chest, dragging her down, forcing her to drop the broken sword. She looked up, eyes brimming with unspoken anguish. Abeni moved to run to her side, but a strong hand yanked her back while another closed over her mouth. She looked up startled to find an unexpected face staring down. The witch!

Abeni struggled against her grip, but the old woman was surprisingly strong! She peered down with those dark eyes, letting out a silencing hiss that sent Abeni immediately still. Sweeping her free arm in a wide circle, she covered them both inside a long shawl. It was thin enough to see through and shimmered—like moonlight on water.

Her mother looked in their direction, tears filling her eyes. She reached out a hand, a palm open, and whispered something unheard—just before the ropes stole her away.

Abeni tried to shout as she watched her mother disappear, swallowed by the gloom. But the old woman held her firm, the rough hand about her mouth tightening. She might have struggled further, had the storm woman not turned to glare at them. She went still with fright as those eyes fixed on her—the flames behind burning fiercely. But to Abeni's surprise, they didn't linger long. Instead, they looked right past her, searching into the distance.

"Now where have you gone to, little one?" the storm woman murmured.

Abeni's eyes rounded. The warrior couldn't see them beneath the shawl! This was . . . magic! She looked up to the old woman. Maybe she really was a witch!

The storm woman frowned, searching about. Tilting her head, she narrowed those burning eyes, until they were just small dots of light. She stepped forward, stopping right before them. Abeni's heart pounded like a drum. The storm woman reached out a hand, grasping so close that Abeni inhaled and shrank back. But those fingers only snatched at air, missing them completely. The storm woman made a frustrated sound in the back of her throat, looking set to try again when something else caught her attention.

Abeni gritted her teeth as a horn blared, so deep and rumbling it rattled the whole of her—inside and out. It rose high and then fell, like the roar of some monster. She thought it might have been the most terrible thing she'd ever heard.

At the sound of it, the storm woman looked up, peering off into the distance. Then she walked away. Abeni let out a held breath. All throughout the ruined village the other storm women were doing the same. Wherever that awful horn had come from it appeared to be a summons of some kind, and they were now preparing to leave. The gloom that had surrounded her village began to thin, like mist clearing away. What it revealed made Abeni's heart lurch.

Her entire village was there—everyone who had been snatched away. Cords of rope were wrapped about their wrists, while longer pieces circled their necks, linking each one to the other. Around them the storm women barked orders, pushing people who wailed and huddled in fear together at the end of spears.

A man who dared talk back was struck with a lash across his

bare back that sent him howling. Searching the crowd for her family, Abeni made out the dejected face of the Chief Elder. He had been stripped of his crown. And his rich robes had been torn away. It was amazing to her how, without those things, he now looked like nothing more than a little old man.

It was as Abeni watched them that she heard the song.

It was muffled. And though it tickled her ears, she had to strain to hear it.

But who could possibly be playing music in all this? Was she imagining things?

No, there was a man. She could see him now. A man she didn't know, walking through her village. He was taller than any man she'd ever seen, broad with big thick arms. And he was dressed in the oddest clothing—a vest of shaggy white goat's fur, and pants made from the same. Even his feet were wrapped in goat's fur, and he wore tufts of it on his forearms. His face was hidden, concealed beneath a frightening mask made up entirely of goat horns of every type: twisted and poking out in every direction. In his hands he held what looked like a long wooden flute. And as he walked through the fire and smoke, he played. When he reached the villagers, he stopped walking but continued to play—as if waiting.

Someone came forward. Even through the veil of the old woman's magic shawl, Abeni could make the person out. Danwe. One of the blacksmith's sons. She'd know those stork legs anywhere. He stumbled towards the stranger in the goat horn mask. Someone else joined him. His brother. The two stood before the man, swaying slightly like thin trees in a breeze. Something about their faces didn't look right, Abeni thought. They were expressionless, as if the two boys were awake but dreaming.

A third person walked up. A girl. Two more followed. Then several more. Soon it was a stream of people—all moving to surround the stranger in the goat horn mask as he continued to play his flute. They swayed to his music, that dreamy look on their faces. No, not people, Abeni realized. Children! They were all children. None of the grown-ups walked to the man. But as their children left, the grown-ups began to wail all over again. One woman tried to hold on to her daughter. Sowoke! Still in her fancy blue dress. But the girl struggled, slipping free from her grip.

Something in Abeni's throat caught at the sight of another familiar face. Fomi.

Only her friend didn't seem herself. There was no fear on her face, no sadness, no anger. It was just empty. Dreamy. She walked right up to the crowd of children, her body swaying in that odd way.

Abeni tore her eyes away, to stare at the man in the goat mask. Who was he? What was he doing to her friends? Then she remembered. The song! They'd all dreamt about a song! Could this be the same one? Before she could think on it more, the strange man turned and walked away, still playing his flute. The crowd of children surrounding him followed. He was leaving the village—and all the children were going with him!

The grown-ups really began to shout now. Some sought to tear off their bonds, to fight back. But the storm women only laughed. They pushed back anyone who tried to break free, lashing backs and outstretched arms.

It was in the middle of all this confusion that Abeni saw her mother. She was there! Holding close to another woman who wept, the two of them bound in ropes. The sight was more than Abeni could bear. With a burst of strength that surprised even her, she tore free of the old woman, running from beneath the shawl and crying out. Her mother never looked up. She was far away and there was too much noise between them. But someone else had heard.

The storm woman who had hunted Abeni turned at her voice. Her painted face broke into a wide smile that fell away just as fast. Those fiery eyes stared past Abeni to something behind her. The old woman. She had taken off her shawl, revealing herself. At sight of her the storm woman's face contorted with anger. Pulling out her knife, she drew back her arm and hurled it towards them.

But Abeni hardly paid them any mind. The song had seized her as soon as she stepped from under the old woman's shawl. And it was perhaps the most beautiful thing she'd ever heard. How had she forgotten that from her dream? It felt warm, filled with whispered promises. Suddenly she was very eager to follow after the other children—to go wherever that beautiful song was going. To not be left out in the cold, away from that terrible warmth. She never even saw the dark blade tumbling end over end, erupting into bloodred flames as it came.

The old woman was before her in an instant, swatting the knife away with her staff in a shower of fiery sparks. She snatched up Abeni's hand—and the song went faint again, just beyond hearing. The warmth and the promises faded into nothingness and Abeni blinked. Her head swam. She looked up, struggling to think, and met the old woman's gaze.

"Run when I run!" the old woman ordered sharply. "And do not let go!"

Then she bent her body low and took off in a run. Abeni was jerked forward with such force her insides shook. Her feet moved without her thinking as she ran alongside. The storm woman with no color went by in a blur as they passed. Abeni glanced back to see her sent flying by the gust of wind they kicked up. She flipped end over end before landing again on her feet in a crouch. Loosing an angry snarl, she bounded after them.

Abeni looked back again, to find the storm woman running in their direction. Others joined the chase. And they were frightfully fast! Each one moved in terrific leaps that brought them closer and closer! The old woman glanced back and let out a grunt. Bending lower she put on another burst of speed, heaving Abeni along with her.

The two pulled away from the pursuing storm women. Sunshine danced over them as they broke through the gloom. They passed the bound villagers in a flash. A sadness washed over Abeni as they receded in the distance, and she wondered if she would ever see them again. In the time it took to blink twice they were in the forest, trees and bushes speeding by. Glancing to her feet, she didn't think they were even touching the ground. A carpet of green became dark soil and after that a wide transparent sheet that rippled.

Abeni gaped at seeing fish swimming below. They were atop a river—running on water! The transparent sheet gave way to land again. The world was one big blur as they zigged and zagged.

Then with an abruptness, they stopped.

Abeni pulled away from the old woman's grip. Her legs felt like water, and she stumbled. They were standing on a grassy hill surrounded by thick forest. In the distance was a river. She guessed it was the one they had crossed moments before. Far beyond that, hidden by trees and bush, a line of black smoke snaked into the sky. Her burning village. It seemed impossible that it could now be so far.

Abeni couldn't say if it was the running, which had to be magic, or all that she'd seen and been through. But she suddenly felt sick—sicker than she'd ever felt before. Her stomach gave a sudden lurch, and all the good Festival food and sweets she'd eaten that day came up in a sick rush. Everything was spinning—the land, the old woman, even the sun and sky above. Then she was falling, into a darkness so deep it seemed to go on forever, and she thought she might never stop.

CHAPTER FIVE

PRISONER

Abeni squinted at the bits of sunlight touching her face. She woke up, feeling exhausted. It was an effort just to sit up, and she immediately regretted it. She put a hand to her head. It was spinning and her stomach felt queasy. Her legs were the worst. They ached. As if she'd been running for miles. She closed her eyes, waiting for the dizziness to pass before opening them again.

For a moment, she was confused. She was inside, lying on sky blue blankets with golden patterns atop a giant cloud of white cushion filled with something soft. The cushion sat on a long bit of red-brown wood with legs carved and painted like a cat's. It put her somewhat off the ground, and she leaned over the edge to peek at the polished floor below.

The earthen walls surrounding her had been polished smooth too, until they gleamed like stone. Drawings in colorful chalk covered them in a pattern: deep blues and bright reds, stark whites, shining golds, and vivid purples that took up every space. She thought she could just make out the shapes of people and animals. In another drawing she glimpsed a lush forest and a moonlit sky. Others, she couldn't say what they were precisely. There were so many it was hard to tell where one began and another ended, all connected like a great big painting. She looked past the strange drawings to where a round hole had been cut into one wall. It let in the sunlight, which made her eyes squint. Through that opening she could see outside to what looked like a garden. Tall green stalks stood up straight from the ground in rows, amid thick leafy bushes and bright flowers. Altogether, it was a beautiful sight and she gazed in wonder. Birds flew throughout the garden, calling to each other in musical chirps and melodies that reached her ears. One, with blue and yellow feathers, flew right through the hole and into the room. She ducked low as it circled her head once before rising higher, whistling a tune and flapping about.

Abeni watched the bird in a daze. The way it went on, she couldn't help but wonder if it was here to welcome her. She frowned. But birds didn't talk. And welcome her where? This wasn't her home. This wasn't her sleeping mat. She peered down at herself, for the first time noticing what she wore. Why, these weren't even her clothes! She was wrapped in unfamiliar brown cloth, which was odd because last she recalled she was wearing her special dress. Her birthday dress. That's right. It was her birthday . . .

The memories came back at once.

The dark gloom. The storm women. The living ropes. The man in the goat horn mask. The song. The fear, the fires. All of it flashed through her mind while screams and cries filled her ears. She could almost smell the burning—the hot smoke filling her nose and chest until she wanted to choke. Her hands clenched into fists, clutching the blankets about her so tight it hurt. The dizziness quickly returned. And her body shook, reliving all those terrible moments. How could she have forgotten?

She looked around again, forcing her mind to think. To remember. How had she gotten here? Someone had taken her. Yes! They had fled her village and the storm women. Fled the man in the goat horn mask and his strange song. She had felt sick and then it was like she was falling into a deep darkness. But someone had caught her, carrying her here.

The witch!

As if summoned, the old woman appeared.

She walked through an open space like a door, entering the room. Abeni inhaled sharply, drawing into herself. The witch was just like she remembered: a tall old woman in a plain brown dress, wearing colorful shawls about her shoulders and long beaded necklaces that jangled as she walked. Her thick white locs were pulled back and hung to near to her waist, tied up with a bit of bright green cloth. In one hand she carried a clay plate, and in the other a bowl. At seeing Abeni, her white eyebrows rose. Not in surprise—more like a patient expectation.

"You're awake," she said by way of greeting. "Good." Glancing up, she noticed the bird still flapping about the room, and the lines on her brown skin drew into a frown.

"Shoo! Away with you now! She's had a long sleep but still needs her rest."

The bird whistled back.

"Well, you'll just have to wait until she's feeling better," the old woman replied briskly. "Now out of here. Go on!" The bird chirped something back that sounded like disappointment, and then flapped through the hole and away.

Abeni stared, stunned, as the old woman set the dishes she held down on the round flat top of a small wooden table with three legs like a stool. The bowl was made of dark wood, and intricate black carvings covered its surface. It was filled with food—some kind of fish stew. Round balls of fufu sat on the nearby plate. All of it smelled quite good and made Abeni's stomach grumble, a reminder that it had been emptied earlier.

"I've brought you some food," the old woman said. She lowered to sit at the edge of the long cushion, draping her shawls more closely about her and looking at Abeni awkwardly. She seemed unused to talking to people—much less twelve-year-old girls. Her wrinkled face was blank, not angry yet not smiling either. But those dark eyes stared with interest.

Abeni stared back, saying nothing. Was this really happening? Was she really in a witch's house, being offered witch's food? She'd heard tales like this from storytellers in her village. They didn't usually end well.

"You've been asleep for some time," the old woman began, as

if talking might help ease the moment. "In the past three days, you've done little else."

Abeni's eyebrows jumped. She'd been asleep for three whole days?

"It was the magic," the old woman explained, reading her face. "The spell was stronger than I would've liked. But it was the only way to escape. And I've never used it on someone so . . ." She fumbled for a word, then settled on one. "Small."

Abeni just continued to stare. Magic. She remembered now. They had been running, so fast that everything around them went by in a blur. Was that why her legs hurt so much? Her feet had even touched water, running across a river. She'd run across a river! It had all been magic—a witch's magic. A brown wrinkled hand with fingers adorned with rings reached out for her forehead, and she shrank back.

The old woman stopped short and frowned. She pulled her hand away but kept talking. "You had a fever. Strong magic can do that. But it looks broken now. I'll bring you some water and . . ."

Abeni listened as the old woman went on about rest and food and where some fresh clothes could be found in the corner. After everything that had happened, these seemed the wrong things to be discussing. And why was she going on as if Abeni would be staying here for some time? Why weren't they talking about getting her back home? Someone somewhere must be looking for her. After three days? They had to be. Opening her mouth, she found it dry. It took some swallowing, and even then, her voice came weak and thin.

"I want to go home," she croaked.

If the old woman heard the words, she didn't acknowledge them. She just kept on, talking now about her garden, where Abeni could get some sun when she was better.

Abeni frowned. She didn't like being ignored.

"I want to go home," she repeated, this time making her voice stronger.

But the old woman kept talking. Something about gathering

plants in the forest. And that she might be gone from time to time.

Abeni glared now, her anger rising. She wanted to get back to her village. There had to be others who'd escaped. She needed to find them. Then they could . . . they could . . . Well, she didn't know what they would do. But she couldn't just stay here, eating and sleeping in a witch's house as if that was the most normal thing in the world!

"I WANT TO GO HOME!"

Abeni's shout echoed in her ears. She hadn't known she could yell that loud. The effort left her tired and dizzy all over again and her throat hurt. She had to fight to not lie back down. Finding her anger, she held on to it, the strongest thing she had right now.

The old woman went quiet. Then with a sigh she shook her head. "There is no home for you to return to, girl. You saw what happened as well as I."

At her words, fresh memories flashed through Abeni's head. People tied together like animals by the storm women. The other children of the village, led away by the man in the goat mask. She shuddered, trying to shake the visions away.

"Liar!" she shot back.

The old woman's white eyebrows drew together, and she leaned close. "Little girls should mind their words to one my age. Would you speak this way to your mother?"

Abeni glowered. She wasn't a little girl. She'd seen twelve harvest seasons. And this woman wasn't some village elder. "You're not my mother!" she spat. "My mother isn't a witch!"

The old woman's eyes narrowed, becoming two black points. She looked ready to retort and for a moment Abeni wondered if she'd perhaps gone too far. But a change passed over her face and it smoothed out, becoming calm again.

"You should eat," she said. "You haven't rested fully. And it is making you say foolish things."

Abeni's eyes rounded, her anger flaring up like her nostrils.

Swinging out an arm, she swept the bowl and plate from the small table. Hot stew and fresh doughy fufu went splattering onto the floor. She glared at the mess then looked back up in satisfaction. How was that for foolish?

The old woman eyed her coolly. "I didn't know you were still such a child."

Fresh embarrassment replaced satisfaction and Abeni felt her face go hot. Before she could respond, the old woman casually lifted a hand, moving her forefinger in a small looping circle. A clattering came. Abeni looked down to find the bowl and plate stirring! They rattled and jumped as if they'd come alive. With a sudden flip, they righted themselves. Spilled food lifted from the ground and returned to fill them. She gaped as both dishes leaped into the air to land back onto the table. Every drop of stew and bit of fufu had been rescued, like they'd never been undone—steam still rising from both.

"You need to eat whether you know so or not," the old woman said. "The food will remain warm and unspoiled." She rose to her feet, gathering her dress about her. "I'll return with water. Perhaps when you're ready to not behave like a child, we can talk." With that she turned and walked away, disappearing back through the open door.

Abeni watched her go, fuming. Child? She'd show her a child! Glancing at the food she lashed out once more, knocking it back to the floor. Her tantrum didn't last long. Like before the bowl and plate refilled and returned to the stool. She put her hands to her head in frustration and yelled at the top of her lungs all over again.

The rest of the day went by very slowly. The witch—Abeni had decided that was exactly what she was—did return a few times. Once she bought a small stone jar of drinking water that somehow always stayed cool. She came in another time to leave some fresh clothes—another bit of brown cloth to wrap in—and a larger clay jug with water for bathing. Then just as the sun fell, she stuck in her head one more time.

"Get your sleep," she said. "You will need to rest." Then, almost as an afterthought, "Oh, and don't mind the wall."

Abeni didn't understand that. But as night came on and the room grew dark, the many colorful drawings that covered the wall began to glow. Then they started to move. She gasped, staring in wonder and fright as the drawings jumped and danced, taking on different shapes. Sometimes they formed people or animals, or creatures that couldn't possibly exist. She thought they might have even been telling a story, though of what she had no idea.

She might have asked the witch, but she'd resolved to ignore her altogether, and had made it a point to look the other way whenever she entered the room. She made certain to just sit there, keeping her face sullen. Her anger showed no signs of easing, and she had no intention of giving it up. She would outlast this witch!

There was, however, the problem of food.

Abeni awoke late that night to a loud grumbling. It was her stomach. Curled into a ball, she didn't dare turn to look at the bowl of stew and plate of fufu that were still there. She could smell them. If she saw them too, she might give in. And she'd rather starve than eat any of the witch's food.

Morning came and she hadn't touched a morsel. She'd dreamt of them though. At one point she even thought she'd woken in the middle of the night to see them drawn onto the strange walls. Dancing fufu balls and a stew that begged to be eaten. Now, she snuck glances. Her stomach didn't help, growling and begging to be fed. Traitor. As morning stretched into afternoon, it only grew harder to ignore the food and her grumbling belly. She couldn't remember ever being this hungry in her life.

The stubborn part of her didn't want any part of the food. The hungry part—the one her stomach ruled—insisted on eating right now! The stubborn part wanted to stand up to the witch. The hungry part said starving wouldn't hurt the witch any. The two went back and forth that way, until the hungry part tried a new tactic. If she was ever going to escape from here—she was determined to do that—she certainly couldn't do so hungry. The stubborn part considered this for a bit, admitting it was a good point. And that was how Abeni found herself eating.

She gulped down the stew. Made of spicy fish and okra, it was quite probably the best thing she'd ever eaten. Like the witch promised, it was still warm, hot in fact, almost burning her tongue. But she was too hungry to care. She licked away every last drop, using the fufu to sop it up. In among the jumble of images on the wall, she thought she saw a drawing of a girl, rubbing her belly with contentment.

She was still sucking the tiniest bits of stew from her fingers when the witch walked in. Her white eyebrows drew together at the emptied dishes, but she said nothing. Instead, she gathered them up and left. In moments she returned with more, setting them atop the small table. Abeni never looked at her, staring elsewhere in silence.

It went on like that for a few days.

Morning and night the witch brought food—soups, meats, fruits, and more. Some of the dishes Abeni knew, like the mix of beans and spices and the peanut chicken. Other things, all delightfully delicious, she couldn't name. She ate it all, never offering thanks but leaving her bowls piled high. In time, she felt strong enough to walk around the room without getting dizzy. A few more days, and she thought she might be back to herself.

The witch seemed to have given up on speaking as well. She left food and clothes and water as needed, then went about her day—all of which was fine by Abeni. From the window, she could see the witch spent most of her time in her garden, planting and caring for the many things that grew there. It looked like hard work. Once, while hauling some rocks, she glanced up, with a look that might have been asking for help. But Abeni turned away. She had no intention of lifting as much as a finger.

She'd heard so much about "the witch" in her village. Now here she was living in her house. If only Fomi could see her now! As always, thoughts of home came with sadness. Sometimes she'd just stare at nothing for a long while, thinking about her brother's jokes, her aunts' doting, or her mother pounding yam. Fomi's pranks. Ekwolo's smile. She even sometimes saw that silly Sowoke's face. She missed them all. But strangely she couldn't bring herself to cry. No matter how sad she felt, she hadn't shed a single tear since coming here. It felt like a part of her was gone, taken with her village—leaving an empty place inside. She worried that if she didn't find them soon, that emptiness would grow and swallow her up entirely.

So, she plotted her escape.

The witch sometimes disappeared for a whole day, not returning until sunset. Abeni had no idea where she went and didn't much care. But the second time the old woman did so, she took the opportunity to slip from her room—and gaped. She was standing in a hallway that curved in a wide circle. Above her was another floor much the same, and a third above that, under a high roof covered with what looked like flowers—a thick and colorful blanket at the height of bloom. All along the hallway were doors. Some were tall rectangles of black or brown wood, with designs on their surface: colorful beadwork, bits of glass, even shells arranged into patterns. Others looked made of stone and were etched with symbols she couldn't understand. At least one door was a wide round circle painted a bright yellow. No two were alike. And she thought there might have been dozens. This place was larger than any house she'd ever seen. Even her village's meetinghouse was tiny compared to this!

She glanced back to the room where she'd been staying. There was no door there and she wondered if she should go back. Was it safe to go wandering about a witch's house? She was certain that in the stories, that never ended well. But she was curious despite herself. Plus, she was getting tired of just lying about. If she was going to escape this place, she needed to know something about it. Maybe in these rooms there was even something that could help. Taking a deep breath and trying to ignore all the warnings buzzing in her head, she set out. Her hands traced along the doors she passed, feeling their surfaces. She passed several before stopping at a tall black door. A small carving like a face sat in its center, staring out with blank eyes and lips pursed into a slight smile. Gingerly touching a silver handle, she grabbed hold and pushed.

The door opened easily, as if in invitation. She peeked her head inside before stepping in fully and stared in wonder. The room was bigger than she could have imagined. It extended far into the distance, beyond what she could see. And if it had a ceiling . . . well, she wouldn't know. There was just a shadowy gloom high above. Like the room went on forever. That was impossible of course. Then again, so was what she was looking at. The room was filled with masks. Masks of every type. Many were carved of wood, but some of iron, or silver, or other things. They were in the shapes of people, sometimes with bushy manes or wide scowling mouths. Some were small enough to fit her face. One that she walked around, carved of black and red wood, was at least three times her size—and she shivered to think of whatever face wore that! There must have been dozens of masks. No, hundreds. All stacked atop each other or laid out in orderly rows. The sight made her think of Harvest Festival, sending a sharp pain of longing through her. Backing out of the room, she closed the door, and moved on to another.

Behind a red door she found a room filled with carved wooden stools, all jumbled up in one big heap like a small hill. A narrow green door led to a room of statues, some small enough to fit in her hand and others so big they towered up into the shadowy ceiling. She never got to see what was behind the round yellow door. She'd only opened it a crack before a howling wind came from inside, blasting her with chill air. She had to use her full weight to close it again and when she was done stood shivering— covered in something cold and white that melted to water before her eyes. And she decided that maybe those old stories had been right.

The next day that the witch was gone, she was more careful

about her exploring. Now she opened doors gingerly, peeking inside to make certain it was safe. She never saw the round yellow door again. Or the doors that led to the rooms full of masks, or stools, or statues. She'd gone to exactly where they'd been, only to find them gone—replaced with completely new doors that led to completely new wonders. But none of it was helpful. None of it told her how to escape this place.

After a few days, she decided she'd had enough of doors that led to strange rooms. Instead, she stepped through the one that led outside. She hadn't been out of the house since she arrived here. But the witch had been gone since morning and she thought it was safe. Stepping into the sunlight she blinked at its glare and smiled. It was good to feel the warmth on her skin again, and she took her time walking through the garden—spreading her arms wide so that the tips of her fingers brushed the tall green stalks of grass. More than once, she thought she heard voices, a slight whispering that tickled her ears. But when she looked about there was no one. Odd. Then again, what about this place wasn't?

Still searching for the source of the whispering, she turned back to glance at the house and stopped in her tracks. She was looking at a small round earthen building covered in green vines and topped by a straw roof growing with flowers. It was a tiny, rickety looking thing. Her own home was at least three times its size. But how was that possible? She'd been going from room to room inside the place for days. Some had ceilings so high that she couldn't see where they ended. How could something be big on the inside but small on the outside?

"Crazy witch house," she muttered, shaking her head.

It was two days later—a total of fourteen, from the markings she kept on the wall behind her bed—that she made her first escape attempt. The witch was gone for the day again, so the timing was perfect. She didn't take much, just a few chewy fufu balls she'd stashed away. She pushed through the green stalks, which annoyingly clung to her—almost like they were trying to hold her back. Leaving the garden, she made a dash for the forest. She had only taken a few steps inside when she stopped. Turning in a circle, she stared at the trees and bushes that went on without end. And she came to a sudden realization. She had no idea where she was going. For a long moment she stood there, trying to find a path of some kind. But it was no use. Each direction looked as unfamiliar as the other. With a heavy heart, she turned and tramped back to the witch's house, feeling defeated.

The failed attempt left Abeni even more dejected. She'd really believed she might be able to find her way home. But she was no hunter. She'd never wandered more than a few steps from her village. The witch had taken her a long way and nothing here was familiar. She couldn't just wander in the forest. She needed a better plan than that. Yet no matter how hard she thought on it, she couldn't come up with a way to find her way home. Each day that passed she grew more hopeless, and her nights were little better.

Abeni's dreams were no longer about food. Instead, she relived that terrible day. The dark gloom and black ropes were there. So were the storm women. The woman with no color stood at their head, laughing as they burned everything and stole everyone away. In the middle of it all the man in the goat horn mask played his song, as all the children danced in the flames.

It was on a night of such frightening dreams that Abeni came awake with a start. Her night tunic stuck to her skin with sweat. Sitting up, she swung her feet over the edge of her bed—so the witch had called this thing—and sat trying to push the nightmare away. She followed the moving images on the wall, which surprisingly calmed her after bad dreams. But whenever she closed her eyes, the frightening memories were there again. She wouldn't be getting any more sleep tonight.

Sighing, she turned to gaze out the window. The sounds of the forest drifted into her room. Chirps, howls, and cries. Sometimes, she'd awaken to find the witch sitting in her garden and staring up at the night sky—as if looking for something. On a few occasions, she would even sing—though Abeni could never make out the words.

Tonight, however, the witch wasn't out in her garden. And Abeni had an urge to take in some of the night herself. Slipping from her room, she tiptoed across the smooth ground, ignoring the new doors that had sprouted up, and made her way outside. Striding through the stalks of tall grass that swayed gently, she touched them with the tips of her fingers. The familiar whispering came as usual, buzzing in her ears. She stood still, straining to listen. But beyond slight bits of laughter, she couldn't understand anything.

Giving up, she shook her head, muttering for the hundredth time about the strangeness of this place. Finding a patch of earth, she sat down, not caring if her clothes got dirty. The witch would bring her new ones in the morning anyway.

She couldn't remain like this. A prisoner. Somewhere out there was her village. And she believed—needed to believe—that others had escaped. It wasn't impossible, she insisted, arguing against her own doubts. She just needed to find a way to get closer to home, so that anyone looking could find her.

Amid her thoughts her eyes drifted up to the sky. There were stars everywhere. It looked like someone had thrown glittering jewels across a wide black cloth. They shimmered and shined— subjects in the kingdom of the moon spirit, who today covered one side of his face because he was in a bad mood.

Abeni smiled, recalling the stories from her village about the stars in the night. She found the ones said to be a herd of galloping bison. Behind were two bright stars that were the lions chasing them. A long set of twisting stars was a river. And the three stars that made a point above them formed a giant crocodile that lived there. His jaws were so big that if he opened them, they could swallow the whole moon, and make the night dark forever.

Luckily the moon had a protector—the hunter. She looked to the familiar pattern of stars. The hunter wore his hunting dress. He held up a spear, whose tip was the brightest star in the sky. The crocodile feared the hunter and his bright spear. So he kept to the river and didn't bother the moon spirit or his subjects.

Abeni sat gazing at them, surprised that she remembered those old stories so well. They were for children after all. But she was forgetting something. It nagged at her, like an itch she couldn't reach. When she remembered, she jumped up to her feet.

Her father had told her the story of the hunter among the stars, who all hunters looked to for good fortune. Most important was his spear. What was it her father used to say? She racked her brain to remember, and his voice came to her in answer.

In the forest at night, it is easy to get turned around. But any hunter who has lost their way can always look up to find the tip of the great spear—that points home.

All this time she'd been trying to find a way home and it was out here all along! In a children's story! All at once she started thinking, planning how this might work. She'd finally found a way of escaping from this witch, and she intended to take it!

CHAPTER SIX

INTO THE FOREST

It took a few more days to set her plans into motion. Unlike her last attempt, this time she'd be prepared. She stashed away fufu, bits of fruit, and other edibles behind her bed—leaving her plate empty. It meant that some days her stomach grumbled with hunger. But she steeled herself to it. Food wouldn't be enough. She'd need something to drink. It was as she was pondering this while walking in the house that she noticed a brown door. New of course. Only it was slightly ajar. That was different. Her curiosity getting the better of her, she moved close to peek inside—and stared. It was full of gourds. All dried and hollowed out, and of every conceivable size. There were some that could fit in her hand and great big ones she could easily crawl into. She took a small one and filled it with water. There was one problem solved. Now, she just had to find a way out.

It was one thing to leave the house in the day when the witch was gone. It was another to try and sneak out at night. The witch was always here at night. When she wasn't sitting in her garden, she could be heard walking her house—wandering in and out of those strange rooms.

It was on the fourth night, as Abeni lay in her bed watching the pictures on her wall shift about, that she heard the witch walking about her house. Unlike past nights, however, it didn't sound like she went into any of the rooms. Or outside. Instead, her footsteps disappeared into the distance. Abeni waited. The witch had been gone most of the day, not returning until just before sunset. After bringing some food she'd yawned loudly, as if tired. Letting some time pass, Abeni crept from bed into the darkened house. The witch's room was just down the hall. Like hers, it had no door. She tiptoed towards it, heart pounding, to peek inside. If she was caught, she wondered what the witch would do. She smiled in relief at what she saw. The witch's room was nothing fancy— just a rounded space with a high bed. Right now, she lay atop it, fast asleep. Whatever she'd done today, it had left her exhausted. With luck, she probably wouldn't wake until morning.

Abeni didn't waste time. Returning to her room she pulled out the bundle of hidden food and the filled gourd. Hurriedly, she got out of her night tunic and wrapped herself with one of the thicker fabrics the witch had provided. Her own gold dress she folded neatly around her jewelry. She placed everything—food and clothing— into a bag she'd spirited away. The gourd with water she hung at her waist. When she finished, she slipped into her sandals and slung the bag across her shoulder. She was set to leave when the pictures on the wall caught her attention. They were flickering quickly, showing a girl running through a forest. All about her things shifted with big eyes and even bigger mouths, until the girl was swallowed by darkness. Abeni gave a start. Was that supposed to be her? For a moment she shrank back, fearful. Then, catching herself, she shook her head. No! It wasn't real. Just some pictures on a wall. She wasn't going to listen to this witch house. She was leaving—now! Doing her best to ignore the images, she left the room, walking past all the strange doors, and slipping by the slumbering witch, into the waiting night.

The warm night air blew soft against her skin as she stood outside. Looking to the sky she found the hunter easily and followed the length of his spear to the bright star at its tip—looking in the direction it pointed. Right into the heart of the forest. Home. She was going home. With a deep breath, she took her first steps. She didn't run through the garden, fearful she might cause too much noise. But she walked as fast as she could. As she passed the tall grass stalks, they again stuck to her—and she was certain this time they were trying to hold her back! She had to put up a small fight to get through, shoving and pushing them aside. When she finally cleared free of them, she turned back to glare.

"I certainly won't miss any of you!" she whispered sharply.

Walking a bit further, she left the odd garden behind and came right up to the forest's edge. It looked different at night—bigger and darker than she expected. And it was filled with all sorts of unsettling forest sounds: growls and cries and howls. Remembering the pictures on the wall made her hesitant, and her stomach fluttered nervously. No. None of that. Her father was a warrior. She'd watched her mother fight with a sword! She could be brave too, like them. Besides, who knew when she'd get another chance like this. Pushing down her fears, she took one step into the forest. Then another. And several more. Soon she was in the thick of it, surrounded on all sides by dark bushy shapes. A tremor of panic went up her back, but she quickly looked up again and breathed a sigh of relief. The hunter's spear still shined in the night, as big and bright as ever. A beacon to guide her home.

She set out on a brisk walk—never once looking back at the witch's house she left behind.

There was no trail or path to follow in the forest, just lots of green intent on getting in her way. She stepped over plants, pushed through thick bush, and made her way around trees. It was hard to see in the dark. And sometimes low-hanging branches snagged her hair and thorns scratched her skin. It felt at first like she and the forest were fighting. And she wasn't certain she was going to win. But things got better as she went. Her eyes got used to the dark. Or at least she could see things more clearly, and she was able to watch her footing to avoid roots that poked up from the ground and places where the earth was uneven. She settled into a steady pace, glancing up every now again at the hunter to make certain she was going the right way.

When she got thirsty or hungry, she drank from the gourd and nibbled on chewy balls of fufu. She was too excited to be tired. She passed her time just thinking. Mostly about her village, imagining who might be waiting when she returned. People had probably started rebuilding the burned houses by now. She couldn't wait to see everyone again. She *would* see them again. She just knew it! A song came to mind, and she began to hum. It was the hunters' chant. Her father and uncle sang it whenever they went out into the forest, asking the spirits to see them home again. She was still humming when she heard a rustling.

Abeni looked up. The sound had come from the trees. There hadn't been much to see in the forest—just a few night birds, funny looking bugs, and one time a red-haired monkey who glared as if she didn't belong here. But there was nothing there now: just the leafy forest canopy that swayed idly in the night breeze.

"Stop being so scared," she muttered to herself.

Shaking off her unease, she picked up the hunter's chant again. However, she hadn't gone more than a few steps when the rustling came back—only louder. This time she stopped. That hadn't been in her head. And louder meant closer. Squinting up at the trees, she searched their leafy branches—thinking to find some small forest animal up there. But still there was nothing. Now that she thought on it, there was no sound at all.

Abeni listened carefully to the night. There had been noises enough since she entered the forest—bugs chirping, birds calling, frogs croaking. But now there was nothing. Not a single chirp or call or croak. The whole forest had gone suddenly quiet, so that she could only hear her own breathing. She was thinking of how strange this was when she saw the eyes.

Abeni went absolutely still, staring up at two red eyes that gazed out from the trees—like pieces of wood left in a fire until they glowed. She bit her tongue to stop from yelping and crouched quickly behind a bush. The eyes hadn't seen her, had they? She stayed hidden for a long moment, waiting, dreading at any moment a pair of glowing red eyes would appear right above her. When nothing happened, she crept to the edge of the bush and peeked out, fearing what those eyes might belong to.

At first she thought she was looking at a humongous bird, all covered in black. But squinting, she saw what she'd mistaken for feathers was actually fur. The creature—and it was definitely a creature—had wings that were all wrinkled, with bony hooks at the tops like small hands. And it didn't have a beak. Instead, there was a snub nose and sharp pointed ears. It clung to the side of a tree with curved black claws, sniffing the air while its red eyes searched the night.

A bat, Abeni realized! She was looking at a bat! Only who'd ever heard of a bat big enough to carry off a goat! She gawped at the size of it. Two goats! Maybe three! The thing was as big as a water buffalo! A sudden dreadful thought came to her—it could probably carry her off! She sunk lower behind the bush, trying to hide herself, and noticed something even more startling.

There were wide straps of leather wrapped around the giant bat's belly. They led to what looked like a seat, where a man sat. At least she thought at first that he was a man. Only now that she looked him over, he was small, no taller than her in fact, and dressed all in black that blended with the night. As he turned, she glimpsed his face and sucked in a breath. That was definitely not a man's face! It was painted red, with lips that curled down and eyes that glowed as fiery bright as the bat's! His ears were pointed and pierced with gold hoops. For the first time, she noticed that the bat had gold hoops in its own ears. One thick loop hung from its nose too!

Abeni's heart pounded as she stared at the two. She'd heard stories in her village of all sorts of monsters, but none of them included giant bats. Or men that were not men, with glowing eyes! And none of those stories were supposed to be real! They certainly weren't supposed to be in her forest! She had no idea what these things were or what they were doing here. But she wanted to be far away from them. Still crouched, she started to back away, hoping to find some other part of the forest—where there were no strange red-faced riders or giant bats! She glanced to the sky, finding the hunter. As long as she could still see the spear, she'd be fine. She just needed to—

A slow hiss froze her in place. It came from right above her.

Every part of her screamed not to look up. Not to see what hovered above. But slowly, she lifted her head and felt her belly quiver as her eyes made out the large black shape.

It was another giant bat!

This one hung upside down by its black claws, long sharp things that curled around a thick branch. And it was staring right at her with those glowing red eyes. Its rider twisted in his seat, peering down. At seeing her his lips curled upward in a smile, showing sharp yellow teeth. Abeni stared back. She was shaking all over but couldn't move. It was like her legs had grown roots that pinned her to the ground. As she watched, the bat opened its mouth wide to show long white fangs—then shrieked! The high-pitched sound echoed into the night, jolting her from where she stood. She shrieked back in terror—then ran!

Abeni fled headlong through the forest. Above, the giant bat leapt into the air. It was joined by the first, the two soaring above the canopy. She could hear their leathery wings beating after her, creating a wind that buffeted her like a small storm. *Whoosh! Whoosh! Whoosh!* Claws snatched and tore at branches, showering her with bits of splintered wood and leaves. Bushes tore at her dress and fresh scratches stung her skin as she crashed through them.

Twice she stumbled, almost going down but catching herself. The third time her foot caught on something—a root perhaps— ripping her sandal off and sending her flying. She tumbled across the forest floor before scrambling onto her back just in time to see one of the bats diving down through the trees right for her! Branches snapped like twigs as it came, barreling through the canopy with a fierce cracking. Its bony curled claws were opened wide, ready to wrap around her and snatch her up! She found now that she was too scared to even scream.

Suddenly there was light—a flash so bright it lit up the forest like it was day. Abeni was blinded by the glare as everything went white. The bat shrieked again. But this sounded like a cry of pain. It beat its leathery wings hard, pummeling her with wind, to pull back from the light. For a while, all she could hear were those beating wings like drums in her ears. Then they began to grow faint, becoming weaker until she could no longer hear them at all. The light vanished, and she had to blink several times before she could see. Someone was out there, walking right up to her. She stared open-mouthed, able to form only one word.

"You!"

"Me," the witch replied.

CHAPTER SEVEN

HOME AGAIN

Abeni came to her feet, stumbling back a few steps.

"Out for a night stroll?" the witch asked, scowling.

Abeni fumbled to reply. "You followed me!" It was all she could think to say.

The witch let out a long *humph!* "I came after you," she corrected, jabbing with her gnarled and knotted staff. "Fortunate for you that I did. Did you really expect to outrun Mmoatia raiders? On sasabonsam?"

Abeni stared. Mmo who? Sasa whats? "You mean the riders on the giant bats?" Her eyes went nervously to the skies, expecting them to return—swooping down on them at any minute. "What were those things? Why did they chase me?"

"Mmoatia on their black steeds, the sasabonsam," the witch repeated, as if that explained everything. "A hunting party. And like a mouse out where it doesn't belong, you make easy prey. A fine thing too if you'd ended up in their cooking pots!"

Abeni shuddered. Cooking pots? She looked up again to the skies.

"That danger has passed," the witch said. "I've sent them to hunt elsewhere." There was a frown, her gaze going vacant as she muttered to herself. "Though when have Mmoatia raiders ever ranged so far from their hunting grounds? Most unusual. What next? Zimwi pulled from their caves and sent up from the south?" Her eyes fluttered and she returned a scolding gaze back to Abeni. Lifting a long finger, she wagged it hard. "But there are more things in this forest, girl, that could spell your end! You're not in your little village any longer! The world is bigger and more dangerous than you know!" With another *humph!* she turned about. "Now come along and let's return home."

A part of Abeni wanted very much to follow the witch, who had already begun walking. But she hadn't run away without a good reason.

"No," she said. The witch turned about, raising one white eyebrow. Abeni almost stepped back under that stare. But she thought of her mother, holding that sword to defy the storm woman, and held her ground. "I'm going back to my village. I'm going back to see if anyone's still there. I don't care if a hundred monsters chase me, I'm going to get there!"

The witch glared at her for a long moment, before shaking her head with a sigh.

"Stubborn child," she muttered. "You insist on doing this foolish thing?"

Abeni nodded. "Yes. And I'm not a child."

The witch snorted at that. "And if I force you back, you'll just find another time to sneak off?"

"Probably," Abeni answered. Then, finding more courage, "Yes."

The witch threw up a hand in exasperation. "Cha! What have I done to be cursed with such a hard-headed girl? Fine. But *I* will take you. So you might arrive with your skin!"

Abeni released a held breath. "You'll come with me?"

The witch lifted a white eyebrow. "You would prefer I left you here?"

Abeni glanced around at the forest, which seemed darker and more foreboding than ever. She didn't like the witch. She didn't *trust* the witch. But she thought she disliked the idea of being out here alone even more. She nodded once.

The witch just gave another *humph!*, gathering a shawl more tightly around her shoulders. "Well?" she growled, already walking off. "Don't stand there like a monkey waiting for fruit to ripen. Move! And you dropped this." Abeni caught something thrown her way. Her sandal. She slipped it on and ran to keep up.

The witch kept a surprisingly fast pace. Abeni ached and stung all over. And one of her legs had a slight limp. But she didn't complain or ask the witch to slow down. The two walked in silence as the forest returned to normal—with all its forest sounds.

They had walked for some time when the witch stopped before a sloping grassy mound between some trees. Abeni had to look close to see it was the mouth of a cave, so well hidden she might have passed it up.

"We stop here for now," the witch said.

"Why?" Abeni asked, suspicious. She'd kept an eye on the hunter's spear still visible in the sky, to make certain they were moving in the right direction. But the witch could still be trying to trick her.

"Because my body is too old," the witch snapped. "And yours too battered to go on without rest." Turning, she bent down and ducked into the small cave, her voice echoing from inside. "And there's the rain."

Rain? No sooner had Abeni thought the word than thick, fat droplets came falling from the sky. Cold pounding rain soaked her in moments—as if some cloud spirit had overturned a jug on the world. With a squeal, she ran for the shelter of the cave, squeezing herself inside.

It shouldn't have surprised her that, much like the witch's house, the cave was bigger on the inside than it looked on the outside—roomy and with a rounded ceiling high above. The witch herself was already seated cross-legged before a bundle of sticks. Touching them with the tip of her staff, she started a fire that was soon crackling.

Abeni walked to sit on the other side, shivering and damp from the rain and thankful for the warmth. As she watched, the witch unslung a bag from her shoulder: a sack woven of plain brown cloth. Reaching inside, she amazingly pulled out an un-spilled bowl of steaming soup—complete with a spoon—and began to take slow slurping sips. As Abeni stared in astonishment, she remembered the fufu balls in her own bag. She fished them out, only to find they'd gotten soggy. Grimacing, she nibbled at them anyway. Catching her stare, the witch stopped her slurping and grudgingly reached into her brown cloth bag to pull out a *second* bowl of hot soup, with a spoon. She slid it across the ground to Abeni without a word, then returned to eating.

Abeni licked her lips, accepting the bowl.

"Thank you," she said—it was the first time she'd thanked the witch for anything. Something about that made her face heat in embarrassment. The witch answered with a grunt, and the two of them sipped and slurped without speaking.

When they finished, the witch just as impossibly pulled out two long thick blankets—handing one to Abeni. "No need to walk in the rain. We'll sleep until it's done, then be on our way." Abeni wanted to protest, but she *was* tired. And her body ached. As the sound of rain and the warm food in her belly made her eyelids heavy, she promised herself she would only sleep for a few moments. Just enough to . . .

Abeni awoke at a snort. She sat up quick, realizing she was the one who had snorted.

"Awake," the witch said. She sat at the cave's mouth, peering outside. "Good. We can go now." Never turning around, she stood up and ducked out of the cave, disappearing. Abeni jumped up from her blanket, rolling it up and hurriedly following.

When she poked her head out of the cave, she squinted. Sunlight! The rain had stopped, but she'd slept clear through to morning! Looking up, she saw with dismay that the hunter was gone, the stars of night replaced by a blue sky still tinged with the bronze, orange, and yellow of dawn.

"Do not fret," the witch said, seeing her face. She opened her small bag, beckoning for Abeni to drop in the blanket—which she did, not even bothering to ask how something so big could fit inside. "I know the way," the witch went on, closing the bag shut.

They walked for a while in the early morning and Abeni was surprised to find how rested she now felt. Her limp and aches were gone. She looked at her palms. The scratches and cuts there were gone too. A hand went to touch her side, which had been sore from a bruise, and felt nothing. Magic. It had to be. Her eyes went to the witch, not sure how to feel. She was still contemplating this when there was a familiar sound. Water. But not rain, running water. Pushing through some tall reeds, they emerged to find a sight that made Abeni's breath catch. A river. She ran hurriedly to the bank, excitement welling up. This was the same river she had crossed with the witch! Somewhere on the other side was her village!

But there was one problem.

"How will we cross?" She looked to the witch, hesitant. "Will we run . . . like before?"

"No one is chasing us this time, girl," the witch replied. "We will use the boat."

Boat? Before Abeni could ask, the witch lifted her chin and nodded at something bobbing near the water's edge. A small boat, painted green and almost blending with the tall reeds that surrounded it.

They had barely sat down before Abeni was sent flying at a sudden lurch, landing on her back. The witch glanced down with an amused stare. Grabbing hold of the boat's sides, she hoisted herself up and looked out over the edge. They were moving fast across the water. No one rowed, but they were moving!

There was another lurch when the boat slid up onto the dirt bank before going still. Abeni didn't waste a minute, jumping out and looking down a path cut into a grass field. She'd been here before. This was where villagers like Fomi's family came to fish. This was the path home! She set out, not waiting for the witch. Things were becoming familiar—an oddly shaped tree here, a rise in the land there. And a sound came in the distance.

Chok. Chok. Chok. Chok.

Abeni almost shouted as she broke into a run. She knew that sound! Someone was pounding yam! Maybe, she dared hope, it was even her mother! As the tops of straw-covered homes came into view between tall trees, her legs pushed harder. She entered her village at a full run, laughing giddily. She had done it! She was back home!

Her laughter faded as her eyes took in her surroundings and her smile slid away.

The houses she had glimpsed between the trees were intact only on one side. Now she could see where they were eaten away by fire. Charred remains showed where straw roofs had burned, and earthen walls had been torched. Some were just mounds of ash, unrecognizable as homes. She walked between them silently, putting names to the families that had lived in each before stopping at the crumbling ruins of the village's granary. The wooden gate was ajar. It swung loose in a slight wind, repeatedly hitting a wooden bowl that lay discarded nearby.

Chok. Chok. Chok. Chok.

Abeni stared at both for a while before walking deeper into the village, drawn to the place most familiar to her—home. The straw roof had fallen in, giving the house the look of a man who had lost his hat. Hesitating, she went to the door and peeked inside. Here, it barely looked like her home at all. Black marks on the walls showed how high the flames had reached. Bits of the straw roof were scattered all over. Pots and gourds were smashed, spilling all her mother's spices. And there was a sharp smell, so smoky and pungent she could taste it on her tongue.

Abeni pulled her head back out. Turning from her house, she started walking again. What she'd just seen should have horrified her. But she didn't feel anything as she wandered the deserted streets like a ghost. Here and there she recalled things—the fire pit of the blacksmith, the house where women spun cloth, the place where the Chief Elder heard disputes. The meetinghouse. Or what was left of it.

In front of where the meetinghouse once stood, there was a curious thing—a spear, the sharp point planted into the ground. Dangling from its top was a long strip of black cloth painted with what looked like an orange teardrop, fiery like the sun. Nearby was a pile of twisted and charred wood, mingled with bits of metal and shell. Abeni had to look closer to make out what it was. Masks, drums, costumes. They were from the Harvest Festival—depictions of the spirits her people held important. Some were newly created. Others old and passed down through the ages—items she would not have dared touch. All of it had been tossed aside and set on fire, like garbage—as if all they had believed was worthless and could be so easily erased.

The screams, the smoke, the living ropes, the man in the mask of goat horns—everything about that day came back to her all at once. No one had escaped. Everyone was gone.

It hit like a blow to her middle, doubling her over.

Abeni's legs felt suddenly weak, and she dropped to her knees. Deep inside, in the pit of her stomach, which she now curled around, something fought its way up, pushing to make its way out. It sent her breathing deep and fast and when it reached her mouth, it came in a long shuddering breath. Tears—the first she'd shed since that awful day—filled her eyes. And she cried. It came like a river that had been held back too long. She sobbed in great gulps of air that shook her whole body.

"Stop it! Stop your stupid crying!" Her voice trembled. "What did you think you'd find here?" She balled her hands into fists, digging nails into her palms until it hurt. She wanted to hit something. Wanted to shout and scream until there was nothing left. She cried long and hard, and she hated herself for it.

"There is no shame in tears," a voice came.

Abeni jumped up, whirling to find the witch.

"If you held it all inside much longer," she went on, "you would hollow yourself out like a gourd." She settled onto the ground, grunting at the effort and crossing her legs. "Mothers shed tears as they birth children. The bravest warriors shed tears in battle. The young mourn for the old that pass away. And the old, for those they must leave behind. Even spirits shed tears. Do not find fault with yours."

Abeni wiped at her cheeks, not sure she understood.

"You have questions," the witch said. Her dark eyes stared

knowingly. "Questions, I think, that you are at last ready to ask. I will answer as I can. But if they are many, I suggest you sit. This could take some time."

The witch was right. She did have questions. Things she wanted to know but had been too frightened to ask before. Sitting down, she ran through them, uncertain where to begin.

"Start with the one that confuses you the most," the witch offered.

Abeni thought on that, settling finally on one word. "Why?" Her voice came hoarse. She gestured to the heap of burned masks and her destroyed village.

The witch gripped her staff tight. She had laid the long piece of wood across her lap, and her dark brown hands tightened about it as she spoke. "Beyond this forest, in lands you've never heard of, there is a war."

War. Abeni repeated the word in her head. She remembered the day the witch had come, speaking to the grown-ups about a war. "What does my village have to do with a war? We've never done anything to anyone."

"War is like a fire," the witch answered. "It starts with a spark in one place. Stamp it out and you may stop it. But let it keep burning, or feed it, and it grows. There's no telling where it will go when unleashed, or who it will strike. Your village was hidden from that war. And while so, you were safe. I regret you could not stay hidden longer."

"But who?" Abeni pressed. She wanted answers she could understand. "Who started this war?"

The witch scowled, etching deep lines in her face.

"He names himself the Witch Priest," she said. "Behold his standard." She gestured to the strip of cloth attached to the spear, the one with the teardrop painted like the sun. "The eternal living flame, which will set the world afire. He has built himself a throne, and sends his armies across the lands. He claims to bring freedom—from the spirits and the gods, from rulers and priests. He urges the people to turn from them, to accept his one rule and his one wisdom. Through this, they will find peace." She snorted, leaning forward to tap beneath one eye. "But I see through his deceptions. I know what he is truly after."

"What?" Abeni asked. "What is it that he wants?"

"More power!" the witch stated hotly. "It is all their kind ever wants! Power to control! To dominate! To make all bow to their will. And they are never content! So now this bringer of freedom has declared war upon all who do not accept his rule. To his side he calls those who are easily led, whose minds can be bent to his will by awe, fear, or whispered promises. They come to him, answering his summons." She paused, her eyes intent. "You saw some of them this very night."

Abeni shuddered. "You mean the riders on the giant bats?"

The witch nodded. "Mmoatia raiders do not normally hunt so far beyond their lands. They have been promised spoils by the Witch Priest and now fit their great winged sasabonsam for war beneath his banner."

Abeni readied her next question. "Those storm women. The ones who attacked my village. They follow this Witch Priest too?"

The witch nodded again.

"They must be demons, like the Mmoa—" She struggled at the unfamiliar word.

"Em-mo-AH-tee-uh," the witch helped. She shook her head. "Mmoatia are not demons. Not men, true. But not demons. Some can even be pleasant."

"But you said they eat people," Abeni reminded.

"Well . . . yes. There's that." The witch moved on, as if people-eating was a matter up for debate. "In any case, the women who attacked your village are little different from you."

Abeni frowned, disbelieving. "But their eyes! And the way they moved!"

"The Witch Priest is a great seducer," the witch said. "Those women were warriors from a land far to the west. Guardians to a king once. His daughters pledged to the sword. Then the Witch Priest came to them, promising immortality, bestowing upon them gifts for their fealty, which they accepted. He has renamed them now his Isat—his fire, from an old tongue from the East."

"But the woman with no color," Abeni pressed. That face still haunted her, even awake. "She has to be a demon. Her skin!"

The witch shook her head again. "Just another mind corrupted by her new master. She was born with such skin, to a mother and father with skin no different than your own." Seeing Abeni's skeptical face, the witch nodded. "Yes, it is a rare thing, but it has happened among your people. It is even said those born with such skin are closer to the spirit world. Though there's no real truth in that either. They are only who they are. Nothing more."

Abeni listened, trying to make sense of things. It seemed that there was a lot about this world she didn't know about or understand. The bigness of it was overwhelming and made her feel small. Looking to the witch she bit her lip. Her next question frightened her the most. It took a great effort just to say the words.

"What happened to my family? To my village? My friends?"

An unsettled look crossed the witch's face, and she gripped her staff tighter. When she spoke her voice came low, almost at a whisper. "Beyond this forest, and farther still, there is a thing called a sea. A river so large you can't see where it ends. So much water, it covers the land, and you can watch the sun sink into it."

Abeni's eyebrows rose trying to imagine it. Could there really be such a place?

"From across this sea come the ghost ships—great canoes bigger than houses, guided by wraiths. The Witch Priest has made some bargain with these foul spirits to whom he barters the living. What he receives in return, I do not know. But he sends out his servants to capture fresh souls to feed this dark trade." The witch's eyes fixed grimly on Abeni. "I have seen them in dreams—ships that carry hundreds in their bellies. I have glimpsed the wraiths that guide them, with bodies little more than mist—like white smoke that walks. I have seen them take the living and make them into wraiths like themselves. Whole villages have been emptied and sent to them, like yours."

Abeni listened in horror. Ghost ships? Wraiths that stole people away?

"But what do they do with them? What do these wraiths want?"

The witch shook her head. "Only those taken by the ghost ships can say for certain. And they . . . never return."

Abeni sat in stunned silence. Her family, everyone she had ever known, was gone forever? Traded away to these ghost ships the way goats were traded at market? How could such a thing be? How could no one have ever told her? Another thought came.

"My friends. The storm women didn't take them. There was someone else. The man in the mask of goat horns. And that flute—with his song. Did he take them to these ghost ships too?" She swallowed. "Is he this Witch Priest?"

The witch's face became unyielding stone for a moment. She seemed to weigh something before shaking her head. "That one, I do not know. But he is not the Witch Priest. Merely another servant gifted power with that foul song. He has stolen the children of your village away—to another place. Though I cannot say why."

Abeni remembered her friends all walking to the man, standing about him and swaying. She could still see Fomi's blank face. She couldn't remember at all how the song went. But she could recall how it made her feel—like it was calling her to see the most wonderful thing ever.

"We all dreamt about a song," she said absently. The witch's eyebrows rose in question. "The night before," Abeni explained. "We all heard a song in our dreams that we couldn't remember. Do you think it might have been the same one? Of this man with the goat horn mask and his flute?"

The witch scowled. "Perhaps. It is a foul magic that would steal into the dreams of children."

"There was a woman's voice too," Abeni said, recalling the memories she'd buried away. "She was crying. 'He has taken the children . . . the Children of Night.'"

The witch stared back with an expression that might have been surprise. "It appears many strange things occurred that night," she murmured.

Abeni wasn't certain what to make of that answer. She wasn't even certain it was an answer.

"Where are my friends?" she pressed. "Where did that man take them?"

The witch shook her head. "Their path is lost to me. Somewhere far beyond my power."

Abeni's mind swirled. Why had this happened to them? What had her village done to deserve it? Her frustration and confusion quickly turned to anger. It flared up, wanting to lash out, seeking someone to hurt.

"You let it happen!" she accused the witch. "You could have stopped them! You can do magic! But you just let everyone be taken! Why didn't you stop it?"

The witch flinched, as if the words hurt. Then she straightened and glared back.

"I did what I could!" she said between bared teeth. "I told your people to leave this place, to go deeper into the forest! I gave warnings! I sent visions! I even walked their dreams! But they wouldn't listen! Do you think I wouldn't have spirited everyone away if I could?" Her hands gripped tight about her staff, stretching her skin taut over her bony knuckles. Closing her eyes, she took a deep breath. When she spoke again her voice was calm, but tired. "In the end there was nothing I could do."

Abeni listened. It was the first time the witch had shown emotion over what had happened. The first time she showed that she cared. "So the dream we all had about the song and the woman crying, that wasn't you?"

The witch shook her head. "No. That was something else."

Abeni sighed. "Maybe you should have sent us some visions like you sent the grown-ups," she whispered. "Maybe you should have warned the children too."

The witch regarded her for a moment. "Perhaps."

The two sat in a long stretch of silence. Abeni watched as beams of sunlight flooded the burnt-out houses as if searching for the missing people. The deep sadness filled her again, but she pushed back the tears this time.

"Why did my mother give me away to you?" She spoke hurriedly, fearing that if she didn't get it all out now, she might never dare ask again. "I saw the two of you talking. I heard you. She had to choose between me or my brother. Why me? Was she angry with me?"

The witch's eyes rounded. "Angry? No, child. Your mother did what she did to protect you. She understood what was to come that day. The choice she made, to save you and not your brother, that was not an easy one. No mother should ever have to make such a choice."

Abeni stared back in surprise. Her mother had given her to the witch to save her?

"Is that why you came that day? For me?"

"I came for a child. I made an agreement long ago with your village. I would look over them, and one day they would give me a child—when I asked."

That was an odd agreement. Abeni paused. "So, you didn't know it would be me. I'm not special."

The witch shifted slightly, fidgeting with her shawl. "I had a vision the night before I arrived," she said at last. "Of a girl. That girl turned out to be you. But I didn't come seeking you out," she added hastily, as Abeni's eyes rounded. "Whatever forces are at work in this world, they brought you to me. That makes you special, I think, in your own way."

The thought that she'd survived when so many others hadn't didn't make Abeni feel special at all. It only made her feel guilty, and sad. "I miss them," she said, a deep longing in her voice.

The witch's eyes softened. "I miss them as well. You have seen me in my garden, sitting at night. Do you know what I sing? It is the song of this village, of each person born into it. I remember them all. There's even a place for you—little rain bringer." She stared out at the burned and emptied houses. "They tried to destroy this place, vanish your people, make it as if you never were." Her voice turned defiant. "But I have kept their memories! That, they could not take from me!"

Abeni stared at the witch in wonder.

"I want to hear the song," she said at once. "Will you sing it to me?"

The witch raised an eyebrow. "It's hard to sing for someone who doesn't listen. Who sits sullenly in her room. Who runs off into the forest at night."

Abeni winced, recalling her rude and terrible behavior. She had been blaming the witch for what had happened. But she'd had it all wrong. Her eyes went momentarily to the dark banner with the fiery flame. This was all someone else's doing. "I'm sorry," she said, then worked up her nerve before venturing a question. "Are you . . . a witch?"

The old woman drew up indignantly. "And if I am? I've known a few witches in my time. Some admittedly unpleasant. But a few were decent enough." She gave a great huff. "But no, I'm not a witch. I'm an old woman who lives in the forest. It makes people think all sorts of things."

Abeni breathed a sigh of relief. Though something in that answer seemed only part right. Not a lie, but not the whole either.

"Why did you make this agreement with my village?" she asked. "Why do you need children—?"

"A child!" the old woman broke in. She held up a finger. "Only one."

"Only one, then," Abeni corrected herself. "But why do you need me?"

"Because I'm old. And old people sometimes need help." She seemed annoyed at the question. "Anything else? Would you care to know how the stars are born and die in the heavens? Where babies come from? Or perhaps the meaning of existence?"

Abeni shook her head. How old did this old woman think she was, that she didn't know where babies came from? She was surprised to feel the corners of her mouth tug up in a small smile, despite her sadness. Oh, there was definitely something off about that answer. Not a lie, but again not the whole either. Still, she decided she'd let that go—for now. Grown-ups always seemed to keep secrets.

"Good," the old woman said. "When you're ready, we can start our walk home."

Home, Abeni thought. She gazed around the deserted village. That was no longer here. She came to her feet and walked up to stare at the black cloth with the painted flame hanging from the spear. Grabbing hold of it, she felt the rough fabric—before tearing it away. Her first intent was to rip it to shreds or stamp it into the ground. Instead, for reasons she couldn't quite say, she rolled up the banner and tucked it into her bag—next to her gold birthday dress and jewelry. The old woman regarded this curiously but said nothing.

"I'm ready," Abeni said. "But why are we walking? Can't you just do some magic? Fly us back?"

"You know how to fly?" the old woman asked sourly. "No? Then we walk." She stood up using her staff, muttering about ridiculous requests.

"I don't know your name," Abeni said, coming to join her.

"Asha," the old woman replied. Abeni nodded, remembering now. But she certainly couldn't call her that—not someone her age.

"Auntie Asha then," she decided.

"If it pleases you."

Abeni felt it did. "You say you've been looking over my village since it was first founded? That would make you how old . . . ?"

"*Very* old," Auntie Asha replied tartly.

Abeni felt another smile forming. That was probably the best answer she'd get.

"Auntie Asha," she asked teasingly. "Where *do* babies come from?"

The older woman groaned. And Abeni managed a real smile now. Oh, she had many more questions than that.

CHAPTER EIGHT

TALKING TO POTS

W ake up!"

Abeni's eyes flew open with a start. She had been having the most pleasant sleep she'd had in a long while. No burning village. No frightening women with spears and swords. Closing her eyes, she tried to return.

A rough shake jolted her back awake. Uncurling, she turned around to squint at her tormentor. Auntie Asha stared back, bending close.

"What is it?" Abeni asked sleepily.

"Time to wake up," Auntie Asha retorted.

Abeni eyed the window, where only faint sunlight peeked in. It couldn't have been much past dawn.

"It's too early," she whined. "I'm not ready yet." Turning about, she lay back down to sleep. Her eyes had barely closed before she was attacked—by her blanket! The cloth came alive, wrapping about her tight. She yelped as it tugged her hard from bed, dropping her onto the floor with a thud! Struggling to untangle herself from the deranged fabric, she looked up to find Auntie Asha glowering down, hands balled into fists on her hips.

"Time to wake up," she repeated slowly.

"But I'm still tired!" Abeni protested, pushing away the blanket. "We were out all day!" It wasn't an exaggeration. They hadn't returned from her village until close to nightfall. After eating and a bath, she had stumbled into bed and fallen right asleep.

"All the more reason not to squander this one," Auntie Asha replied.

Abeni frowned at the logic. "I'm still growing, you know. I need my rest."

That earned her a *humph!* "Growing girls also need not spend their days lying in bed. I allowed it when you first arrived. But time enough has passed. There's work to do."

"Work?" No one had said anything about work.

"Yes, work," the older woman repeated, meeting her puzzled stare. "Or did you think your food, water, and clothes just appear by magic?"

Abeni said nothing. Actually, that was exactly what she'd thought.

"Well, it comes from work," Auntie Asha lectured, wagging a finger. "And it's time you started doing some. It will be good for you, both in body and spirit."

Abeni muttered grumpily. She hated when grown-ups made you do chores for them, and then said it would be good for you.

"So that's why you brought me here? To be your servant?"

Auntie Asha laughed so hard, the wrinkles on her skin grew smooth. "A servant knows how to clean, to cook, to spin cloth, to plant. Which of those can you do?" When Abeni didn't answer she laughed again, as if it was the funniest thing she'd ever heard. "There's food outside, and from now on it won't stay warm. If you want to eat, I suggest you hurry. And stop your pouting!"

Abeni glared at the older woman's back as she left the room. "I'm not pouting!" she called. "That's just how my lips are!" She wasn't enjoying this turn of events at all. But there seemed little she could do about it. Narrowing her eyes at the blanket, she gave it a smack. "Traitor!" Then she yelped again, as it smacked her back.

After losing a second fight with the blanket, she washed up, got dressed, and left the house to meet Auntie Asha out front. Wooden bowls of food were waiting—hot porridge doused with honey, fresh cut fruit and small rounded pieces of sweetened bread. She ate up all that she could and washed it down with a cool tea brewed with red leaves. Finishing, she sat back and gazed out across the garden, letting her eyes wander to the house and back again. *This isn't going to be so bad,* she thought encouragingly. How much work could there be for one old woman in this place?

It turned out the answer was a lot.

Her first task was washing their bowls. To do this she had to get fresh water. That meant a long trek to a forest stream with a large jar. The walk itself was difficult, and she could barely remember the old woman's directions, which consisted of "look for a green bush here" or "a tall tree there." The forest by day wasn't like at night, and she wasn't going far. But it was still filled with cries and hoots that made her jump. Things buzzed in her ears and at least once she walked through a cobweb so big, it covered her hair and face—and she tried not to think of the spider large enough to make it. By the time she reached the stream she panted from the effort and was itchy and sweaty besides. Getting the water back was another headache.

Seeing older girls and women in her village balancing jars atop their heads was common enough. But it turned out to be much harder than it looked. She sloshed water everywhere in her first attempt, getting drenched in the process. When she finally managed to get the jar back half full, she found six more, empty and waiting!

Water-carrying took up most of the morning. By the time it was done, she was already tired, and soaked besides. But there was more work waiting—lifting heavy rocks in the garden and pulling up unwanted plants. When she was done her clothes and skin were dry but caked with dirt. She didn't even want to imagine how she smelled. And still there was more! She helped grind grain, dry leaves, and collect wood for the cooking fire—she even had to scale and clean fish, which helped her appreciate Fomi's strong dislike. Fish guts smelled awful! Blech!

When the day ended and night came, Abeni ate a meal of peppery fish she helped prepare, washed the sweat and grime from her skin, and then collapsed face-first into her bed where she promptly fell asleep. Her last wish before drifting off was that hopefully tomorrow wouldn't be as bad.

But it was. So was the day after that. And the ones after that. Every morning she got up as the sun rose. If she didn't, her fussy blanket would throw her from bed. She tried to fight it several more times, the two of them circling one another, its ends knotting into little blanket fists. And she lost each time. The thing took its job very seriously! She ate, and then set about her chores. She helped in the garden. She helped fish. She helped beat and pound yam, which wasn't at all fun anymore. No matter how much she did, it seemed there was always more work!

And the old woman was not the best living companion. Most times she just gave orders or scolded when something was done wrong. She wasn't mean, exactly. She just didn't seem to be one for idle talk or play. More than once, Abeni had tried to start a conversation. But she only got short responses, and a "concentrate on your work!"

The worst of it was the house.

"You want me to clean the rooms?" Abeni asked one morning.

"That's what I said," Auntie Asha replied. She sat in front of her house weaving together a basket of long brown reeds, not bothering to look up.

"Are you sure I should go inside them?"

"You had no problem going inside before."

Abeni's eyes rounded. So, she knew about her earlier exploring. Of course she did. "They're not all . . . safe."

"Then you'd best be careful."

Abeni glanced to the house, uncertain. "How many rooms are in there?"

"Just as many rooms as are needed," Auntie Asha answered.

Abeni frowned slightly. Who knew what that meant? The old woman was especially short on talk when it came to magic. She performed very little of it in front of Abeni now and was reluctant to explain other things—like her bizarre house.

Grunting in resignation, Abeni trudged inside. As usual, she didn't recognize any of the doors—they came and went by the day. There was no way to tell what lay behind each, and picking one was just a matter of choice. She remembered, however, that the room with all the cold had been bright and yellow and round. Maybe the prettier doors were the more dangerous ones, she pondered. It would be just like this house to do that. Singling out the drabbest door she could find, she walked up and put a hand to the rough brown wood—before gingerly pushing it open. And gasped.

The room was filled with drums. Endless drums. Drums, in every shape and size—sitting about or all stacked one atop the other. Round drums and long drums and some that looked like you should hold them in your hand or slung over your shoulder. She walked past a drum so big, she craned her neck to look up at it—and still couldn't see the top. They were all covered in dust, and she thought they might have been here for some time.

"What am I supposed to do with all of you?" she asked aloud—then stopped as her foot struck something. She looked down to find a large clay jug, filled with soapy water. Next to it was a thick white cloth. Not very subtle. Sighing, she picked the cloth up, looking around again at all the dust-covered drums. "This will probably take all day," she muttered.

It took three. Three long days. And that was just the beginning. The next room she encountered was overflowing with giant hollowed-out gourds so large she could easily fit inside. She wiped them clean, then rolled them out on their bulbous bodies to be arranged neatly. Cleaning the rooms always took a long time. If she didn't finish in one day, it would still be waiting there the next—not disappearing until she was done. Or the room decided she was done. Then there would be another one waiting, with more odd things in need of cleaning or rearranging or tidying. It was tiring work. But at least alone, she had time to think, without the old woman's commands or fussing. Her thoughts often went to home—what had once been home anyway.

When she was with the old woman, she tried her best to learn more about this Witch Priest and his war. She especially wanted to know about the ghost ships and the man with the goat horn mask. But Auntie Asha avoided all such talk, often changing the subject or giving curt answers—as if she'd revealed more than enough already. It left Abeni frustrated. But becoming angry or throwing a tantrum wouldn't help. She and the old woman were past that. So, she settled on being patient, and determined to learn what she could.

Sometimes at night, when she hadn't yet fallen asleep, and the moving images on her wall no longer amused her, she reached into her bag and took out the cloth she'd brought back from her village—the banner with the orange flame of the Witch Priest. She didn't know what she was looking for, but she stared at it, wishing it would give up its secrets. Mostly though, the sight of it left her cold and brought fitful dreams.

It was on a day after one such restless night that she found the sword.

The door had appeared that morning, a thing of iron with sharp edges. Behind it was a room filled with weapons. Many were so sharp and dangerous looking she had to be careful not to cut herself. The cloth had been waiting too, this time with some white cream in a small bowl. Her task was to shine and polish each weapon. And from the amount of them she guessed she'd be doing so well into nightfall.

It was in the middle of her cleaning that she saw the sword. It was short and small, with a dark, sharp, and pointed blade. She picked it up, amazed at how light it was. Many of the weapons here she could barely lift. This one she could hoist above her head.

She recalled her father—how good he had been with a sword. And her mother, standing with a sword raised up to the fierce storm woman. She got the sudden impression that this room had been meant for her. Maybe all her troubled thoughts the previous night had made it appear. Without giving it a second thought, she knew then she was going to take the sword. Sneaking it into her room wasn't hard, and she slid it behind her bed where no one would look. She fell asleep staring at it, running a finger carefully along the dark blade.

That night she dreamt of her village and that terrible day. She'd had this dream many times before. But this time was different. This time she was there, older and stronger. She wielded a sword—the same one she'd stolen—against the storm woman with no color. And she won! With her mother and father beside her, they fought off the remaining storm women, cutting their cursed ropes and sending them fleeing. She confronted the man in the mask of goat horns, slicing his flute in two and rescuing her friends. It was the best dream she'd ever had.

When Abeni woke the next morning, memories of it flittered in her head. She knew then why she'd taken the sword. Why the room had appeared. It was too late to save her village. But she refused to believe it was too late to save her family and friends. Somehow, someday, she would find them again. She would rescue them from ghost ships and storm women and men with cursed flutes. But she'd have to be strong—much stronger than she was now.

That morning, just before the sun rose, she went outside with the sword. Standing in the back of the house, she began to practice. She didn't think she even knew what she was doing. She'd never paid much attention to her father or uncle as they sparred. But she practiced anyway, depending on her memory and what seemed right. She especially thought of her mother—the way she had stood holding that sword, the way she wielded it. One day she'd be able to do that.

She practiced with the sword whenever she got a free moment. When the old woman had gone out. Or had left her to her own designs. Once she found a room filled with nothing but mirrors. She spent most of the day practicing in front of them—watching her reflection from every angle. Suddenly, her daily tasks seemed less dull. Between the water-carrying and grain grinding and endless rooms in need of cleaning, practicing with the sword had given her something to focus on. Something that was all hers. Holding it made her feel powerful, brave. Not a girl who cowered at storm women with fire in their eyes or fled before bat riders swooping through the skies. She was a hero with the sword, like in her dreams. Wherever her friends and family had been stolen to, she'd find them. She'd bring them back!

Still, she wasn't naïve. Taking on a whole army of those storm women might work in a dream, but this was real life. She was going to need more than a sword. She would need something powerful. Something strong. She would need magic.

And she knew just the person to teach her.

One day, as she and the old woman sat in the early morning shelling peas on straw mats in the middle of the garden, she decided to bring it up. They were plucking the peas from green pods and dropping them into a large bowl. She'd practiced how she would go about her question. All she'd been waiting for was the right moment.

"Auntie Asha," she began, "I was thinking." The older woman continued her work, not looking up. Knowing this was just her way, Abeni continued. "I've been doing all this work, and it takes me so long. The rooms alone can take days. I was thinking how much easier it could be."

"Yes," Auntie Asha said, eyes on her peas. "How much faster it could be if you didn't sit about staring at nothing, dreaming while awake."

Abeni blinked. She didn't know the old woman had even noticed.

"Well, yes. But I was thinking you could help, by teaching me."

"There's only so much instruction for sweeping or cleaning."

"No, I don't mean that. I meant . . ." She held her breath. "Magic."

The old woman's hands stopped their work—going still. She looked up, her black eyes unblinking. Abeni swallowed, meeting that gaze. A part of her wanted to say *never mind* and return to shelling peas. But she needed this, not just for herself, but for her village. It was now or never. "What I was thinking, um, saying . . . if you could teach me magic . . . I could get my work done . . . more quickly." She swallowed again.

"You want to learn magic," Auntie Asha said finally. "To help with your chores."

Abeni nodded. Her heart thumped hopefully. Maybe she'd made her case well after all.

"And to think," Auntie Asha continued in a rueful tone, "so many children must complete chores each day, without a bit of magic to help. How terrible for them!"

Abeni was set to nod again, until she read the old woman's blank stare. This wasn't sympathy. She was mocking her—making fun of her request. Hope faded, then fled, as Auntie Asha leaned closer, those dark eyes scrutinizing, as if she could see right through her.

"Now what would a girl like you possibly want with magic? A girl who, when I found her, feared magic. Certainly not just to do her chores. That would be lazy. And she's not lazy, is she? No, her mind is forever working at things. Maybe she needs magic for something else? Maybe for the same reason she thinks she needs to steal a sword?"

Abeni's eyes widened. If she hadn't been sitting down, she would have jumped back. She had done her best to keep her sword practicing secret!

Auntie Asha's voice hardened to stone. "Maybe the girl thinks she can learn magic and how to swing a sword, and then go out chasing after ghost ships and storm women and men in goat horn masks? Could *that* be it?" When Abeni didn't answer, she flared her nostrils in an angry snort. "Magic! Cha! What a day that would be, when I teach magic to a girl who dreams of being a hero! Teach you just enough to end up in more trouble than you can handle! This is the last I want to hear about teaching you any magic! The very last!"

Abeni turned her eyes downward, her facing burning with embarrassment. She didn't answer back. She just kept her eyes on her hands as they began to shell peas again, in silence.

The next day, she found herself cleaning out a new room—this one filled with feathers. Of every color imaginable—spotted

or striped or in bright hues. Some were small enough to fit in
the palm of her hand. Others were so large she couldn't imagine the bird they came from. Didn't want to imagine either. She
sorted and arranged them, placing the smaller ones into wide
woven baskets and laying the larger ones on the floor. When
she had finished she was exhausted and covered in feathery bits
that stuck all over. She walked to the back of the house, where
a plate of covered food—white fufu balls with a spicy melon
soup—waited.

The old woman had left earlier that morning—off on one of
the forest hunts she took from time to time—leaving Abeni up
to her waist in feathers. She sat glumly eating her food, picking
feather bits out of her hair and grimacing when a few made it onto
her tongue. Auntie Asha's refusal to teach her magic had robbed
her of her fire. She hadn't even bothered to practice her swordplay
that morning. Without magic her plans seemed empty dreams.
How would she fight women who wielded flaming knives and
men with cursed flutes with her one sword? She scowled, biting
down hard on a fufu ball and chewing furiously. Did that old
woman expect her to stay here for the rest of her life? Cleaning endless rooms and pulling weeds? Surrounded by magic she
couldn't touch?

A stray feather floated up from her clothes to land on her
cheek. She swiped at it angrily. In her dark mood she almost
didn't hear her name being called.

Abeni.

She turned around, stopping her chewing, and looked about
behind the house. No one was there. The garden was empty. And
that hadn't sounded like the whispering grass stalks. Oh, that was
just perfect, she thought glumly. Now she was hearing things. All
this work was making her crazy!

Abeni.

She stood up now, putting her food down. Okay, that hadn't
been her imagination.

"Auntie Asha?" No answer. It hadn't sounded like the old woman anyway.

Over here, Abeni. You have to look for us. Want to find us.

She turned, following the call, and stopped in surprise. There was a door. It was tall and made of plain-looking wood, the rough surface painted white with red symbols. Right out in the middle of the garden! Only, she'd never seen a door that wasn't in the house before. *But why should that surprise you?* she thought. *If rooms in this strange place can come and go as they please, why not out here?*

But why had it appeared now? And why was it calling her?

Come find out.

Abeni's eyebrows rose. She hadn't asked that aloud! Unable to resist, she set down her food and took cautious steps towards the door. She made a full circle around it, finding the same white paint and odd symbols on the opposite side. An idle thought came to her. The door wasn't attached to anything, just a bordering red frame. If she walked through it, wouldn't she just come out the other side? Right here in the garden?

"Only one way to find out," she mused.

Gingerly, she lifted a hand to push the door open—just a bit. But before she'd even touched the wood, it cracked open on its own. She jerked her fingers back. None of the other doors had ever done that before. They'd never called her either. Licking her lips nervously, she dared a peek inside. But she couldn't make out more than shadows. Gathering up her courage, she first poked a head inside and then followed with her whole body, gaping at what she found.

Behind the door, standing impossibly in the middle of the garden, there was a room. It was much like the others she'd become used to cleaning, though perhaps larger than any of them. It was dark inside, but she could see it filled with the most unexpected things yet—pots! Every kind of pot she could think of! Giant pots and little pots, round pots and skinny pots. Some were painted in vibrant colors. Others were plain dull clay. There were so many different kinds she couldn't describe them all. They sat everywhere, upright or on their sides, all atop each other in great big heaps like small hills. As she stood staring, the strange voice came again.

Wouldn't you like to see us, Abeni? Wouldn't you like to do some magic?

Abeni's heart leapt at the question.

"Yes!" she answered, uncertain who she was talking to.

Then we'll teach you. Just repeat after us. Reveal!

"Reveal?" Abeni asked with a frown. That didn't sound like much.

You'll have to do better than that. With magic, you have to mean it. Say it with your very heart. Now—Reveal!

"Oh," Abeni said, abashed. She cleared her throat. "Reveal!"

Something flickered before her eyes before returning to darkness. Then the entire room burst into brilliance! Abeni let out a small squeak. Had she just done magic? A tingle of excitement ran through her. She had just done magic! With the light, she now realized how big the room truly was. It went on and on, so that she couldn't even see an end. And that wasn't all. A low humming had begun, growing louder by the moment. The humming was made up of voices. Dozens, perhaps hundreds of voices—all talking at once. The voices were coming from the pots! They were talking! These pots were *alive*! They moved about, twisting and jostling each other. Some yelled. Some whispered. Some laughed. A few even sang. Excited at this new discovery, she tried talking back.

"Excuse me?" she began.

"You're excused!" one retorted. Several pots howled in laughter.

Abeni frowned. That wasn't very nice. "I just wanted to know—"

"I just wanted to know," some pots mocked in unison.

Okay. This was getting annoying. "What are you?" she asked.

"What do we look like?" one shot back. "We're pots! What are you?"

"I'm a girl," she replied indignantly. "And I've never seen talking pots before."

"Well, we've never seen a talking *girl* before!"

Abeni gritted her teeth. This rudeness really wasn't necessary.

"Did you call me?" she asked. "I heard a voice. Was that you?"

"Yes. But you called us first," a pot said.

"Me? How did I call you?"

"I wish I knew magic," several mocked. "I wish I didn't have all these chores. I wish I was big and strong! Waah! Waah! Waah! You called us up with all that sitting around and moping, you great big lump! We answered back so you'd shut up!"

Abeni's cheeks heated. She *wasn't* moping.

"But where'd you come from? I've never seen this place."

"It's magic, you dolt! Just like us! You can't see it unless you're looking!"

Abeni supposed that made sense. As much sense as talking pots. She shook her head. This place had a surprise around every corner—and there were many corners!

"Over here, Abeni!" one of the pots called. She looked down to where a shallow bowl like a basin sat. "Why don't you let me show you what I can do? Touch my side and say, Reveal!"

She reached a hand down, then hesitated, thinking of Auntie Asha. If the old woman had hidden this room away, it was probably for a good reason. She wouldn't look kindly on Abeni even being in here, much less touching her magic pots. "I don't know. Auntie Asha might not like it."

A roar of angry cries rose from the pots that made Abeni jump.

"That old tortoise!"

"Dried up hag!"

"We're not afraid of her!"

"She's not the boss of us!"

They went on that way for a good while, saying the most awful things.

"Just touch my side, Abeni," the shallow bowl urged. It spoke with a pleasant voice, not rude like the others. "I want to show you something. Asha doesn't need to know."

Abeni bit her lip. She *did* want to learn magic, didn't she? This pot just wanted to show her something. What harm could there be in that? Reaching a hand to the bowl again, she touched its side with her forefinger, uttered the magic word.

"Reveal!"

The bowl quickly filled with liquid. It looked like milk but shined bright with light. Abeni leaned in and gazed down in wonder as images began to show across the glowing surface: a shadow that moved in the sky, a girl with orange eyes like a cat and another with black eyes who disappeared in a blink of pink mist, a strange village with tired grown-ups walking towards a pit at the crack of a whip. A dark red stone that pulsed and beat like a living heart. And monsters behind masks of wood and iron, with mouths that roared. She reared back, as the monsters rippled away, and a new image came. She gasped! She was staring at herself! But bigger, stronger! There was a sword in her hand, and she held it high—as if to say nothing could frighten or challenge her again! She leaned in to see more of the image, but it too rippled away and was replaced by another. It was of a little girl. She looked familiar somehow, although Abeni was almost certain they hadn't met before. As if the girl could see out of the bowl, she suddenly looked up with dark piercing eyes above a bright smile and spoke.

"Hello, little rain bringer."

Abeni jumped back. The girl vanished and was soon replaced by more images—so many it made her dizzy. She looked away, trying to clear her head, and wondering what that was all about.

"Things that could be," the bowl said, reading her thoughts. Its voice became a low whisper. "Watch out for shadows, Abeni!"

She was about to ask what that meant when a larger pot adorned in colorful beads pushed itself forward, knocking the shallow bowl to the side. The glowing waters rippled, and the images disappeared, leaving behind glowing white liquid.

"Enough of that bore!" the bigger pot said. "Let me show you some real magic!"

Abeni hesitated. But hadn't she come this far? Touching the pot, she rubbed its side and said, "Reveal!" In an instant, it filled up with something—what looked like thick blue soup.

"What is it?" she asked in wonder.

"Maaaagic." The pot purred the word like a cat. "This is where the old hag keeps it all, hidden away. You wanted some, didn't you? Here's your chance. Have a taste!"

Abeni stared into the pot. Back in her village the local healer would make potions. She'd gotten sick and had to drink one down. It had made her better but tasted terrible!

"I'm not some little village healer," the pot snapped. "This isn't brewed out of bitter leaves or ground-up cow horns. This is magic—pure magic! Just taste! Come on!"

These pots certainly were fussy! Not to mention impatient. Just a taste, then. She dipped the tip of a finger into the blue goop. It was very cold, and she shivered! Bringing just a bit to her tongue, she licked lightly—and her eyes lit up.

"Good, right?" the pot asked.

Abeni nodded vigorously. It was delicious! The most magnificent thing she'd ever tasted. Like milk and flower nectar and maybe what sunshine tasted like after a rainfall!

"Have some moooore," the pot purred. "Heh heh. Have as much as you like."

Abeni grinned. Reaching a full hand in this time, she took a scoop of the cool liquid and drank it down. Every bit of her seemed to come alive, and she shuddered. The more she tasted, the more she wanted.

"Oh, try me! Try me!" another pot urged, pushing forward.

Abeni paused her drinking, her lips and mouth smeared blue. Touching the new pot, she commanded it to reveal itself. A heap of what looked like colorful stones appeared. But they were soft and squishy to the touch. She put one in her mouth and was surprised to find it sweet as a melon—and chewy! Another tasted like a sugared tamarind. She gulped it down.

"Try me! Try me! Try me!"

Abeni looked to find more pots had surrounded her on all sides, urging her to make them reveal their contents. They bustled and pushed to reach her, and she had to tell them one at a time. But she granted their wishes, saying the magic word eagerly, then stuffing her mouth with their deliciousness!

"Abeni," a voice came, in the middle of her eating. It was the shallow bowl, its glowing waters gone still. She wondered what that tasted like? "You might want to stop."

Stop? She'd stuffed her mouth with some pinkish crunchy things that squirted liquid like fiery honey on the inside. Why would she want to do that? If someone had told her before that magic could taste so good, she would've been eating it every day! She sat on the floor, shoving new things into her face, not stopping until she was too full to take any more. Lying back, she rubbed her swollen belly as more pots clamored for her attention.

"Give me a moment," she muttered tiredly. "I'll get to the rest of you. Just need to—*hiccup!*"

Abeni sat right up. That hiccup was so strong, it had made her jump. She put a hand to her chest. Maybe she had eaten too fast. Leaning back, she tried to get comfortable again, but couldn't. What was she sitting on? Looking down, she found something thick and long poking out from beneath her dress. It was covered in green scales and had a pointed end. Oh, she thought absently. Just her tail.

She bolted straight to her feet. *Her tail?* She spun in a circle, frantically trying to see the thing. She could feel it at her back, swishing and curling about! A tail! How had it gotten there?

"Hiccup!"

She covered her mouth with a hand. That hiccup had made her feel funny. She noticed the pots were no longer calling to her. Instead they giggled, as if at some joke. When she turned to them, they only laughed louder. What was so funny?

"Abeni." It was the shallow bowl again. "You might want to take a look at yourself." Frowning, she leaned her head over the milk-white waters. There were no images this time, just her reflection. She squealed at seeing two furry things on either side of her head. She squealed again when her fingers touched them. Ears! Long, and covered in gray fur. She had grown rabbit ears!

Don't panic, she told herself. *Don't panic!* There had to be a perfectly reasonable explanation. She glanced to the pots and their emptied contents. Magic! More strong hiccups made her double over, shuddering. When she looked back up at her reflection she had grown a pair of curving horns, white and streaked with brown like a cow's, and her forearms were covered in shaggy white dog hair! Okay! She was panicking! She was *definitely* panicking!

She turned to run from the room and away from these crazy pots! But she had only taken a few steps when she tripped. She would have fallen flat on her face if she hadn't caught herself. Pushing up with the flat of her palms, she looked at her feet and it was little wonder. One was a bird's foot, all skinny with four claws. The other ended in a black hoof! Not knowing what else to do, she sat down and was racked by constant hiccups—which caused new things to grow or change upon her.

The pots roared their laughter at each one.

It was in the middle of her despair that the door to the odd room burst open. Standing there was Auntie Asha. The old woman somehow seemed taller than usual, filling up the doorframe. Her dark eyes shined as she glared across the room. As one, the many pots shrank back, some of them shrieking, the smaller ones trying to hide. When that dark gaze fell over her, Abeni cowered too. She must have looked a sight—by now having grown a bushy lion's mane and a twitching nose like a baby elephant. But the old woman's anger seemed to melt away, turning to a look of concern. Walking over, she bent down, and with surprising strength lifted Abeni into her arms, taking care to be gentle with her tail. As they neared the doorframe, she turned a parting glare on the pots.

"Do not think I will not deal with all of you later!" she said coldly.

The pots wailed. Soon an argument erupted, as they all turned to blame each other. The old woman left them there, stepping through the door to outside. Abeni was surprised to find the sun sat low and lazy on the horizon. It was almost sunset! How long had she been in there?

Auntie Asha took her to the house and set her down in her bed. She disappeared for a moment, then returned with a small wooden cup and a large clay bowl. In the cup was a green liquid that made Abeni's elephant nose wrinkle. It smelled horrible!

"You'll need to drink this and quick," Auntie Asha instructed. She pressed the cup forward. "Unless you want to stay like this forever."

That was all Abeni needed to hear. With the old woman's help, she held up her elephant nose and drank down the green liquid. Blech! It tasted even worse than it smelled!

"Good." Auntie Asha nodded, accepting the drained cup. "Now, the bowl."

Abeni looked to the empty bowl, wondering what she was to do with it. Then her stomach made a terrible sound. A deep gurgling that roiled her belly. She grabbed the bowl, hanging her head over it just in time as everything came up in a rush—a rainbow of colors, whole stones, and chewed up bits of unrecognizable things. She panted when it ended, wiping at her mouth. Then she noticed her nose, wrinkling it in relief. It was hers again! Looking to her arms she found the fur was gone. She was about to cheer when she noticed her feet—still a chicken foot and a hoof. Her stomach grumbled noisily.

"You swallowed a lot of magic," Auntie Asha said. Her tone wasn't angry, but it held a scolding note. "You are about to learn that all magic comes with a cost. It will be a long evening."

Abeni only partly heard. Her head was once again over the bowl, her belly heaving.

It was well after nightfall when she finished emptying her stomach. It had been harrowing, but she was herself again—no more tail, rabbit ears, or anything else. Certain that nothing else was coming up, she pushed the bowl away and sat back, exhausted. Auntie Asha, who had stayed with her the whole time, handed over a cup. Abeni took it, peering inside hesitantly.

"Just water," the old woman assured her.

"Thank you," Abeni said, taking a sip. Or at least that's what she intended to say. Only it didn't sound like that. She was speaking words she'd never heard before. In another language! She could tell what they meant—she just didn't know why she was saying them. Looking up, she found Auntie Asha appeared just as confused.

"What was that?" Abeni asked. These were new words, as unfamiliar as the last. The old woman leaned close from where she sat on the bed's edge, to place a palm to her forehead, bending low to meet her at eye level.

"Do you understand me?" she asked in some odd language.

Abeni nodded. Like before, the words were nothing she'd ever heard. But she could understand them all the same.

"Tell me all that the pots made you eat," Auntie Asha said. "Leave nothing out."

Abeni did so. The words that tumbled from her lips were so unfamiliar she didn't know her mouth could make those sounds.

"Hmmm," Auntie Asha said when she'd finished. "I believe I know the problem."

Abeni breathed a sigh of relief. "You understand me, then?"

"I speak many tongues. Now it seems, so do you. You swallowed a prattle stone."

Abeni stared blankly. "A prattle what?"

"Prattle stones form in the bellies of giant fish that swim the seas of the world," the old woman explained. "Holding one in your mouth allows you to speak and understand many tongues. It seems swallowing one whole has a lingering effect."

Abeni grimaced, feeling queasy again. She had swallowed something that had grown in a giant fish's belly? Disgusting! "Can you get it out of me?"

Auntie Asha shook her head. "I wish I could. A good prattle stone is a rare thing. But all that's going to come up has done so." She pointed to the bucket full of colorful goop. "That prattle stone seems to have taken a liking to you. Out of one belly and into another, I suppose."

"But I don't want it in there!" Abeni whined. She didn't like the idea of some magic rock making a home in her stomach. "I want to talk normal again!"

The old woman clucked her tongue, rolling her eyes. "Cha! Do young people ever listen? You can speak any tongue you wish, silly girl. Just stop and think before you talk. What a day it would be if everyone did so now and again!"

Abeni wasn't sure she knew what that meant, but she tried. She thought of what she wanted to say and how she wanted to sound. It took a few wrong tries and more chiding from the old woman to concentrate. But finally she was successful. The words she spoke sounded familiar again. "That's better," she said, relieved.

"Keep practicing," Auntie Asha urged. "It will get easier with time. Hopefully you've learned not to go around talking to strange pots."

Abeni nodded, rubbing her aching stomach. "Why are they so mean?"

Auntie Asha moved to sit on a nearby stool, adjusting her shawls about her shoulders. "Because I made them that way. I need them to be difficult, to keep their secrets. That's why they often speak in riddles. I'm afraid it's also made them cruel." She paused. "But this is my fault. And for that, I am sorry."

Abeni stared in surprise. That was unexpected. The old woman was silent for a long moment, her face drawn up. Abeni had seen that look before—on people who were trying to decide whether they should say a thing or not. It was best to keep quiet, she'd learned, and let them choose.

"I have a sister," the old woman said finally. "She lives far from here, beyond the forest, in a valley. Much like me, she is a caretaker—of a small village."

Abeni's eyebrows rose. Auntie Asha had a sister? She hadn't ever thought of the old woman as even having family. But she supposed everyone had a family. Even when they were stolen away.

"The night before I came to your village," she went on, "my sister spoke to me. In my dreams."

Dream-talking should have sounded crazy to Abeni. But this was a day when some talking pots had tricked her into eating magic. And now she had an enchanted stone in her belly. So what did she know?

"It had been a very long time since my sister and I had last spoken," Auntie Asha went on. "I almost didn't recognize her voice."

The old woman went quiet again, and a far-off look entered her eyes. "What did your sister tell you?" Abeni asked, genuinely curious.

Auntie Asha's dark eyes focused, returning from wherever she'd gone. "That the children of her village had been taken. By a song. And that *he* was coming."

Abeni's body went stiff and cold at once. "The man with the flute," she whispered. "The man in the mask of goat horns!"

The old woman nodded gravely. "You heard her too that very night. All the children of your village did."

It came back to Abeni suddenly. The woman in the dream the night before Harvest Festival. The one who had been wailing and crying.

He has taken the children. Taken them from me. The Children of Night.

She looked to the old woman, a hundred questions forming. "How . . . ?"

Auntie Asha shook her head, white locs swaying. "I do not know. When you told me that you and all the children of your village had heard my sister's cries, I was unsure what to make of it. I still am. Perhaps, in her desperation, she sent her call far and wide so that it crept into all your dreams. Or it could be that my dream of her spilled over into all of yours. Perhaps even the flute's cursed magic played some role." She gave a frustrated grunt, throwing up her hands. "Cha! As I said, I do not know."

Abeni stared. "Why didn't you say this? When I told you what we heard that night?"

Auntie Asha shrugged. "It would have done little more than confuse you."

"It's my right to be confused," Abeni protested.

Her tone must have been sharper than she realized, because the old woman's dark eyes narrowed. But Abeni didn't look away. Grown-ups were always hiding things and then telling you they had a good reason.

"I did not know at first what my sister spoke of that night," the old woman went on. "So I went to that very room of pots where I keep my magic concealed. There is a basin there filled with moon water that allows me to glimpse things to come."

Abeni nodded. "I saw it. The glowing water that shows you images."

This time it was Auntie Asha's eyebrows that rose. "A scrying pot. It will show you tomorrow or the many tomorrows that might be."

"I saw—" Abeni began, but the old woman held up a hand.

"What the waters show is for you only. But be mindful. The further away from now, the more unreliable the visions. The tomorrows you saw are not yet written."

"Is that why you came to our village? Because of your sister's warning?"

Auntie Asha's face darkened. "No. Before I ever heard her call, I sensed . . . a darkness . . . in the forest. When I consulted the scrying pot, it showed me the fate of your village. That the darkness would consume it. That I was already too late."

Abeni tried to imagine what the visions in the pot must have showed Auntie Asha and shivered again. "What happened to the children of your sister's village? Does she know where the man with the flute took them? The one in the goat horn mask? Maybe we can . . ." She trailed off at the troubled look in the old woman's eyes.

"We have not spoken since that night. I have called. But she does not answer."

The hope Abeni had dared to let herself feel evaporated. And she sank back down. There was a long stretch of silence, so that all that could be heard was the wind blowing through trees and the early chirping and calls of night.

"You mean to go after them." Auntie Asha said at last. She looked at Abeni, her expression unreadable. "The storm women, the ghost ships, the man in the goat horn mask. You mean to find them. And nothing I say will dissuade you. Is this true?"

Abeni met the old woman's gaze, which did not blink. She was surprised by the question. But those eyes seemed to demand she give an answer. So she did. "Yes. I promised you I wouldn't run off again. And I won't. But I'll never stop looking for my family or my friends. Never." She meant it more than anything.

The old woman released a sigh, leaning back heavily on her stool. "You asked to learn magic. I didn't approve, for precisely this reason. I thought keeping you busied at other tasks would stifle your desire. But I see now I was wrong. That desire only grew. How else could you have called up the door?"

Abeni blinked in confusion "Me? I didn't—"

"The magic that gives the pots life felt your longing," Auntie Asha cut in. "Being mischievous, they took advantage of that. That was my fault. I shouldn't have dismissed you so readily."

And you need to stop keeping secrets from me, Abeni thought darkly. Wait. Had the old woman just *apologized*? To her? That was new! The two sat in silence again for a while. The room had darkened since they'd entered, and the images on the wall now stirred to life. They told a story about a hapless girl and a set of pots. She frowned. *Cheeky thing.*

"I will teach you," Auntie Asha declared suddenly.

Abeni looked away from the moving images. "What?"

"If you wish to go out into the world to find your family and friends there is little I can do to stop you. I will not keep you here while your heart aches for such a thing. You are, after all, a strong-willed girl. But I insist on teaching you. If at the end of your lessons you still wish to go chasing after storm women and men in goat masks, then you may go. But if you decide otherwise, know that this can still be your home."

Abeni's heart leapt. Despite her still queasy stomach, a slow smile crept across her face.

The old woman scowled. "Do not be so pleased with yourself. What I'm going to teach you isn't the kind of thing you *think* you must know."

Abeni's face fell, then scrunched up in confusion. What did that mean?

Auntie Asha put on a rare smile. "Don't worry. I promise it will be fulfilling—more than swinging that sword around." With that she rose again, smirking at the puzzled look on Abeni's face. Picking up the filled bowl, she prepared to go. "I must return this magic where it belongs. And have a word with those pots. Get your rest. Tomorrow, you will need it."

CHAPTER NINE

LESSONS

Abeni winced, clutching a hand that stung from where it had been hit. She glared at Auntie Asha, who stood across from her, leaning against the familiar gnarled walking stick.

"Enough?" the old woman asked. Abeni didn't answer, instead glancing to the sword that lay on the ground.

Auntie Asha huffed. "Stubborn child. If you must, try again."

Abeni quickly reached down to pick the weapon up, gripping the hilt. She'd barely pointed the blade before the old woman's staff came whirling. The thick wood struck her sword hand, and the weapon tumbled away. She winced, sucking in air and shaking her fingers—as if that might somehow relieve the stinging.

This had been going on now for much of the early morning. Auntie Asha had instructed her to bring the sword and show what she'd practiced. Abeni was eager, wondering if the old woman would gift her with magic that would make her skilled at the sword. Maybe even a magic sword! But each time Abeni even tried to lift the weapon, the old woman's staff rapped her hard on the hands. It was embarrassing. And it hurt!

"Have you had enough now?" Auntie Asha asked. "Or is there still something you want to show me?"

Abeni looked to the sword, then to that gnarled staff—and flinched. She shook her head. She didn't think her hands could afford any more of her pride.

"Good," the old woman said. "Consider this your first lesson—don't take things not meant for you. Now go and put that back where it belongs."

Abeni didn't argue. In the house she found the iron door already waiting. At a push, it opened to reveal the room of weapons. She hesitated briefly before putting the sword back. How many nights had she spent dreaming of wielding the thing? How many mornings and stolen moments had she used to practice with it? Or at least, she had thought she was practicing. Her throbbing hands made her think otherwise. She placed the sword back where she'd found it and left the room, not looking back to the door—which she knew was probably already gone.

Outside, Auntie Asha was waiting in the same spot, holding something in her other hand now. It was a long slender piece of wood. Shorter than her own staff, and straight, with no twists or knots. When Abeni reached her, she handed it over.

"Here."

Abeni took the staff. Made of smooth hard brown wood, the thing was about her height and just wide enough to get her fingers around.

"You'll find this more useful than any sword," Auntie Asha said.

Abeni eyed her doubtfully. "But it's just a piece of wood."

The old woman humphed. "A piece of wood you can lean on when you tire. That can support you when your legs give way. That you can use to carry things or defend yourself. Can a sword or spear do all that?" When Abeni didn't respond she just went on. "No, swords and spears are only good for cutting and poking and stealing life. And once you have done so, it is a darkness you cannot be rid of." She snorted in disgust. "Do you know why I keep such a room? Filled with weapons? As a reminder of people's stupidity! What a day it will be when the proud warrior with a sword or spear understands they are still a fool!" Abeni frowned at that. Her father and mother weren't fools. She thought to say as much, but the old woman tapped the piece of wood with appreciation. "No, this is much better than any sword. Come, I'll show you."

"I'm going to fight you?" Abeni asked uncertainly.

"Me?" Auntie Asha chuckled, turning to go. "No. These bones are too old to jump about all day. I found you a proper partner."

Puzzled, Abeni followed her around the side of the house to find a peculiar sight. It was a man—only he was made completely of straw. The yellowed fibers bunched and wrapped together, giving him lanky arms and legs that fit onto a long torso. He towered over them both, his chest and back bent slightly. He even wore clothes—a long blue robe with white curving designs that fit over broad shoulders to hang down to just above his ankles. Here and there bits of bright red string wrapped around where elbows and joints would have been, as if to keep his constructed body in place. He didn't have a face, just a head made up of straw, partly hidden by a wide round wooden hat that sloped up to end in a knot. He stood waiting for them, holding a long staff much like her own in one hand.

"This is Obi," Auntie Asha said. At her words, the straw man unexpectedly came to life. Abeni jumped back, startled. But he only removed his hat and bent down to give a flourishing bow. His body rustled as he moved but stayed firmly in place. Auntie Asha put on a proud smile and winked. "Didn't you say you wanted to see some magic?"

Abeni nodded in wonder, taking a while to remember to close her hanging jaw.

"So then," the older woman said with a clap of her hands. "Let's begin!"

The rest of the morning Abeni practiced with the wood staff. She learned how to hold it, how to balance it and move it properly. Obi was her instructor and sparring partner. The straw man moved nimbly and he never tired; it was all she could do to keep up. But Auntie Asha kept her at it, with commands and instructions.

"Everything you need to know to wield that staff can be found all about you," the old woman said. She tapped her own staff as she spoke. "The fisher bird scoops its catch. The sun touches the horizon. The wind whistles in the trees."

Abeni listened, moving alongside Obi as the old woman spoke and her staff pounded out the rhythm. Her body leaned back, staff held before her, for the small tree sways in the wind. She planted feet firm, the staff this time pointed straight ahead, for the boulder parts the stream. Obi lifted her arms or made her bend her knees when she was doing it wrong, and Auntie Asha called out new forms to learn.

They practiced the whole day like that. And the one to follow. And the one after that. Each time it ended, Abeni was left exhausted and aching. But she got up every day, eager to start anew. At night, she found herself getting up to practice in her room. Her wall often displayed images of the forms. Even that stupid blanket helped, pulling her into the correct stances. She would work at the forms until she got them right or fell asleep, clutching the staff to her.

And that wasn't all.

Auntie Asha set about teaching Abeni many things, starting with the forest. As they did their daily chores, Asha no longer sat in silence, but spoke at length. She named the trees about them and how they grew. She pointed to the grass and the plants and explained how they could be used for food or healing. She showed where to find the burrows of animals and how to listen to the calls of birds. She even walked with Abeni to the stream to fetch water, demonstrating how best to balance a jug on your head—finally!

Abeni devoured it all, like a hungry person eager to be fed. She had no idea the forest was filled with so much to know about. The two of them ventured out to places where strange plants grew or climbed tall trees just to pluck a special leaf. She would spend whole afternoons with Auntie Asha lying on the ground, watching ants go about their work while the old woman explained it in detail. She claimed there were little people, so small that they sometimes rode on the backs of ants. Abeni had looked hard for them, but so far had never found any.

They even dared to go out at night. Those were frightening

at first, given her last time out at night in the forest. There were so many calls and cries and shadows. And she often scanned the skies, fearful the bat riders would return. But Auntie Asha explained the many sounds of the forest at night, the things to beware of and the things that were of no danger. She showed how to hide, if need be, and how to use the stars to guide their way. Slowly, Abeni found her fears retreating. She actually began to look forward to their night trips, out to find flowers that bloomed only when the sun had gone down and colorful frogs that croaked and sang to the moon. She quickly learned there was magic all throughout the Jembe forest. Maybe not the magic she had first thought to learn. But it was magic just the same. She'd just never noticed.

Sometimes she sat out in the garden at night, just listening and trying to place a name to every sound—if they could be heard over the whispering grass. The old woman had explained that the tall green stalks were enchanted, and spoke often, if anyone bothered to listen. Now that Abeni knew how, she heard them all the time. Mostly they just gossiped—quite a lot, in fact.

Auntie Asha also told her more about the wider world, of other forests, bigger even than the Jembe; of things called mountains; rivers so long they seemed to go on forever; places so cold that flakes of ice rained from the sky, like beyond the door to that room she'd opened, and others swirling with thick dust called sand. Abeni had been surprised at that. It turned out Sowoke's desert was real after all! Auntie Asha spoke as well of lands both near and far, with people as many as they were different. Abeni had never known there could be so many types of people! There were those from the far south, warriors who herded cattle and carried long spears and brightly decorated shields. Others in the east were said to build their houses from cut stone that towered into the sky. And there were people to the west who Auntie Asha claimed had so much gold, they covered their skin in shimmering dust. She even described things called kingdoms that held even more wondrous things called cities—which the old woman claimed were like villages, only much, much larger, and with thousands of people! That, Abeni found, was perhaps the hardest to believe. How could thousands of people live in any one place? She couldn't even imagine what thousands of people might look like! And how could anyone be a chief over anything so big? That had to be impossible!

A few times, the old woman also spoke of the war.

Her voice would become a whisper. She would tell of the Witch Priest and his army, made up of frightening things like hyena men, giants called zimwi who lived in dark caves, creatures like the night riders and their monstrous bats, and even worse things. She claimed that with each passing day the Witch Priest's power was growing. Whole peoples and even some of these great kingdoms had fallen to him. The ghost ships came more now, and everywhere he touched burned with fire.

Abeni was always silent during these talks. She knew this was never supposed to be part of her lessons. And when Auntie Asha caught herself, she'd stop abruptly and turn to something else. But one day, as Abeni listened to stories of war and troubles in the wider world a question came that she couldn't hold back.

"Where are the spirits?" she blurted out. Auntie Asha went quiet where she sat, patting pounded balls of plantain to eat with their meal. But Abeni pressed on. "My mother told me the spirits watch over the world, to make certain everything is right. Where are they? Why haven't they stopped this Witch Priest?"

Auntie Asha stayed quiet for a long while before shaking her head, her hands continuing their work. "There are many kinds of spirits in the world. Some are flighty, and care only for themselves. Some are of the dark. Those would gladly join the Witch Priest, for they delight in wickedness. Others are merely spirits of small places—streams or trees—too weak to stand up to him. But there are powerful spirits, who strive to keep the world in balance. They have not come forward. The Witch Priest uses their absence to turn the people from them."

"Why haven't they come?" Abeni asked. "Why don't they stop him?"

The old woman frowned, shaking her head. "Perhaps they have stopped caring."

That left Abeni shaken. She had been taught the spirits were the life of the world. If they had gone from it, if they had stopped caring . . . the thought made her feel empty and suddenly alone.

But she didn't have to dwell on such things long, because there was always something new to do or to learn. One day, as she sat grounding up dried plants and placing them into gourds, Auntie Asha came and sat across from her, nodding appreciatively. Abeni smiled at the unspoken compliment. She was making the herbs and powders often mixed with mud or honey to make poultices, used for everything from mosquito bites to burns. Abeni recalled her mother's many herbs, though they'd never been so many. She had enlisted Obi's help. The straw man sat beside her, cross-legged and using a rounded stone to mash his own leaves. As he did so the jewelry around his wrists clanked together noisily.

"You've given him more of those things?" Auntie Asha grumbled. She tapped disconcertingly at the jewelry. "By the time you're done with him he'll not be fit for sparring. A straw man with jewelry. Cha!"

Abeni grinned. She had gotten used to the older woman's gruff ways. "Oh, I think he's still good enough." It was true. Though the straw man sat tame now, his daily lessons hadn't lessened by a hair. And she had the welts to show it. "Besides, I think he likes them."

She had been stringing together bracelets from painted wood beads and bits of stone. Some she kept for herself, others she offered to the straw man. She didn't think he was accustomed to getting presents. He lifted his arms to show off his gifts, shaking them until they rattled. Obi was as silent as a statue. Still, he talked in his own way. Abeni didn't know what magic kept him alive. But he now helped with chores and traveled with them into the forest, carrying baskets to help their gathering.

"Show-off," Auntie Asha muttered.

Abeni smiled. "I've been wondering at something. Your sister, who takes care of people—the way you looked after our village. Are there more like you two, who look after other places?"

Auntie Asha fidgeted with her shawls, the way she always did when asked a question she didn't quite like. "There were once many of us—until people decided they didn't need us anymore. Didn't want us anymore. They called us witches and drove us away. Or built great cities we couldn't possibly tend to. I am the last of my kind in this forest. Beyond my sister, I do not know how many of us are left in the world."

"Is your sister as old as you? What's her village like? How far—?"

"Eh!" Auntie Asha exclaimed, throwing up her hands. "Do young girls ever tire of questions?" She let out a breath. "My sister is *older* than me in fact, if you must know. And her village is much like any other, I suppose. Our kind tend to keep to the places we look over. This forest is my home, and hers is the valley. We used to talk often, before these dark times . . ." She stopped, an unreadable expression coming over her face. Then, with a shake, she seemed to catch herself. "Enough of this work for the day. I have something new."

Abeni stopped her grinding, wiping her hands on her dress. She had learned not to press on things like this. A few nudges at a time worked best.

"I want to sing you the song of your people," Auntie Asha said.

Abeni's eyes rounded. It had been a long time ago that the old woman had promised to sing it for her. So much had happened since that she'd put it out of her head. Or at least she'd found other things to take up her time. But now she was eager to hear it. Nodding, she settled back to listen. Obi did the same, stopping his mashing and going still. Auntie Asha closed her eyes and took a breath, then began.

Her voice was beautiful, strong but surprisingly soft. It came through clear, momentarily drowning out the sounds of the forest. Abeni listened, entranced. As the words flowed from Auntie Asha's lips they painted images, creating a tale that fit together like a pattern on a piece of cloth. It told of the first people who had come to the place where her village stood. How they had decided this was where they would build their homes. Of how they had met the old woman, who was old even then. And how they made their pact with her, to watch over them, to help guide them. How she promised to be with them, for as long as the village stood. The words and the story they wove filled Abeni with wonder. This was a kind of magic she'd never felt before, and the day fast slipped away as she listened. The song turned sad as it reached the destruction of her village and the story of the one girl who survived. Then it stopped.

"What's wrong?" Abeni asked, yearning for more.

"Nothing," Auntie Asha answered. "The song is simply at an end."

Abeni sat back. "I'm the girl who survived."

"You are all that remains of your village, all that remains of my song."

Abeni felt a pang of sadness. "Will you finish it?"

The old woman shrugged. "How am I to sing a song that has not yet happened? No, you will have to learn the song of your people, and then make it complete."

"Me?" Abeni exclaimed. "I don't know anything about magic songs!"

"Then I will teach you."

"But—"

"I sing that song to keep your people close," Auntie Asha said, cutting off her protests. "If this song is not passed to you, who will sing it when I am gone?"

Abeni went quiet. This task seemed more than she could handle.

"You are a clever girl," Auntie Asha said, reading her doubt. "I have faith in you. Now you must have the same."

Abeni bit her lip, casting a glance to Obi. The straw man's

faceless head bobbed up and down beneath his wide-brimmed wooden hat.

Abeni nodded. "Teach me."

Auntie Asha smiled. "Let us start at the beginning."

For the rest of the day the old woman taught her the song and continued to do so each day after that. She sang bits of it while Abeni practiced her sparring, or at meals or through their forest gathering. Whenever a spare moment presented itself between her other lessons, Abeni learned the song. Soon she was able to practice parts of it herself and hummed idly as she did her chores or before bed. Sometimes she sang it to Obi, who shook his head if she skipped a verse or got it wrong. Other times she sat in the garden at night, singing to the whispering stalks of grass, which swayed and sang it back.

This was how she spent her days, which became so many she stopped counting. Instead, she measured time by the moon, or when rains came and went, causing the plants to flower and change with the seasons. She became used to the forest, this home, and those who dwelled there—a girl, an old woman, and a straw man. They were a family, even if a decidedly strange one.

It was the morning after a particularly strong storm that Abeni was awakened by noise. She jumped from sleep, muttering to her feisty blanket that she was awake before it could throw her. But she stopped at the strange sight of a figure in a large wooden mask peering down at her, dancing about and beating a rounded drum. Green vines surrounded its face, where a mouth of yellow and green beads was fixed in a smile. Accompanying the dancer was a tall figure in a red and white mask like an animal—either an anteater or an elephant. He juggled brightly colored balls filled with seeds or stones that rattled while he hopped back and forth on straw legs.

Abeni sat up now, rubbing her eyes. Was she dreaming? No. The two masked figures were Auntie Asha and Obi. Upon seeing her awake the pair went still and opened their arms wide. The balls in Obi's hand fell to the ground, exploding into bright bits of blue and red light before vanishing into colorful smoke.

"Happy birthday!" Auntie Asha cried out.

Abeni frowned before her eyes rounded. Birthday? Could it be?

"It's your birthday, little rain bringer!" Auntie Asha confirmed, removing her mask to show an uncharacteristic smile. "Or at least the one your village celebrated."

"Harvest Festival!" Abeni breathed, hardly believing it. Had it been so long?

"I thought you might like to look nice on your special day," Auntie Asha said. She motioned to Obi, then frowned when he didn't react. "Did you forget them?"

The straw man put a hand to his head before gliding hurriedly from the room. Auntie Asha sighed, muttering something about having straw between the ears. When Obi returned, he carried a bundle in his arms. It was her gold dress, the one with the red spirals, along with her sandals, and even her mother's jewelry— everything she'd worn on her last birthday. They'd been folded away all this time. The straw man moved to offer it but stopped.

"Not so soon," Auntie Asha said. She looked down with one raised eyebrow. "If I recall, someone is supposed to be going through her first rites!"

Abeni's eyes widened. "First rites," she murmured. How could she have forgotten! This was her thirteenth Harvest Day! She'd finally seen thirteen harvest seasons!

"So then," Auntie Asha declared with a toothy grin. "Let us start the ritual!"

Abeni yelped as she was pulled from the bed by the blanket. She'd thought they were on better terms now! The thing was a menace! With Auntie Asha and Obi flanking her, she was led away into the hall to stop before a door—round and yellow.

"I remember this one," she said, surprised at finding the door again.

"Good." Auntie Asha nodded. "Then you will have no trouble going inside."

Abeni looked up in surprise. "Inside?" She remembered what opening that door had led to—a windy place that rained wet and cold flakes. She thought it was what the old woman had once described as snow.

"Inside," Auntie Asha confirmed. "You will bring me back the berries of a red tree. That will be your first task."

A red tree? Abeni wasn't sure what to make of that.

"Here," the old woman said. "This might prove helpful." She offered up, of all things, Abeni's blanket. The very one that tried to yank her from bed each morning. She accepted it, frowning. What was she going to do with a blanket?

Before she could ask the question, the door swung open. A blast of frigid air shook her to the bone, and she immediately wrapped up in the blanket. Well, she supposed that answered that.

"Remember," Auntie Asha said, looking down at her sternly. "Help may arrive from where you least expect. You are readied?"

Abeni wasn't certain what that meant. "I think I am . . ."

"Good," the old woman broke in—then promptly pushed her inside.

Abeni squawked as she stumbled into the cold. Wind howled in her ears, and the stinging bits of snow tried to cover her all over. She pulled the blanket even tighter and turned back to see—the door already gone. Her heart leapt in her throat. Had the old woman trapped her here? But no, she said this was a task.

"Well, you'd better get on with it," she said through chattering teeth.

She looked about. Wherever she was, there was snow everywhere, covering everything in a sheet of cold white powder. She didn't think there was a sky here—or at least she couldn't see one. There was just a shadowy gloom obscured by the swirling flakes.

Her eyes were still searching about when they fell on something in the distance—a speck of red. Setting out, she trudged towards it, pushing through snow that chilled her sandaled feet. As she neared the speck, it grew larger until she could make it out: a tree, which looked as if it were growing right there out in the open. She stooped before it, gaping. The tree didn't look like any tree she knew. Instead of bark, it was made from something red and almost translucent. She put a hand to it. Smooth and hard. Cold too, as cold as the snow. She looked up its length to bare branches, stripped of leaves. Wait. Not completely. Squinting, she made out one lone leaf high above—with red berries that glinted.

"There you are! Just need to get you."

That turned out to be easier said than done. The tree wasn't just cold, it burned to touch it too long. She shook her hands, trying to get warmth back into them, hopping from one of her cold feet to the other. How could something so cold burn? It was also slippery. She was a good climber and had scaled more than a few trees. But she couldn't even get to the first branch of this thing—sliding down the smooth trunk at each attempt. She fixed an infuriated glare up at the leaf. It might as well be as far away as the moon, for all she could get to it.

"Where's that help you said might arrive?" she muttered, thinking of Auntie Asha's parting words.

A sudden yanking almost took her off-balance. She caught herself in surprise, and the yank came again. Her eyes found the blanket. The thing had come alive again and was tugging at her. Another pull sent her stumbling and she tried to tear it off. But the blanket wrapped about her face, stifling her muffled cries. Fighting to get free, she finally succeeded and looked to find it had slipped between her hands and was now standing straight up— gone stiff. She stared at the crazy thing, wondering what could have possibly possessed it to behave so bizarrely, when she noticed its tip almost reached the leaf above.

She inhaled sharply, understanding. "Can you get it?"

The blanket made a movement that she hoped was a nod. Gripping the thing, she lifted it higher and watched as the tip reached just beneath the leaf. The forms she practiced with the staff came without thinking. *Cricket Hops the Bush* sent her leaping, and *Cat Swishes Its Tail* made her flick the blanket's stiff end at the branch. There was a quick snap, and the leaf fell away. Abeni caught it before her feet met the ground, smiling in triumph. As she held the leaf in her hands, the blanket folded itself back around her shoulders, bundling her in its warmth.

"Thank you," she whispered.

The blanket responded—with a sharp slap at her face.

"Oww!" she cried. "What was that for?" Her words stopped at seeing the door had reappeared. "Oh. Right."

When she trudged back through the opening, Auntie Asha and Obi were there. The straw man shook a rattle while the old woman hurriedly bundled her in a thicker blanket, dusting away flakes of snow.

"You did well," she said. Her hand produced a small jar of white paint. Dipping a forefinger inside, she applied a small dot on Abeni's forehead. A branch with colorful leaves came next, brushing cool wetness upon her cheeks. "The dot is to mark you. The waters of the branch to sweep away some part of the child in you and make clean the path to come. You have completed your first ritual and learned your first lesson: sometimes you must work alongside those you might not always get along with, to achieve a greater goal. Do not let your pride, or theirs, be your undoing."

Abeni looked to the blanket about her shoulders. She supposed they had worked together, at that. Opening her hand, she showed the old woman the leaf. But before she could present it, the thing began shriveling before her eyes. In a few blinks, she was holding nothing but water, which ran through her fingers to drip onto the floor.

"Another lesson," Auntie Asha said. "Sometimes the things we seek and work hardest to obtain may not be possible."

Abeni shook her head, confused. "Then why bother trying?"

The old woman smirked. "To try, girl, is sometimes all we ever have. We cannot know the outcome of any task if we do not start there. Speaking of tasks, are you readied for your next?"

Abeni looked down to where the water now pooled and then back up to Auntie Asha. "I'm ready to try." That actually made the old woman smile.

The rest of the morning held more rituals. Abeni thought some might have been from her village. Others had undoubtedly been the old woman's creations. She was sent to rooms twice again, and set upon strange tasks. Auntie Asha whispered secret things in her ears, told her new truths to remember, and some things she should never repeat. When it was finally over her face bore many more white dots and her cheeks were brushed one last time with the wet branch and leaves.

"Let this water wash away much of you that was as a child," Auntie Asha intoned. They stood now in the garden, amid the tall grass stalks, who all chittered excitedly. "But not all, as we must hold on to some bit of that time. Let it wash away childish things but allow you to remember them too. Now, put on your finest garments so that you might be properly presented."

With Obi's help, Abeni wrapped herself in her gold dress and fitted her jewelry about her neck and fingers. All the things she had kept with her since her last birthday. When they were done, she walked out as a young woman, to be presented to her small village—an old woman and a straw man. There was great applause alongside the noise of rattles and drums. Even the grass stalks cheered. And Abeni found herself grinning under it all.

The rest of that day there were no chores or sparring. Instead, the three of them celebrated. Abeni clapped and laughed as Auntie Asha and Obi dressed up in different masks, taken from one of the rooms. Some of the masks seemed to come alive and made odd faces and sounds. She joined them, singing and dancing in memory of Harvest Festival. They ate and drank and even splashed around in the stream, while Auntie Asha set instruments to make music on their own and caused bowls and plates to prance about. It was the most fun Abeni could remember having in a long time—which made it even odder when she began to cry.

It was almost night when the tears came, heavy and without warning—like a storm out of a blue sky. One moment she was laughing, the next her eyes burned and cheeks were wet. She cried so hard her body shook. Obi paused in his juggling. The instruments went quiet, and the bowls and plates ceased their prancing. Auntie Asha walked over then, wrapping long arms about her and holding her close.

"I'm sorry," Abeni stammered. "I was just enjoying all of this and then I remembered Fomi. We couldn't wait for this, to complete our first rites together. Now it's here, but she isn't. She's gone. They're all gone. It seems wrong to celebrate."

Auntie Asha put a hand to her chin and lifted it up so that their gazes met. Those black eyes held her firm. "It is fine to feel sadness. This day was a sad one. It will likely always be. But I wanted to show you that there is also happiness. Let this be the final lesson for you today. Life is filled with moments that can bring pain and joy at once."

That night Abeni dreamt of Fomi, her family, and her village. It was Harvest Festival. Everyone was celebrating. Everyone was happy. And as she slept, she smiled.

CHAPTER TEN

SHADOW

It was many days later that Abeni found herself in the garden late at night. She lay lazily in Obi's lap, leaning against him as he braided her hair. The straw man was as comfortable as any bed. And his straw fingers parted and twisted her hair just right—never pulling hard enough to make her cry out. She had a very tender scalp. The cool night breeze washed over her as she sat gazing up at the stars, humming her song. About them, the tall green stalks swayed and whispered, trying to get her to listen to some idle bit of news that had drifted their way.

"And there's the crocodile the hunter keeps away," Abeni said, pausing to point out the star to Obi. "His spear is the one I followed back home—my old home—when I ran away. I think I can fit it into the song. I just need to come up with the right words."

She'd learned the entire song by now. It was still hard to believe, but Auntie Asha had managed to teach her the whole thing. She'd gotten it down so well that some parts—namely where she was concerned—she had changed slightly. To make them better.

"I'll sing you what I have so far," she yawned. "If you don't like it just shake your head." The straw man nodded, silent and patient as always, nudging her head to the side so he could start on another set of braids. She hummed the new verses between several more yawns. But her eyelids grew heavier by the moment under his nimble fingers, and she soon drifted away.

Abeni shivered awake at a sudden chill. Opening her eyes, she found she was still in Obi's lap. How long had she been asleep?

She hugged herself, shivering. And why was it so cold? Gazing up at the night she saw the stars staring back. Then, some of them disappeared. Not twinkling—just . . . gone. It happened so quick she thought she was seeing things. But no, a group of stars had vanished. Sitting up, she was about to mention it to Obi when the stars reappeared.

There was a shadow.

It was so dark it cut even against the black of the night sky. She couldn't make out a shape exactly, just large wings like some giant flying thing. Her heart pounded as she first thought of the bat riders. Only this was bigger than even the giant bats. Wherever it passed its darkness swallowed the stars, blocking them from view until it moved on. She was certain it was where the coldness came from, as if it stole the very warmth from the air. Something in her mind nagged. Something about this was familiar.

Before she could even comment aloud on it, Auntie Asha suddenly came running from the house. The old woman dashed through the garden and past them, holding the hem of her brown sleeping tunic above her bare feet. Stopping in the middle of the tall stalks she glared upward, following the shadow. Her feet quickly dug into the soil, moving in a blur to bury her up to her ankles. Then, with her eyes closed, she tilted her head back until her white locs fell in a long shroud—and moaned.

Abeni gasped as that deep moaning reached her ears and something powerful washed over her. Magic! She could feel its tingle on her skin, making the fine hairs there rise on end. Her head swam beneath the strength of it, scattering her thoughts like a wind blowing through dandelions. She could even taste the magic—pungent and sweet. It filled her nostrils with the scent of rich toiled earth and the air before a storm. It pushed out from Auntie Asha in waves, drowning everything in its depths. The grass stalks grew taller as they swayed in that torrent of magic, going high to tower over them. Fresh green vines crept up to encircle the walls of the house while the roof burst open into colorful flowers. Abeni watched in amazement. Everything was growing! She tried to sit up further, wanting to see more. But Obi draped his body over her, curling up in a ball and holding her tight. She remained beneath him, peeking up at the sky. At one point the shadow passed right over them, so close that the cold of it made her very breath visible! Then it was gone.

When the straw man lifted back up, she stared in awe out across the garden. It looked as if all the plants and flowers had grown taller or their branches and leaves had spread out farther. Auntie Asha stood with her feet still rooted into the ground. But where she seemed so powerful moments ago, now she only looked tired. Her body drooped and she seemed older, as if she'd aged in that brief time. Frowning up at the sky, she was talking to herself, murmuring loud enough to be heard.

"The pots. I have to consult the pots . . . I thought I had more time." Her head moved about absently, and when her eyes fell on Abeni their gazes connected. The old woman's face showed surprise before turning hard as stone, deepening into something terrible.

Abeni shrank back, suddenly fearful of that look. She didn't think she was supposed to have seen or heard any of what had just happened. Before she could speak, Auntie Asha gestured with a hand and uttered one word like a command that echoed and rang in her head.

"Sleep!"

And that's exactly what she did.

@   @   @

Abeni woke the next morning and went about her usual tasks. She sparred with Obi—she had gotten so good now that he barely ever managed to touch her. As he came at her with *Farmer Beating the Ground for Snakes*, she dodged and struck back with the high-sweeping *Monkey Knocking Down Fruit*. She shouted with success as the wooden wide-brimmed hat flew from his head at the blow. Running to pick it up, she put it on and did a little dance. His staff dropped to his side immediately and he bowed low.

Strutting to the front of the house, she found Auntie Asha peeling fruit. The old woman glanced up, taking note of her.

"And why are you wearing a straw man's hat?"

"I won it!" Abeni proclaimed, sitting down. It was the first time she'd managed that. And she was quite proud! She deserved a reward, she thought—and grabbed a piece of fruit.

The old woman's face put on a half smile. "You should give it back. He's quite prideful—for a straw man."

"Oh, I will," Abeni said, chewing noisily. "But he'll have to win it back!"

Auntie Asha shook her head, then looked down to her peeling. "Sleep well?"

Abeni shrugged. "Well enough, I guess." She had to guess. Because she couldn't really recall. In fact, she couldn't remember how she fell asleep at all. She had been out in the garden with Obi, and then this morning had awoken in her bed. Something about it nagged at her, but she couldn't say what. Her eyes ran across the garden and the house, where vines entwined the walls and flowers covered the straw roof. That had always been like that, hadn't it? And the grass stalks were always that tall, weren't they? She stared at them, feeling as if she was missing something.

"Good," Auntie Asha said, breaking into her thoughts. "Because I have a task for you, out in the forest." Abeni's eyes lit up, and she promptly forgot whatever it was she had been thinking. Despite her first harrowing trek into the forest, she enjoyed it now. And it was on rare occasions that the old woman let her venture out alone. "I want you to go and bring me back some morning mushrooms."

Abeni's excitement melted away. "Morning mushrooms?"

Auntie Asha nodded. "And I need them still jumping, so mind how you do so."

Abeni groaned out loud. They'd gone out to get morning mushrooms before. The plants were far from here, at least a quarter day's walk. What's more, they only came out at dawn, with the first hints of sunlight. After that they disappeared into the ground and wriggled so far down you'd never reach them. Even if she left right now, she'd spend the whole night waiting for them to appear.

"I'll have to spend all night out there," she complained, slurping down more fruit.

Auntie Asha nodded. "No other way for it."

"Why do you need them?"

The old woman stopped her from taking a last piece of fruit. "Because I do. Stop asking questions. You can pack whatever you need."

"That's a lot to carry," Abeni grumbled.

"Yes," Auntie Asha agreed. "So, I thought you might take the big bag."

Abeni's eyes lit up. "The big bag?" she all but squeaked.

The old woman gave her a knowing smile, and pulled out a plain sack weaved of brown cloth. Abeni accepted it excitedly. The big bag! It was Auntie Asha's favorite magic bag—the one she'd brought along on the night Abeni had run away. Much like their odd house, it was larger on the inside than the outside. It could hold all sorts of things, but never grow any bigger or heavier. And if you put food in there, it stayed fresh or warm even when you took it out days later. A cup of water could go in and never spill. Abeni clutched it to herself eagerly. This was the first time she'd ever been allowed to use it!

"I thought you might like that," Auntie Asha said approvingly. "Set out whenever you like. Though you'll have to leave in time to reach the place where the morning mushrooms grow. Just be certain to get as many as you can. You recall how to get there, yes?"

"I remember," Abeni said, fitting the bag's straps over her shoulder. The old woman had taught her many tricks of how to find her way through the forest. And she'd made her memorize the path to most of the places they visited. "Can I take Obi?"

Auntie Asha shook her head. "No. I'll need him here."

Abeni made a disappointed sound "But I could do it faster with him. Maybe I'd even get back sooner."

"No!" Auntie Asha's voice was suddenly strong, and she looked up with a stern glare. Dropping her fruit, she put a hand to Abeni's shoulder and gripped tight. "I need you to remain out there, all night! Do not return here until you have gathered as many as you can! Do you understand me? Tell me you do!"

Abeni looked back, startled. Had she said something wrong? "I understand."

The old woman released her grip and returned to peeling fruit.

"I really need those mushrooms," she muttered. There was a pause as she began again, eyes still on her fruit. "I've tried to recall memories of my life when I was still young, before I became the old woman in the forest. But it's like . . ." Her brow furrowed as she searched for words. "Like trying to remember someone else's dream." She looked up, her dark eyes glittering. "Before you came, I'd grown so used to being alone I'd forgotten what it was like to be around others. But you, Abeni, filled with so much life and will, so much wanting . . . you have managed to remind me of that. Remind me maybe of what I used to be. Remind me that I am more than just the old woman in the forest who your people visited now and then. I want you to know, I've learned lessons from you as well in your time here."

Abeni listened quietly, accepting the praise, unsure of what to say. She'd never thought she had anything to teach anyone, especially someone who seemed to know so much.

"Just be careful when you're out there," the old woman said, ending the odd moment. "I'll pack along a few extra things. Keep to the paths we've taken. Don't go looking for shortcuts. Stay out of the darker parts of the forest." She took another pause. "And watch out for shadows."

That last part caused a flicker in Abeni's memory.

"Watch out for shadows," she repeated. "That's what the pot said." Auntie Asha frowned at her, puzzled. "The scrying pot told me that too—watch out for shadows. I'd forgotten."

Auntie Asha looked away, returning to her peeling. "It will be a long trip. Best prepare."

It was well into the afternoon when Abeni set out, waving goodbye to Auntie Asha and Obi. This was her first night trip alone, and the two had busied themselves helping her pack. There was food, water, blankets, and a lot of other things. Luckily the magic of the bag kept it light. She was wrapped in a brown dress and had two more in case this one got dirty. Her staff came along, of course. And sandals good for walking.

Auntie Asha had given very precise instructions, making note of trees, plants, rocks, and other sights along the way—in case Abeni had forgotten. With little to pass the time, she practiced her song, going over the harder parts. The sun drooped low and she stopped to eat, taking out a bowl of soup from the bag, warm as if it had just been made and not a drop spilled. The trick, Auntie Asha had explained, was to think about what you wanted before reaching inside. Of course, the bag only held what you filled it with. If you tried to get something you hadn't put in there, your hand just came out empty.

Finishing her meal, she started out again. It was twilight. After her last trek alone at night she had stuck to the path Auntie Asha said was safe. But for good measure, she brought protection. She held it now: a round, smooth ball of stone. Shaking it made it glow. The harder she shook, the brighter it got. If she shook strong enough, it would make a blinding light—like the one that had chased those bat riders away. Hopefully, she'd never need that. Right now, she just used it to light her way.

She reached her destination sometime after nightfall. It was a patch of dirt beneath a big tree with a tall trunk and twisted roots going in every direction. She knelt to look over the dark soil. The morning mushrooms were in there, she knew, but wouldn't come out until dawn. If she tried to dig them out now, they'd just burrow deeper and then might not come out at all. That meant a long wait until dawn when they would appear with the first rays of sunlight. Sighing, she pulled a blanket from the bag—not the one with the habit of fighting her—and sat down to wait.

Time seemed to pass slower than usual. With nothing else to do, her mind wandered back to her earlier conversation with Auntie Asha. The old woman was behaving oddly. Well, as odd as you could expect from a witch. *Watch out for shadows.* A strange thing to say. Strange also that she'd heard it once from a pot. Stranger still that Auntie Asha ignored it. Now here she was, bundled off and sent to gather mushrooms.

The more she thought about it, the more it confounded her. And she found herself unable to sleep. Instead, her thoughts drifted again to the garden, the house covered in vines and flowers—how it all felt somehow off. Like she was forgetting something. Or worse, she wasn't being told something. It gnawed at her, like a root jutting in her back. And she tossed and turned, wanting to go back home now, to get to the bottom of things. It was annoying knowing she'd have to wait until dawn.

Suddenly, she was struck by an idea. She looked down to the faint glow coming from the stone she still held in her hand. Maybe she could make the sun come out early, in a way!

She moved to kneel over the patch of dirt. Putting the stone right above, she shook it slightly. The glow grew a little. But in the dirt, nothing happened. She shook it again and the light grew more. Still nothing. This time she shook the ball until it became so bright she squinted at it. And waited, holding her breath.

Just beneath the dirt, there was faint movement—little things wriggling about. She bent down, waiting to see if the mushrooms would make an appearance. But the wriggling stopped, just near the surface. They seemed hesitant. She thought about reaching in and trying to grab them, but that wouldn't do. They'd just burrow deeper, and might not come back out for days. But if she made the ball any brighter, they might think it was midday and disappear back into the soil.

"What do I have to do to get you out?" she murmured.

Thinking, she remembered something Auntie Asha did each morning. She sang to her plants. When she did, they seemed to perk up, their leaves sitting just a bit higher or their stalks straighter.

She'd always thought it was some kind of magic. But maybe it was the song itself.

Bending low, just above the dirt patch, she began to hum. It was a soft song about morning and waking up. Her mother used to sing it to her. And though she didn't know all the words, she could hum it easily. As she watched, the wriggling in the soil started up again. It grew more intense the longer she hummed. The soil began swirling about like the surface of a small pond. One by one, small forms pushed up from the dirt. Morning mushrooms! Each was big enough to fit in her palm. They freed themselves by the dozens, touching the night air, drawn by her humming and the glowing light. Their white and purple spotted hoods spread wide as if yawning awake.

Still humming, Abeni reached for her bag, opening it wide and lightly shaking the ball of light. The mushrooms followed, hopping on little white stems, chasing after what they thought was the sun. First one at a time, then in bunches, they jumped into the gaping bag. In moments, she had enough to fill a basket. Flicking the ball of light once, she let it go dark again. The remaining mushrooms outside the bag squealed in alarm, snapping their hoods shut and diving back down into the soil.

No matter. She already had all that she needed. Opening the bag, she peered inside. The morning mushrooms she had caught jumped about, squealing and mewing as they wriggled against each other. But they were trapped all the same. She closed the bag shut and thought of nothing. Just an empty bag. When she opened it again, the mushrooms were all gone. They were somewhere in there, she knew—wherever things in the bag went. But she'd have to think of them to find them again.

Sitting there, she realized her work was done. She no longer needed to be out here. Without a second thought, she slung the bag back across her shoulder and started back home. As she walked, she thought over Auntie Asha's insistence she stay out the whole night. But that had been to get the mushrooms. And she'd done so—only a lot earlier. She thought of the feelings that had nagged at her. If the old woman was really trying get rid of her for the night, she wanted to know why.

"When will you stop trying to keep secrets from me?" she spoke softly.

◎ ◎ ◎

It was in the very late night, later than she would ever normally be awake, that she found herself finally just outside their garden. Nothing seemed amiss. Everything was like she'd left it. So why couldn't she shake whatever was bothering her?

Walking through the tall blades of grass she found them surprisingly quiet. They were usually forever chattering and giggling. But now they just clung to her silently, some getting in her way. She pushed past them, wondering at their odd behavior, until she noticed they weren't all that was quiet.

Abeni stopped to listen for the sounds of the forest—and heard nothing. There were no night birds, no animal calls, not even a chirping cricket. Something definitely wasn't right. Not knowing why, she crouched low in the stalks of grass. A chill crept through her, the night air gone suddenly cold. And she saw it.

A shadow.

That was the only word for it.

Darker than the night, the shadow looked like it belonged to an unusually tall and slender man. Only there was no unusually tall and slender man to cast it. This shadow moved on its own! And it looked as solid to the touch as she was. The shadow walked about the front of their house on long spindly legs that made no sound, almost gliding across the ground. Coming to a window it stopped, its neck stretching impossibly long as it poked a faceless head to peer inside.

Abeni clamped a hand over her mouth to stop from crying out. The shadow thing was looking inside their house! It seemed to be searching. But what was it? And what did it want? She had to warn Auntie Asha! The old woman was probably asleep. She might not even know—

Her thoughts were broken as their front door flew open with a loud bang. The shadow thing seemed equally surprised, pulling its head from the window and stepping back as someone appeared.

Abeni gasped. Obi!

The straw man stood tall, blocking the doorway, his staff in hand. The shadow thing studied him for a moment, its head twisting this way and that. Obi kept still, his featureless face unreadable beneath his wide-brimmed hat. The odd standoff lasted only a moment, as the shadow surged forward.

It moved as oddly as it walked, more gliding than running—and amazingly fast. Obi came to life at once, staff whirling in his hands as he swiped the shadow thing right across its middle. Its dark body was cut clean in two as the thick sturdy wood passed through it, sending the top half flying. When the staff came back up, only a pair of long spindly legs were left standing. Abeni sighed in relief. But as she watched in dismay, the head and torso that had flown away stretched back down, reaching the legs. They came together and settled to become whole again!

When Obi struck out a second time the shadow thing slipped aside, stretching its long body. An arm wrapped around the straw man's staff like a snake, wrenching it away and snapping the thick wood in two! The shadow latched another snaking tendril onto one of Obi's arms, pulling hard until it was ripped from his shoulder. The same was done to Obi's other arm, then his legs, and last his head. When the shadow thing was done, it tossed what was left of the straw man aside.

Abeni stared in horror, watching Obi be torn apart. The scattered pieces of his body still twitched, hands and feet groping about in the dark to find one another. She wanted to run and help him. But she found she couldn't move. It felt like something held her to the spot. She was terrified. All that training, and when it came time to fight, her own body betrayed her. Still hidden, she watched as the shadow thing again prepared to walk into their house.

Get up! she shouted in her head. *Move! You have to warn—*

Suddenly the shadow thing stopped in its tracks. It backed off hurriedly, away from the door. Someone was coming out of the house.

Auntie Asha! Abeni's heart leapt.

The old woman walked from her home, her face a scowling mask as she held her gnarled staff before her. She stared at the shadow thing with eyes that could cut stone.

"So," she said in a tone to match her dark look. "You have found me at last."

The shadow thing stared back at her with an eyeless face. Then, to Abeni's shock, it spoke. It didn't have a mouth. And she couldn't understand what it was saying. But it was definitely speaking. Its voice was a buzzing, like the sound of endless bees right in her ears—so that she felt the urge to swat about her head. Hearing it made her feel cold all over again and her body shook.

"Join you?" Auntie Asha asked, seeming to understand the buzzing. She barked a sharp laugh. "Go back to your master! Tell him he has nothing I want. And do not darken my door again, if you know what's good for you!"

The shadow thing reared up at her response, its slender body stretching until it became taller than the old woman. The buzzing grew louder, almost tickling Abeni's ears now. But it wasn't bees, she realized. It was voices, dozens, perhaps even more, all talking at once. And they sounded very angry.

Auntie Asha glared back. "Try, then," she growled in a low voice. "If you must."

At her words, the shadow thing leapt for her. But Auntie Asha was quicker. She brought her staff up, chanting aloud. The gnarled and knotted wood grew bright with light. When it struck, the shadow thing's body trembled—and it shrieked.

Abeni clamped hands over her ears at the awful sound. It was like dozens of mouths all opening and shrieking at once. Now she understood. The shadow wasn't one thing. It was many things. And they were all screaming—screaming and cursing in pain.

The light! they cried. *Cursed light! It burns! It burns!*

With a violent tremor the shadow thing's body broke apart and a river of smaller shadow things scurried away. Some slithered. Others ran on legs—two and as many as ten! They sought out the dark, fleeing from the staff's light. In moments they were gone. And there was silence.

Abeni clutched her chest, heart pounding as she took in shallow breaths. She was still frightened beyond belief. But she was also thankful to see the shadow thing fleeing. Auntie Asha looked relieved too. Her staff slowly dimmed and she leaned against it heavily, looking weary. Even her locs hung limp. All that magic must have tired her. She needed help. Abeni was starting to rise from her hiding place when a sound sent her still again—buzzing.

It started as a low hum, but grew steadily. The many dark things were returning. They ran or slithered or crawled, meeting and joining together again, merging into one another, the buzzing of their many voices growing louder as they spoke.

Cannot destroy us. We are forever, like you.

In moments, the shadow thing re-formed into the tall, slender man. Auntie Asha stared at it grimly. Tightening her grip on her staff, she stood up straight and rolled her shoulders.

"Back for more, then?" she asked.

A hundred terrible voices laughed. *You are old now, and weak.*

"We shall see," Auntie Asha replied gruffly. "Or is talking all you do?"

She lifted her staff and with a yell struck again. The wood flickered back to life, though its light was not as strong this time. The shadow thing staggered back at the blow. But its body didn't fall apart like before. It lashed out an arm, extending it like a whip to wrap around the staff. The old woman uttered a word and tiny needles of light erupted all over the snaking tentacle, forcing it to pull away.

The shadow thing hissed with its many voices and this time lunged for the staff, wrapping several snaking arms about it. Wherever that darkness touched, the light drained away, leaving the wood rotted. The old woman dropped the staff quickly, but not fast enough. The sickness spreading along the wood had touched her, and one of her hands began to wither. She bent over, clutching it in pain.

The sight of Auntie Asha hurt made Abeni jump, causing the stalks of green to rustle. The sound was so slight that no one should have heard it. But the shadow thing twisted a faceless head to the garden. Auntie Asha looked up as well, following its eyeless gaze. Abeni did not dare to breathe. What the shadow thing was seeing, she didn't know. But Auntie Asha's eyes went wide, staring directly at her.

Something in the old woman came back alive then. She stood tall, letting out a sharp yell that drew the shadow thing's attention. Every part of her seemed to fill with life. Her withered hand healed and her long locs rose up on end like white snakes as her body turned bright until she was glowing. Chanting in words that echoed through the night, she flung her arms out wide and called. From inside the house came a sudden clatter—and as Abeni watched in awe, an army emerged.

Weapons, masks, drums, even plates and bowls, all came charging. They were all things from the many rooms she had cleaned! They poured out of the house, streaming past Auntie Asha in a wave to attack the shadow thing. Spears thrust at it. Drums beat upon it. Crocodile masks snapped at it while plates and gourds crashed against it. They fought with a fury, brought to life by Auntie Asha's magic and channeled by her anger.

The shadow thing lifted its many arms to protect itself, retreating under the barrage. For a moment Abeni thought it might even break apart again. But it quickly sought Auntie Asha out, realizing she was the source of the attack. Its shadowy body twisted and slid about, leaping this way and that, avoiding sword swipes and baskets that came hurtling at its head. Slowly it waded through the mayhem, until it stood right before the old woman.

Abeni held her breath as everything seemed to slow. Auntie

Asha stared up at the shadow towering before her. Then she gave the slightest nod.

The shadow thing reached into its own body to pull out a long spear made of darkness. Drawing an arm back, it gave a sudden quick thrust, plunging the weapon down into Auntie Asha's chest. The old woman's face knotted up in pain and her dark eyes went black as the night. She hung there for a terrible moment that to Abeni felt like an anguished forever. When the spear was pulled free, the old woman dropped to the ground and did not get back up.

Abeni watched in horror as Auntie Asha lay sprawled in front of the house. *This can't be happening! This can't be real!* The shadow thing stared down at the old woman's unmoving form before its gaze turned to look around. The many objects that had attacked it had gone still, no longer animated.

In a fit of anger, the shadow thing kicked away one of the baskets. Then it crushed a drum beneath a foot. It picked up a spear and snapped it in two. Lost in a senseless rage, it destroyed whatever it could get its hands on, its many voices buzzing angrily. When it grew bored with that, it turned to the garden.

Abeni's stomach fell away as the faceless head swiveled in her direction. The shadow thing glided forward, grabbing a nearby flower between dark fingers. The colorful petals blackened at its touch and the stem shriveled away. Ripping the dead plant from the dirt it moved on to another. She watched as it set about tearing up and killing the garden in delight. And it was getting steadily closer to her.

The grass stalks crowded in close, trying to hide her. But she knew that once the shadow thing touched them, they would wither away too. And she would be exposed. She shuddered to think what it would do once it found her.

Suddenly, a dreadful sound cut across her fearful thoughts.

A horn. Deep and rumbling in the night. She thought it might have been the most horrible thing she'd ever heard. Only she'd heard it before—on the day her village fell. The horn had sounded, and the storm women had ended their attack.

It had the same effect now. The shadow thing stopped its mayhem, turning to stare in the direction of the horn. It looked back to the house and uttered something like a curse. At once, the whole structure burst into roaring flames. The shadow thing stood watching the fire for a while before stretching out its arms and transforming into something that looked like just two large wings. They flapped up into the air, soaring high into the sky, and wherever they passed, the stars faded away. A memory flooded Abeni's mind. *Seeing the shadow thing soaring and searching. Auntie Asha running out to make the green things about them grow, hiding them away. Being told to sleep.* And as the sound of that awful horn came once again, it drew out an even deeper memory. The day her village had been attacked. Sitting up on the roof of the meetinghouse she had looked up and seen something dark moving through the gloom. It had, she knew, been this very shadow thing. And that horn meant it was a servant of the Witch Priest.

As soon as the shadowy wings vanished into the distance, she dashed from her hiding place, running and stumbling down to reach Auntie Asha. She grabbed her, shaking her and calling out her name. But the old woman was still. Not knowing what else to do, Abeni grabbed onto Auntie Asha's dress, trying to drag her away from the burning house. She strained at the effort. The heat and smoke were unbearable, and she coughed beneath them. She was beginning to lose hope when a hand touched her shoulder.

She shouted and whirled around, imagining every horror possible, only to find—

"Obi!"

The straw man had somehow managed to pull himself together. Or mostly so. He looked like a poor version of himself, missing bits of straw and singed all over. But he was standing. He too took hold of Auntie Asha, and together they pulled her away from the burning house.

When they had gone a good way, Abeni fell to her knees,

coughing from the smoke. Wondering what to do, she heard someone call her name. Not Auntie Asha, who remained still. And of course not Obi. When the call came again, she turned back to the burning house. There was a door in front of it now, made of plain brown wood and painted white with red symbols. She recognized it—the room filled with the pots. And the call was coming from inside.

"Wait here!" she told Obi. Rising, she ran to the door, pulling it open to find—fire! Everything was smoke and flames in here too, just like the house. The pots that filled the room burned, some cracking from the heat. It was such a terrible scene that the last thing she expected was singing. But the pots that remained were all singing mournful songs and bidding each other farewell. They swayed back and forth, bellowing at the top of their lungs—or whatever they spoke with.

"Abeni!" one called.

She looked down to find the bowl with the glowing white waters. The scrying pot, the old woman had called it. Strange images appeared on its surface, showing things she didn't fully understand.

"I needed to find you!" it said. "Almost time for us to go now!"

Abeni looked to the burning pots. They hadn't been nice to her. But they didn't deserve this.

"I can get some of you out of here, in the big bag! Just let me—"

"No!" the scrying pot shouted. "The magic I alone hold is too great. Better we end here. I called to give you something. Look down."

Abeni did. Sitting at her feet was a small, cracked pot with three stones—one blue, one red, and one gold. They reminded her of colorful eggs. She bent to pick them up, finding each cool to the touch.

"Take them," the scrying pot said. "You'll know when you need them—the cat will help. I've seen your many tomorrows. Have trust in what I say."

The *cat* will help? These pots and their riddles! Unable to argue with what she didn't even understand, she hurriedly placed the stones into her bag.

"One last thing, Abeni." The scrying pot's tone turned stern. "Beware the Children of Night."

Abeni frowned. Another riddle? "Who are the—?" Her eyes rounded. The Children of Night. That's what Asha's sister had said. *He has taken the children. Taken them from me. The Children of Night.* Her mind ran, frantic. "Do you mean my friends? The ones taken away? Are those the Children of Night?"

"They become hidden in darkness," was all the scrying pot said. "To free them you must seek them. But in finding them, you risk losing yourself."

Before she could think on the words some part of the room fell away, bringing down a heap of pots in flames.

"Go, Abeni!" the scrying pot shouted. "Leave this place and take Asha with you!"

"But I want to know more! You have to tell me more!"

"I've told you all I know! It's your tomorrow, after all, not mine."

Abeni didn't have a chance to say anything else, because flames arose suddenly all around her, so hot they burned her skin. Running from the room she stumbled back to the garden. Behind her, the door slammed shut before going up in a whoosh of fire. She wondered then if all the doors were burning, and if all the rooms were now being destroyed. Her eyes settled on Obi standing and waiting, with Auntie Asha held in his arms. Walking hurriedly to them she looked around. Where to now? Where could they go? She settled on a place she was familiar with—where they could hide if the shadow thing returned.

Beckoning to Obi, she dashed through the garden where the tall blades of grass whispered their goodbyes. She paused only to retrieve her staff, then led the way into the forest. From behind, she could hear the straw man trudging along with Auntie Asha in his arms. When she reached their destination she stopped, out of breath.

They were at the stream she gathered water from each morning. She had come here so many times she could find it without thinking. Obi laid Auntie Asha beside her and she knelt to hold the old woman's head in her lap, splashing water onto her face. Nothing happened. She tried to push some water past her lips. But they didn't open. Putting a hand to Auntie Asha's skin, Abeni trembled. It was cold. So, so cold. She looked up to Obi, shaking her head.

"I don't know what to do. I think she's . . . She might be . . ." Her voice cracked as she struggled to say the word *dead*. "What are we going to do, Obi?"

The straw man stared down in silence. Bending low, he brought fingers to gently brush her cheek—catching a lone tear. Then, with a sudden jerk, he pulled away, standing straight up. Lifting the wooden hat from his head he gave a dramatic bow like the first time they'd met—then burst apart.

Abeni blinked through the haze of straw falling about her, all that was left of Obi. It took moments to realize what had happened, and what this meant. The magic that had created the straw man was now gone. So he had simply ceased to be. That magic had come from Auntie Asha. And if her magic had died, then . . .

She's dead, Abeni forced her mind to say. Auntie Asha was dead.

PART II

CHAPTER ELEVEN

ASHA

Abeni lay on her back in Auntie Asha's garden, gazing up at a blue sky and slow-moving wispy late day clouds. Sitting up, she saw she wasn't alone. Across from her sat a little girl who stared up at the sky as well. She looked down to Abeni with large dark eyes, then waved and smiled. Abeni lifted a hand and waved back uncertainly, then stopped.

This was a dream.

The call of birds brought Abeni awake. Opening her eyes, she shifted her cramped legs, coming out of the ball she'd curled into. The flowing stream nearby babbled softly with the other sounds of the forest, and through the trees she could see the sun halfway rising in a dull sky. No wispy clouds. It was still morning.

Pushing up, she spied a broad wooden hat with a pointed top sitting alone on a mound of straw. Her heart sank. Obi. Oh, poor Obi. *That* hadn't been a dream. Memories of the past night came rushing back—the shadow thing, the fire, Auntie Asha. The loss hit all over again and a familiar numbness crept over her. Not sadness, but a feeling of emptiness. As if nothing mattered. Maybe she should try to cry. That seemed the proper thing to do.

Crying won't bring them back, a voice whispered. *You should know that by now.*

She let out a long breath. The emptiness sat on her shoulders like a heavy stone. And she didn't know how to rid herself of it. Maybe the way to start was facing what she was avoiding. Bracing herself, she turned to the one place she didn't want to look. There, under the shade of a tall tree that grew up and bent over, lay a brown dress and several colorful shawls. Auntie Asha. Just where she had left her before collapsing into sleep. A sharp pain cut through the emptiness at seeing the old woman's body, still and—

Wait.

Abeni frowned, squinting through the morning sunlight. Something was wrong. Going to her hands and knees she scrambled over for a better look and stopped in disbelief. There were only clothes here. Empty clothes. Auntie Asha was gone! As if someone had just spirited the body away. What in the world was going on?

A sudden squeal made her jump. She spun around, looking about, to find—a girl?

Abeni blinked. Was she seeing things? No, the girl was still there. She couldn't have seen five—certainly no more than six— harvest seasons. Her hair was a deep black that hung in thick twisted locs down her back. And she was as naked as a baby, showing every bit of her rich brown skin. She sat in a shallow part of the stream, splashing and laughing giddily.

Abeni stared. Since she'd begun living with the old woman, she hadn't seen or met any other people. Rising, she got to her feet and walked to the edge of the stream.

"Excuse me," she began.

The girl looked up and Abeni gasped. The large dark eyes staring back were more than familiar. This was the little girl from her dream! The one who had waved to her! At seeing Abeni, she smiled a big bright smile.

"Good morning!" she greeted her in a high voice.

"Good morning," Abeni replied slowly. A thought came to her. "Am I in a dream?"

The girl scrunched up her small face, sticking out a pink tongue to lick at the air. "No," she said. "Dreams taste different."

Abeni blinked. *What?* "Are you from a nearby village? Where's your family?"

The girl shrugged.

Abeni tried again. "There was someone, over there. Did your

people take her?" The girl's eyes followed to where she gestured at the bundle of Auntie Asha's clothes before she gave another shrug.

Abeni was growing irritated.

"I don't know what's going on," she said, putting on the voice grown-ups did when they meant to be serious. "But whoever you're with, I want to talk to them. I want to know what they did with the old woman. Right! Now!" The blank stare she got back only fed her frustration. "Are you even listening?"

The girl nodded slowly, but still said nothing.

Abeni put her head in her hands, trying to contain her temper. "Little girl. You can't be out here alone. Just tell me who you're with."

The girl smiled at that. "I'm not here alone. I'm here with you, little rain bringer."

Abeni started. Little rain bringer? How could this girl know about that? The last person who'd used that nickname was . . .

Something in Abeni's mind flicked to life. She glanced to the empty clothes where the old woman had vanished, and back to the little girl who sat naked in the stream. Then she looked at her—bent down low, and *really* looked at her. That thick hair of locs. That face. Those dark eyes. *Familiar* eyes.

No! She shook her head. It couldn't be! It *can't* be.

Her voice came in the barest whisper. "Auntie Asha?"

The girl scrunched up her face again in thought. "Ahh-shaa," she sounded. Her head bobbed up and down, as if remembering. "Yes. I think I was Asha once."

That was when Abeni fell down.

Her legs went weak, like they'd been turned to water. She landed hard on the ground and just sat there, her eyes wide and round. Was this a trick? Yes, someone had to be playing a joke on her. That was it. Yet there were those eyes!

"But I saw . . ." Abeni stammered words through clenched teeth. "You died!"

The girl lifted her fingers to draw a big O in the air. "Death. Life. All a circle."

Abeni shook her head. "No! Not for people. People grow old, then they die! They don't come back! They don't turn into . . . children!"

"No," the girl agreed. "Not people."

Abeni glared. What did she mean, not people? If not people, then . . . When the answer came, she might have fallen a second time if she wasn't already sitting down.

Not people. NOT people. NOT PEOPLE!

It came out in a breathless gasp. "You're a spirit!"

The girl smiled in answer before looking down to find her refection in the water, bending close to inspect it.

Abeni's mouth hung limp. The girl—Auntie Asha—was a spirit! People had called her an old woman. Some said she was a witch. But all of them had been wrong. She was really a spirit! A spirit! How could no one in her village have known? How could *she* not have known? After all this time! Not living in a witch's house! Not living with some old woman! She'd been in the home of a spirit!

Her mind was ajumble. She ran through everything she knew about spirits—which admittedly wasn't much. In her village people offered prayers to spirits or called on them when needed. Sometimes, like during Harvest Festival, they honored them and gave them thanks. They were supposed to be everywhere—in the rivers, the trees, the sky. And they could look like anything. She supposed that included old women and little girls.

Abeni wet her mouth, realizing it had gone dry. "You said you *think* you were Asha once. Are you still . . . her?"

"No," the girl answered, still staring at her reflection. "And yes."

Abeni shook her head. "I don't understand."

"I'm not Auntie Asha anymore," the girl said. "Not exactly. If I think really, really hard, I can remember being her. But it's not the same. It's like . . . like . . ." She fumbled for words.

"Like trying to remember someone else's dream," Abeni finished.

The little girl's eyes went round, and she nodded eagerly. "Yes! Like that!"

"You told me that once," Abeni said. "When you were still . . ." She couldn't even find the right words. A sudden thought occurred. "Have you ever been . . . little . . . before?"

The girl didn't answer right away. She'd taken to making faces at her reflection, wrinkling her nose while pushing out her lips. "I've been a girl. A woman. And an old woman. Lots of times."

Abeni gaped. "Lots of times? You've done this . . . died . . . many times already?"

The little girl lifted small hands to make the O again. "Like I said, all a circle."

Abeni frowned at this. From what she knew, Auntie Asha had been around since her village's founding. Before her parents, their parents, and their parents . . . well, it had been long ago. In all that time, she'd been called the old woman. If she'd been a little girl, it was before her village even existed. That meant she stayed old a *very* long time.

"That's why you wanted a child," she whispered. "The agreement you made with my village. You didn't just need someone to care for you because you were old. When you die, you become a little girl. You needed someone to take care of you when you became little again."

The girl looked up. Her face was serious now, at least as serious as a little girl's face could be. "I needed a guardian. I still do."

Guardian? Abeni reared back. "But I can't look after you! You need a grown-up!"

The girl sighed, an odd thing on her small face. "I was supposed to have more time. To teach you. So when I was ready to be small again, you would be grown-up already. Then you could look after me, until I remembered how to look after myself. Only . . . it didn't work out that way."

Abeni stared as it all sank in. She was supposed to look after a little girl—who was really a spirit? She was supposed to raise her and take care of her? She hadn't seen but twelve harvest seasons when she arrived in the old woman's house. She'd only seen thirteen now! "I can't do this." Her voice shook. "You expect me to take care of you? *You* were supposed to take care of *me*! Instead, you've left me here alone! You've left me alone all over again! And now you're asking me to do things I can't do!" She was shouting, her confusion turning to hurt, and anger that made her head throb. It *wasn't* fair that anyone expected so much from her!

The little girl shrank into herself, dark eyes widening as fear spread across her face. Then she did something completely unexpected—she began to cry. Abeni was so surprised that she stopped shouting. For a moment she knelt there stunned, not knowing what to do. She'd never seen Auntie Asha cry. She couldn't even *imagine* the old woman crying. But this little girl was weeping, tears streaming down her cheeks as her lips trembled. The hurt on her small face was more than Abeni could bear, and she felt suddenly ashamed. She reached out, pulling the girl into an embrace.

"No, don't cry! I shouldn't have yelled at you. Please, Auntie Asha, don't cry!"

The girl sobbed against Abeni's chest, her face buried in a nest of thick locs—now the color of black earth instead of ivory. "I'm sorry!" she wailed. "I didn't mean for this to happen, not so soon!"

Abeni hugged her close. None of them had meant for any of this to happen. Who could have possibly known that she would be sitting here, holding a small girl who had once held her? It was all so strange! She needed to know more.

"The shadow thing." She shuddered to even name it. "You knew it was coming."

The little girl pushed back to look up with puffy eyes. "I hid from it for a long time. And it found me. But then you came back. You saved me. I wonder if that's what was supposed to happen?"

Abeni couldn't make sense of much of that, but she nodded anyway.

For a long while the two sat there, quiet in their own thoughts. Something still tugged at Abeni, pieces of the puzzle she was trying to sort out. "The shadow thing works for the Witch Priest, doesn't it—like those riders on the giant bats?"

The little girl's eyes drew tight. For a moment her face looked a lot like Auntie Asha's—filled with a dark and knowing intensity. When she spoke, it even sounded more like the old woman's voice. "The shadow is one of his oldest minions."

"Why did he send it after you? What does he want?"

"He wants me to join him. He believes I can make him stronger. It's why he keeps hunting me, why he sent his armies into this forest."

Abeni frowned. Her mind latched onto those words *why he sent his armies into this forest.* "The storm women. They were looking for you."

The little girl lowered her head to stare at her hands, not meeting Abeni's eyes. "The night before I came to your village, I saw the shadow in the sky. I hid myself away, hid my home. But the magic . . . I couldn't . . . Your people have cut back the trees to graze goats, to build your homes. There were not enough green things to grow up and conceal you."

Abeni listened, feeling as if she'd been struck. The Witch Priest's armies hadn't come to her village by chance. They had come for Auntie Asha. And their village had just been . . . in their way. If the storm women hadn't been hunting her, they might have never come into the forest at all. Her village might never have been destroyed. No one might have ever been taken away. That terrible day might have never happened.

Auntie Asha hadn't told her. It had been another one of her secrets.

Abeni should have been angry—furious. But she was angry with an old woman. Not a little girl. And she just felt tired. Tired of grown-ups and their secrets. Her parents and all the adults of her village had kept secrets. Auntie Asha kept many, many secrets. And where had that gotten them all? Closing her eyes, she took a deep breath and buried away those thoughts. Because she didn't know what to do with them. Not now. When she opened her eyes again, she found the girl looking at her with an anxious expression.

"What are you going to do now?" Abeni asked. "Where are you going to live?"

The little girl shook her head, her thick locs swaying. Of course, she didn't know. Auntie Asha would have known. But whatever this little girl was, she wasn't the old woman. Not anymore. The two of them were out here alone, without a home, without a village, without family—

Abeni stopped. No, not without family. She looked at the little girl as an idea took root: an idea formed from hope, desperation, and—if she was being honest—a bit of spite.

"You have a sister. Do you remember?"

The little girl stared blankly before her eyes grew wide. She bobbed her head in excitement. "Yes! I have a sister!"

"Is she a spirit? Like you?"

The little girl nodded again. "She takes care of a village, like I took care of yours!"

"Then you should go there," Abeni said. "To your sister. She can take you in."

The little girl beamed at this suggestion before her smile faded. "Oh no! I remember now. My sister's village. The children. He took them!"

Abeni had already thought of this. She leaned forward. "You mean the man in the goat horn mask? The one with the flute?"

The girl made a face. "He's very bad."

"But you need your sister's help," Abeni urged her. "What if that shadow thing comes looking for you again? Or those riders on the giant bats? You need someone who can protect you."

Someone who knows about a man in a goat horn mask with an enchanted flute, a voice in her head whispered. *Who knows about ghost ships.* She faltered for a moment. *Who's keeping secrets now,* the voice whispered guiltily. No, this was different. Grown-ups were the ones who started this whole business of keeping secrets. If she wanted to save her family and her friends, she would need to learn how to keep secrets too. She wouldn't like it. But she would do whatever it took. Besides, the scrying pot had said, *The Children of Night . . . To free them you must seek them.* Well, the pot had actually said more than that. It'd said to *beware* the Children of Night. That to find them she risked losing herself. But she was certain it was talking about her friends. And she intended to save them, whatever the risk.

"I think you must go to your sister," she said. "Do you know the way?"

The little girl looked confused—like any little girl would, unsure of the questions being put to her. "My sister is very far away. Outside this forest. I don't know if I can get there alone." Her dark eyes brightened. "Will you come with me, Abeni? I'm sure my sister will take you in too!? Please say you will! You're the only one I can trust!"

Abeni had been waiting for this. She wanted this. But that last part still made her voice catch and her face flush with guilt. She would never have been able to convince grown-up Auntie Asha of such a thing—to go chasing after the man in the goat horn mask. She was taking advantage. She knew that, and it was wrong. But they *did* need to find Auntie Asha's sister. Abeni couldn't be a guardian—not to some little girl who was really a spirit, who was being hunted by shadow things! Getting her to her sister would be best, for everyone. She told herself that made all this alright. And she thought she mostly believed it.

"Of course," she answered. "I'll come with you."

The little girl squealed and wrapped her in a tight hug. Abeni sat there, feeling awkward at first, then slowly hugged her back.

"What do I even call you now?"

The little girl pulled away. "What did you call me before?"

"Auntie Asha."

She wrinkled a small nose. "That might sound silly now."

Abeni managed a faint smile. "It probably would."

"Then just call me Asha."

"Fine, 'just call me Asha.'" She reached out to tweak her

nose—which felt just like any other little girl's nose. "Let's find you something to wear."

They spent a while rooting through the discarded bundle, ripping pieces of clothing and cutting them to size. Abeni wrapped the girl in the brown fabric, which made a nice little dress. She made out several other pieces, folded them, and placed them into the magic bag—which she'd thankfully held on to. Shoes were another problem. But with a lot of cutting and stitching, they turned the old woman's sandals into something useable.

Abeni got a bit sad as she remembered her gold dress. It had probably burned up in the fire. Or so she thought, until she reached inside the bag and felt something familiar. Pulling it out she found in surprise it was a smaller bag—the one that held her birthday dress, sandals, and jewelry!

"I thought you might want that," Asha said. She was wearing a yellow shawl that draped her small body, and she sat picking through her many necklaces and bracelets. "So I put it in there before you went out."

"Thank you," Abeni said. She paused. "I thought last night I'd lost you forever. I'm glad to have you back, even if . . . different."

The little girl gave her a bright smile. "I'm glad to be back, little rain bringer."

Abeni shook her head. How could she ever get used to that? Then something came to her. "Asha, were you in my dream earlier? Just this morning?"

The girl nodded. "Mm hmm. I miss my garden. And you remember it better."

Abeni didn't reply to that. Oh yes, the time ahead was going to be very strange.

Suddenly, the weight of what she was about to do fell upon her. She was set to follow this girl, this spirit, into the bush. She knew nothing about the rest of the forest, or the world outside. It could be dangerous out there. It *was* dangerous! Panic seized her. Her heart pounded. Sweat broke out across her skin. And her legs refused to move.

Asha looked up at her, then quietly placed a small hand inside her own.

"I remember your mother," the little girl said. "She was very strong—even when she was afraid. You remind me of her."

Abeni stared at the girl, recalling her mother standing before the storm woman. Frightened, but determined. At once, her fears receded. Not gone completely, but enough to let her draw in deep calming breaths as her legs took the first few steps into the unknown.

CHAPTER TWELVE

SPIRITS

Over the next few days, Asha led them through the forest as they made their way to her sister. At times Abeni let her walk ahead, following at a safe distance. But most often the girl liked to hold her hand, tugging to signal the direction they were to take. How she knew what that was exactly, Abeni had no idea. She had asked as much, eager to learn where the little spirit was leading them. But Asha responded each time with a shrug.

"It feels right," was all she would say.

Abeni eyed her doubtfully while taking in their unfamiliar surroundings. They had gone far now, roaming into parts of the forest she no longer recognized. It was hard to wander around the bush on just feelings—especially when the one you were following looked and acted like a little girl. Asha's attention drifted. A lot. She stopped to ooh and aah at colorful beetles or hooted up at monkeys sitting in trees. More than once, Abeni had to stop her from running off to chase after butterflies!

At times she couldn't help but just stare in wonder. This was the same old woman who had once saved her, who she'd lived with, who had taught her, who had made a straw man come to life! Now she was . . . this. How was she to ever get used to that?

It was hard to tell how much of the Auntie Asha she knew was even left. Sometimes she asked questions of the girl, things she thought the old woman might know. But she got only a few answers, and mostly shrugs or blank stares. And this girl couldn't do much of what the old woman could. Much? Make that most! Abeni had tried to get her to help fish once. But the girl had run laughing and splashing through the water, trying to catch fish with her hands. Having her help prepare food was just a mess. She didn't dare let her start a fire!

But her magic, at least, wasn't gone entirely.

Abeni knew all spirits held magic—how else to explain changing from an old woman into a little girl? Asha still held some bit of it. Entering Abeni's dreams was her favorite trick, especially dreams of Asha's garden. When asked how she did it, the girl only giggled. But other than those tricks, this Asha didn't seem able to work any great magic like before. Not the kind that created living houses with fantastic rooms. Or that might help or protect them.

"Even spirits have to learn," she told Abeni that first evening. The two sat on a big rock, watching the sky turn red then orange and almost pink with sunset. Asha strung together a necklace as she spoke, made up of leaves and flower petals. "I'll have to spend another lifetime rediscovering everything I've lost." She grinned, holding up the completed necklace as Abeni bent her head to have it slipped on. "I think it might be fun!"

Not everything had been lost. Asha may not have known every plant or bush like before. She couldn't put a name to each tree just by sight of a leaf. But she had a sense of things. One time, she knocked some red berries out of Abeni's hand, warning they were poisonous—though she couldn't say how she knew. If she sniffed the air and claimed it might rain, it usually did. She always managed to find water, or a clearing and shade to rest. And she steered them away from parts of the forest she said looked *wrong*. Abeni was certain to listen to her about that.

The next day as they walked, she tried a new topic. "You told me your sister is like you. The one we're going to see. Who are the people she looks after?"

"The people in the valley," Asha answered. She was balancing on a fallen tree branch on one foot. "She takes care of them. And the valley."

"So, she's not a little girl, then?"

Asha shook her head, laughing. "I've told you already. She's big! Very, very big!" She extended her small arms as far as she could and puffed out her cheeks.

Abeni had asked that question three times since they'd set out. And had gotten the same answer each time. Even the "very, very big" part. She just wanted to make sure. A fine thing it would be to find out this sister had become a little girl too. No one to give her the answers she sought. And she'd probably have to take care of them both.

"Are all spirits like you two?" she asked. "Do they look after people?"

Asha laughed a little girl's laugh. "Of course not! There are all kinds of spirits. Some look after rivers. Or rocks. Or mountains. There are spirits who look after plants and trees. I once knew a spirit who tended a small field of yams! But lots of spirits don't really look after anything. They just . . . are. And most don't have much to do with people. Some even pretend you don't exist."

"Then why do you and your sister look after people?"

Asha only shrugged. "Someone has to."

Abeni didn't know what to make of that answer. But before she could ask anything else, Asha gave a big-mouthed yawn. "I'm tired," she whined. That was another thing. Asha could be all bursts of energy one moment, then needing to rest the next. She supposed those little legs could only walk so much.

"We'll rest here," she sighed, stopping beneath a tree with wide leaves for shade. She reached into the big bag and pulled out a blanket, spreading it for them to sit on. Then she pulled out a honey cake, a gourd of water, and two cups. She broke the cake apart and the two sat down, nibbling. Abeni had finished one piece and reached for another, but found it gone. She frowned. That was odd. She had broken the cake into four pieces. They'd eaten two, but now there were none.

"Asha, did you take the other pieces of cake?"

The girl shook her head. She was eating and counting her fingers and toes—something she'd done at least three times already, as if expecting some to go missing.

Abeni sat, puzzled. This wasn't the first time food had vanished. Yesterday she'd set out pieces of bread with some smoked fish for dinner. But when they were ready to eat, some had gone missing. She thought she'd counted wrong. Now it was happening again. What was going on?

Looking around, her eyes caught something on the ground. She walked over, bending down to inspect it. Crumbs. She picked up a bit and sniffed. Honey cake! The crumbs left a trail, which she followed to a set of bushes. She was about to inspect them when their leaves suddenly shook.

Abeni jumped. Something was in the bushes! Running back to the blanket, she snatched up her staff. "Asha!" she whispered. "I think we're being followed!"

"Yes," the girl agreed, still counting toes. "Since yesterday."

Abeni glared. "What? Why didn't you say anything before now?"

Asha looked up and blinked. "You didn't ask before now."

Abeni had no idea how to even respond to that. The bushes shook again and she bit her lip in worry. "Is it something dangerous?"

"I don't think so," Asha said. "Ohhh! I've lost my count!"

Abeni kept her eyes on the bushes. Whatever was in there, Asha would have at least warned if it was dangerous. Still, she didn't like being followed. Crouching, she crept towards the bushes, trying to make out anyone in there. But she saw nothing. Bracing herself, she lifted her staff to push the leaves aside. Still nothing. Just a strong smell like flowers that tickled her nose and then was gone.

She poked all through the bushes, until she was convinced they were truly empty. Giving up, she walked back to Asha.

"Well, whatever it was seems to be gone," she said.

"You probably scared them," the girl responded.

Abeni's eyebrows rose. "They shouldn't be following us. You aren't worried?"

Asha shook her head absently. "No."

Abeni sighed. If the girl wasn't concerned, maybe she shouldn't be either. After all, a thief who stole pieces of cake and who smelled like flowers couldn't be much trouble.

When they started out again, she was more mindful of her surroundings. Every now and then she peeked back, but didn't turn around. Their follower left clear signs. Bushes moved here, plants shifted there; one time, a small branch fell from a tree. Whoever this was, they were terrible at sneaking. It was a wonder they'd stayed hidden this long. But even if they weren't dangerous, she couldn't have someone skulking behind them. And she couldn't spend the rest of this journey looking over her shoulder. Worse, they were running out of cake!

Her mind made up, Abeni stopped.

"Are we resting again?" Asha asked.

"Yes." She pulled a blanket from the bag and laid it out. "Let's play a game."

Asha's dark eyes lit up, and she clapped. The girl loved a good game. One of her favorites was waking Abeni up with tickling. Those little fingers went everywhere!

"Let's pretend we're asleep," Abeni said. "And see who can go the longest."

"I can! I can!" Asha shouted.

"We'll see." Abeni chanced a glance behind them and took out some pieces of honey cake. One she gave to Asha and kept another for herself. A third piece she set nearby. Asha quickly chomped hers down but Abeni ate slowly, a hand on her staff.

"Time to play," she said, finishing. "And no tickling!"

Asha lay down right away, squeezing her eyes tight. Abeni followed, resting her head on her palm. Then waited. It didn't take long before a familiar scent tickled her nose—like flowers. It was followed by the sounds of someone eating noisily. Lots of smacking and swallowing. Gripping hold of her staff, Abeni jumped up from the blanket.

"Thief!" she cried out.

But that was all she could say. Because she wasn't even sure what she was staring at. The person in front of her with a mouth stuffed full of honey cake looked like a girl, maybe her own age, though a little shorter. Bits of fur covered her brown skin and each of her fingers ended in a small, curved black claw. But it was the long thin striped things covering her that stood out, each ending in sharp points. Were those . . . quills? Like a porcupine? Come to think of it, she sort of looked like a porcupine.

At seeing Abeni, the girl's eyes rounded—her pupils growing impossibly wide until they were like black plums. She dropped the honey cake and let out something between a choke and a shriek. There was a sudden burst of pink mist followed by an even stronger smell of flowers. And she was gone.

Abeni gaped. What had she just seen? Their thief was a porcupine. Or a girl. Or both! A porcupine girl? And she could make herself disappear!

"Wait!" she cried. "I'm not going to hurt you!" But there was no answer. She picked up the dropped piece of cake. "Here, you can have this if you like. I just want to see who you are."

For a while there was only quiet. Then there came a voice—squeaky and shaking.

"You scared me!"

Abeni looked up to find someone sitting on a tree branch high above. It was the porcupine girl. Her quills were raised, and they quivered with her trembling.

"I'm sorry," Abeni said, staring at the girl in wonder. "I didn't mean to scare you. I just wanted to know who was following us. Please, come down. I have more cake."

The porcupine girl frowned, looking uncertain. But as she eyed the honey cake she licked her lips. There was another burst of pink mist and she disappeared. A second slight explosion nearby also let off the scent of flowers. Abeni whirled about to find the porcupine girl standing across from her. Her black eyes were wary. But she also licked her lips, glancing at the honey cake.

"I meant what I said," Abeni told her. "You can have it."

The porcupine girl hesitated, then quickly snatched the cake away before jumping back.

Abeni crouched, watching. Those quills had settled a bit. A good sign, she hoped. Now that she'd had a better look, she saw that the girl didn't have them everywhere. The larger ones mostly covered her back, chest, and torso, almost like clothing. Her arms and legs remained exposed, showing limbs that looked like any other girl. So did her face, though tufts of gold fur sat on her cheeks. The quills even covered her head, flat and sloping down like hair.

Asha, who was still playing the sleeping game, opened her eyes.

"Oooh! Prickly!" Jumping up, she bounded over. Abeni tried to stop her, fearing the flighty porcupine girl would vanish. But she only glanced sideways at Asha, who was playing with the sharp tips of her quills.

"You're a spirit," the porcupine girl said in her high voice. She turned to Abeni. "You're a mortal." Abeni nodded, though she'd never been called a mortal before. "A mortal and a spirit walking through the forest. How strange."

"Abeni's my guardian!" Asha blurted out.

The porcupine girl eyed Abeni, her small flat nose wrinkling with doubt as she finished off the honey cake. "You're rather small, for a guardian."

Didn't she know it. "And what are you?" she asked, hoping that wasn't rude.

The girl seemed puzzled at the question. "I'm a porcupine spirit, of course."

A porcupine spirit! That explained why she was . . . well . . . the way she was.

"I don't suppose you've seen any others?" the girl asked. "Porcupine spirits? Like me, but taller? Pretty quills? Great dancers?"

Abeni shook her head. "You're the only one I've seen . . . ever."

The porcupine girl sighed. Then she scowled. "You know you shouldn't go around scaring people like that with your big stick. It's not polite!"

Abeni was taken aback. "You shouldn't go around sneaking behind people and stealing their food. That's not polite either."

The porcupine girl puffed up, offended. "I wasn't stealing! I was just borrowing!"

Abeni stared at her. How did you borrow food?

"Why were you following us?"

The porcupine girl's scowl evaporated, and she shrugged sheepishly. "I thought you might make good company."

"Oh!" Abeni said in surprise. "You could have just come out and said so."

"I was scared."

Scared? Abeni couldn't imagine what was so frightening about her and Asha. "Are you alone?"

The porcupine girl nodded.

"Prickly's lost," Asha said.

The porcupine girl nodded again, and sat on the ground.

"We were fleeing the war, my family and I," she told them.

"You mean the war against the Witch Priest?" Abeni asked.

The porcupine girl's face turned fearful. "Don't say his name! Anyway, we left our home to escape all the fighting. I was following, like I'd been told. But I saw some butterflies and wanted to dance with them."

"I love butterflies!" Asha exclaimed.

"Aren't they the best?" the porcupine girl agreed. An excited grin lit up her face before dying away. "It was a wonderful dance. But when I tried to find my family again, I couldn't. I looked everywhere. I waited for them. But they were gone. And I was alone."

Abeni knew all too well what that was like. "How long have you been out here?"

"Four days . . . or maybe sixty." The spirit frowned. "I'm not sure how it works in mortal time. Is your family nearby? Mortals do live in families too, don't they?"

Abeni opened her mouth to answer but found she didn't want

to retell that story. "My family's gone," was all she said. "It's just the two of us."

"Oh. Where are the two of you going?"

"To see my sister!" Asha blurted out, extending her arms. "She's very, very big!"

"Oh," the porcupine girl said again. "That sounds nice." Her shoulders drooped and she stared down at her hands.

Abeni studied her. Another spirit. She'd never thought she'd see a spirit in her life. Now here were two she'd met. Neither looked anything like she'd expected. They weren't big or fantastic or scary, like the masks at Harvest Festival. They were just . . . girls. Like her. As bad as she thought she had it, being out here alone must have been worse. She had barely thought out her next words before she posed the question.

"Do you want to come with us?"

The porcupine girl shot up to her feet.

"Oh yes! Most definitely so! I mean to say, if it's not too much trouble?"

Abeni smiled. "No trouble. Asha says her sister knows lots of things. Maybe she knows where your family is." The porcupine girl perked up at that. "I can't promise anything," Abeni added hastily. "But there's a chance." Chances seemed the most anyone could hope for right now.

"Prickly's coming with us!" Asha cheered, doing a little dance and shaking her locs from side to side.

"Asha," Abeni scolded. "I'm sure her name isn't Prickly."

"I'm Nyomi," the porcupine girl put in. "My mother says spirits shouldn't give names so easily. Especially to mortals. But if we're going to be friends and travel together, I think we should know each other's names. And you don't seem so bad—for a mortal. Though come to think of it, I don't know any—mortals, that is."

"Now you do," Abeni said. She introduced herself and Asha.

"Abeni and Asha," the porcupine girl repeated. "Do you have any more cake?"

Abeni reached down to her blanket, where her portion remained. She broke it into three smaller pieces, so they could all share.

"Abeni," the porcupine girl asked, munching. "How is it you can understand me? Spirits understand all tongues. But you're just a mortal—no offense."

Abeni chewed down a bit of cake, and rubbed her belly.

"I swallowed a rock," she said.

Nyomi looked at her, puzzled. "Is that a mortal joke?"

"It's an actual story," Abeni replied. "But not that interesting. Tell me more about you." The porcupine girl's eyes lit up and she eagerly began to talk, continuing long after the sun had descended behind them.

Over the next two days, they got to know Nyomi more, and she turned out to be the strangest person—well, spirit—Abeni had ever met. She spent a lot of time dancing—something porcupine spirits were supposedly very good at. At any moment she could vanish to chase fireflies or a beetle, both of which it turned out she ate. Abeni tried not to stare as the girl slurped down worms and bugs she found under rocks. Porcupines she'd seen around her village mostly ate flowers and the bark off trees. And so did Nyomi, but she also liked her share of crawly things. Maybe this spirit was part mole. Asha loved it, of course, and more than once Abeni had to stop her from trying to gnaw on a tree or slurp down worms as well.

The porcupine girl's most favorite food was honey. They couldn't come across a beehive without her trying to get some. Twice they'd been forced to run from angry swarms as Nyomi made off with dripping combs—their only warning a shout to run as she charged past. After a harrowing flight that ended with them jumping into a small pond, Abeni convinced the spirit to at least warn them first when she went honey stealing.

And the porcupine girl could talk. Goodness, could she talk!

Nyomi talked about her family, about the things she'd seen, the other spirits she'd met, and just about everything. That second day after their meeting, she spoke through the afternoon and into the night. Fortunately, it seemed spirits needed their sleep too—though the porcupine girl muttered even then.

Abeni didn't mind it so much. She supposed after being alone, Nyomi just needed to talk to someone. She'd calm down eventually. At least she hoped. Besides, if the porcupine girl did all the talking that meant Abeni didn't have to speak about her own past—or Asha's. Some things she didn't feel like sharing. Maybe she was getting better at keeping secrets.

In her endless talks, sometimes Nyomi mentioned the war. Abeni listened close at those moments, hoping to pick up things she couldn't learn from Asha.

"And we saw a whole bunch of mortals," the porcupine related once. "They were all carrying great big shields of cowhide with spears fitted onto their backs—long ones and short ones. One of my cousins, on my mother's sister's side, said they were warriors from somewhere far in the south. And that they'd come up to join other mortals here in the west, against the—" She lowered her voice to a whisper. "—the Witch Priest! There were so many, and with those spears with black sharp tips! We all stayed hidden while they passed. No one thought it was a good idea to dance for them!"

The west? Abeni mused. She never knew she lived in the west. *West of what?* she wondered. "Have you ever heard of ghost ships?" she asked.

Nyomi shook her head while digging through some dirt. "No. They sound scary!"

The porcupine girl appeared to be scared of many things—an almost endless list.

"How about storm women?" she pressed. "Warriors with fire in their eyes?"

This time Nyomi shivered down to her quills. "No! They sound even scarier!"

"What about a man in a mask made of goat horns? With a magic flute?"

Nyomi shook her head again. "Sorry." She plucked some fat white grubs from the soil and plopped them in her mouth, chomping as she talked. "I have met some goat spirits. They just sit chewing all day. Chew, chew, chew. And they'll eat anything!"

Abeni sat back, disappointed. She'd put those questions to the younger Asha more than once. But the little girl only shook her head blankly.

Nyomi did provide some useful information. Though she had never spent time among mortals, others in her extensive family had visited mortal towns, even these things called cities. She related their stories, confirming what the old woman had told Abeni. She listened to it all, half in fascination. She wondered if she would ever see such places.

It was on their third day since meeting, as Abeni listened to Nyomi go on about some very rude meerkats, that she heard a faint sound. She had to drown out the porcupine girl to listen properly.

"Did you hear that?" she asked.

The porcupine girl went quiet. "Hear what?"

"A sound. Like someone crying."

Nyomi tilted her head, eyes going wide. "Oh! I do hear it!"

"It came from there." Both turned to find Asha gesturing in the distance.

"You're not going to try and find them, are you?" Nyomi asked worriedly.

Abeni thought on that for a moment. They had their own way to go. And they certainly couldn't be stopping for everyone. On the other hand, people didn't cry for no reason. "Someone could be hurt," she said. "Or in trouble."

Nyomi's hands fidgeted. "But shouldn't we stay *away* from trouble?"

Abeni ignored the girl, who muttered something about not doing well with trouble before vanishing into pink mist. Well, at least this way she'd remain quiet. As she and Asha got closer the crying grew louder. It did sound like someone was in trouble.

Pushing past some brush they entered a clearing and found an unexpected sight—a girl.

She knelt in the grass, wearing a dress that glistened like black fur. Her head lifted at seeing them, revealing a strikingly pretty face framed by long black hair, braided and parted down the middle.

"Help me!" she pleaded, her big brown eyes streaming tears.

Abeni ran over. "What's wrong?"

"I'm trapped!" The girl lifted an arm. Around her wrist was a small rope knotted with bits of red cloth. It was tied to an iron spike driven into the ground.

"How did this happen?" Abeni asked, bending down to inspect the rope.

"Men from a village nearby!" the girl cried. "They tied me here!"

"Why?" Abeni asked. She couldn't imagine men of her village doing such a thing.

"They say I'm a demon! They're crazy! Get me out! Please!"

Abeni looked over the rope. The knots didn't seem hard to undo.

"Please hurry!" the girl begged, her face frightened. "They might come back!"

"Just a moment!" Abeni said, her fingers already working on the knots. "There, it's loose! You can—"

Abeni blinked. The rope was somehow tied again. How could that have happened? She set to loosening it a second time. Asha came over, crouching to stare at the girl, who stared right back. Undoing the knots seemed harder, but they finally gave way. Abeni let out a relieved breath. But no sooner had she done so than the knots quickly retied themselves! She glared at the rope in exasperation.

"What is this thing?"

"Just a rope!" the girl said. "Try again!"

Abeni shook her head. "It won't stay loose!" Thoughts of the ropes that had snatched away the people of her village came to mind, and she flinched away. Memories flashed. Her trying to cut at those ropes to free her brother. His screams as they tightened about him. The fear on his face as they pulled him into the dark.

"Please, you have to try!" the girl wailed. She cast frantic glances into the distance and looked like she might cry again.

Abeni pushed away the haunting images. This wasn't the same thing. It wasn't! Gritting her teeth, she gingerly put fingers to the odd rope, starting on the knots a *third* time. Asha moved to hover over her, watching with interest.

"Abeni!" She jumped. It was Nyomi. Or at least her voice. "People are coming!"

The tied-up girl looked around confused, searching for the voice. Abeni turned at Nyomi's warning. Sure enough, there was movement in the bush—and voices. She grabbed her staff, standing up just as three men stepped into the clearing.

One, tall and thin with a long face, carried a spear. Another, with nostrils that flared as he breathed, also held a spear, and a short bow. A third man, bigger than the others and with tiny eyes for his face, carried a stick with a bulging knot at the end. The three stopped in their tracks, staring at Abeni in surprise. She stared back. She hadn't seen people who were just people since her village. These men dressed differently, in bright red cloth that was slung over one shoulder and hung to their knees. And they wore their hair shaved except for little tufts dyed red in the front. But otherwise they could have fit right in at her village. She almost smiled at seeing them, until she noticed their faces—hard and cold as rock. Their eyes went to the tied-up girl. At the sight of her they grinned and cheered, as if at some great victory.

"Caught you!" the tall man with the spear shouted.

"Thought you'd get away, eh?" another said, shaking his cudgel.

"Not from us!" a third echoed with a whoop.

Abeni frowned. These men were happy at catching a girl?

"Good day, uncles," Abeni said, bowing respectfully.

The man with the long face fixed on her again. His smile vanished.

"Who are you?" he asked.

"My name is Abeni, uncle," she answered, bowing again. "This is Asha. We were just passing through. May I ask, why have you tied up this girl?"

"That's no girl," the big man spat.

"The rope doesn't catch girls," the man with the bow added. "Only demons."

"A demon has been raiding our village," the tall man said. "Making off with our goats. We set a trap. A magic rope she couldn't undo!"

Abeni looked to the girl. Her large eyes stared up in fright and she shook all over. A demon? These men weren't making sense. She turned back to them.

"I'm sorry, uncles, but I find that hard to believe."

The narrow-faced man scowled. "We don't care what you believe! We don't have to explain ourselves to some disrespectful child! We've caught this demon and we're going to make sure it doesn't menace us again." He lifted his spear, stepping forward.

"Wait!" Abeni cried. "Uncles, look at her. She's just a girl!"

The three men did look, but nothing in their faces softened.

"Just a girl," the narrow-faced man mocked. "First some of our children run off, then our goats are snatched away—are we to believe some demon is not involved?"

Abeni went still. "Your children? What's happened to your children, uncle?"

The man seemed puzzled by her question, but he answered. "Not all our children. Just some. They claim they hear a song calling to them. At night, when they sleep. Then the next day, they vanish. We caught one as she left, brought her back and tied her up. But in the morning, she was gone, the ropes we'd bound her with at her feet. It looked as if she'd . . . chewed through them." He shook his head. "That is why we set a trap, to capture the evil that plagues us."

Abeni's mind was ajumble. All she could think of was the day her village had fallen. Her friends walking off in a daze. The man in the goat horn mask with his flute . . . and his song. It was happening here too. Only he was stealing away children through their dreams!

"Do you hear it?" she asked. "The song?"

All three men shifted uncomfortably. "Never," the narrow-faced one said. "It is only the children who hear it. Only they who it calls."

"What do they tell you about the song?" Abeni pressed. "Do they speak about a man in a mask of goat horns? Or storm women? Living ropes that steal away people?"

She spoke in a rush. The men stared at her like she might have sun sickness. But something in their stricken faces said her words were not all unfamiliar.

"I know nothing of storm women or living ropes," the narrow-faced man said quietly. "But the children, those we were able to hold back for a brief time, spoke of seeing a man concealed behind a mask of goat horns in their dreams—a man who walks with monsters."

Abeni's breath caught. It was him! But monsters? That was new.

"Why do you ask such questions?" another man asked. She turned to find his eyes glaring in unmistakable suspicion. "How do you know what was in the dreams of our children? Where do you come from? Who are your people? You say you are passing through our lands, but you speak our tongue with ease. How is that possible?"

Abeni stumbled. That would all be hard to explain.

"She's with the demon!" the big man barked. "Probably a witch!"

The narrow-faced man's eyes widened at Abeni as if she'd sprouted horns. He gripped his spear tighter. "We capture the demon and arrive to find you trying to free it. Now you ask about the song. Who are you? *What* are you? Do you work with the one who stole our children? What have you done with them?"

He was shouting now, his face moving from fear to growing

rage. Abeni stared at them all. They thought she was working with the man in the goat horn mask? They had it all wrong! But she didn't know what to say. How could she explain?

"I'll get the witch to talk!" the big man growled. He stalked forward, lifting his cudgel. Abeni stared in shock. Was this big man going to try and hit her? She brought her staff up hurriedly. *Farmer Beats for Snakes* rapped him on both hands. He dropped his cudgel, crying out and grabbing his injured knuckles.

"She put sorcery on my hands!" he bawled. "Witch! Witch!"

Abeni glared at the man. Ridiculous! She'd just hit him was all, the big baby. She was set to say as much but never got the chance—as his companions charged.

Abeni's staff came up to block them. Until today, she'd never used her training on anyone but Obi. Sparring with the straw man hadn't been easy. But this was an actual fight! She was surprised how easily the forms came to her. *Tree Sways in a Breeze* let her duck a cudgel swung for her head. *Frog Hops the Pond* kept her nimble to avoid darting spear points. And *Seeding the Field* sent fast strikes to arms and shins. The men were surprised too, yelping in pain and growing angrier by the moment. A thrust of a spear came much too close, and she was reminded that unlike Obi, these men would truly hurt her! She glanced to Asha. But the little girl paid no attention to the fight at all. Her eyes stared at the rope as if nothing else were happening.

"Abeni! Look out!"

She was suddenly pushed away by something unseen just as an arrow whooshed past—hitting a tree with a loud *kerthunk*! One of the men had shot at her! There was an explosion of pink mist accompanied by the smell of flowers, and she found the porcupine girl standing there.

"Thank you!" Abeni stammered. "I think you saved my life!"

Nyomi didn't respond. Her large black pupils were wide with fear, and she was staring at the man with the bow, who looked back dumbstruck. With a shriek she disappeared again, releasing a volley of quills—right at his face. The man howled as the needles peppered him. Spinning about, he got another set to his backside. He dropped the bow and jumped higher than Abeni thought he could, trying to pull the quills out.

The two other men paused at seeing the porcupine girl, but they didn't give up. They looked ready to charge again—just as Asha exclaimed: "There!"

Abeni looked to find she had loosened the rope. This time it didn't retie itself, but fell away limply. The trapped girl pulled her arm free and stood, rubbing the mark on her wrist. She smiled, setting her gaze on the three men. Then, the girl changed.

Her brown eyes turned a bright orange. She no longer seemed afraid at all. The corner of her lips curled up into a growl and she went down on all fours. Hands and feet became paws with sharp claws. Her black dress seemed to grow until the dark fur covered her completely. Her ears turned sharp while a tail twitched behind. Abeni had barely blinked before it was all over. In the girl's place, there was a panther—sleek and black as night! The big cat wasn't fully grown, but not small either. It stalked towards the three men, a low rumbling coming up from its throat. Then it roared!

The sound shook the air and the three men screamed. They turned on their heels and ran, stumbling over themselves to get away. The big man ran fastest of all, quills still in his backside. They crashed headlong through the bush, crying of demons in the forest. The panther kept roaring until the three were finally out of sight. Appearing satisfied, the big cat turned back and changed once again.

Abeni watched, mouth open. The panther didn't become the girl in the trap. Her dress had been replaced by a band of black fur around her chest and another bit at her waist like a skirt, leaving her middle bare. Her long arms showed off muscle, and each finger on her hands ended in sharp curving claws—much like her feet. She seemed taller too. Her hair was no longer neatly braided and instead fell in a tangle of black locs that covered half her face. Her dark skin now shined like polished stone and her cat eyes nearly glowed in the sunlight. She was still striking, just in a different way.

What was she, Abeni wondered? Her answer came with the scent of flowers.

"Panther spirit!" Nyomi appeared suddenly. "I knew something wasn't right!"

The panther girl pushed aside the locs in her face and sniffed. "Porcupine spirit." Her low voice carried the hint of a growl. She waved at the air as if clearing it. "I thought I smelled flowers."

Nyomi whirled back to Abeni. "I told you not to stop! She's trouble!"

The panther girl yawned. "Shouldn't you be dancing or jumping at your own shadow, porcupine girl?"

"Better than being disliked by everyone you meet!" Nyomi shot back.

The panther girl's eyes narrowed. "Go chew on a tree."

Nyomi opened her mouth to retort and Abeni decided to step in.

"Hello," she said. "I'm Abeni."

The panther girl didn't look her way, instead turning from Nyomi to Asha. She crouched and smiled, showing a set of gleaming teeth—some of them sharp.

"My little rescuer," she said. Asha stared at the sharp teeth in wonder, then bared her own and growled in imitation. The panther girl threw back her head and laughed. "What manner of spirit are you? So small, but much more!"

Abeni looked on awkwardly. It was nice of the panther girl to thank Asha. But she was the one who had come to her rescue. Clearing her throat, she stepped forward.

"I'm Abeni," she tried again.

This time the panther girl turned to look up at her with flat orange eyes.

"I heard you the first time, mortal. I just wasn't interested."

Abeni stepped back, stunned at the rudeness.

"That's not very nice, *Zaneeya*," Asha scolded.

The panther girl's head snapped about in alarm. She shot to her feet. "You know my name! And you speak it in front of a mortal! Why would you do such a thing?"

Asha shrugged. "It's only a name."

"To tell a mortal a spirit's name is to grant them power over us!"

"That's silly, Zaneeya," Asha snapped, sounding for a moment very much like the old woman. "Abeni doesn't want power over you. She's the one that came at your cry. You should be thanking her."

Zaneeya stared down at Asha, who stared back, unblinking. Whatever passed between them, the panther girl broke away first and turned to Abeni. She bowed her head stiffly. "You stopped to free me when you could have walked on. For that, I owe you thanks. It should not be thought that panther spirits are ungrateful."

"It's nothing," Abeni said. "I'm sure you would have done the same." When there was no answer, she spoke again. "So, you're a spirit?"

"And you a mortal," the girl replied flatly. "There, we both know things."

Abeni felt her face heat. Why did this girl make her feel stupid just for talking?

"Those men said you stole their goats?" she asked.

"I was hungry. Goats are for eating."

"Oh, I know what that's like. Back home, when my friend Fomi and I were hungry, we'd taste soups or steal fried yam . . ." Abeni trailed off as she saw the other girl's disinterested look shift between her and Asha.

"Where is this home of yours?" Zaneeya asked. "Not here, since those other mortals didn't know you."

"I'm from another part of the forest," Abeni answered.

The panther girl cocked her head. "Out here alone? Strange for a mortal girl. And in the company of two spirits. Very strange. Where is your family? Where is your mortal . . . settlement? What do you call them? Villages?"

Abeni's mouth went dry. She hadn't had to answer much of that with Nyomi. Obviously, panther spirits were more curious than porcupine spirits. Or maybe it was just this one.

"Abeni's my guardian," Asha put in.

Zaneeya frowned, looking Abeni over. "You're small, for a guardian."

Abeni returned a tight smile. Second time she'd heard that in two days.

"Are you out here alone?" she asked.

The panther girl's face darkened. "I've lost my sisters."

"I'm sorry," Abeni said. "How did you lose them?"

She snarled. "We were attacked by mortals. Mortals who think of us as nothing more than demons. Mortals like you!"

"I'm not like that!" Abeni protested. "I fought those men to save you."

"Because I looked like a helpless mortal," Zaneeya retorted. In a blur she was the pretty girl again, with big brown eyes on the verge of tears. "She's who you want to help, to save." Another shift, and the panther girl was back, orange eyes flashing. "If you had seen me as you do now, would you have been so quick to help?"

Abeni was taken aback by the question. The panther girl now looked admittedly more frightening. But she'd like to believe she would have done the same thing.

"Yes," she said. "I would have. Because those men were wrong."

Zaneeya said nothing, then shrugged. "Perhaps you are better than most mortals. The men who attacked my sisters and me marched beneath the banner of the Witch Priest. He gave them weapons made with dark magics to hunt us. When they came, we fled. I have been lost from them since."

Abeni found the tale too familiar. Had everyone been hurt by this war?

"You must have been frightened," she said.

"I was not frightened!" Zaneeya retorted hotly. "I'm no coward!"

"No," Abeni apologized. She was a touchy one! "I'm just saying I understand."

The panther girl looked away, sullen. "What would you know of it?"

Abeni didn't answer. More than most, she'd wager.

Zaneeya let out a breath, and the anger seemed to slip away. She sat down heavily, drawing her knees to her. "I've walked with my sisters all my life. To now walk alone is a hard thing."

"You should come with us," Asha said.

All three girls turned to the little spirit in surprise.

Nyomi shook her head. "That's not a good idea! You heard those mortals. It wasn't only their goats who have gone missing." She leveled an accusing stare.

A rumble came from the panther girl's throat. "I do not eat mortal flesh. I understand it to be . . . unpleasant." She showed a wide sharp grin. "Porcupines, on the other hand . . ."

Nyomi squeaked—disappearing in a pink mist.

The panther girl chuckled. "Too easy." Her attention turned to Abeni and Asha. "Where are you going?"

Abeni hesitated. Nyomi was one thing. But a panther was much different than a porcupine. What if she got hungry and decided one of them was a meal? *Now you sound like those men*, she thought, and felt a bit embarrassed. No, she knew better. Whatever else this panther girl was, she was lost and out here alone. Abeni wouldn't wish that on anyone. And a spirit who could turn into a panther might be useful.

"Asha has a sister," she said at last. "Yes," she said, as the little girl extended her arms wide. "She's very big. And she knows things. We're going to see her. She might know where your sisters are."

The panther girl's orange eyes blazed bright with hope.

"No, Abeni!" Nyomi reappeared suddenly. "This is a bad idea!"

"We're all alone out here," Abeni told the porcupine girl. "There'll probably be trouble—like those men, or worse. Better we're together than apart."

"But you don't know what she is," Nyomi protested.

Zaneeya grunted. "The talking prickly bush is right. Do you know what I am?"

Abeni met that fierce face. "A girl who's lost." She turned to Nyomi "We should all be able to see that."

The panther girl's eyes narrowed to orange slits. "I will not follow a mortal."

Can't say she doesn't speak her mind, Abeni thought. "Then follow Asha."

Zaneeya looked to the little girl before nodding.

Asha cheered, going down on all fours while growling and pretending to tear up the ground like a panther. Nyomi continued to shake her head. Abeni watched them all. Each had started out alone. But now they were together. Something about this seemed right. She just hoped she knew what she was getting herself into.

CHAPTER THIRTEEN

BUSH BABY

The next few days made Abeni wonder if her hopes had been misplaced.

Zaneeya and Nyomi fussed constantly, about just everything. When the porcupine girl tried to tell one of her stories, Zaneeya cut in to point out where she was wrong. They argued about the names of plants and animals. They fought over where to sleep at night. The two even bickered over the shapes of clouds in the sky.

For Abeni it was all exhausting! She tried her best to steer clear of the two when they argued, not taking sides. Both of these girls were spirits, with magical powers she didn't understand. She wasn't about to get between them. Her mother used to warn that when elephants argued, mice could get trampled!

The source of the trouble wasn't hard to figure out. Zaneeya. There was no way to say it nicely, but the panther girl was not easy to get along with. She was haughty, surly, quick to anger, and just overall impolite. Not even that silly Sowoke had been this bad! About the only person she was nice to was Asha. The rest of them she seemed to just tolerate. Abeni had never met anyone so sure of themselves. It was admirable, in a way. But also very irritating.

"We panther spirits are strong," she said to Abeni as they walked. "Do you know how fast a panther spirit can run? We're feared because we're fierce!"

The only thing Zaneeya liked more than bragging about panther spirits was complaining about mortals.

"Mortals get sick," she would say. "Mortals are greedy. Mortals lie. Mortals steal from each other and even kill other mortals." Abeni had no idea how many mortals—people—the panther girl had ever met. But it seemed impossible to change her mind. Abeni didn't think Zaneeya even realized she was being insulting!

"I'm a mortal, you know," she'd pointed out after one of the panther girl's tirades.

Zaneeya only nodded. "Then you know what I'm saying is true."

Despite the girl's difficult nature, Abeni did her best to get along. She hadn't been around other children since . . . well, since her village. Fomi had been her best friend. The two could talk about anything. Now she felt awkward. Like she had to learn how to talk to other children her age all over again. Then again, these two weren't *her age*—not really.

When Abeni mentioned in passing that she'd counted thirteen harvest seasons, Zaneeya shrugged it off.

"I have counted eighty of your harvest seasons," she replied casually.

Abeni stopped in her tracks, staring. "Eighty?"

The panther girl yawned to show sharp teeth. "Give or take a season."

When she turned to Nyomi the porcupine girl shrugged as well, munching on some flower petals. "I think I've counted sixty. Or maybe seventy? I forget."

Abeni gaped at them both. "Is this a trick? The two of you can't be that old!"

Zaneeya rolled her eyes. "We are spirits. We do not age like mortals, whose lives are as brief as . . . flies." The panther girl snickered, eyeing Abeni as if looking for a response. She didn't take the bait, turning to Nyomi instead.

"If you're so old, why do you still look like girls . . . my age?"

The porcupine girl thought on this for a moment. "Maybe since spirits live for such a long time, we stay one age for a very long time. Or maybe mortals don't stay the same age long enough. My father thinks it's a shame that mortals have such short lives.

He says if you lived longer, you wouldn't be so excitable. You'd fight less, and dance more."

Abeni bit back a smile. Let the porcupine girl tell it, dancing solved everything.

"Asha was an old woman once," she related. If the two found anything odd about an old woman turning younger, they didn't show it. "Is that going to happen to you? Will you grow old and then . . . start over?"

"Of course not," Zaneeya answered. "All spirits aren't the same." Abeni wanted to reply that neither were mortals, but she held her tongue.

"She's right," Nyomi said. "Asha is different from any spirit I've ever met."

"How?" Abeni asked. She looked to the little girl, who skipped along ahead.

"She's old," Zaneeya said. "The oldest spirit I've ever encountered. It is a strange thing, that she has chosen you for a guardian. Panther spirits, of course, do not need such things. But some spirits choose mortals to look after them. Perhaps they are a tree or pond that requires tending. Or they are spirits too weak to defend themselves. Others involve themselves in mortal affairs." She said this with a particular distaste. "They grant power to mortals on their behalf, making them great wielders of magic or warriors. Have you been given such?"

Abeni shook her head. "All I have is a staff, a straw man's hat, and a magic bag."

Zaneeya snorted. "As I said . . . you are a strange guardian."

That was how their first two days went—bits of conversation where Abeni tried to learn as much as she could, between Nyomi and Zaneeya's never-ending bickering. She tried to make the best of things, which meant helping everyone get along. One night as they sat to eat, she averted an emerging spat—over where the sun traveled when it set—by quickly changing subjects.

"Zaneeya, where do panther spirits come from?"

The panther girl turned to her, orange eyes flickering annoyance at the interruption of a good argument. "Everywhere. We roam as we please."

Abeni tried not to grimace as the girl prepared her meal. Zaneeya caught her own food. But she refused to cook it, balking at what she called "burnt meat." Instead, she ate everything raw. As Abeni watched, the panther girl used the sharp claw on a fore-finger to slice open the belly of a hare. She sank sharp teeth into it, ripping away pieces that she gulped down.

"Disgusting," Nyomi said—crunching away at snails. Zaneeya swallowed, wiping away blood on her cheek with the back of her hand. Leaning forward she looked ready to reply something, but Abeni hurriedly stepped in again.

"So, then you've seen a lot of the world?" she asked.

Zaneeya sat back, forgetting the porcupine girl and chewing.

"I've seen some. My sisters move often. Mother doesn't stay in one place long."

"You have a mother?"

Zaneeya gave her a flat look. "Doesn't everyone?"

"How many sisters do you have?" Abeni tried. She snatched a bit of raw hare from Asha, who was set to bite into it.

"Many," Zaneeya replied.

"I never had a sister," Abeni said. "I had a brother. Do you have any brothers?"

The panther girl laughed. "It is only my mother and sisters. All panther spirits are women and girls."

Abeni's eyebrows rose in surprise. "No men? No boys? Not even a father?"

"You should ask her about her father," Nyomi muttered. Zaneeya's eyes narrowed to slits as she and the porcupine girl stared at each other quietly. But she soon turned back to Abeni with a lopsided grin.

"Not even a father," she repeated.

Abeni glanced to Nyomi, who had gone back to her snails—now sucking out the insides. She wanted to ask more but didn't want this to become an argument. So, she turned the topic to something she really wanted to know.

"Out there in the world, have you ever seen ghost ships?" She cast a glance to Asha, who didn't appear to be paying them much mind.

"No," Zaneeya said. "But I've heard of them."

Abeni sat up, her heart thumping. "You have?"

"Crafts sailed by wraiths from across the sea," the panther girl replied. "Mortals who serve the Witch Priest barter other mortals to the wraiths."

"Do you know where they take them?"

"Across the sea, I would think," the panther girl said, as if she were dense.

"But why?" Abeni pressed.

She shrugged. "Who is to say? Mortal doings are not my concern."

"What about storm women? Or a man in a goat horn mask?"

Zaneeya frowned, and Abeni realized she was talking and breathing fast.

"The only goats I've come across were those good for eating." And with that the panther girl turned away, seeming bored with the conversation.

Abeni fell back, quiet. She wanted to ask so much more! Zaneeya was the first person other than Asha who had spoken of ghost ships. She would have to work on coaxing the panther girl to recount every bit she knew. There might be a clue to what became of her village buried in there somewhere.

For the next few days, Asha led them through a part of the forest where the land was no longer even, rising and falling as they walked. Sometimes they were made to cross steep ravines, scrambling down carefully and then pulling themselves up on the other side by fleshy tree roots that grew up out of the ground. Other places sloped so high, it felt like they were walking sideways to climb them. They had to be careful in places where the land dropped off completely, leading down into dark crevices. They encountered no more people, and no signs of villages—which was for the best, given Zaneeya's fondness for goats. It was all exhausting, at least for Abeni, who had to stop and drink water often. Each time she did so, Zaneeya muttered about the softness of mortals.

It was at the end of a morning of long walking that Abeni found a large rock to sit on. Its smooth surface was covered in green moss that was cool and soft beneath her. She sipped water from her gourd and wiped sweat from her brow. As usual Zaneeya stood by impatient, arms folded and grumbling. Nyomi meanwhile chatted on about some singing frogs. Asha lay beside her, watching a red caterpillar inch its way across the rock.

Abeni was nodding absently to Nyomi, trying to ignore Zaneeya while keeping an eye on Asha, when she glimpsed something moving nearby. A flash of bright green. And it looked big. It was hidden behind a thick tangle of trees that grew up like a wall. Returning the water gourd to her bag, she got up and walked closer. The trees were so knotted together that she had to search for an opening to fit through. When she finally managed to push her way inside, she gaped.

It was a garden of flowers—about the biggest flowers she'd ever seen! The bright green she had glimpsed turned out to be a stem, nearly as thick as she was. She craned her neck to follow its length, as it extended up, up, up, into the air to end in a rounded sky-blue bulb. She gawped at the size of the thing. And it wasn't alone. Dozens of the giant flowers spread out across a vast clearing. Their bright green stems swayed in the breeze, rocking immense bulbs back and forth.

Abeni let out a breath of awe. They were beautiful!

"What are those?" Nyomi asked. The porcupine girl had followed her into the hidden garden and now peeked curiously over her shoulder.

"I don't know," Abeni answered. She wondered what those bulbs looked like when they opened fully.

"Where are you two going?" Zaneeya shouted.

"I found something!" Abeni called back. "Asha, come look!"

Both girls emerged through the tangle of trees into the garden.

"You stopped for flowers?" Zaneeya asked, staring up at the things.

"Not just any flowers," Abeni said. "Look at the size of them!"

The panther girl sniffed and wrinkled her nose. "They smell funny."

Abeni inhaled a sweet tickling scent. "They smell beautiful! Do you know what they are, Asha?"

The little girl didn't answer, her gaze fixed intently on the strange flower.

"Asha?" Abeni asked again.

"We should leave," she said suddenly. Her small face looked troubled.

"What's wrong?" Abeni asked.

Asha shook her head. "This isn't the way we're supposed to go."

"I agree," Zaneeya put in. She eyed the flowers like she expected them to bite. "Something about this place doesn't feel right. Or *smell* right."

Abeni looked at the two and then back at the flowers. She didn't feel anything. And they smelled wonderful. But she knew better than to ignore Asha's warnings.

"Fine," she said. "Maybe we'll see some again." As the others walked away, she lingered to look out at the flowers one last time. Putting a hand to a giant stem, she touched its smooth surface before turning to go. A sudden tremor shook the plant, making her jerk her hand back. It traveled up its length until reaching the top, setting the bulb to shaking. The green stem began to curve and bend, dipping low until the giant blue bulb hovered right in front of her.

As Abeni watched in amazement, the tightly wrapped petals broke apart, opening and spreading wide. Lying in the bed of the giant flower was a creature. It was as big as she was, with a body covered in thick orange-brown fur and bands of white around its arms and legs. Its head was huge, round like a monkey's but with the whiskers and oversized pointed ears of a cat. They twitched from beneath shaggy hair, as a small black nose wrinkled and a faint yawn escaped a broad mouth. She thought the thing might have been sleeping. But now it was coming awake. Two large eyes that took up much of its face slowly parted, and deep black pools ringed with brown stared out. They blinked lazily, fixing on her. Then without warning, the creature began to cry.

Abeni jumped back. Crying? No, it was screaming! At the top of its lungs. And it sounded like, of all things, a baby. Only so loud it was nearly deafening. The wailing quickly became a shriek, and she had to cover her ears.

"Sorry!" she tried. "I didn't mean to wake you up!"

But the thing just cried louder, tossing its head and throwing a fit.

"What's happening?" Zaneeya called.

"I don't know!" Abeni began. She could barely hear herself above the screams.

She bent down and tried to quiet it.

"Shh! Don't cry!" she pleaded.

As she got closer, the creature's wail faltered and it went suddenly still. She smiled with relief. "See there? Nothing to be upset—"

Her words cut off as the creature suddenly leapt up, its broad mouth open wide. She stumbled back, fearing it was going to bite her! But instead, it drew a deep breath. Abeni was tugged forward and felt herself held fast, her mouth frozen open in a cry that never came. The creature inhaled and a trail of white vapor left her mouth to enter its own. It did so again, sucking the air right out of her. It hurt! Like her chest was on fire. But she couldn't break away. She couldn't even scream. She remained locked with it, unable to free herself.

Suddenly hands grabbed at her, yanking her away. She fell back, tumbling to the ground. She found Zaneeya and Nyomi sprawled out beside her. She scrambled from atop them, bending over and coughing harshly.

"Abeni!" Asha cried. The girl had a small hand to her cheek. "Are you okay?"

Abeni took in gulps of air. "I think so," she croaked.

Or at least that's what she intended. Instead, an odd wailing came.

What was that?" she tried. But her mouth only made a shrieking cry like a baby. She clutched at her throat. What was happening?

"Delicious," a voice said. Abeni froze. That was *her* voice! Turning, she stared at the creature in the flower. It was rising, pushing up from the petals to stand. Licking its lips, it smiled. "You taste absolutely delicious!"

Abeni gasped. The creature had her voice! It sounded just like her!

Seeing her stricken face, it laughed—*her* laugh—from its broad mouth.

"Oh no!" Asha said.

"A bush baby!" Zaneeya growled. She'd gotten to her feet, baring sharp teeth at the creature. "Silly mortal! You woke up a bush baby!"

Abeni stared in confusion. *A bush what?*

"It stole your voice!" the panther girl said. "Don't you stupid mortals know better than getting close to a bush baby?"

Abeni wanted to yell back at the girl. They could talk about how stupid she was later. Right now, she just wanted her voice back!

"Abeni!" Nyomi cried in alarm. "Your ears!"

Abeni put hands up to her ears and squealed. These weren't her ears! They were big, pointed, and furry. She could even twitch them. Hearing a laugh, she turned to the bush baby and inhaled in horror. The thing's ears had changed—into her own!

"Mine now," it teased in a singsong. "Ohhh! Nice arms too!"

As it lifted two brown-skinned arms, Abeni lifted her own to find two long shaggy things that ended in claws. She fought not to scream.

"Bush babies don't just steal your voice!" Zaneeya said. "They steal you—all of you! When the change is complete, you'll be a bush baby and it'll have your body!" She glanced up to the giant plants. "Hope you like living in a flower."

The very thought brought Abeni to action. She bounded up, lunging for the bush baby. But she didn't get far, stumbling on her own feet. The creature laughed, leaping from the flower on sturdy brown legs. Abeni looked down. Sure enough, her legs were now short stumpy furry things that ended in a pair of big feet with toes that curled.

"Give those back!" she yelled, only managing to wail louder.

The bush baby whooped. "What was that? Can't understand a thing! Bush baby got your tongue?" It tittered at its own joke. "The best part is that I don't just get the body. I get what you keep in here too." It tapped the side of its head—mostly her head now. "You've got some tasty memories!"

Abeni scowled at the thought of this creature rummaging through her memories.

"Auntie Awami and Awomi," the bush baby murmured. "Mother and father and brother. Fomi. A Harvest Festival? That looks fun! Ohhh! What's this? Secret things. Things you haven't even told your new friends about."

Abeni stiffened. Those were hers! It had no right!

"Storm women," the bush baby said. "And a man in goat horns with a flute. Scary! Oh dear, they took everyone in your village away. Left you all alone, and—" It stopped, swinging its gaze to Asha.

"So *that's* who you are," the bush baby said. "Now, there's a surprise! Do you know he's looking for you? Oh yes, he didn't believe a fire could end you so easy." Abeni frowned in confusion. He? Who was the creature talking about? As if hearing her thoughts, it turned to smile her own smile back at her. "Oh, you know who *he* is. You've seen his banner. You keep one hidden in that bag. It's all here with me, in your memories. One single flame to set the world afire!"

Abeni's insides went cold in horror. The Witch Priest!

"I hear him day and night," the bush baby said. "Even when I slept. He calls us to him. But we're not fighters. We have no wish to join his war. Still, what reward might I get when I give him what he wants!"

The bush baby leapt in a flash. Bounding past the others, it grabbed hold of Asha. The girl squealed as she was picked up—and then they were speeding away.

There was a piercing cry that Abeni didn't recognize at first as her own voice. She'd tried to yell Asha's name, but there was only a shriek. With determination, she pushed back up to her feet and managed to stand. Her first steps were wobbly. But after a few tries she stumbled into a run. Snatching up her staff, she tried to hold it between her new claws and tore after them.

The bush baby was fast—faster with her legs than she had ever been. It zipped away, ducking between the thick green stems and leaving echoing laughter in its wake. It was stronger too, carrying Asha as if she were just a doll! The girl cried out, but didn't seem able to break free.

Luckily, Abeni was getting a handle on her new body. The bush baby's short legs couldn't run very fast. But they could jump. The first time she tried, she was surprised when she went sailing high and landed again on her feet—those long curling toes clutching the ground. Her eyes had grown too, and could see a long way. She easily made out the bush baby in the distance, her stolen body appearing every now and again between the maze of giant flowers. Zaneeya now ran along beside her, changing to panther form and joining the chase.

Still, the bush baby was hard to catch. At one point, they got close enough for Zaneeya to pounce. But it slipped out of her way, laughing as the panther girl went sliding and tumbling. Abeni tried too, using her new legs to make terrific leaps. She almost landed right on top of the creature once. But it grabbed onto a giant green stem with one hand and swung about, holding on to Asha and using the momentum to sling away. It landed nimbly, heading back the way they had come. Turning to look at them, it grinned and stuck out a tongue at Abeni—just before it unexpectedly stumbled.

The bush baby let out a sharp squeak as it flew into the air, flipping end over end. Asha flew from its grip. And the two came tumbling down, bouncing across the forest floor several times before coming to a stop. Abeni winced at the fall, hoping neither Asha or her own stolen body had been hurt! An explosion of pink mist revealed Nyomi—with a leg stuck out. She'd tripped the thing!

"Prickly got it!" Asha cheered.

Abeni reminded herself to give the porcupine girl a big—but careful—hug! The dazed bush baby sat up, preparing to run. But Abeni leapt high, letting her new legs carry her, and landed right beside it. Before the creature could stand, she knocked it back down.

"Give me back my body!" she demanded. Whatever she sounded like the anger in her voice was clear enough. The bush baby looked up with defiant eyes—her eyes—and a tight-lipped smile. She yelled again, but it didn't budge.

Zaneeya trotted up beside them, changing back into the panther girl and picking pieces of the forest floor from her hair. "It won't open its mouth," she said. "Not before the change is complete. It knows once it has all of you, there's no going back."

Abeni glared down at the creature. It smiled wider, not showing a shred of teeth. Zaneeya was right. It wouldn't open its mouth now, not even to gloat. It just had to wait her out. She looked down at her body. Most of it was furry now. Only her hair and nose were left. And soon they'd be gone too.

Frantic, she shook the bush baby, fearful at the same time she might injure her body. It seemed to know this, and smiled up smugly. Nearing her wit's end, Abeni felt a hand touch her shoulder. She turned, worry painted on her furry face, to find Asha.

The small girl nudged past her and came to kneel before the bush baby.

"You shouldn't go taking things that don't belong to you," she told it. "See, I'm familiar with what you stole. And I know something about it you don't." For the first time the bush baby looked confused. Asha leaned closer. "It's ticklish!"

Before the bush baby could stop her, the girl's tiny fingers sought out the tickle spots she knew well on Abeni's body. Like little wriggling worms they burrowed between armpits, dug beneath rib cages and under its chin. Unable to contain itself, the bush baby opened its mouth wide and howled with laughter.

"No fair! No fair!" it bellowed.

Abeni didn't hesitate. She wasn't certain how this worked, but she'd felt it done to her. Bending down, she opened her mouth and drew in a long deep breath. The bush baby froze, its mouth gaping wide as white tendrils of vapor rose from its throat. She inhaled again, pulling and pulling, until there was nothing left—then fell back.

The bush baby scrambled away, going to its knees and coughing fitfully. It turned to her with a grimace, and she noticed its ears—they were big and twitchy. She touched her own, now back to normal.

Abeni gave a happy cry, hearing her own voice. Her arms came next, followed by her legs. Very quickly, the rest of her returned. Her dress was torn where her changed body had stretched it or fur had pushed through. But that hardly mattered. She rubbed her wonderful brown skin, glad to have it back.

Hearing a whimpering, she looked up. The bush baby was itself again, a squat monkey-cat-looking thing. Its big round eyes were filling with tears, and its bottom lip trembled. She didn't feel the least bit sorry for it! Opening its mouth wide, it shrieked so loud they all covered their ears.

"You might as well quit your crying!" Zaneeya growled. "You know you can't steal the same body twice! And your magic doesn't work on spirits!"

The bush baby stopped, glaring at them ruefully.

"Oh, I wasn't crying," it said in its odd baby voice. "I was calling."

They followed its large eyes, which turned upward. Everywhere, the giant flowers were swaying and their bulbs trembling.

"I don't like this," Nyomi said. Abeni agreed, gripping her staff and pulling Asha beside her. Zaneeya crouched low and growled warily.

They watched as one by one, the long green stems curved and dipped, their bulbous flower heads hanging low. Each of their petals slowly peeled back, opening to reveal . . . Abeni gasped! More bush babies! They yawned and stretched, coming awake and blinking sleepy eyes at the four girls.

"You're right," the first bush baby said. "We can't steal a body that's already been tried. And we can't take your spirit bodies. But we can still take her. *He* would like that!" It glared at Asha, ears twitching excitedly. "The rest of you, we'll just have to eat. Baby's hungry!" It snarled, opening its mouth wider than ever before to show off rows of pointed teeth dripping with saliva. Every bush baby that had come awake fast did the same. Then as one, they came for them.

Abeni swung her staff, *The Water Buffalo Charges* coming to her at once, knocking aside the first bush baby that lunged for her. Beside her Nyomi squeaked in terror, sending off quills more by fright than on purpose. They caught bush babies in the face and arms, who leapt back, wailing in pain. Zaneeya roared, slashing with her claws. But the bush babies were too many. If they remained here, Abeni knew, they wouldn't last. They needed to get out of this garden—now! Lifting her staff above her head and sweeping wide circles with the form *Raining Down the Leaves*, she made a clearing.

"Run!" she yelled, pulling Asha with her.

Zaneeya shifted into a panther, plunging through the tall flowers. She took the lead, slashing and snapping at anything that got too close. Abeni and the others followed, running through the path she created. Behind, the bush babies thundered after them.

Abeni wielded her staff as best she could with one hand, her other holding tight to Asha. Some of the smaller bush babies, no bigger than cats, tried to drag the little girl away—their tiny teeth and claws biting and scratching. Abeni flung them away, swatting one so hard with her staff it went flying. Glancing up, she made out dozens more bush babies emerging from newly opened flowers, all jumping to the ground below. The things were coming from everywhere! They ran with wide-open mouths, gnashing sharp teeth and wailing their strange baby cries.

Abeni felt relief when the girls finally broke free of the giant flowers. Maybe the bush babies would stay in their garden. But looking back she found they hadn't slowed at all. The creatures poured out from the garden in a swirling mass of fur and claws, crashing through the dense bush to get to the fleeing figures. The four girls ran faster now, struggling to put some distance between themselves and their pursuers.

Abeni suddenly felt the ground change beneath her. Looking down she saw she was running on the edge of deep crevice, hidden by thick trees and bush. She tried to keep her footing, but she was going too fast. It only took one wrong step and she stumbled, losing her balance. Her fingers slipped from Asha's, and she pitched over the side! Her own scream filled her ears as she fell to the darkness below.

CHAPTER FOURTEEN

THE VALE OF LOST THINGS

Abeni was still screaming, clutching to her staff as she tumbled. Her arms reached out frantically for something to hold. But there was only air. She was falling and there was nothing she could do! She took in a gulp of air, and was set to scream again when a pink mist suddenly surrounded her.

"Got you!" someone said. And then they both disappeared.

Abeni realized she wasn't falling anymore. Instead, she floated in a place of swirling pink mist. Wherever this was, the scent of flowers was overwhelming. She remained there for a moment. Then abruptly, she was on solid ground again, back where she'd fallen. Stumbling, she managed to stay on her feet, moving away from the edge of the crevice. She looked to Nyomi in shock. The porcupine girl hadn't just become invisible. She had . . . jumped somehow, from one place to another and back again, plucking her right out of the air!

"How'd you do that?" Abeni asked.

Nyomi stared back at her, just as stunned. "I don't know!"

"Prickly has surprises!" Asha said, hugging Abeni tight.

"Why have all of you stopped running!" They looked to find Zaneeya changed back to a panther girl and gesturing behind them. The bush babies were still in pursuit—and nearly on top of them!

All three cried out before bounding away. They ran, catching up to Zaneeya. She led them through bushes and beneath fallen trees, anything to throw their pursuers off. But the bush babies kept coming, biting and ripping through dead wood or shrubs to get to them. Wherever they were now, it was filled with tall twisted trees with even more twisted roots snaking in every direction—making them easy to trip over. The ground had turned soft and squishy, making it hard to run. Then abruptly they came to a stop as Zaneeya suddenly halted. Catching up to the panther girl, they soon realized why. There was no more ground. Abeni peered over a ledge that dropped away into white mist. Turning back around, she found the bush babies still coming, teeth and eyes gleaming greedily.

"They'll be on us soon!" Zaneeya said. She had changed back to her panther girl form, and her sides heaved with her panting.

Abeni's mind raced. She peered back over the ledge. It was another one of those crevices—so wide she couldn't make out the other side.

"Nyomi! Can you do that thing again? Jump us all out of here?"

"I don't know how!" the porcupine girl said, her frightened eyes locked on the approaching bush babies. "When I did it before, I was scared for you! Now I'm too scared to do anything!"

Abeni sighed. "Asha! Do you have any magic? Anything that can help us?"

The little girl looked up fearfully, shaking her head.

"All my magic got burnt up in the fire."

At her words, Abeni had a sudden memory. "Not all of it!"

Thinking of what she wanted, she pushed a hand into her bag and pulled out three stones—one blue, one red, and one gold. The last bits of Asha's magic that the scrying pot had made her take. It had said she would know when to use them.

"If anyone is going to do something, now would be good!" Zaneeya shouted.

Abeni looked at the panther girl. *The cat will help.* That's what the scrying pot had said. It didn't make any sense at the time, but here was a cat!

"Zaneeya!" She thrust the stones forward. "Which one?"

"What?"

"Which one do I use? The scrying pot said you would know!"

Zaneeya glared as if Abeni were crazy. Abeni looked up to find the bush babies almost upon them. Their hungry cries and wailing were deafening!

"Now, Zaneeya! Pick one!"

"This doesn't make any sense!"

"That doesn't matter! Just pick one!"

Zaneeya growled. "Fine, then! Blue!"

Turning, Abeni hoisted the blue stone in her hand, not certain how to use it. But as the first bush babies to reach them leapt forward she wound her arm back and threw the stone at them. It sailed through the air, striking the closest bush baby right on the nose—then exploded.

A cloud of shimmering blue dust filled the air, covering the bush babies. And then, there were flowers.

In a series of small pops, blue flowers sprouted from the bush babies. Pop! Pop! Pop! They grew on their arms. Pop! Pop! Pop! They came out of their ears. Pop! Pop! Pop! They even pushed up from their open mouths. The closest bush babies to them turned completely to flowers. They landed just at their feet, taking root in the moist ground. Everywhere there was popping, as the bush babies became flowers. Some fell right where they stood; others drifted off with the wind. Soon they were gone entirely, leaving a blanket of flowers that grew up alongside the twisted trees. The four girls gazed up in wonder as a shower of blue petals fell all around them.

"Oooh!" Asha whispered.

Abeni nodded her agreement. Carefully, she placed the remaining stones back into the bag—as everyone let out long sighs of relief.

"That was close," Nyomi said. "I hope that's all the excitement we'll—"

Abeni never heard what the porcupine girl said next because she was gone in an instant. That was odd. Because there wasn't any pink mist. Zaneeya looked up, confused, but then she was gone too with a yelp. Abeni looked to her feet. They were sink-ing into the moist ground that she could now see was mud. This whole area was mud. And she realized the others hadn't vanished, they'd fallen! She only had time to lift Asha into her arms before the ledge of mud and roots under her feet broke away—taking her with it.

The world turned upside down as they fell. Several times Abeni tumbled head over heels, carried along by a river of mud. She held tight to Asha, though she couldn't tell if the little girl was screaming or laughing. The jutting roots of trees and vines poked and scratched her all over. It seemed they fell forever before finally there was nothing but air. She glided for a moment and then landed with a thick splash!

Abeni lifted her head, spitting out mud. She looked around to find Asha sitting nearby, a bright smile on her muddy face. Somehow, impossibly, her long thick locs remained clean—with not so much as a speck on them.

"Again! Again!" the girl cried, clapping.

Abeni rose up fully, checking herself. Nothing appeared bro-ken, though she felt battered enough. She was covered in mud. In fact, she was sitting in mud. It was surprisingly warm, even some-what comfortable—but it was still mud! She wiped some from her face and turned to find the others.

Nyomi waved to her, caked in so much mud it was hard to make out the girl beneath. Zaneeya was just getting up, growl-ing irritably as mud dripped from her arms and legs. She shook fitfully, trying to get it off. Both looked unharmed, though very dirty.

Abeni reached around, managing to find her wide-brimmed wooden hat and her staff. She pushed up to her feet and peered around. There was mud as far as she could see. Though that wasn't very far because a hazy white mist blanketed everything, like a cloud on land. Looking down she realized it came out of the mud, which bubbled and burped.

"Excuse you!" Asha said, as a brown bubble burst noisily.

"What happened?" Nyomi asked, shaking mud from her quills.

"We fell," Abeni said. She looked up but could only see the roots of trees in the mist. "A long way too." They were likely at the bottom of one of those crevices.

"I should have known!" Zaneeya growled, trying to walk in the oozing mud. "I should have known something like this would happen! By myself I never had these kinds of problems. But I join up with a dancing porcupine and a mortal too stupid to stay away from bush babies and I end up—" She flung out her arms at the expanse of mud. "I end up in this!"

Abeni flinched, stung. She already felt guilty as it was.

"I'm not stupid," she said tightly. "I didn't know what that thing was."

"So you walk up to it?" the panther girl asked. "And stick your face close? Maybe all mortals aren't stupid. Maybe just you!"

Abeni's face grew hot. She stomped over to the panther girl, though in the mud that took a lot of effort. Spirit or not, she wasn't going to be talked to like that!

"If I remember right," she said, "someone—not a mortal—was *stupid* enough to get caught in a trap! Over some goats!" A rumble sounded in Zaneeya's throat, but Abeni pressed on, heedless. "If I also remember right, I got you out of that trap. And just now, I saved our lives! But as usual, you've been nothing but ungrateful! So maybe the only stupid thing I've done was inviting you to come along!"

Zaneeya leaned forward, her teeth bared. "And what a fine idea that was! You think I didn't hear what that bush baby said? That you keep a banner, with the single flame? When you invited me along, you didn't say the *Witch Priest* was after you!" Her eyes narrowed. "Who are you *really*? What was all of that about everyone in your village being taken away? What secrets are you keeping from us?" She gestured to Asha. "Why is this little spirit being hunted? What kind of trouble are you getting me into?"

Abeni clenched her jaw tight. "I told you what you needed to know," she said flatly. "If you don't like it, you can go off on your own. That way, we won't have to listen to you complain!"

Zaneeya growled openly now and stepped forward, burning eyes peeking from between a tangle of muddied locs. The panther girl was tall. And there were those claws. Not to mention she was a spirit. But Abeni wasn't about to back down. She bent her neck to meet that orange gaze. The two stood glaring at each other for a long while before someone finally spoke.

"That way." They turned to find Asha staring into the mist. "It's where we need to go."

Both looked at her for a while. Finally, Abeni pulled away. The panther girl wasn't worth her time. Taking Asha by the hand she stalked off. Well, tried to stalk—but with all the mud she just ended up kind of trudging. Nyomi soon followed, casting glances back to Zaneeya, who stayed where she was, her orange gaze still smoldering. The panther girl became a faint figure in the mist before she began to trail behind them.

Their walk through the mud was a quiet one. Even Nyomi was silent for once. Abeni was still angry at the panther girl, yes, but also at herself. Zaneeya—rude and irritating as she was—had also been right. She'd woken that bush baby up. She should know better than to poke around at strange things in the forest. That wasn't even the worst of it. The bush baby's words kept playing in her head. *Do you know he's looking for you?* She shuddered.

Her eyes went to Asha, who walked along humming lightly. She was supposed to be her guardian. Against this Witch Priest or whatever he sent for them? What if those bat riders were looking for them too? Or worse, that shadow thing? All her doubts hit her at once. The old woman had placed so much responsibility on her. How could she possibly live up to it? Putting her head down, she trudged along glumly through the mud and mist, feeling as if she carried a heavy weight on her shoulders.

Things got no better as the day wore on. Mud sucked and oozed at their feet. If you stood too long in one spot, you sank and had to work hard to get back out. The mist didn't help either. It was thick to breathe, hot, and muggy. Worse, there didn't look to be any end in sight—like the whole world had become mud!

It was getting late when Abeni stared up at the sky. She couldn't make out the sun through the mist, but she could tell there was only a little daylight left. If they didn't reach solid ground soon, they'd be forced to walk through the night. Because trying to rest on oozing mud would be impossible—why, they'd sink right into it! Her rumbling belly reminded her they had little food left as well. And out here she doubted they'd find anything more.

Stopping, she waited for the others. Nyomi walked up, dried mud caking her quills. Zaneeya lingered quietly some ways off, still not speaking. Realizing she'd have to talk first, Abeni voiced her concerns.

". . . and that's where we are," she finished.

No one said anything. "I think we should keep walking," she offered. "Maybe we'll find . . ." She trailed off as Nyomi's large pupils widened and she let out a sharp squeak. She turned to Zaneeya. The panther girl's eyes were wide as well, her jaw slack. She quickly realized they weren't looking at her—but past her. Turning, she followed their gazes until her own eyes rounded.

There was something rising out of the mud. Something big! Its massive body was covered in the oozing muck, as if it was made of the stuff. Thick legs rose into view, four in all, and a fifth limb that had to be a tail. An immense head with a long snout was soon visible, and it turned to regard them.

Abeni stared up at the thing, too stunned to even cry out. It looked like a lizard the size of an elephant, dripping in mud. The only parts not covered were its eyes: two clear pearls, on either side of its head, that reflected their images like mirrors. The giant mud lizard looked down at them, opening its mouth to show sharp teeth, gleaming like knives.

Abeni had seen enough. Pushing Asha behind her, she lifted her staff and struck out—hoping to drive the thing back. Only the wood went right through its body! The mud swallowed her arm up to the elbow. She tugged hard, trying to get free. But neither the staff nor her arm was coming back out.

A roar announced Zaneeya at her side. The panther girl slashed claws into the thing's flank. But her hands passed right through too, sticking in the oozing mud. The two girls struggled to break free, but the more they fought the deeper into the creature's body they went.

Tiring, Abeni released a ragged breath. The giant lizard moved its head closer to Zaneeya, sniffing her through muddy nostrils. Sticking out a long pink tongue, it licked the panther girl, leaving her dripping in gooey warm saliva.

"Blech!" she growled in disgust, twisting away from another lick.

Nyomi, who remained with Asha, shrieked in terror. "It's tasting her!"

"He is doing no such thing," someone chided.

Everyone jumped, startled at the voice. Leaning to one side, they all looked past the creature to find a man. Or at least a man's head—small and brown and framed by curly black hair showing bits of white.

At first glance Abeni feared they had come across a talking head, like she'd heard about in stories in her village. Then she saw wriggling brown toes farther away. The man was lying in the mud, buried in it almost completely. He beamed up at them with a pleasant smile.

"Is this your monster?" Zaneeya asked hotly.

"Monster?" The man chuckled. "Moshi is no monster. He's a friend, and quite harmless." He turned to the mud lizard. "Let them go, Moshi. I don't think they want to play."

The mud lizard sounded a rumbling bellow like disappointment before puffing up and pushing outward. The two girls went stumbling back, freed from the oozing thing. The man rose from the mud. He was small, Abeni noticed—no taller than most of them. His entire body was covered in mud, including a long cloth wrapped about his waist.

"Don't all of you look a sight," he remarked. "Been walking the mud sea long?"

Abeni nodded, eyeing the giant lizard warily. *Did he say mud sea?* "Do you know how far it goes, uncle?"

The man picked bits of mud from his beard. "Oh, forever, I think."

Abeni frowned. "Nothing goes on forever."

"Hmmm," the man murmured. "Tell me, did you fall here somehow? Maybe into a river or a deep hole . . . ?"

"A crevice," she answered.

The man nodded. "Yes, that can happen too." Seeing their odd looks he gestured about. "Do you see the other side of this crevice? Do you think a whole sea of mud can fit into a crevice?"

Abeni wasn't sure what he was getting at. "There has to be way out," she insisted.

"There is," he replied. "But you won't find it here."

"Where are we, uncle? What is this place?"

The man was climbing onto the mud lizard. Seating himself, he looked down. "This is the mud sea. It surrounds the Vale of Lost Things. And, if you don't mind me saying, the four of you look quite lost."

Abeni looked at him, perplexed. *The Vale of Lost Things?* "But we're not lost."

The man lifted a muddy eyebrow. "Hard to reach here otherwise."

"We know where we're going," Abeni insisted. She looked to Asha. "Don't we?" The small girl nodded, gawping at the mud lizard. "This is where we should be."

"Hmm," the man murmured again. "Maybe you are lost *on purpose.* Either way, you'd best come with me, then. Moshi's big enough to fit us all."

Abeni looked at the man uncertainly. It was a friendly offer. But she was wary about riding on a giant lizard with some stranger. She glanced to the others. Asha's dark eyes were locked on the mud lizard in fascination.

"I want to ride the big cow!" she exclaimed.

"Salamander," the small man corrected with laugh. "Moshi is a salamander."

"I want to ride the big samamander!" Asha exclaimed.

Abeni looked again to the others. Nyomi seemed wary, but she hadn't disappeared. Now she just shrugged. Zaneeya stared at the giant salamander uncertainly, but she didn't say no either. Abeni supposed she'd have to take that as agreement enough.

The four managed to scramble onto the giant salamander's back. Their hands and feet seemed to stick into its muddy body as they climbed. When they were settled behind the small man, he gave a shrill whistle. With a lurch the salamander took off at a scampering gallop across the mud, swinging its head and wide flat tail from side to side.

"My name is Tutuo," the small man called back to them. "Or at least that's a name I took. I didn't get yours." They each answered—except Zaneeya, who had to be prodded. "Two spirits and a mortal girl," the man remarked. "An odd pairing."

"Three spirits!" Asha corrected between gleeful shrieks.

"Three spirits, then," the man agreed. With another shrill whistle he urged the giant salamander to run faster. Abeni clenched her teeth as they picked up speed. Beside her, Asha threw up her arms and whooped in delight.

As she looked out at the drab landscape, Abeni wondered if they would ever stop seeing mud. As if in answer, the giant salamander banked suddenly to the right, heading for a thick cloud of mist. She inhaled as they pushed through it and then squinted in surprise at sunlight. It was the sky! She was relieved to see it again. Even better, there was no more mud! They were on solid ground now, dark rich soil. She glanced back to see the wall of mist swirling in their wake, then yelped as the giant salamander's body began changing beneath them. Brown mud vanished, becoming something darker. She ran her hands over it in surprise. The creature's body had changed into dark soil—like the ground they ran upon!

"Moshi is a mimic salamander," Tutuo remarked, catching their startled looks. "He can become whatever he wishes, though most times he just takes on what's closest."

As the salamander started climbing a set of big gray rocks, he did just that—turning to stone.

"Uncle," Abeni called. "You said this was the Vale of Lost Things? But we were in a forest when we fell. How did we get here?"

"I don't understand it all myself," he answered. "Sometimes people and things just show up. Even fall right out of the sky. But if they come here, they're certainly lost."

"Umm, uncle?" Nyomi asked. "What's a vale?"

Tutuo chuckled. "You'll soon see!"

The giant salamander Moshi continued climbing the rocks. When he reached the top everyone's breath caught. Sloping down and spread out before them was what looked like a great bowl filled with lush grass, trees, and bushes. A large blue-green lake sat in its center, fed by a small waterfall. But it wasn't just the land. Scattered everywhere were an odd assortment of things. A bunch of woven baskets made a small hill. The curving red-painted wall of a house with no roof stood covered in a thicket of vines. What looked like a giant carving, made of black stone, of a woman's head lay almost buried on its side. There was more, including things Abeni couldn't put a name to. It reminded her of the rooms in Asha's house—and she wondered if somewhere here there might be a bunch of magic pots.

"Welcome to the Vale of Lost Things," Tutuo told them. "You can get off here. Though you might want to get out of all that mud. There are heaps of clothes down there you can rummage through. Sandals too, though often there's only one side. Seems people don't lose their shoes in pairs. Isn't that odd? Anyway, water's good for swimming and cleaning." The giant salamander lowered its now grassy body, and they climbed off.

"I live there." The small man gestured up, past a set of winding stone steps, to where a piece of rocky green earth curved over the edge of the lake like a hook. At its tip sat a small round house with a pointed roof. It leaned slightly to the side.

"Be some food waiting if you like," he said warmly. "I don't get too much company in the vale. More things come here than people—or spirits. I'd welcome sharing a meal for some good stories." With a whistle he was off, the giant salamander scampering up the winding path to his small home.

The four girls watched him go. In a blink, they were dashing for the inviting waters of the lake—eagerly jumping in.

Abeni broke the lake's surface for about the third time, washing the last bits of mud from her hair. Tutuo hadn't been wrong. The water was great for swimming! Nearby, Asha helped clean Nyomi's many quills while Zaneeya floated on her back. By the time they finished they all looked and felt refreshed.

Abeni rested on some rocks, wiping her hair dry. She had changed into another dress pulled from the bag, and had Asha do the same. Though there was indeed a nearby heap of clothes that she wanted to rummage through later. Asha was eyeing another heap made up completely of necklaces. A delightful scent drifted past them and Abeni inhaled deep. It was coming from Tutuo's small house. Clearing her throat, she got the others' attention. They hadn't really spoken much, not since her big argument with Zaneeya. Now she was rested and clean—not to mention hungry—their fight seemed distant and maybe silly. Despite their harsh words, the panther girl had been the first to run to her aid when they thought Moshi was a mud monster. One of them needed to be the first to talk. She wasn't about to apologize—they'd both said unkind things. But she could talk.

"We need to decide whether to go up there or not," she said. "Do you think we can trust him?" She directed her look to Zaneeya, who lounged on a set of rocks—very much like a cat.

The panther girl shrugged. "I don't trust most mortals. This one is friendlier than most—and that makes me trust him less."

Of course, Abeni thought wryly. She looked to Nyomi. The

porcupine girl chewed her lip, glancing up at the small house and grimacing.

"I'm scared of heights!" she said.

Naturally. Still, Abeni needed some help here. After their run-in with the bush babies, she was uncertain about her own judgment. She leaned in towards Asha, who was collecting colorful stones.

"Do you think he's safe?" she asked in a low voice. "That bush baby said you were being hunted. What if this Tutuo was sent by—"

"No," the little girl cut in. "I told you. This is where we're supposed to be."

"But we're lost!" Abeni said, exasperated. "This is a place for lost things!"

Asha looked around, and a great big smile spread on her small face.

"Exactly." Jumping up before Abeni could respond, she started up along the winding path towards the house. The three other girls exchanged gazes filled with unspoken questions, then got up and followed.

Reaching the leaning house, they found a large straw mat spread out with bowls of food—cooked fish, pounded yam, cut-up fruit, and more. The small man sat feeding a big yellow melon to the giant salamander. The salamander crushed it messily between its teeth—which were no longer sharp, but instead great square blocks. They had both changed: Tutuo into bright blue robes and Moshi into bright blue matching skin. Tutuo looked up and smiled at seeing them.

"Welcome! Welcome!" He gestured at the straw mat. "Eat as much as you like. There's more than enough. You'd be surprised at the amount of food that comes here!" Turning to Nyomi, he offered a bowl heaped with wriggling things and colorful shells amid flower petals. "I don't have many porcupine spirits visiting, but I couldn't help but notice—you wouldn't happen to be part hedgehog, would you?"

Nyomi's eyes widened. "My mother's father's mother was a hedgehog spirit!"

"Ah! I guessed right, then! I've managed to dig up some earthworms and lake snails. Hope you like them in flowers and honey." The girl squeed in delight.

"And for you." He offered another bowl to Zaneeya. It was filled with what looked like cut-up pieces of fish sprinkled with green leaves and bits of rice.

"I don't eat burnt meat," she told him, sniffing at the bowl suspiciously.

"Oh, it's quite unburnt," Tutuo assured. "Raw, in fact. I just added a few spices."

The panther girl hesitated, but she eventually picked up a bit and plopped it in her mouth, chewing slowly. Her orange eyes lit up.

"Good?" the man asked. She replied with vigorous nods.

The four ate heartily, emptying their bowls and receiving seconds. And thirds. When they finished, they lay about, rubbing plump stomachs. Above them the sun had vanished and the first stars began appearing in the sky. The small man sat with them, leaning against the salamander and gazing up lazily at some buzzing fireflies—like stars that had come down to be among them.

"Have you cast some spell on us?" Nyomi moaned, massaging her swollen belly. "Because I suddenly feel very sleepy."

Tutuo laughed. "The only magic I know is in cooking. But I rarely get to share it."

"Where did you learn to do such things with fish?" Zaneeya asked. "Most mortals can't enjoy meat until they've stuck it in some fire."

"I've traveled the world, wide and far," the man said. "You learn some things."

"You're not from this vale?" Abeni asked.

Tutuo shook his head. "My home is far beyond this place. But I left it to see the world. I was gone a long time. I stayed among the mighty Zhusa—the spear-bearers of the southlands—and played their games of raiding cattle among one another. I saw with my own eyes the great kingships of the west and stood before the wondrous walls of Agadu itself! In the stone cities of the east, I met mystics who live in towers and who claim to have visited the flying people—whose kingdom is said to float among the clouds." A dreamy look came into his eyes as he recounted his adventures. "When I returned home, my people said I had grown odd. That I spoke of strange things. And they didn't care for my new friend." He patted Moshi. "So, I took a new name and began wandering again. Wasn't sure where I was going. One day Moshi and I went swimming in a river. Dived under the waters, and when we came up again, we were in the lake outside—right in this vale. Decided to stay. I suppose we were lost too."

Lost too, Abeni thought. Like they had become lost. Only Asha said they were meant to be here. The girl had crawled over and curled up beside Tutuo, playing absently with his bushy beard.

Abeni gazed out across the darkening vale. It *was* beautiful.

"So that's my story," Tutuo said. "Who wants to go next?"

Nyomi raised an eager hand and quickly launched into a tale. The porcupine girl told of getting separated from her family and meeting Abeni and everything that had happened since. The small man listened intently, stopping to ask questions, and oohing and aahing as Nyomi gave vivid descriptions. He gasped at their run-in with the bush babies and cheered at their escape. When it was done, he leaned back and clapped.

"Well done!" he exclaimed. "You are an excellent storyteller!" Nyomi beamed at the compliment. Abeni thought it was the nicest thing you could possibly tell the girl.

"But she left out the best parts," Zaneeya complained.

"Oh, there's more?" Tutuo asked. "I would love to hear!"

The panther girl cleared her throat and began giving her own version of events. She wasn't as good a storyteller as Nyomi. And she had a habit of making her own role appear very important. But when she finished the man thanked her appreciatively.

"I've always found stories are best told from many sides," he remarked. Turning to Abeni he raised an eyebrow. "And you? Do you have a story you'd like to tell?"

Abeni shook her head. Nyomi and Zaneeya had said it all well enough.

"You should sing your song," Asha suggested, playing absently with her locs.

Abeni went stiff, looking to the little girl in surprise. Had she just blurted that out?

"You have a song?" Tutuo asked, seeming genuinely interested.

Abeni wasn't certain what to say. Her song was her story. Her people's story. She didn't know that she wanted to share it. "I haven't sung it in a long time," she said. "I might not even remember it."

"I'm sure you remember it," Asha said. Her eyes locked on Abeni—looking every bit as sharp as the old woman's. "Songs and stories aren't riches to be locked away. Sometimes it helps to share. Or we carry our burdens all by ourselves."

Abeni found everyone was staring at her. Waiting. Their expectant faces made her mouth go dry. Her chest felt suddenly tight, and it was like she couldn't breathe. She wanted to be somewhere else—anywhere but here. But Asha's words played in her head, like roots digging into soil.

Sometimes it helps to share. Or we carry our burdens all by ourselves.

That's what she'd been doing. Even after meeting Nyomi and Zaneeya, she hadn't shared much about herself. Maybe it was time to see what happened if she did.

Beginning was hard. The first few words were harder. It had been so long. But the more she went on, the more it all came back. The tightness in her chest loosened. And she could breathe again, taking deep breaths as she sang.

She sang of her village, of her people. She sang of the day of the storm women and how she came to live with the old woman. She sang of the night of the shadow thing, and how the Asha they knew now had come to be. Then she sang of meeting Nyomi and

Zaneeya, and even added new verses about a small man and a giant salamander. When she finished, she looked up to find everyone quiet. Nyomi's black eyes glistened. Even Zaneeya looked on in wonder.

"Now that is a story!" Tutuo whispered.

"Abeni, I never knew . . ." Nyomi said. "Why didn't you tell us?"

She shook her head. "I don't know. I wasn't sure what you would think of me."

Zaneeya frowned. "Why should we think less? It is quite a tale." She paused as if catching herself. "For a mortal."

Abeni looked to the panther girl, stunned. Had Zaneeya just given her a compliment?

Tutuo offered a warm smile. "Sometimes we shouldn't face the hardest things alone. As the small one said, sometimes sharing helps, yes?" He looked down. "Eh! Seems someone's had a long day."

They followed his gaze to Asha, who lay sleeping. "I know I said I could show you the way out. But no sense wandering now at night. Sleep and stay the morning—or as long as you like."

Abeni looked to the others.

"I can't walk another step with this full belly." Nyomi yawned.

"I'm sleepy too," Abeni admitted.

Zaneeya grunted. "Panther spirits can travel day or night. But if the two of you are tired, I could use the time to get some rest."

Abeni supposed that settled it. She turned to Tutuo. "We'd happily accept your offer to stay here, uncle—until morning."

He smiled at them. "Until morning, then."

That night they slept as they often did, under the stars. Nyomi curled up in a ball of quills in the cool grass, while Zaneeya climbed a tree and sprawled out on a branch as a panther. Abeni and Asha slept on blankets, pressed up against Moshi—who transformed into something soft and plush. It was the best sleep Abeni had had in a long time.

They ended up staying that morning, the next morning after that, and yet a third. Each day they got up and thought about leaving, but managed to find a reason to stay. It was raining. There was some new part of the vale to see. Tutuo's fabulous cooking! The small man seemed happy to have them. By day he showed them about. Sometimes they helped him fish or gather plants. Or they just lay around lazily, exploring heaps of lost things. Their favorite pastime was playing a game where they got Moshi to turn into everything from gold to pure fire! At night they sat while Tutuo smoked from a long pipe and told fantastic stories from his travels—of kingdoms that rose out of the sand, ghost villages, talking skulls, babies that sprouted out of thumbs, and other bizarre things.

On their fourth day, as Abeni sat on a rock by the lake, Tutuo came to sit beside her.

"Not going in?" he asked.

"In a while," she said, watching Zaneeya splash through the water as a panther, chasing Asha, who squealed and laughed. Moshi rose up in the middle of them, his body made of blue liquid, upending a shrieking Nyomi in the process.

Abeni laughed. "They're so silly."

Tutuo chuckled. "No more than I was as a child."

Abeni looked to him. "But uncle, they're not really children. I mean, they're spirits, much older than me."

He nodded. "Older than me, even."

"Then why do they act so much like children?" She'd wondered that for a while but it seemed rude to ask Nyomi and Zaneeya. Besides, Tutuo had traveled all over and knew lots of things.

"Because in a way they are," he replied. "Spirits are eternal, in a sense. They can die, yes, but not like you and me. And they live many of our lifetimes. Their emotions are strong, and they feel with every part of their being. So, if they appear as children, they will act very much that way—even if they've seen a hundred harvest seasons."

Abeni thought on that. "Asha was an old woman for a long time. Now she's young. And she told me she's been young before."

"Yes," Tutuo said. He looked down to Asha, who had hopped

onto Moshi's back. "That one may look young, but her eyes say otherwise."

"What kind of spirit is she?" Abeni asked. "The others aren't sure."

Tutuo pursed his lips. "Hard to say. I have encountered many spirits in my travels—some smaller than ants, others big as mountains. You can never tell just by looking at them."

"Asha told me that this Witch Priest wants people to turn away from the spirits," Abeni said. "That he's come to free us from them."

Tutuo was quiet for a long time before speaking. "Some people worship spirits. Some call on them. Some even seek to control them. Spirits of course have their own will, ignoring mortals altogether or involving themselves in our lives—for good or ill. I have not ventured back into the world and know nothing of this Witch Priest or his war. But it seems wrong-minded to me to turn away from the spirits. They keep the balance between things. Some say it is the spirits who made people, given that task by the gods. They were our first teachers, showing us how to plant, to sing, and to laugh. A world without them would be a sad and lonely one."

Abeni tried to find some truth in his words. Yet, as she thought of her village, her mood grew dark. "My people called on the spirits often. But that didn't save them."

Tutuo looked to her sadly. He didn't appear to have an answer for that.

"The world outside grows darker," he said. "I can feel it, even here. In the things that come here." His eyes fixed hers with meaning. "I have thought on your song. I believe I understand why you have set out to find Asha's sister. Someone as wise as the old woman—who might know how to lead you to ghost ships, storm women who carry fire in their eyes, men in goat horn masks, and stolen away children."

Abeni didn't answer. But he nodded as if she had.

"And whose idea was it to seek out this sister? The little spirit's? Or yours?"

Her face felt suddenly hot. She started to speak, but Tutuo held up his hands.

"I'm sorry. I didn't mean to make you feel bad."

Abeni looked to the lake, where the others played. "Are you going to tell them?"

"It is not mine for the telling. But . . ." She turned to find him again giving her that meaningful gaze. "That little spirit is very attached to you. If you leave her with this sister, to go your own way hunting after ghost ships or the like, she will take it hard."

Abeni sighed. "I thought you weren't trying to make me feel bad."

He offered a slight smile. "Truly I do not mean to. However, there is another choice. You and your friends don't have to venture out into the storm. You can stay here. No dark flyers on bats will ever haunt these skies. No shadows will enter this place. Just lost things. Maybe that's why you were brought here. To give you a place where you can hide away from the ones who hunt you. Perhaps you should think on remaining lost. At least for a while longer. There's no war here, after all—but there is a great big lake!"

He jumped up suddenly, running to the edge of the rock. Letting out a warning whoop he leapt off, dropping like a rock to land with a splash! Everyone cheered.

Later that night, Abeni lay awake. Tutuo's words played in her head. His questions had made it seem like she was lying to the others. But they had their reasons for finding Asha's sister, and she had her own—even if she hadn't told them exactly what those reasons were. *Does it matter that you didn't tell Asha?* She pushed the question away, turning to what else was said. Tutuo was right. In the vale, there was no Witch Priest. It was certainly safer than trekking through a war. Maybe they *could* stay a bit longer. All wars had to end, didn't they?

The thoughts followed her into sleep. When she opened her eyes again, she lay between familiar tall stalks of green that swayed and whispered beneath a blue sky. But this wasn't the vale. Turning her head, she found Asha lying awake beside her.

"You really like this dream," Abeni said.

Asha grinned. "You remember my garden better than I do."

Abeni still hadn't become used to the girl entering her dreams. There was a rustling through the green stalks and a tall figure appeared, casting a long shadow. With a crash, he fell to lie down beside them.

"Good to see you, Obi," Abeni greeted him. The straw man nodded. She wasn't certain if Obi truly existed here, or if he was just another memory. Either way, she enjoyed his presence.

"Asha, do you like it in the vale?"

"Yes! Very much. Tutuo is nice. And Moshi leaves the best presents."

Abeni smiled. The giant salamander had taken a liking to Asha and often left her gifts—bits of fruit, pulled up flowers, and once a half-eaten fish.

"What if we stayed here awhile longer? Until things are safer. Then we can find your sister. Do you like that idea?"

"Yes! It'll be fun!"

Abeni bit her lip. "Is that what we're meant to do, then? Stay here?"

Asha shrugged. "I don't know."

Abeni frowned. "But you just said you'd like to stay."

"Yes. But I don't know if I should." The little girl pressed small hands to Abeni's cheeks, as she often liked to do.

"I'm not Auntie Asha anymore," she said. "I want to do what's fun, even when I know there's important things that also need doing. Making grown-up decisions is hard. That's why I need a guardian."

"I'm not a grown-up," Abeni protested.

Asha smiled. "But you're all I have. And I trust you."

Those last words stung more than Abeni had thought possible.

The next morning, she gathered the others. She'd made a decision for herself and Asha. But she couldn't do so for them.

"Asha and I are going," she said. "We can't stay here. No matter how nice it is. Or how safe. We have to find her sister."

The two girls were quiet for a while before Nyomi sighed.

"I'll come with you," she said. "I don't like it where it's scary. But I do want to see my family again."

Abeni turned to Zaneeya, who gazed out at the vale. "Staying here would be nice. But . . . it feels too much like hiding." She turned to fix them with orange eyes. "Panther spirits do not hide."

So that was that, then. They were going. All of them. Something about that felt right. When they told Tutuo he looked disappointed, but only asked if they were certain.

Abeni was as certain as she could be. The vale was beautiful and peaceful, but it wasn't where they were meant to be anymore.

The small man spent the rest of the morning preparing their leave, filling the magic bag with bread, jars of honey, fried yams, and more. They took a last swim in the lake, riding Moshi. Then, as the day waned, he showed them the way out.

"Getting into the vale is easy," he told them. "Leaving is more complicated." He led them to a part of the vale they hadn't visited before, where leafy purple plants shaped like elephant ears and big enough to wrap around you grew in great bunches. Moshi pushed through them, leading the way.

"We won't go falling through mud again, will we?" Zaneeya asked.

Tutuo chuckled. "No. Just a door. But it can be difficult."

A door? Abeni thought *Out here? And what did he mean by "difficult"?*

Before she could ask, Moshi pushed through a set of the giant leaves, bringing them to a clearing. In the green grass sat a door.

"That's a big door," Nyomi whispered.

Abeni agreed. It was the biggest door she'd ever seen! It towered high above and was wide enough for them all to walk through at once. The entire thing was made of black wood that glistened like stone. Intricate carvings ran across its length, of people and animals. Or creatures she couldn't guess at—like one with the body of a monkey but the head of a crocodile. In the center of the door sat a giant carving of a face, its closed eyes reminding her of a sleeping man.

"Whose door is this?" she asked.

"I don't know," Tutuo said, staring up at it.

Zaneeya's eyes narrowed. "Who made it? Giants? I don't *like* giants."

Tutuo shrugged. "Don't know that either. It's just always been . . . here."

"What are we supposed to do with it?" Abeni asked.

"What you do with any door. Walk through it."

She thought of the many doors in Asha's house. "But where does it go?"

"Out," Tutuo said. "Though where that is depends on you. The door is the only way out of the vale. But it doesn't lead to any one place. I have brought others here. And the door has taken them to where they want to be. Or, perhaps, where they need to go. I can't say for certain." He patted the giant salamander. "Moshi and I have never walked through it ourselves."

Abeni looked to Asha, who was tracing her fingers along a carving. "So how do we open the door?" she asked. "You said going through would be difficult."

"Noooo." The man drew out the word. "I said the *door* was difficult."

She blinked. What did that mean—?

Her thoughts were interrupted by a loud yawning that made her jump. The giant face in the center of the door was moving, its mouth stretched wide! When it was done, the eyes on the face opened.

"Wétin dey happen?" a loud voice grumbled. "Who is making all this noise?" Carved pupils on the eyes shifted to look down.

Tutuo motioned for Abeni to speak.

"Greetings . . . um, door? My friends and I would like to go through. Please?"

The face frowned down at her, then took in the others. "A lost girl? And three lost spirits?" It huffed. "All of you coming from different places. Nobody knowing where you are going. Abegi! No waste my time!" The eyes began to close again. Tutuo mouthed at her to keep talking.

"Great door!" she called. "We may be lost. But we know where we have to go!"

The eyes came open again and the face regarded her sourly.

"Most don't know where they are going," it grumbled. "Or where they need to be. Your heads like all the rest. Full of want, want, want. Go here, go there!" The face pursed its lips at Asha. "This one want to go see sister." The lips twisted to Nyomi and Zaneeya. "These ones want to see family. And you—" There was a considering pause as the lips fixed on Abeni. "Nawa oh! You want go do big things! Big things! No be so?"

Abeni's heart skipped.

It chuckled. "Make I tell?"

Now her heart pounded. Tutuo had been right, this door was difficult! Like Asha's pots! She was relieved when Zaneeya stepped up to ask her own question.

"You can send us anywhere we want to go?"

The door rolled its eyes to the panther girl, seeming annoyed.

"Yes, yes. Wheresoever you all want go."

"Then can you send us each where we want? To different places?"

"Foolish question!" the door snapped. "You come together, you leave the same!"

"But—"

"E don do! I say you all go the same place!"

"I don't need anyone else deciding where I need to go," Zaneeya argued.

"Eh! Small cat girl wey get plenty mouth! No vex me o! Make I go land you slap!"

Zaneeya bristled. "Try it! You don't even have arms!"

The door's face grew angry, and it shook all over. The smaller carvings along its surface came suddenly to life, sticking out tongues, flicking tails, or shaking fists. Leave it to Zaneeya to make a door mad.

Tutuo quickly spoke up. "She didn't mean offense!" He turned to them. "The door has its own rules. You'll have to follow them."

"Fine!" Zaneeya snapped. "I'll tell you where we need to go."

"No!" the door shouted. Its eyes landed on Abeni, and a mischievous look settled on its carved face. "You *all* choose."

They all had to say it together? Abeni glanced to Nyomi, who looked nervous but nodded. Zaneeya fell back sulkily, giving a curt nod. Asha simply smiled. Okay. They could do this. Gazing up at the door, she was opening her mouth when it cut her off.

"Listen well," it said. "Choose *carefully*. What all of you speak by mouth, your head must also think. If the two no be the same, you go fit land anywhere."

Abeni frowned, looking to Tutuo.

"Wherever the three of you tell the door you want to go," he explained, "you have to *want* to go there. Truly. If there's another place in your thoughts, you might go there instead. You *all* will."

"Be like this thing don happen to you," the door teased. "Maybe luck dey your side this time, eh?"

Abeni was puzzled. Someplace else? They'd all agreed they would be going to see Asha's sister. Where else was there? All at once, Zaneeya's question struck her. This door could take them *anywhere*. It could take her back to Asha's house. It could take her back to her village. Or . . . it could take her to where her village had gone! Through this door, she could find her family! Or she could go to her friends! It was all here! Everything she wanted!

The door gave a low laugh. "So many choices."

Abeni felt a moment of panic. Her mouth wanted to say one thing, but her mind jumped from place to place. She saw herself finding Asha's sister. Next, she was on a ghost ship fighting wraiths to free her village. Or she was finding her friends and leading them to safety. All of it swirled in her head, and she found it hard to talk.

The door tsked. "Eiyaa, small girl wey no know where she want to go. Chicken wey run way from one house go next house go still end up inside pot of soup!"

"What?" she asked.

The door rolled its eyes. "The chicken running this way and that is going to end up in hot water no matter where it runs to! Same way your destiny will find you, no matter how you choose— spirit guardian."

"Umm," Nyomi asked. "Why are we talking about chickens?"

"I have no idea," Zaneeya muttered. "Must be a mortal thing." She looked up to the door. "I wish to go find this spirit's sister, so she may help me find my sisters."

"I also want to find her sister!" Nyomi piped up. "To find my family!"

"And I want to go and see my sister," Asha added joyfully.

Everyone turned then to Abeni. She opened her mouth to speak but found she couldn't. Her mind swam, going everywhere at once. Ghost ships. Storm women. A man in a mask of goat horns. Her friends. Her family. So many places to go. What if she spoke one thing but was thinking something else? What if she took them all *somewhere* else? What if—?

"Abeni." She looked to Asha, who regarded her with calm dark eyes. "Just choose. You know where we all must go. You know where we all must be."

Something in the small girl's voice made the swirling thoughts in Abeni's head go still. Finally, she could see clearly the one she wanted. Closing her eyes, she welcomed the quiet. And chose.

CHAPTER FIFTEEN

WISH SONG

Abeni stepped into sunlight.

The door had split right down the middle, opening. And they'd all walked through.

Under her breath she kept saying the same thing. "Take us to Asha's sister, take us to Asha's sister, take us to Asha's sister." In her head, ghost ships, storm women, and the man with the goat horn mask still called to her. But she pushed them back. She'd given her word to get everyone to Asha's sister. Taking them someplace else wouldn't have been right. Hopefully, she hadn't also given up the chance to see her friends and family again.

Glancing back through the door, she made out the vale. On the other side, Tutuo was there. He waved to them beside the giant salamander—whose body had turned into a clear glass that reflected the sun in a rainbow. She waved back just as the door closed and disappeared.

"Well," Nyomi breathed in relief. "We're here."

"And where is that exactly?" Zaneeya asked dubiously.

Abeni wasn't certain. She lifted a hand to shield her eyes. The sun here was very bright. It sat big and full in a blue sky without a single cloud, looking like a hot round ball. They stood on a wide flat plain, and in every direction was tall, brown grass.

"We're not in the forest," she said. She had never been outside the forest before. The idea staggered her. She reached out to grab a stalk of the tall grass and it broke in her hand, dry and brittle. The soil too was dusty and cracked. Even the one tree she made out grew stunted, the parched ground exposing its dried-out roots.

"This land looks blighted," Nyomi said.

Abeni agreed. She turned to Asha. "Which way now?"

The small girl was kneeling, her hands playing with the cracked earth. When she looked up, her face was worried. Her dark eyes gazed out as she tilted her chin into the distance. And they began to walk.

This dry grassland was hard to travel. There was no water. The few trees they met had no fruit. And there was not much to eat. The panther girl went hunting, returning with some scrawny lizards. Even Nyomi had a hard time finding food under rocks. Abeni made sure she and Asha ate and drink very little to conserve what they had in the bag. That first night out on the plain felt strange. In the forest there were all kinds of sounds. Out here, it was quiet. Not even chirping insects.

It only grew worse. And after two days, the harshness took its toll.

Abeni plodded along wearily. She wore Obi's wide-brimmed wood hat to block out the burning sun. The air was so dry and hot it was hard to breathe and sweat soaked her clothes. Asha had undergone a strange change as well. She was no longer the happy and skipping little girl. She barely talked, only nodding each time Abeni asked if they were traveling the right way. She slept a lot and Abeni was forced to carry her much of the time. Even her thick locs had gone limp. Nyomi walked beside them, her quills and face drooping. For once, she didn't do much talking. Even Zaneeya looked tired. She trotted through the brittle grass in panther form, her sides heaving.

They were on their last gourd of water when Zaneeya suddenly stopped, her ears perking up. Without a word she bounded off, leaving them behind. After what seemed a long while, the panther girl returned, shifting to her near-human form.

"A mortal village," she panted. "Not far. In a valley."

Abeni inhaled sharply. A valley! "Asha! Is that where your sister is?" The girl stirred awake to look up and nod faintly. A wave of relief swept through Abeni. After all this time, they'd arrived! "Let's go! I'm sure they'll have water!" She paused, looking over the two girls—Zaneeya's orange eyes and Nyomi's quills. "Only, I don't know how people might react at seeing two spirits."

"They know Asha's sister," Nyomi countered. "Like your village."

"My village knew an old woman. She never looked like . . . you two."

Zaneeya made a face before closing her eyes and breathing deep. As Abeni watched, the panther girl changed into the quite pretty girl they'd found in a trap. She flashed a smile with no sharp teeth and spoke with not a hint of a growl in her voice.

"I've been around mortals enough to know what they prefer."

"I can do that!" Nyomi declared. She closed her eyes and frowned in concentration. Slowly the quills on her body disappeared, replaced with brown skin. The slight fur on her face vanished, and she was left with a short crop of dark curly hair. Opening her eyes showed pupils still a bit large, but normal enough. She beamed proudly.

Abeni stared at the porcupine girl with raised eyebrows. She had managed to look quite human all over—which was clearly visible, since she wore no clothes.

"Nyomi. Did you forget something?"

Zaneeya snickered.

The porcupine girl glanced down with a shrug. "I've seen mortals before that don't wear as much clothes as you do."

"But they still wear *something*," Abeni said.

The porcupine girl rolled her eyes. "Fine." She inhaled and a pink mist formed about her, shaping into a wrapped dress with stripes of white and brown—much like her quills. "Better?"

"Better." Abeni nodded.

With Zaneeya leading the way, they started their trek to the mortal village. It sat right in the middle of the valley, shimmering in the heat. As they got closer, they could make out a short stone wall. Then houses. Small and bleached white with pointed roofs of wood and straw, as colorless as this land. Abeni drew a deep breath at the sight. She'd never been in a village other than her own. This one was smaller, true. But it was still a village, with people, and families. She wondered if they had Harvest Festivals too? A jumble of emotions ran through her, and she felt momentarily overwhelmed.

"You coming?" Zaneeya asked, eyeing her curiously.

Shaking her head to clear it, Abeni nodded. She stepped forward past a low wall of fitted-together stones into the outskirts of the village, Asha cradled in her arms.

Zaneeya sniffed, looking around pensively.

"What is it?" Abeni asked.

"This place," the panther girl said. "It smells . . . odd."

Abeni could smell nothing. Just the dry scent of dust that swirled in the air and settled onto everything. They continued walking.

There were people. All stopped to gape at the four girls. Some gasped. A few even backed away. Abeni stared up at the many faces peering down at them. They were gaunt, like the unnaturally thin bodies that showed beneath tattered clothing. Their wide eyes all carried a haunted look. She'd never seen people so grim.

"What's the matter with these mortals?" Nyomi whispered. "They look as wilted as this land."

Abeni shook her head. More than once she tried to talk to someone, hoping to ask after Asha's sister. Maybe, as in her village, they knew her as an old woman or a witch. But everyone refused to meet her eyes. She had begun to wonder if they'd come to a village of ghosts when she saw someone walking towards them.

It was a woman. No older than Abeni's own mother. But her face was so sunken it made her age hard to tell. Her dark skin was covered in a light dust like everyone's here, as was her plain brown dress of rough looking cloth. Thin copper loops wrapped her forearms from wrist to elbow while a single band the same color circled her neck. Her cheeks were adorned with intricate scars, while her hair was braided tight to her scalp in rings from top to bottom. She took careful steps to reach them, even as others turned away.

"I have water if you like," she said.

"Yes, auntie." Abeni nodded quickly. "We're very thirsty."

The woman turned, looking about nervously before beckoning them to follow. She led them through the narrow dusty streets to a house much like the others; a part of the straw roof had fallen in and spidery cracks showed in the mud brick. She took them inside, entering a room so small they were forced to crouch. An assortment of items—dried roots and plants and leather pouches—dotted the wall, fitted into small holes. The smell of them tickled Abeni's nostrils. It was enough to even make Asha stir, her nose scrunching. At sight of the small girl the woman's eyes softened.

"That one is only a baby!" she whispered. Scooping a cup into an earthen jar, she brought out some water. Abeni gladly accepted, putting some to Asha's lips. The woman filled up several more cups for the rest of them. She sat and stared while they drank. On her lap, her fingers played absently with one another, like she was trying to stop from reaching out to touch them.

"Thank you, auntie," Abeni said again, wiping Asha's dusty face with some of the water. The girl had come awake, peeking through her locs to take in the small space with interest. "My name is Abeni, this is—"

"Where do you come from?" the woman cut in.

"From the Jembe forest," Abeni answered. There was no reason to lie.

The woman frowned. "That is a long way from here. My people say only bush ghosts live in that forest. How did you make it across the savannah?"

Bush ghosts? This probably wasn't the time to explain about

secret vales and magic doors. "We've walked a long time," Abeni said. "Can you tell us where we are?"

"The village of Kono," the woman answered.

Abeni had never heard of such a place. "You're a healer, auntie." She gestured to the many items tucked into spaces in the wall.

The woman nodded. "You have a good eye."

"I knew someone," Abeni explained, "an old woman, who kept roots and plants. She was good at healing too. Do you have someone like that here in your village? A woman—a very big woman? Who takes care of you?"

The woman shook her head, looking perplexed. "We have no one like that here."

Abeni tried again. "Maybe, auntie, you don't think of her as a woman. Maybe you think of her as . . . a witch?"

The woman's eyes widened in alarm. "We have no witches here!"

Abeni worried she might have said the wrong thing. Most people, after all, didn't take kindly to witches. She was set to try another question, but Zaneeya broke in first.

"What is wrong with this land?" the girl asked. "Everything looks dead!"

Abeni winced at the bluntness. But she had similar questions.

"This valley was once a lush place," the woman answered. "Our village grew food to feed us and to trade. We grazed the finest goats and sold their pelts. People traveled from all over to Kono for those pelts." There was a hint of pride at the memory. "But . . . we have had a drought. Nothing grows now, and the last bits of green have almost vanished."

"You should ask some cloud spirits for rain," Nyomi suggested brightly.

The woman shifted eyes to the girl. "There are no spirits here, child. They have abandoned us."

Abeni shared a shocked glance with the others. She looked down to Asha, whose face now looked troubled. Before Abeni could think on this further someone pushed through to enter the house. A man. His beard was peppered with white, and she first thought him to be the woman's husband. But he didn't greet her like that. There was an important way he carried himself that reminded her of her father—or a chief. He glowered at the four girls before turning to the woman.

"What are they doing here?" he asked in a deep voice.

"They needed water," the woman replied.

The man's scowl deepened. "This isn't wise!"

"I only wanted to see them," the woman countered. "It's been so long . . ." Her words faltered and her eyes glistened with unshed tears. But the man didn't flinch. Turning, he squared up his broad shoulders and addressed them.

"You can't stay here," he said bluntly. "Leave."

Abeni bowed low, her head touching the floor. If the man was a chief, it was best to show him respect. "Forgive us, uncle. Did we do something wrong?"

He grunted, unmoved by her display. "There's just been a mistake. Go. Now."

Abeni stared up at him, then the woman, not understanding their odd behavior. Perhaps it was time just to be direct. "We came looking for someone. A woman—a spirit who takes care of the valley."

The man scowled further and he shook his head. "There are no spirits here, girl. You've come to the wrong place."

Abeni's heart sank. That wasn't possible! Not after all this time. Not after all they'd been through. "Please," she begged. "We came so far. We just need to find her. We're so thirsty and almost out of food."

The man's eyes softened for a moment. But his hard mask returned just as quick. "Nyama will give you some water and food," he said, nodding to the woman. "Then you will leave. Do not ask to stay again." Giving one last stern look to the woman he turned and left.

She released a heavy breath. "I'm sorry. What I did was selfish. He's right. You have to go, for your sake as well as ours." Moving to a corner, she took out flat rounds of brown bread. She folded several into a cloth and began filling small wooden bowls with food from a pot. Abeni received them, placing each carefully into her bag. The woman looked on curiously but said nothing.

"Auntie, is there another village near?" Abeni asked. Maybe Asha's sister was elsewhere.

"Not near," she answered. "But several days walk east, you will find one."

Abeni gaped. Several days? Why, they could die of thirst by then!

"That's all I can give," the woman said, reading her thoughts. "Now, you must go. Please." Walking to the front of her small home, she motioned to the door. As they left she looked each of them over, her face waging some unspoken struggle.

"A safe journey to you," she said. Suddenly she leaned close, gripping Abeni hard by the shoulder. Her eyes were wide and she spoke in an urgent whisper. "The day is almost done! When night comes, keep walking! Don't stop to rest! Keep going, as far away as you can!"

Abeni stared at the woman in bewilderment. She nodded, and the strong hand released her shoulder. The four left the woman's home, glancing back to find her staring after them. They kept walking, past the other hushed villagers who would not look at them, until they had gone back out through the stone walls.

Sunset came quick, before they had journeyed very far—not even leaving the valley. As darkness fell, they found themselves out in the open again. Weary from the day, they stopped and rested in the tall dry grass.

"Those were the strangest mortals I've ever seen," Nyomi said. She turned up her nose at the bit of chicken she now held, glancing around for any stray bug that might wander by.

"The drought has baked their minds," Zaneeya added, sniffing at the meat.

Abeni had to agree. She turned to Asha, who was picking up bits of cracked dirt again and sifting it through her fingers. She hadn't spoken since leaving the village, and her small face remained troubled.

Abeni leaned close to her. "Asha, are we in the right place?" she asked. "Maybe your sister isn't here?"

Asha shook her head. "This is where she should be. She's very, very big."

"None of those villagers have heard of any woman like that, Asha," Abeni said.

The girl shook her head again. "My sister isn't a woman."

Abeni's mouth opened, stunned. "What?"

"My sister isn't a woman," Asha repeated.

Abeni thought her head might explode. "But you said she was a woman!" she sputtered. "A big woman! You told me that!"

Asha looked up. "No, I said she was very, very big." She extended her arms as she'd done many times. Abeni stared at the girl. How could she have a sister who wasn't a woman? She wanted to scream. But instead she took several calming breaths and tried to think. What was it Tutuo had said? Spirits could look like anything. Some were smaller than ants, others as big as mountains. She looked to Asha again, *really* looked to where her small arms extended out across the grassy land, and understanding flooded in.

"Your sister!" she said in wonder. "She's the valley?"

Asha dropped her arms back to her sides and nodded.

Abeni's head spun. The spirit they'd come all this way to see wasn't a person at all? She was a whole valley? Sisters were supposed to look like you! That's how it was supposed to work! *But Asha is a spirit,* she thought. *It doesn't work the same for her!*

Neither Zaneeya nor Nyomi seemed to take this news with too much shock.

The panther girl only raked the ground with her claws and grimaced. "If this land is your sister, I fear she might be just as dead."

"No!" Asha insisted stubbornly. "She's not dead!"

Abeni reached down to grab a fistful of dry dirt, looking it over in her palm. If not dead, this spirit was certainly dying. "How can you be sure?" she asked.

Asha bent over, placing her hands to the ground. Wriggling her fingers into the soil, she took a deep breath. "I can feel her. She's still here. She's still alive."

"Can you talk to her?" Nyomi asked. "I once had a very interesting conversation with a rock spirit!"

"It was probably just a rock," Zaneeya murmured.

Asha shook her head sadly. "She doesn't answer. Someone hurt her, very badly."

Someone? Abeni wondered. She looked out across the blighted land. Who could have done this to a whole valley? "Do you think it was the people in the village?" she asked. "They were acting very strange."

Asha's face turned troubled again and she sat back up. "I didn't like that place. There wasn't anyone to play with."

"What do you mean?"

"There was no one to play with," the girl repeated. "Just sad looking grown-ups."

Abeni's eyes went wide. Only grown-ups. The village had only grown-ups! There had been no children!

"A mortal village without children," Zaneeya pondered. "That seems odd."

"No," Abeni said. "Not odd at all. Asha, when she was the old woman, told me the children of her sister's village had been stolen away. With a song. Like in my village."

"Stolen?" Nyomi asked. Her voice dropped to a fearful whisper. "You mean by the man in your story? The one in the goat horn mask?"

Abeni nodded. She'd been so focused on finding Asha's sister, she didn't even think to notice.

"That wasn't in your song," Zaneeya remarked.

Abeni turned to the panther girl "What?"

"The words you just spoke," Zaneeya answered. "Of this man in the goat horn mask also stealing away the children protected by this spirit we seek. You never told us of this. Not even in your song."

Abeni met Zaneeya's unblinking orange gaze, which seemed to be weighing her.

"I haven't found a way to include it," she said.

"What do you think it means?" Nyomi put in. "Will Asha's sister still be able to help us?"

"How?" Zaneeya growled. "She may be dust!"

"Then what do we do now?" Nyomi asked, sounding distraught.

Abeni shook her head. She wasn't sure, to be honest. Finding Asha's sister was why they'd come all this way. The spirit was supposed to take care of Asha. She was supposed to help the others find their families. And she was supposed to help Abeni find the people stolen from her village. But even if it was possible to talk to a valley, this one wasn't speaking. So what *were* they supposed to do? Had they made the right choice in coming here?

The four girls ate the rest of their dinner in silence. After a while they all lay down early, tired from their long day and lost in their own thoughts. When Abeni fell asleep, the unanswered questions were still rattling in her head.

It was the music that woke her.

Abeni opened her eyes, sitting up to breathe in the warm night air. She hadn't been dreaming. Someone was playing music. It started faint but grew: a soothing melody that rose and fell in waves. It flowed all around her, tickling and insisting that she listen. She sat in her blankets, mesmerized as it grew louder.

Zaneeya stirred awake, tilting her head to listen.

"What's all that noise?" Nyomi mumbled drowsily.

Zaneeya made a face. "Music, I think."

"It's not very good," Nyomi yawned.

"It's beautiful!" Abeni exclaimed. Her companions stared at her strangely and she stared back. How could they not hear the wonder in this music? Wait. Had she heard this song before? A voice in her head cried out a warning. She might have listened, but something in the distance caught her attention. Someone was out there.

Rising to her feet, Abeni gazed into the dark, trying to make out the figure.

"What are you looking at?" Zaneeya asked, coming to stand beside her.

"There." Abeni pointed with her chin. "Who is that?"

The panther girl narrowed her gaze. "I see nothing but the night."

"No, someone's out there. A woman, walking closer. She . . ." Abeni trailed off, the words catching in her throat. What she was seeing couldn't be. She blinked. But the sight remained.

"Mama?" she whispered. Her mother was standing there, wearing the same costume she'd worn on Harvest Festival. She smiled warmly at seeing Abeni and waved.

"Mama!" Abeni cried. The warning in her head grew to a shout. She ignored it, ready to launch into a run. Only something held her back. She looked to find Nyomi and Zaneeya to either side, holding her arms. "What are you doing? My mother's out there! I found her!" The music was stronger now, insistent and pulling.

"Have you lost your mind?" Zaneeya asked. "There's no one there!"

"She's right," Nyomi added, her voice worried. "We can see better than you in the dark, and there's nothing out there."

Abeni glared at the two spirits, then back to her mother—and she gasped! Now her father was there too! Nearby were her aunts, Awami and Awomi, and her Uncle Tawayo. Her brother stood between them, grinning. He even made a face.

"They're all here!" she said, unable to stop her tears or her laughter. "I knew you'd find a way to escape! I knew I'd find you again!" Turning to Zaneeya, she pleaded, "Please let me go! It's alright! They're waiting for me! I need to go!"

"No," someone said. Abeni turned to find Asha. The small girl stood staring up at her with concern. "I remember this—from before. Don't let her go!"

Abeni looked to her in shock, then to Nyomi and Zaneeya. She struggled to break free. But they held her fast. The music in her ears drowned out the warning voice, turning it into a muffled plea as her family beckoned.

"Let me go!" she shouted, angry. "You can't do this! Let me go now!" She glowered at Asha, the anger turning to rage that burned her skin. "This is your fault! You ruin everything! I hate you! I hate you!" She was screaming now. Asha winced as if she'd been struck. But Abeni didn't care. Right now, she wanted this little girl to hurt, the way she hurt.

Then, unexpectedly, someone else appeared, walking toward them.

It was a girl. Abeni had never seen her before. She looked near her own age and wore clothing much like the people of the village. The others turned in surprise at her approach. But even as she spoke to them, her brown eyes remained fixed on Abeni.

"Hold your friend," she warned. "If you let her go, she'll be lost to the night."

Abeni glared at the girl. Someone else who wanted to keep her from her family!

"Here, have her smell this." The girl withdrew a thick black root from a leather pouch that hung from her shoulder. "Hurry. The song is stronger than you know."

Asha took the plant and looked it over with interest. She gestured to Nyomi and Zaneeya. Abeni howled as she was bent down. When she reached Asha's level the girl put the root under her nose and held it there. It stunk! She gagged, trying to turn her head. But everything started spinning. Her eyelids felt suddenly heavy, and she closed them as her family and the music faded away.

CHAPTER SIXTEEN

MONSTERS

Abeni awoke to stare up at an earthen roof. For a moment, she wondered if she was back home. But no, her house's roof was made of straw. This wasn't the old woman's house either. And it was so small. She struggled to sit up. Her head throbbed terribly, and her mouth tasted bitter. Turning, she saw Asha sitting cross-legged beside her. The little girl gave a tiny smile. She smiled back, but her smile slid away as she stared about.

Looking through a large opening she saw that it was morning. And this wasn't a house at all. It was a small cave. There were things scattered on the floor, pouches and bits of dried plants. A few bowls and cups. Even some blankets that might have been colorful once but which were now worn. Her eyes fell on Nyomi and Zaneeya, who sat inside the cave as well. But what held her attention was the person she didn't know—yet still recognized. A girl, short and stout with round cheeks that reminded her of Fomi. She sat at the back of the cave, chewing on a bit of bread.

"You were in my dreams," Abeni murmured.

"You weren't dreaming," the girl replied.

Not dreaming. Memories of the past night came back in a rush, making her bolt upright. That she regretted, as her head began spinning. Asha put out a hand to steady her, but Abeni blinked past the dizziness, focusing on the girl.

"Who are you? Where am I?"

"I'm Damju," the girl answered. "You're in my cave. Do you recall last night?"

Abeni nodded slow. "There was a song."

Not just any song. It was the same song she'd heard the day her village fell. The song that stole away all her friends. She remembered everything from last night. The song calling to her. Sounding so beautiful in her ears. What it had shown her. How badly she'd wanted to answer. The only reason she hadn't was—

She looked to Nyomi and Zaneeya. "You stopped me from going. I got so angry. I said things." She turned to Asha, horror-stricken. "Oh, Asha, I'm sorry! I didn't mean those things!"

The little girl offered a slight smile. "I think the song made you sick."

Abeni put a hand to her forehead. It was like she'd been another person.

"Your friends tell me you've heard the song before," Damju said.

Abeni closed her eyes, trying to clear her head. She could still see her mother, her father and brother, her aunts. All calling to her.

"I didn't recognize it," she whispered. "It was like hearing it for the first time."

Damju nodded. "The song can be like that. It is . . . tricksome."

Abeni's eyes flew open. "How do you know about it?"

"This mortal is from the village," Zaneeya said. "She's told us what has happened to their children—what almost happened to you."

The girl bit off another piece of bread, chewing before talking. "I call it the wish song. I know about it for the same reason you do. The wish song came one night, drifting through our village. It only woke the children. It was the most wonderful thing we'd ever heard. It showed us things and called for us to follow. That was how it took all my friends away. It pulled our greatest wishes from our heads and made them real. Everyone saw what they most wanted, calling to them, and they followed."

"I saw my family," Abeni said. "But they were never here, were they?"

Damju shook her head. "That's what you have to remember. The things the song shows you aren't real. When you realize that, it loses its power over you."

Abeni buried her face in her hands, unable to hide from the visions. It had all felt so real! She looked back up to find the girl still staring at her. "If this wish song took all the children of your village, how did you escape?"

Damju smiled crookedly. "My wishes are a little harder to see."

Abeni gave her a curious look, only then noticing the girl's brown eyes. She'd been mistaken. They weren't looking at her. Not the way others did.

"You can't see," she said in surprise.

"You're bright," Damju replied dryly. "I can't see *like you*. But I see in my own way. Shapes, mostly, and light. I could hear the song that first night, but I don't think it could figure out how to make me see the wish. Whoever cast it doesn't know how to see like I do. So I was able to resist it. The other children couldn't."

"What happened to them?" Abeni asked.

Damju shook her head. "I don't know. The song took both my brothers that night. The families with children too small to have been taken all left the village right after. My mother was afraid the song would come for me again and sent me with them. I stayed away for almost a whole harvest season. But I couldn't leave my home behind. So I came back." She spoke through gritted teeth. "And I learned how to deny the cursed song."

Abeni looked around the cave. The girl had been living here, all alone. "Why haven't you returned home, then?" she asked. "Why are you out here?"

Damju's face tightened. "Because of the monsters."

Abeni stared at the girl, then looked to the others.

"She says monsters come each day to her village," Nyomi explained. "They're led by the one who makes the song. The scary one you told us about."

Abeni felt a coldness grip her insides. "The man in the goat horn mask!" she whispered. "He's here?"

Damju grimaced. "We call him the Goat Man."

The Goat Man. The name made Abeni shudder. She had come seeking information on him from Asha's sister. But she'd never suspected he'd be here! She felt light-headed as she took it all in. When she spoke again, she struggled to make her voice calm. "Has he brought other children here? Children from other villages?"

Damju shook her head. "I can't say. I only know his monsters come each morning to gather what's left of my village. They are made to work for him through the day and returned at night."

"What kind of work?" Abeni asked.

"I don't know," Damju answered. "But it's why my people sent me away. There are no more children in my village. If the monsters found me there, if they thought my people were hiding me, everyone could get in trouble."

"They left you out here alone?" Nyomi asked, horrified. "That's terrible!"

That was terrible, Abeni thought. But it explained why the villagers had stared at them so oddly, and why that man who looked like a chief had made them leave.

Damju shrugged. "I'm not completely alone. My mother visits. She brings food and water. I don't think the rest of my village even knows I'm here."

"Who are these monsters?" Abeni asked. "Do they ride on giant bats? Are they made up of shadow? What do they look like?"

Damju smirked, and she realized the silliness of her question. "I'm sorry! I wasn't thinking!"

"People often don't," the girl said. "I don't know anything about giant bats. Or things made up of shadow. But I can tell you that the monsters are very big—very tall." She paused, her round face thoughtful. "Why didn't the song work on your friends? It only took you."

There was an awkward quiet.

"Perhaps we just didn't believe it, like you say," Zaneeya said finally.

Damju thought on this, then shook her head. "No. There's something about you three that's different. The light around you . . . it's all wobbly."

Zaneeya's eyes narrowed. Nyomi seemed startled. Asha only gave one of her knowing smiles. Abeni looked the girl over appreciatively. Maybe she saw better than they thought. It seemed this wish song didn't work on spirits. She didn't think they even heard the song the same way. Before anyone else could speak there was a rustling of grass from outside. They all turned at once at the sound. Someone was coming.

Damju jumped up from where she sat. "It's my mother! Mama! I'm here!"

"Damju?" a woman's voice called. "I thought I heard you talking—"

The person who appeared crouched at the opening of the small cave went still, staring at them in surprise. It was the woman from the village, the very one who had given them food and water. She looked each of them over before turning to her daughter.

"Damju, what are you doing with these people?"

"I met them last night, mama. The wish song, it came for them too."

Damju's mother didn't reply. Coming into the cave, she laid down a bundled cloth and unfolded it to reveal bowls of food and a gourd of water. As she spread them out, her eyes shifted uneasily among the other four girls.

"You didn't heed my warning," she scolded.

"We were tired, auntie," Abeni said. "We couldn't go any further."

"Mama," Damju spoke up. "The song took the children of her village too."

The woman's face softened, before turning hard again. "We've lost much ourselves."

"What's happened in this place?" Zaneeya asked. "Where are your children?"

Damju's mother released a long breath. "I'm sure Damju told

you. The wish song came one night and stole them away. All except my Damju. They've become lost to us, our Children of Night."

Abeni went stiff. "What did you say?"

"That we've lost our children," Damju's mother repeated.

"You called them your Children of Night. Where did you hear that?"

Damju's mother looked up at her and frowned. "I do not know in truth."

But Abeni knew where she had heard it. Asha's sister's words that had been in her dreams. *He has taken the children. Taken them from me. The Children of Night.* They had also been the last words of the scrying pot: *Beware the Children of Night . . .* All of it was coming together here. In this place.

"Have other children been brought here?" she asked. "By the one who plays the song—this Goat Man?"

The woman nodded slowly. "He has led other children here. Some stay. Others he sends away—though I cannot say where."

Abeni's heart beat faster. Could her friends be here now?

"And these monsters?" Zaneeya cut in. "What about them?"

The woman's face turned grim. "The monsters do the bidding of the Goat Man. They force us to work each day. If we don't, he threatens to keep our children forever."

Abeni stared at her in shock.

"The Goat Man did this," Asha said. She held a brittle grass stalk in her hand.

Damju's mother nodded. "He and his monsters brought this blight. The rivers have dried up. The soil has turned to dust. Everything dies."

Abeni inhaled. So that was who had hurt Asha's sister! This Goat Man!

"Have you tried to fight them?" she asked. "To get your children back?"

Damju's mother looked at her with eyes that quivered. "We don't dare—!"

Her words were ended by a terrible sound. A horn, low and

booming to break through the morning. It blared so loud the air seemed to shake around them. Abeni felt a new chill creep up her back. Like the song, she had heard this horn before.

"They've come!" Damju's mother said. She turned to her daughter. "You can't stay here any longer! It's too dangerous!"

"Mama!" Damju clutched her mother's arm. "Don't go. Come with me. Please!"

The woman's eyes wavered, and her face fell. "I can't, Damju. They'll know one of us is missing. I have to keep your brothers safe." She stroked her daughter's cheek before leaving the cave to disappear into the tall grass.

Abeni watched her go, then jumped up to follow.

Zaneeya grabbed her arm. "What are you doing?"

"I want to see these monsters," she said.

"Are you crazed?" the panther girl asked. "You can't just—"

"I wasn't asking your permission," Abeni said curtly.

Zaneeya stared for a moment before releasing her grip. "So, you're making decisions now for all of us, are you? How very mortal of you."

Abeni didn't respond. She threw on her sandals and crawled out of the cave, squinting at the morning sunlight. Crouching, she crept forward through the tall grass. Behind her, she could hear the others following. Her heart pounded like a drum and her mind was on fire. All she could think about was that horn. Reaching where the grass grew short, she pushed aside the dry stalks to see the nearby village of Kono and gasped.

There were monsters.

They looked like great big men, taller than anyone she'd ever seen. Corded and knotted muscles showed beneath their skin, the color of grayish rock. Their broad bare chests were covered in unknown ghostly symbols, continuing along their arms and legs. She couldn't make out their faces, hidden by large masks of wood and iron, leaving only mouths and chins visible. Each carried swords with jagged edges and spears with twisted blades. Some looked like very tall women. Long sharp curving blades like polished bone grew from the backs of their forearms and hung past their knees. Each was wrapped in tattered crimson cloth, held together with bits of metal.

The monsters gathered up the villagers, with snarls and roars. They pushed the slower ones, dragged them from their homes with whips and threats. The people cowered before them, fear etched on their faces.

"Where do they come from?" Abeni asked Damju, who crouched beside her.

"I don't know," the girl answered. "One day they were just . . . here."

"Your mother said they keep the children prisoner."

Damju nodded, and as Abeni watched, the monsters marched their captives away. They walked out of the village, past its low stone walls and into the valley.

"They're coming this way!" Nyomi squeaked.

The porcupine girl was right. With no time to run, they lay low in the tall grass.

"Nyomi, don't vanish!" Abeni whispered. "They'll smell the flowers!" The porcupine girl's black eyes remained wide, but she didn't vanish. Soon the monsters were upon them. They passed by, trampling the stalks and setting the ground to tremble.

The monster in the lead wore a mask with spikes of iron. When a villager stumbled, he turned with a snarl, showing a mouth of sharp teeth. Another monster grabbed the man by the neck with a clawed hand, lifting him off his feet before throwing him to the ground. Abeni flinched as a whip came down several times before he was pushed roughly back in line. When the procession finally passed, she rose to follow. The others came up behind—all except Zaneeya, who fell in at her side.

"Why are we doing this?" the panther girl whispered urgently.

"I want to see what they're doing," Abeni said.

"To what end?" When Abeni didn't answer, the girl growled in irritation. "Just try not to get us killed!"

They continued to follow the monsters and the villagers, making sure to keep a safe distance. It was a while later that they finally stopped. They were still in the valley, but the village was no longer in sight. Here the land was nothing more than the tall dry stalks that grew out of fractured earth. Then, one by one, both captors and captives disappeared. They were descending into something, Abeni realized. Waiting until all of them were gone, she crawled on her stomach until she came to where the tall grass grew sparse. There, she saw it.

Cut into the ground was a pit, like a giant had dug a square hole into the earth and scooped away all the dirt. It was massive, wide enough that she imagined several houses could fit inside, and so deep that rickety wooden ladders were placed to allow people to climb down. But no giant had done this. Inside were the villagers. Many were digging up and hauling away large rocks. Some crawled along smaller ladders and used clay pots to throw soil onto a growing mound. Most squatted and sifted dirt through flat baskets. It looked as if they were searching for something. Elsewhere, a fire raged inside the pit and numerous villagers worked tending to it. They pumped leather sacs of air and beat noisily on things that glowed orange with heat. All around them the monsters kept a close watch, lashing their captives to work faster.

"What are they doing?" Nyomi asked, looking down, confused.

"Who knows?" Zaneeya grumbled. "Mortals are always digging about for things."

"I don't know what they're looking for," Abeni said. "But the ones near the fires, they're making iron. In our village, the blacksmiths made iron that way. But I've never seen so much."

"Maybe it's for that," Nyomi said.

Abeni followed the porcupine girl's gaze. Rising out of the pit was a towering structure. It looked to her like a giant serpent of dark iron that twisted and curved, growing larger and higher as it went. She'd been so intent on the villagers she hadn't even noticed the thing.

"What is it?" Damju asked. "What is it you see?"

Abeni shook her head. "I'm not sure."

Asha settled beside her and tilted her head. "It's for making music," she observed. Everyone turned to the small girl, whose fingers now traced the air along the strange iron monstrosity. "You blow into it there and then sound will go all around and come out up there." She pointed to a wide flaring opening at the top.

"It's a horn," Abeni murmured. They'd had horns in her village for making music. But they were small things of wood or bone. Nothing like this!

"All this for some music?" Nyomi asked, puzzled.

"For the wish song!" Abeni realized. What else could it be? "But it's not finished." She indicated gaps in the structure, where bits of iron still needed to be fitted.

"Why would these monsters need such a thing?" Damju asked.

Abeni thought she knew. "A horn like that could reach much further than your village. It would bring children from all over."

Damju recoiled in horror. "That's awful!"

"But for what purpose?" Zaneeya asked. "Your mother said the children of your village were stolen to make their parents work. Why force them to build something just to get more children? Why even bring the children of Abeni's village here?"

Abeni bit her lip in thought. Zaneeya was right. They were missing something.

"Maybe we should ask him!" Nyomi said.

She gestured shakingly to a figure who was climbing to stand atop a mound of broken and jagged rocks beneath the iron contraption. He was a monster like the rest, only even bigger. Thick white goatskin covered his forearms, while furry pelts hung from his waist. Most of his face was hidden away—by a great mask of goat horns, some twisted and curving, some straight and jutting in every direction. He looked down at the other monsters and the villagers alike, overseeing their work.

Zaneeya let out a hiss. "The Goat Man!"

Abeni nodded. He looked every bit as terrifying as the day

he'd entered her village and stolen away her friends. But what held her attention now was what stood behind him. It was a large strip of red cloth, hanging from a pole embedded into the rock. On it was a single fiery orange teardrop—the standard of the Witch Priest.

CHAPTER SEVENTEEN

INTO THE DARK

This place is cursed," Zaneeya grumbled.

The four of them had returned from the pit and now sat with Damju in her cave, trying to make sense of what they had seen.

"Why build something to take more children?" Abeni muttered absently. Zaneeya's earlier question burned in her mind. "Why bring my friends here?"

"Maybe the Goat Man just likes children?" Nyomi ventured.

"Don't be thick," Zaneeya scolded.

"I'm just trying to help!" Nyomi shot back.

"Then say something useful—like we need to leave this place!" Zaneeya said.

"I thought you wanted to solve this mystery," the porcupine girl mocked.

Zaneeya grimaced. "Not so much I want to be drawn into anything involving the Witch Priest. Let the mortals sort this out."

"You're spirits!" Damju broke in. Everyone turned to her in surprise. "This one," she gestured at Zaneeya, "keeps saying *mortals*. Who else would talk that way but spirits? That's why the wish song didn't call you!"

Zaneeya made a face as if swallowing something unpleasant. "Maybe you heard wrongly," she suggested.

Damju pursed her lips. "My hearing's just fine, thank you."

Nyomi laughed, her quills quivering in delight. "Now who's the thick one?"

The panther girl growled back and the two launched into an argument.

"We need to find the missing children."

Abeni's words cut through their banter like a knife. Everyone went silent. She wasn't certain what she expected. Partly she had spoken for her own benefit. She needed to know it didn't sound as crazy aloud as it did in her head. From the looks she received, she wasn't so sure.

"That has to be the stupidest thing you've said so far," Zaneeya growled.

Abeni started with an angry retort, then stopped. She knew this girl now. Zaneeya hurled insults when her temper got the better of her. Or something made her uncomfortable. Getting angry in turn never managed to solve anything. So instead she bit back her own retort, smoothed her face, and tried something different.

"The night the shadow thing destroyed Asha's home, I spoke to a pot," she said.

"The magic pots in your song?" Nyomi asked.

Abeni nodded. "The one called the scrying pot. It can see things that are going to happen." She turned to Asha, who stared back curiously. "Your sister, in her dreams. She spoke about this Goat Man taking the children. She called them the same thing Damju's mother did, the Children of Night. Then, on that night, the scrying pot told me, *Beware the Children of Night.*" She looked back to the others. "Don't you see? These Children of Night are the missing children of this village. They must be. And I think we're here to save them."

Nyomi frowned worriedly, biting her lip. "That sounds scary. I don't like scary."

Zaneeya shook her head. "We're supposed to take the words of a talking pot?"

"The first time I talked to the scrying pot it told me to look out for shadows," Abeni countered. "I just didn't know what it meant at the time. Its last words to me were about the Children of

Night. Whatever happened to Asha's sister, this Goat Man, and these monsters—it's all the same thing."

"Wait, who is this sister?" Damju asked, confused.

"Your valley," Abeni explained. "A spirit lives here. I think this Goat Man and his monsters did something to her when he stole away your friends. That's why everything's dying."

"The blight!" Damju exclaimed. "It's why people say the spirits went away!"

Zaneeya scowled, looking annoyed that they were even having the discussion. "Even if all this is true, this scrying pot told you to *beware* the Children of Night. Wouldn't that be a warning to flee here as fast as we can?"

"It told me more than that," Abeni said. "It said: *The children become hidden in darkness. To free them you must seek them.* I think that means we have to search for them. We're meant to free them."

Everyone was quiet for a moment. Finally, Zaneeya shook her head "Do you know what I think?" Abeni opened her mouth to speak, but the panther girl went right on. "I think you've wanted to come here seeking missing children all along. In all your big talk about finding Asha's sister, you just *happened* to leave out that the children of her village were stolen—just like yours. You think I didn't notice you asking this mortal girl's mother if she'd seen any other missing children? Would those be the ones from *your* village?"

Abeni fumbled for words. She thought of denying it. Of telling the panther girl that she didn't know what she was talking about. But the more she kept things hidden, the more they seemed to pile up. She was getting tired of keeping secrets. As those orange eyes bored right through her, she settled on the only answer worth giving. The truth.

"Yes," she said.

"Ah!" Zaneeya exclaimed, pointing an accusing finger. "So, you don't deny it!"

"It's not what you think!" Abeni countered. "I knew the

children of the village Asha's sister looked over were gone, stolen away. I hoped that she could tell me something about what happened to them. That it might tell me more about what happened to my friends. I kept that from you, yes. And that was wrong." She looked to Asha. "But I wasn't expecting the man in the goat horn mask to be here too. I didn't know he had hurt her and caused this blight. I didn't know about these monsters. Now that I'm here, though, what the scrying pot said makes more sense. Finding the missing children of this village could mean finding my friends!"

"You don't know that!" Zaneeya yelled. "Your friends might not even be here! These mortals and their blighted village just remind you of your own. You believe if you can bring back their missing children, it will be like bringing back your village. You think that way you can find your stolen life again!"

Abeni glared, her anger welling up despite her best attempts, ready to pour out. Zaneeya always seemed to know exactly the places to cut at—the ones that hurt the most. But she realized in slow admission that the panther girl wasn't so far off. With a deep breath, she let go of the anger.

"Maybe you're right," she said finally.

"Ah!" Zaneeya exclaimed again.

"Does it make a difference?" Abeni asked, throwing up her hands in exasperation. "This Witch Priest robbed me of my family, and everything I've known. He took you away from your sisters. Separated Nyomi from her family. Now he wants to do it to these people. You're right, I don't know if my friends are here. I don't know if Asha's sister can help you like you wanted. I wish I did. But if we can stop what's happening here, like the scrying pot said, I think we should at least try. Maybe I'll find my friends too. Maybe not. And if all we end up doing is saving the children of this village, that's worth it. Someone has to stand up to this Witch Priest. Show him he can't go around taking who he wants! Ruining people's lives!"

"This Goat Man blighted an entire land!" Zaneeya shot back.

"He has an army of monsters and he's defeated a spirit stronger than any of us! What chance do we have?"

Abeni had to admit those weren't very good odds. But she wasn't ready to give up yet. "We have each other. That magic stone I used against the bush babies? The scrying pot told me the 'cat will know' which one to choose. It *knew* I was going to find you, Zaneeya. I'm betting it knew about Nyomi too. We didn't all just meet by chance. You're always going on about mortals and how we do terrible things to each other. Now together, spirits and mortals, we can try and do some good. I know that you're scared, but—"

The panther girl rose up before she could finish. Her orange eyes were on fire and a growl sounded in her throat. "I'm. Not. Scared," she snarled, biting off each word. Abeni realized she'd said the wrong thing. But it was too late to take it back. "*We* need to do this, you say. *We* have to save these children. But you were the one keeping secrets. *You* were the one who jumped up after those monsters. Now it's about *we*?" She shook her head. "None of this is my concern. I came here to find out about my sisters. To return to them. Not to go chasing after the riddles of some pot. Throw away your short mortal life if you want. I won't join you!"

With that she shifted swiftly into a panther and trotted away into the tall grass. Abeni watched her go with disappointment. That hadn't gone the way she'd hoped. She turned to look at the others. Nyomi's eyes slid down to stare at her hands.

"I wish you had told us why you wanted to come here," the girl said, and Abeni flinched at the disappointment in her voice. Nyomi had been the first one she'd met out here. The first one who had trusted her. "What you want to do might be right. But we're only small spirits. And you're just a mortal. What can we do against monsters? Against the *Witch Priest*?" She still said his name in a whisper. "Besides, I'm not the brave person you're look-ing for."

"Nyomi," Abeni said. "I think you're very brave. You saved me."

But the girl shook her head. "Porcupine spirits live to dance and eat, not fight. We flee from danger, not run to it. I'm sorry, but I can't help you."

Abeni reached out to say something else. But there was an explosion of pink mist and the girl was gone.

"Flowers?" Damju asked, sniffing the air.

Abeni sighed and turned to Asha. "Do you think I'm making a bad decision too?"

Asha looked back at her and smiled. "You're trying to save my sister, even though you know it's going to be very difficult. I think that's a *hard* decision—and sometimes we have to do things that are hard. I'll go with you, if you like."

"I will too," Damju put in fiercely. "It's my village, after all."

Abeni nodded at them both in thanks. At least she had that. Sitting back, she began to think on what to do next.

◎ ◎ ◎

Of course, she had no intention of taking either girl. What she was going to do was dangerous. Asha, as she was now, was too young. And she wasn't certain how Damju could manage. No, she would do this alone. She waited until late that night to head out. Both Damju and Asha had fallen asleep, expecting to be awakened. But she let them slumber, sneaking away from the cave. She'd investigate the pit and return by morning to tell them what she'd found. Then, maybe, they could come up with a plan and convince the other villagers to go along.

Whatever Zaneeya or Nyomi thought, she wasn't reckless. All she intended to do tonight was look. The scrying pot had said as much: *They become hidden in darkness. To free them you must seek them.* So that's what she was doing—going off to seek them in the dark of night. That made sense. And that *Beware* part was probably because this was dangerous. Of course, the pot had said more. *But in finding them, you risk losing yourself.*

She hadn't mentioned that to anyone. In part, because she knew it sounded bad. And because she had no idea what it meant. How could she lose herself by finding them? Those pots and their riddles, she muttered silently. Her doubts clung to her like heavy weights, but she shook them off and resumed her walk.

She made her way through the night, following a trampled path. When the tall grass stopped like before she dropped low and crawled until she reached a place where the ground fell away off a rough edge. It was the pit. And inside were monsters.

As she'd hoped, the monsters were all sleeping. They lay about everywhere inside the deep hole, sending up rumbling snores of snarls and growls into the night. Here and there a few torches burned. But not one of them was awake.

Good. The question now was, where were they hiding the missing children? She'd already reasoned out it had to be wherever the monsters were. They wouldn't hide the children where they couldn't keep watch on them. So if the monsters were in the pit, the children must be there too. She spied the top of a ladder emerging from the pit and moved quietly towards it. Finding her courage, she fit her staff across her back, then began her descent. The rickety ladder made more noise than she would have liked, and she couldn't help but imagine she was entering some giant's open jaws.

When she reached the bottom, she let out a thankful breath—so far, so good. Gazing around the pit, she stared at the sleeping monsters, who were even more frightening up close. She made out sharp teeth that jutted from their downturned mouths and muscles that bulged beneath their odd clothing. They smelled too. She wrinkled her nose with distaste. Like unwashed goats! She scanned the pit. These monsters slept without concern. They didn't appear to fear the children escaping. Maybe they had locked them somewhere they couldn't get out, somewhere hidden. She kept searching, uncertain what she would find, until her eyes spied something of interest.

There were great openings on the side of the pit wall. Three in total. Each was wide and tall enough for people—even these monsters—to pass through. She guessed they were probably tunnels dug to mine for iron, or whatever else the villagers were made to look for. But they would also be a good place to hide things. Like children! *They become hidden in darkness.* Unfortunately, the openings were on the other side of the pit—straight through the sleeping monsters. She could turn back now—go up the ladder and return with what she knew. Maybe then she could get Zaneeya and Nyomi to join her. But even as she said it, she knew she wasn't going back yet.

"Just a little bit more," she mouthed quietly—and started her way across the pit.

Each step was a careful one, navigating through the sleeping monsters and trying to avoid sprawled out legs or twitching fingers. One wrong move could bring the entire place alive like a hornet's nest. She got a good scare when one of the monsters shifted as she passed, swinging an arm beneath her just as she was lifting a leg. She froze, leg held up high, and waited. When the arm settled back down, she continued walking, trying to slow her thumping heart.

Reaching the three openings, she stared up at them, wondering which to choose. Light showed from the one in the center, a glow that steadily increased. A torch, she realized. Someone was coming out of that thing! Without a second thought, she ducked into another of the dark tunnels, pressing against the earthen wall—just in time to see a figure emerge. Her breath caught in her throat.

The Goat Man!

He strode out of the tunnel, a towering figure in shaggy goat fur and a face covered in a mask of horns—as frightening as that day she'd first glimpsed him in her village. Two monsters flanked him on either side. The three strode through the sleeping camp until they came to the mound of jagged rocks at its front. Climbing them with ease, they reached the top and then turned to look out across the pit. The Goat Man reached for something at his side. It looked like a long wooden flute. Bringing it to his lips, he blew—and music poured out.

The wish song! Abeni felt the magic in the music wash over

her as it had the night past. As it had that first day in her village. It was still beautiful, and she gasped at hearing it as her
feet walked forward. No! The warning that had come last night
sounded again in her head. This time she forced herself to listen,
planting her legs and fighting to keep them from moving. What
was it Damju had said? The only way to beat the song was to not
believe it. To know it was a trick. To accept that it was a lie. So
that's what she told herself. She whispered it under her breath.

It's not real. It's not real. It's not real.

She said those words even as the song made her fondest wishes
form before her eyes—her family, Fomi, her friends. All beckoning her to follow the sweet music. She shut her eyes tight and
fought. She no longer just whispered the words, she shouted them
inside her head. And with her whole heart, she embraced them. She
had seen this Goat Man work his magic. She had seen him among
the storm women in her ruined village. She had seen him steal
away her friends. She had seen what he had done to Damju's village
and this valley. What he was showing her now was a lie. And she
would not believe. She! Would! Not!

She exhaled a long breath—as if hands that had been trying to squeeze her suddenly let go. When she opened her eyes,
the visions had grown dim and transparent. The song itself had
changed. It was no longer beautiful. It was . . . a mess. Just a lot
of blaring noise. She felt a pang of loss as the visons of her family
faded away, knowing they would never come back.

However, she didn't think the song was intended for her ears
alone.

Everywhere within the pit, the sleeping monsters began to
stir. Arms stretched and legs shifted as they shook their heads and
came to their feet. Soon they were all standing, their masked faces
turned towards the sound. Suddenly there was rumbling. Abeni
gripped the earthen wall. The ground was moving, trembling beneath her feet! As she watched with ever widening eyes, something
began to emerge right out of the ground in the pit behind the
mound of rocks where the Goat Man stood.

A great mask of dark iron appeared first, its sharp edges surrounded by twisted barbs. Massive shoulders came next as it pushed upward, followed by a chest and torso and legs. It was a giant man! He sat on a stool, big enough to fit his enormous frame. All of him, even his chair, was molded from rough and uneven earth, held together by bits of rock. As the carving came to a stop, the rumbling ended. Sitting upon his throne, the figure molded of earth and rocks towered higher than the pit itself. Then, without warning, his earthen head burst into flames! Fire white and hot spewed from the mouth and eyes of the iron mask and Abeni silently mouthed his terrible name.

The Witch Priest.

Not him, of course, but something created in his image. As one the monsters fell to take a knee, staring up into their master's fiery eyes. But Abeni's gaze drifted elsewhere.

Nestled on the lap of the giant was a great crimson gemstone. Cut on every side with flat surfaces and sharp edges, it glowed bright, pulsing alongside the music that still played into the night. There was something else coming from it as well—voices, the voices of children.

Abeni first thought she was hearing things. But the voices were coming from the stone, faint yet unmistakable. They were crying and pleading, as if trapped. The monsters went silent, listening to the music and the strange voices. On each of their chests something glowed red as well, pulsing in time to the stone. She strained to make it out but couldn't see. A horrible thought came to her. Were these the voices of the stolen children? Was she hearing the voices of her friends? Had these monsters somehow locked them inside the giant stone?

No. That didn't make sense. How could a stone—even one so big—hold the children of an entire village? Whatever was happening, she wasn't going to figure it out standing here. Pulling her eyes from the monsters and the statue with the flaming mask, she turned and with cautious steps walked farther into the tunnel.

It was darker inside than she'd thought. She couldn't even

make out her hand in front of her face. Luckily, she had brought along some light. From her bag she withdrew the stone ball Asha had given her. Shaking it slightly brought a faint glow that cut through the dark. She held it up like a torch as she went, letting it illuminate her way.

Inspecting the tunnel walls, she found she'd been right. These weren't natural. The villagers had dug them. She put fingers to grooves cut into the rough earth. How long had these people toiled here?

Walking on she hunted for any sign, any hint, of the missing children. She didn't know what she was looking for, exactly. Perhaps a carved-out space, or a gated pen. Even if she did find them, she'd never get them all out. But maybe if the monsters fell asleep again, she could spirit away one child or two. And then . . . well, she'd figure that out.

But after what seemed like endless walking, she hadn't found anything. There were no signs of children at all. The tunnels weren't simply straight either. They twisted and turned, branching into separate parts. She'd gone so deep inside that she could no longer hear the music in the pit. Worse, wherever she was now, she had no idea how to get back to the entrance.

In finding them, you risk losing yourself. Was this what the scrying pot had meant? She grunted in frustration as she rounded yet another corner. These passages were all starting to look the same. Stopping, she leaned against a wall. This wasn't going at all as planned. She hadn't managed to find a clue to the missing children, and now she was lost.

"A fine hero you're turning out to be," she muttered.

Her eyes roamed the dark, landing on something that glinted nearby. She walked over, shaking the ball for more light. There were baskets. She counted six of them, woven from brown straw. They sat against the tunnel wall, each filled with small sparkling things. Reaching inside one, she scooped some into her hands. They looked like glass beads worn in her village, only much harder, each one glimmering as if they held their own light inside. Was this what the villagers had been digging for?

She was still staring when she heard a faint sound. She went still, straining to listen. It came again—something falling, one after the other. And it grew louder. Footsteps! Someone was in the tunnels! Someone was in here with her!

Panic gripped her. Dropping the shiny things back into the basket, she made ready to leave, eager to put some distance between herself and those footsteps. Holding up the light, she moved to turn a corner—and ran right into a monster.

Abeni cried out before she could even think.

The monster was right in front of her. His huge, muscled gray body blocked her path, and his head grazed the ceiling. At her yell he glared down from behind a mask covered in iron spikes. Eyes bright like fire gazed at her, up and down. Then, opening a downturned mouth to reveal jagged teeth, he let out a deafening roar. Abeni stumbled, managed to spin around without falling—and ran!

She could hear the monster in pursuit, roaring as his clawed hands scraped the walls. She ran faster, rounding corners, hoping to throw him off. But he kept coming, following just behind—enough so that she could hear those lumbering footsteps always getting closer. At least twice she fell, scraping her knees. But she scrambled back up quickly. If she was caught, she'd be taken to the Goat Man. Maybe locked away with the other children. Or worse. She recalled those jagged teeth. What if this monster was just hungry? A shiver ran through her, and she ran on. Rounding yet another corner, she dared a glance back. No one was there. She allowed herself a moment of relief. Maybe she'd lost him after all.

A sudden roar made her almost jump from her skin. The monster appeared out of the darkness—directly in front of her! She braked hard, this time falling completely onto her back. He must have gone through another tunnel. Now he towered before her—cutting off her path. Scrambling backward on heels and palms she managed to evade a clawed hand that snatched for her. Somehow, she got her staff out. Not even bothering to think of a form, she swung it as hard as she could. The thick wood struck her pursuer across his exposed jaw with a loud crack!

The monster reared back, roaring in anger. He grabbed at the staff like it was some annoying thing, and with one hand lifted and hurled it away. She went flying with it to slam against the tunnel wall. The blow was enough to knock the breath from her and she fell to the ground senseless.

Bits of light danced before Abeni's vision. A voice in her head was screaming to get to her feet. To run! But her ears rang, and she couldn't remember how to make her legs work. As the monster stood over her, a terrifying image of those jagged teeth flashed through her mind.

Suddenly there was growling. Only it didn't come from the monster. And it sounded familiar. Was that . . . a cat?

Abeni twisted her head to find two orange eyes staring out from the darkness. There was a roar as a black shape soared over her. It struck the monster squarely in his chest, knocking him down.

Abeni struggled to sit, watching the monster that now lay on his back. He bellowed in pain and anger, as claws and teeth tore into him. Two massive arms finally managed to wrap themselves around the black shape, flinging it away. His attacker sailed through the air, changing and landing in a familiar crouch.

"Zaneeya . . ." Abeni whispered.

The panther girl glanced to her from beneath a tangle of locs before returning her gaze to the monster, now risen to his feet. He roared at her and charged. With a fierce growl she ran for him, teeth bared and claws ready. Abeni watched as the two clashed. Zaneeya's claws raked the monster's torso, tearing through his crimson fabric. He howled in pain, trying to grab at her—but she was fast! In a move that Abeni could barely follow, she flew up to flip off his back, coming back down to slash from behind and setting him to howling anew.

But the panther girl could only hold off the monster for so long. One of his long reaches managed to catch her by the arm. She struggled, but he was strong, pulling her towards him. Grabbing one of her legs, he lifted her high above his head before throwing her down with great force. Abeni watched horrified as Zaneeya hit the ground hard, bounced once, and did not get up.

The monster snarled in victory. Reaching to his side he pulled out something long, iron, and jagged. Abeni gasped at seeing the sword, surrounded with sharp barbs like teeth. Lifting the blade, he aimed at the fallen spirit and readied to finish what he had begun.

Abeni was up on her feet and moving, crying out at the same time. She didn't know when she thought of it, but her hand was already digging into her bag. Reaching the monster, she opened it wide, and threw its contents at him.

Morning mushrooms in the dozens came flying—the same ones she'd captured that night long ago for Auntie Asha, kept fresh in the magic bag. They streamed out, emitting tiny squeals as they jumped onto the monster, hopping and spreading across his body in a white mass. He looked down, lowering his sword arm as he tried to brush them off. But they kept crawling over him, wriggling to get beneath his clothes. Soon he dropped his weapon altogether and began an odd dance as he tried to rid himself of the things.

Abeni thought they must have tickled. Dashing to Zaneeya, she flipped her over, fearing the worst. She was thankful when the panther girl blinked her orange eyes open and groaned—glancing to the struggling monster.

"Morning mushrooms?"

"Come on!" Abeni said, not bothering to explain. She helped the girl up. "Can you run?"

"I can try," Zaneeya panted.

That was good enough. Grabbing her fallen light and staff, she supported the panther girl as they made their way down the dark tunnel, leaving the monster behind.

"Turn here!" Zaneeya said.

"You know how to get back outside?" Abeni asked.

"I can smell it," she replied.

"What are you doing here? How'd you know where I was?"

"I returned to find you gone," Zaneeya said. "This was not a very wise thing to do, mortal—brave, but not at all wise. Asha was sick with worry. So, I came after you."

Abeni flinched with guilt. The two made their way through the tunnels, the panther girl guiding. When they emerged into the pit, she thought she'd never been so happy to see the night. But her joy faded as she gazed around.

There were monsters. They were awake, still standing and staring up at the giant earthen statue of the Witch Priest, listening as the Goat Man played his music. As the two girls emerged from the tunnel he stopped, lowering his flute and staring at them from behind his mask of horns. The monsters turned to follow his gaze, every last eye fixing on them.

Abeni felt her stomach go hollow as those hungry gazes set on them. There was a brief silence as the two girls stared back. The awkward quiet was broken by the Goat Man, who pointed at them and let out a terrible roar. His monstrous army responded to his cry, roaring and breaking into a run for the two girls.

Zaneeya bared her teeth. "Take whichever you want!" she growled. "But the one in that mask of horns is mine!"

Abeni wasn't sure if the girl was serious or if that was some bizarre joke. For the moment all her attention was on the approaching horde. A separate roar came from behind and both girls spun to find the monster they had fought in the tunnels. Free of morning mushrooms, his eyes blazed with fury as he raced for them. Abeni grimaced. Now they were trapped on both sides! Her mind went to the magic stones in her bag. Would one of them help? Her thoughts were broken as a cloud of pink mist suddenly ex-

ploded around them with the strong smell of flowers—and Nyomi appeared.

"What took you so long?" Zaneeya snapped. "I thought you'd
run away!"

"I made Prickly wait," someone said. Abeni watched as a small
form stepped from behind the porcupine girl. Asha! "I needed
to time this just right." The little girl turned to the approaching
monsters, opened her mouth, and then quite unexpectedly began
to sing.

Abeni listened in surprise. It was just a tune with no words,
but strong—a sound that seemed too powerful for someone so
small. It flowed through the night, and the monsters stopped
their run, going still as statues. Abeni gaped as Asha walked towards them, still singing. What was she doing? They'd tear her
to pieces! But as the little girl entered among the monsters, they
didn't lift a hand, instead breaking apart to allow passage, their
baleful gazes transfixed.

As fast as it started, the song abruptly ended. The night went
quiet as the monsters shook their massive heads as if clearing
them. One by one, they roared in rage at the small spirit now in
their midst. Asha looked up at them with little concern, long locs
falling back from her face. Her eyes locked briefly with those of
the Goat Man, who now crouched on the rocky mound, before
she turned back to the others.

"Go," she ordered.

Abeni stared at her, stunned. "What? No!"

"Go!" Asha said again, forcefully. "Leave, Prickly! Now!"

Nyomi jumped at the command, grabbing hold of both girls.
Abeni could hear her own screaming as Asha disappeared between the towering monsters—and then the world went pink.

She was floating in that place that smelled only of flowers.
There was that odd feeling of moving while not moving before
another explosion of pink. Then she was falling, landing in the
middle of tall dry stalks of grass.

She looked around to find Nyomi and Zaneeya sprawled nearby. Someone running towards them. Damju.

"What happened?" the girl asked.

"Asha!" Abeni cried, frantic. "We left Asha!"

"I'm sorry!" Nyomi squeaked. "She told me to go! I just did!"

"You have to jump back, then!" Abeni pleaded. "We have to go get her!"

Nyomi closed her eyes and there was a hint of flowers, but no pink mist. She shook her head. "I can't. Too tired. When did both of you get so heavy?"

Heavy? What did the girl mean by—

A deep growl sent everyone still. As one, they turned. And Abeni gasped.

It was a monster. The very one she and Zaneeya had fought in the tunnel. He had been right behind them when Nyomi jumped. Somehow, he must have gotten caught in her mist. They'd brought him with them!

He stared around, trying to make sense of what could have happened. But catching sight of the girls, he roared angrily as he lifted his sword—and ran for them.

Abeni sprang to life. Zaneeya was still recovering. And Nyomi could barely sit. She had to fend him off. Staff in hand, she got to her feet, moving to meet his attack.

The monster swung his jagged sword with both hands as she reached him. She ducked, going into the form *Cutting the Grass Low* to strike his legs. It was like hitting rock, and her arms hurt with the effort. He lifted his sword to swing again. Then someone else was there. Damju! The girl reached out to lob a fistful of yellow powder that hit the monster squarely in his face. He jerked back—then let out a great big sneeze. He sneezed again and again, so hard it shook his entire body.

Abeni took the opportunity to bring her staff up, sending it straight at his head, hoping to knock him senseless! But another strong sneeze made him twist aside just in time. The sturdy wood only grazed him, pushing along his shoulder and entangling in a necklace of iron ringlets he wore that held a small dark red stone that pulsed like a beating heart.

As she pulled her staff one way, he sneezed again and pulled the other. The ringlets broke apart, raining down in a shower, and the dark red stone fell away with them. All at once, the monster stumbled back as if struck. Dropping his sword, he clutched his head in both hands and fell to his knees. Then, as Abeni watched, he changed.

His body shuddered, the corded muscles of his arms and legs rippling and growing smaller. In fact, he was shrinking—fast! Rough gray skin turned brown and smooth. Claws became fingers. Sharp yellow teeth rounded to white. Soon he was no bigger than any of them. Small trembling hands reached up to the spiked mask that hid his face. Like his clothing, the thing was now much too big for him. He lifted it away, dropping it to the ground.

The monster was gone. In his place was a boy. Still kneeling, he cowered away from them, eyes wide with terror as he trembled all over.

Abeni stared. What had just happened? What was she seeing? She tried to put words to it. But her mind had gone blank. Zaneeya limped to stand beside her, looking just as stunned.

"What sorcery is this?" the panther girl whispered.

Abeni shook her head. "I think," she said, "we just found the missing children."

CHAPTER EIGHTEEN

BLOODSTONE

Abeni stalked angrily through the night, the others trailing behind. Her mind was ajumble—images of Asha swallowed by that dark pit, the monsters, the Goat Man, and now . . .

She glanced back to the boy wrapped in torn crimson cloth who walked hand in hand with Damju. It was hard to believe he was the same monster that had chased her through the tunnels of the pit. But she had seen it with her own eyes. They had all seen it. After his transformation the boy just knelt there sobbing. Only Damju had moved; the rest of them were too numb. He had flinched from her touch. But as her hand closed around his own, he went still and lost some of his tension.

Songu, she called him, a boy from her village. He was near her age. The two had even played together. He had been stolen like the other children, taken by this wish song. No one knew what had happened to him or any of them—until now. Abeni stared at the boy, still trying to make sense of what he had been. But nothing made sense anymore. Turning down a path, she glimpsed the bleak homes of the villagers ahead. It was still some time until dawn. But she had questions too urgent to wait.

Walking through the stone wall, she reached the first of the houses and rapped it hard with her staff. She did the same to the next, and the one after that, making as much noise as possible. People began to appear, emerging from their homes startled and frightened—as if expecting the monsters that tormented them to appear. At seeing Abeni and her friends they seemed confused.

When they saw Songu, they looked like they might faint. They huddled close, whispering. Finally, a familiar face ran forward.

It was Damju's mother. At first she looked at Abeni, not understanding what she was doing here. Then her eyes found her daughter, and they rounded. When they fell on the boy, she staggered like she was staring at someone returned from the dead.

"Songu?" she asked. The boy didn't answer, hiding his face from the villagers.

"He doesn't talk, mama," Damju said. "Not anymore."

Abeni glanced to the boy, who remained as silent as stone. He hadn't spoken a word since changing back. He just stared at them with eyes that seemed empty.

A familiar man pushed his way to the front of the crowd. Abeni remembered him, the one with white in his hair she thought was a chief, who had made them leave before. He scowled as he saw the girls again. But when his eyes took in the boy, his steps faltered.

"Songu, Songu," Damju's mother repeated, tears in her eyes. She moved to touch him, then pulled back—instead clutching her hands together. "How did you make your way back, Songu? How did you return?"

The boy remained quiet. Abeni stepped in.

"By removing this." She hadn't even bothered to bow or show proper respect to people more than twice her age. She was just angry. She reached into her bag, withdrawing the red stone that had sat about the boy's neck. The woman reached out trembling fingers to touch it.

"It's warm!" she said. "Almost alive!"

Abeni had felt the warmth of the thing already—pulsing like a heartbeat.

"You told us the monsters appeared after your children were taken," she said loudly. "But they weren't just taken, were they? Your children *are* the monsters!"

Beware the Children of Night. They become hidden in darkness.

The words of the scrying pot had played in her head repeatedly since this revelation. And still, each time they struck with new meaning. These monsters were the Children of Night. They had been all along—the missing children hidden away in darkness, right before their eyes!

None of the villagers answered. Some looked away. Others put their faces in their hands and wept. Damju's mother, however, gave a weary nod. The man like a chief put a hand to quiet her but she pushed it away.

"The time for silence and secrets is over," she said, meeting his stare. He gave her a disapproving look. But when he didn't move to offer a challenge, she turned back to the three girls.

"We didn't know at first," she said. "But then the Goat Man told us who the monsters were—our children changed by his sorcery. And we knew them then, the way only a parent can."

"My brothers?" Damju asked.

"Lost in the night to darkness," her mother answered gravely.

Damju's face took on a pained look, and she clutched Songu tight.

"These monsters are your very children," Zaneeya said, aghast. Abeni didn't think much fazed the panther girl. But seeing the monster that had nearly killed them turn into a trembling boy had left her shaken. "They whip and beat you, force you to work. Your very children do this to you!"

"Or worse," Damju's mother said. She glanced to Songu, who still wouldn't meet anyone's eyes. Then she turned back to the villagers. "Komba, show them." At her words, someone shuffled forward, and the small crowd parted to let him through. It was an old man whose bent body looked more bone than flesh. His mouth was drawn tight and he averted his gaze as he held up an arm with a missing hand.

"Before this blight came upon us, Komba had two hands," Damju's mother said. "The other was taken, as punishment. The Goat Man had his grandson commit the deed."

Abeni and her companions gaped in fresh horror, unable to speak.

"He renames our children, changing them in body and spirit," the woman went on. "This one," she turned to Songu, "he is called Mosquito." The boy flinched at the name. "He makes them do terrible things."

Abeni forced herself to ask the next question. "The other children this Goat Man takes. The ones he brings here. Does he do the same thing . . . to them?"

Damju's mother nodded, her look pitying. "The friends you search for. He has already made them his own. Like Songu. Like my sons."

Abeni's stomach went hollow. She had known already. But it was another thing to hear. *Oh, Fomi. Is this what's been done to you? I'm so sorry. I'm so, so sorry.*

"How can you live like this?" Zaneeya asked, appalled. "How can you allow this?"

Most shied away from the girl's questions, but the man like a chief spoke up. "What would you have us do?" he asked.

"Fight back!" Zaneeya growled.

"You would have us fight our own children?" he asked evenly. "We went to claim them from this Goat Man, the very day he stole them away. When we saw it was our daughters and sons that stood against us, we dropped our swords and spears and wept. He has taken all we hold precious."

Abeni stood quiet. She had come here to accuse these villagers, to blame them for what had happened to Asha. But as she watched their hopeless faces it was hard. She thought she'd never see anything as terrible as what happened to her village. Yet this competed with even that nightmare.

"What does this Goat Man want from you?" she asked.

Damju's mother reached into a slight fold in her tattered dress, drawing something out. Leaning forward, she opened her hand, where a small rock sat in her palm. Much of it was clear enough to see right through. Other parts were dull brown or yellow. Many of the villagers gasped at the sight of it. Some turned their heads. The man like a chief scowled.

"You should not have taken that," he said in a low voice. "He will know."

"We find him so many," she countered. "How can he miss one?" She returned to Abeni. "It looks like nothing now. But it's harder than almost anything. And when the Goat Man uses his magics to cut and polish it, he can make it shine like a star."

Abeni eyed the stone. "I saw baskets of them in the tunnels."

Damju's mother nodded. "The Goat Man keeps them there, always guarded."

Abeni glanced to Songu. She had met one of those guards tonight.

"A stone?" Nyomi asked, confused. The porcupine girl tilted her head to look at the thing upside down, as if that might bring understanding. "This is the price of your children? A pretty stone?"

Damju's mother shrugged. "Some must think it great, for the Goat Man sends them to the Witch Priest, who trades them for gifts of his own."

Abeni stared at the bit of rock. How could so small a thing cause such suffering?

"And the iron monstrosity that would make music," Zaneeya said. "You build this for him too?"

"Yes. We find him iron to build his great horn."

"And you know what he intends with it?" the panther girl asked.

Damju's mother said nothing, looking down. Many villagers did the same.

"The horn you build is for the wish song," Abeni spoke loudly. If they didn't want to say it, she would make them hear. "When it's complete, he'll be able to send its magic far past your village. It will call to other children, in other villages. They'll become monsters too. This Goat Man isn't just trying to get more workers. He's building an army!"

"We know what he intends," Damju's mother said in frustration. "To steal children from other villages. But . . . he has promised to free ours!"

Abeni stared at her in dismay. Yet she couldn't match Damju's disappointment.

"Mama, how can you do this? To other people's children? It's wrong!"

The woman turned to look at her daughter, hurt and shame in her eyes. "None of you can understand. You can't know what a mother or father would do to save a child!"

Abeni thought of her own mother. Would she have done such a selfish thing? To save her? The thought made her sick.

"This Goat Man came to my village," she said. "He took my friends. Now he's taken someone else from me, this night. She's just a little girl."

Damju's mother exclaimed, now noticing Asha was missing.

"Then she's a monster now," the man like a chief said.

"No!" The force in Abeni's yell surprised even her. Nyomi touched her shoulder gingerly, likely to ease her trembling. "We know how to free them." She pointed to the dark red stone Damju's mother still held. "Remove that, and they're no longer monsters. Together, we can get your children back. We can get my friends back. We can end this."

The whole village went silent, every eye on the red stone. Some faces even held hope—a thing she hadn't seen since entering through their walls.

"How do you propose that?" the man like a chief asked. "Are we to snatch these stones from our children's necks? Do you think they will just give them to us? Do we go into battle against them—led by three girls? The Goat Man wields strong magic. What magic do you have?" He shook his head when she didn't answer. The hope on some faces dried up like a scorched river. "We asked you to leave before, but you stayed. Now your friend is lost to you. Go now, before you lose yourselves."

With that he turned to go. Several of the villagers went with him. Abeni stared after them, the man's words stinging like a blow.

"He won't give them back to you!" she called out. "No matter how you serve him, the Goat Man won't give you back your children! He'll keep them forever!"

The man stopped, as did those who walked with him. For a moment his shoulders slumped before they lifted again, going stiff. He turned and looked back along with the others. From their weary gazes Abeni realized they already feared as much. They just didn't want to face it.

"Enough," the man said in a stern voice. "Go away now, please. Go away."

He turned again and even more followed, going back to their homes. A few lingered like they might speak. But in the end only Damju's mother remained. She walked up and offered back the red stone to Abeni.

"The Goat Man will be hard on us today, after what you did last night." She spoke like someone resigned to her fate. "But I will look for your friend. Wait for me and I will bring what news I can." Kissing her daughter, she turned to go. Her eyes remained on Songu for a moment before leaving them to stand alone in the emptied streets.

"We should go," Zaneeya said.

"No." Abeni shook her head. "They have to help us! We need them—"

"They will not," the panther girl said.

Frustrated, Abeni turned to nod at Songu. "What about him? Where's his family? Won't they at least come to take him back?"

"The scent of fear clings to these mortals," Zaneeya said. "It has left them broken in mind and spirit. Let us not be here when their children come for them."

She turned to go, and the others followed. After a while, Abeni joined them, walking in silence from the now quiet village. They had gotten just a short way from Damju's cave when she stopped.

"It's my fault," she whispered. Her eyes looked up to meet Zaneeya's orange gaze. "You were right. I thought if I found these missing children, I could find my friends too. But all I did was put everyone in danger. And now Asha is . . ." There was a tightness in her throat. "I'm supposed to be her guardian."

"You were foolish to run off," Zaneeya agreed. "Headstrong and rash—so much like a mortal! You made choices for us, without asking first! That was wrong!" Abeni flinched, feeling each charge like a blow.

"I'm sorry," she said. "I shouldn't have done that."

"No, you shouldn't have," Zaneeya snapped. Then her voice went surprisingly calm. "But you were also right."

Abeni's head whipped up.

"We spirits are here to keep the balance of the world," Zaneeya continued. "This Goat Man upsets that balance. He leaves a spirit and the valley she protects blighted. He steals children, turning them into monsters who harm their families. Not even mortals deserve such an evil. You saw that imbalance, better than the rest of us."

"And you found the children," Damju put in. She stepped forward with Songu in hand. "You freed him. You showed us how."

"But Asha's still gone," Abeni said. "What if she's been turned into . . ." She couldn't bring herself to finish.

"No," Zaneeya assured. "His magic will not work on our kind."

Abeni hoped that was true. She needed to believe it. She drew a breath before speaking. "I'm going back for her. I'm going back for all the children."

She had already known she would. The scrying pot, after all, had said as much about the Children of Night. *To free them you must seek them.* Her mind, however, tried not to think on the other part. *But in finding them, you risk losing yourself.* What that meant, she still didn't know. But she wouldn't give up.

She was surprised again to find Zaneeya the first to nod. "I will join you. I will not leave Asha in the hands of this Goat Man. Nor will I leave these lost children to darkness or allow this foul magic to spread."

"I'm coming too," Damju piped in. "Those are my brothers, my friends, who've been stolen away. You shouldn't have left me last time."

"But you're . . ." Abeni began.

The short girl put fists to her hips. "I'm what? A person who sees different than you? Is that supposed to make me helpless?" Her gaze swept over them all. "Has it occurred to any of you that I managed to live out here by myself before you came along? That I've been able to evade monsters and the Goat Man, better than you have?" Abeni closed her mouth at that. She had a point. Damju sniffed. "Besides, my mother works with roots and plants. I've learned a few things that can help us." She patted the leather pouch at her side.

Abeni remembered the girl's sneezing powder. "You're right," she said. "I'm sorry. The only way we're going to do this is together. That means all of us."

There was a slight squeak. Everyone turned to Nyomi, who had listened quietly until now. Her large black eyes quivered, and her quills seemed to droop.

"I don't want to go back there!" the porcupine girl whimpered. "Every part of me says I should run away. I tried before, but I couldn't." She put on a sheepish look. "I never really left, you know. I just vanished and kept my distance. I even followed you last night to that pit. But I was too scared to go after you. So, I came back and told Asha. If she hadn't pleaded with me, I don't know that I would have jumped back to get you."

"But you did," Abeni pointed out. "Maybe you're braver than you think."

"Oh! I'm decidedly not!" the porcupine girl said indignantly. "Porcupine spirits aren't brave and have sense enough to know it! We're quite proud of being cowards! It's how we've survived for so long. As my uncle taught me, when you're scared—run away!" She ignored Zaneeya's snort and let out a long sigh. "But I'll still come with you. Not because I'm brave. But because you and Asha are my friends. And friends help each other, even when they're scared."

Abeni blinked in surprise. Friends. She had been looking for her lost friends for so long. But somewhere along the way, these spirit girls had become her friends too. Something about that made her feel good, despite everything else.

"We will need a plan," Zaneeya said.

Abeni nodded. She lifted up the red stone. It seemed a good place to start.

Her eyes went to Songu, who had yet said nothing.

"Do you know anything about it?" she asked, lifting the stone towards him.

But he shrank away, covering his face with his hand and not answering.

"I don't think he knows any more than we do," Damju said.

Zaneeya hissed. "It is dark magic. Only a sorcerer or a witch could speak on it."

"Asha might know," Abeni murmured. "I wish she was here. I wish I could talk to her." A sudden thought sent her eyes wide. She could talk to Asha! How could she have forgotten?

"I need to sleep!" she exclaimed.

Nyomi frowned. "You mortals tire very quickly . . ."

"No. I mean I need to sleep to visit Asha!" At their confused looks, she explained about the dreams she and the girl often shared.

"A dream walker!" Nyomi gasped. "I have a cousin who can do that . . ."

"You think you can find the small spirit in a dream?" Zaneeya asked.

Abeni nodded. "She often finds me. But I need to sleep first."

"I can help you go to sleep," Damju offered.

"The black root you used before?" Abeni asked.

"Too strong," the girl said, already rifling through her pouch. "You'll sleep half the day. But I can make you a tea with a little less kick. Come, let's go inside."

Back in the cave, the girl took some brown leaves out of her pouch and began grinding them in a small wooden bowl with a round stone. When she was done, she sprinkled the bits into some water in a clay pot and struck up a fire. As the tea heated, she stirred it and put in a few green and red leaves. Abeni watched her work.

"How can you tell which leaves you're searching for?"

"By how they feel," Damju answered. "Or smell." She added a vial of dark liquid.

"Can you feel or smell better because you can't see? I mean, can't see like me?"

Damju leaned in to sniff the boiling pot. "I don't think so. I'm just good at it because I do it more. Ah, it's ready!" She poured the concoction into a cup, making sure to strain out all the leaves and bits, then handed it over.

"Drink all of it."

Abeni took a sip—and almost gagged at the bitterness. This had less kick? Holding her nose, she drank it all down and grimaced.

"How do you feel?" Damju asked.

"Fine," she answered, stifling a yawn. "How long before—?"

Abeni didn't finish the sentence. It seemed she blinked and when her eyes opened again, she was in Asha's garden. Standing, she looked about. It was a bright day and the green stalks swayed back and forth, whispering as usual. The dream was as she remembered. But there was no Asha. Maybe the little girl had to fall asleep first. A tap at her shoulder made her spin around—to look up at a blank straw face.

"Obi!" she exclaimed. "Have you seen Asha?"

The straw man nodded, turning into the garden and beckoning for her to follow. Abeni sprang after him. The green stalks grew higher as they went, and thicker. Soon they were surrounded on all sides, so that not even sunlight entered. She'd never seen any place in the garden like this before. Even the whispering stalks had gone silent. Finally, Obi stopped and pushed aside a curtain of green—to reveal a surprising sight.

It was the pit. It was still night here. The monsters had gone back to sleep, sprawled out like before. The giant statue of the Witch Priest remained standing, his face hidden behind iron and flame. But the rocky mound where the Goat Man had stood was empty—except for one figure.

"Asha!" Abeni ran to the girl, past the sleeping monsters, which never stirred. Reaching the mound, she climbed to the top, where a rounded cage of iron sat. Asha lay curled up inside, her long locs twisted about her. The sight made Abeni sad and angry at once.

"Asha! Can you hear me? Asha!"

The girl slowly opened her eyes. "Rain bringer," she said in greeting, sitting up with a smile. Abeni smiled back, reaching her hands inside the cage. The two of them grasped fingers and held tight. "I couldn't meet in the garden," the girl said. "So I asked Obi to bring you here."

"Oh, Asha! Are you hurt? Are you alright?"

"Not hurt. I'm glad you got away."

Abeni felt a stab of guilt. "I shouldn't have gone off like that. I'm sorry."

Asha didn't say anything, biting her lip and lowering her head.

"What is it?"

"I . . ." the girl began. "I didn't know if you'd come back for me."

Abeni started in shock. "Of course I would! Why would you think that?"

"Because you're mad at me."

"Mad at you? Is this because of the other night? Asha, that was the wish song. It made me say those things."

"I know," Asha said. "But you're still mad at me. For what happened to your village. For me becoming like this." She looked down and her voice became a whisper. "I know you only came to find my sister. So you wouldn't have to take care of me anymore. And you could leave to find your friends, the ghost ships, and your family. I've always known. I thought now that I was gone, you could just go."

Abeni opened her mouth to deny those things, to tell the girl she was wrong. But she couldn't. Not anymore. *No more secrets.* Her voice came, choked. "You keep things from me, Asha. You kept secrets from me when you were an old woman, not telling me you were really a spirit or that you needed a guardian. I don't think you've really told me why the Witch Priest came after you. Why the shadow thing was searching for you and found my village instead. Why he's *still* after you. I'm not angry with you, Asha. But I don't like the secrets you keep."

Asha looked at her for a long moment. A calm came over her face and she nodded. When she spoke, her voice was strong and clear.

"Then I'll tell you what parts I remember. I'm a very old spirit, Abeni. Old enough to remember when the world was not at all like it is now, and there were only a few of us. No panther spirits, or porcupine spirits. Certainly no people. Everything was new. We spent our time discovering and exploring all there was to see. We didn't notice at first when the others arrived—the spirits of rivers and hills and things that live and grow. All children to us. Then there were people! We were curious. We came to see. Many of us stayed among you. But not all."

"Is that how you came to be the guardian of my village?" Abeni asked.

"In a way," Asha said. "But I think I have been the guardian of many, many villages before your own. As I've said, I can't recall it all. The memories are . . . blurry. But I do know that some of my brothers and sisters didn't like the change. The world was now too crowded, they thought. We'd been alone for so long, it seemed like all of you were everywhere all at once. And there were so many of you! All different kinds of you!"

She shook her head in wonder, as if still fascinated by the memory.

"Some who didn't like this new world went away. To live in dark forests, on high mountains, or even at the bottom of the sea. Anywhere to be left alone. They became much like the places they escaped to, distant and unmoving. No one has spoken to them since, and they do not speak at all. One, however, wasn't willing to just go his own way. He wanted the old world back, the one we'd had to ourselves. He spoke of making war on the younger spirits and mortals. Of driving them away. Most of us refused. But a few listened. With their help, he worked to convince the younger spirits to abandon people, and people to abandon them."

Abeni had heard that last part before. "Wait. This spirit, who is he?"

"He has many names," Asha replied. "His most recent title is the Witch Priest."

Abeni could scarcely believe it. The Witch Priest. He was a spirit! "But I thought he was a person," she stammered. "A man?"

Asha pursed her lips sourly. "My brother's very good at veiling himself in lies. In making himself be seen as he wishes. That's how he gets others to follow him. Even now he has mortals and all manner of creatures fighting each other in his great war. None of them realize that in the end, he just wants the world to burn—so there'll be nothing left. He thinks that way, it can be like it was before."

"You told me once that the Witch Priest—your brother." Abeni stumbled over those words. "You said he wanted you to join him. Why?"

"I'm one of the last of the older spirits he hasn't turned to his side, or imprisoned, or worse. I think he believes I could hurt him."

Abeni's eyes grew at that. "Can you?"

Asha's face clouded over in thought. "I'm not sure. At least, I don't see how. I'm no longer the spirit I once was." She paused. "I'm sorry I kept secrets from you, Abeni. I thought no one would want me around if they knew. And I don't want to be alone."

Abeni was taken by the fright in the girl's voice. Tutuo had told her as much: that spirits felt with their whole being and were often just who they appeared to be. She wasn't looking at some elder spirit. She was looking at a little girl, thrown into the world before she was ready—much like her.

"Asha, look at me." The girl gazed up with sad dark eyes and

Abeni tightened her grip on her fingers. "I won't leave you. Not ever. Do you understand?" Asha nodded slowly. "Just promise me, no more secrets."

"I promise," the girl said.

"Good, now tell me how to get you out of here." She ran hands across the cage, searching for an entrance.

"It's sealed by magic," Asha said. "You won't find a way to open it."

"Nyomi! She could jump in and—"

Asha shook her head. "Then she would be trapped in here too."

Abeni banged her hands against the cage in frustration. "We're coming back for you! We're going to get you out of here!"

"I'm not the only one imprisoned," Asha replied. "You have to free the others."

"The missing children! You know, then? They're the monsters!"

Asha nodded. "I didn't see it at first. But when I sang to them, I understood. They've been hurt so much. Can I see what you're holding?"

Abeni looked down in surprise to find the red stone clasped in her hand, still warm and pulsing. She handed it through the cage to Asha, who cradled it between her small palms, inspecting it closely before speaking.

"A bloodstone," she said, "made from the same shiny rocks the villagers search for. The Goat Man has placed a drop of blood inside."

"Why blood?" Abeni asked, appalled.

"Mortal blood is rich with spirit, and it is the spirit of the children he traps inside. A child's spirit is still quite innocent, and thus very strong. Only powerful dark magic could trap it. Still, this bloodstone can only hold a part. Something larger is needed to hold them all." She turned to look up at the statue of the Witch Priest that towered in the night, and to the great crimson gemstone nestled in its lap.

"It's a bloodstone!" Abeni realized. "I heard voices inside it, of crying children!"

Asha nodded sadly. "An entire village of children crying."

Abeni stared at the giant gemstone in revulsion. What had this Goat Man done?

"My sister made herself a part of this valley," Asha said, "tying herself to the people in it. When the Goat Man took the children away, he also took much of her power. I think that's how he's been able to at times walk in the dreams of children. Be thankful he doesn't understand how to fully use that talent and so must rely on his horn. Destroy that great bloodstone, however, and you can break his magic—free all these children from his curse." She went suddenly stiff. "You have to go now! I've kept you too long! I told you he knows how to walk the dreams too! He's coming!"

Abeni stared. Who was coming? Before she could ask, a dark shape reared up before her. She jumped back, finding herself staring at burning eyes beneath a mask of horns. The Goat Man! He snarled like some angry beast, and a monstrous hand reached out, grabbing her arm tight. She gasped in pain as he squeezed hard, and she thought he might crush it in his grip. A cry was set to leave her lips when someone grabbed her from behind. There was a strong heave and the monstrous hand released its grip as she tumbled back amid tall green stalks.

Abeni sat up, taking deep breaths. She looked down to find she was lying atop Obi. The straw man had pulled her free. And they had returned to the garden.

"Thank you." She hugged him tight. It felt good. "I miss you." The straw man hugged her back. "I made some new friends out there. You'd like them. They're going to help me free Asha. And rescue the children. I'm going to get them all back, Obi. I promise."

CHAPTER NINETEEN

THE CHILDREN OF NIGHT

I t was well into the next night when Abeni and the others made their way back to the pit. She crouched in the tall grass, looking down below. They had waited here, keeping watch of the tunnels and the slumbering monsters. As expected, the Goat Man had emerged. Like the night before, two monsters walked with him. Only this time they carried a round iron cage that hung from the middle of a long pole. Inside it sat Asha—just like in the dream.

Abeni clenched her teeth at the sight. That evening, Damju's mother had explained the cage's purpose. The Goat Man kept the girl for her voice and made her sing for him throughout the day. He called her his songbird. Now he walked through his sleeping army and climbed the mound of broken rocks. Standing there he pulled out his flute and blew.

Abeni wanted to cover her ears. The song sounded terrible now.

"It's awful," Damju agreed. "Once you break its spell, it only sounds worse."

"This is what I've always heard," Nyomi muttered.

Abeni tried to ignore the terrible music. The monsters had all awakened now and stood there listening as if entranced. There was a familiar rumbling, and they watched as the massive statue pushed up from the ground to tower above the pit. They squinted as the earthen head and iron mask burst into flames, lighting up the night. Abeni looked away from the fiery eyes and to the great bloodstone that sat in the figure's lap. It was what they had come for.

"Everyone ready?" she asked. There were nods all around.

She looked over her group: two mortal girls, two young spirits, and a boy who didn't talk. They were going to attempt what the grown-ups of this village would not. To fight this Goat Man. To rescue the children.

"It's time, then," she said. "Just like we planned." They had done so all day, coming up with different ideas until arriving on something they all agreed on. She hadn't thought all of them agreeing on anything was even possible! But they'd done it. This wasn't just her plan. It belonged to all of them. Now she just hoped it worked. "We can do this. We just need to stick to the plan. Damju, Songu. You go first. We'll be right behind you. Zaneeya—"

"I will keep the monsters at bay," the panther girl assured her.

"I was going to say, be careful," Abeni finished.

Zaneeya gave a sharp grin. "The same to you. Good hunting, Abeni."

Abeni grinned back. Turning to the others, she motioned to begin.

Damju and Songu walked ahead, finding the rickety ladder and climbing down into the pit. She and Nyomi followed, staying close. Damju had been right about her abilities. She made her way without anyone's help and moved easily. Songu came right behind. When the two reached the ground he took hold of her hand, and they walked forward.

At sight of the pair, the monsters turned, glaring and sending up growls. But none attacked. Instead, they shifted apart, making a path. Abeni and Nyomi followed close behind, unseen and hidden by the porcupine girl's magic. Still, it was unnerving to walk between the monsters. Abeni looked up as they passed, into fiery eyes behind masks of wood and iron. It was hard to believe these were all children, like her.

When Songu and Damju stopped at the front of the monstrous crowd, Abeni and Nyomi stopped with them. The four gazed up to the towering statue of the Witch Priest. The iron mask shrouded in flames glared back down at them. Behind it stood the twisting giant horn for making music, which looked near completion. Far below, atop the mound, stood the Goat Man.

Lowering his flute, he looked upon the new arrivals from behind his mask of horns. The music he played still echoed into the night as if it had a life of its own.

"Songu," he said in recognition. His voice was a deep and threatening rumble, like thunder speaking. "And little Damju."

Abeni's eyes rounded from where she and Nyomi remained hidden. He knew her name! If the girl was surprised, she kept her face blank.

"Do you see, my mighty warriors?" he gloated to the gathered monsters. "Your brother the Great Mosquito has returned. And with a present! Someone who has escaped us for some time. Such loyalty is to be rewarded. Do you see now why I named him Mosquito? Because though he is small, his sting is deep."

Songu said nothing, only lowering his head.

With a wave of his hand the Goat Man called to one of the monsters that flanked him. She stepped forward, handing a necklace of ringlets to him with a small dull-colored stone.

"Little Damju," he said. "You've never truly seen the world. Not with your flawed eyes. But with this, I can grant you sight." He held the necklace high.

Damju huffed, unimpressed. "My eyes are fine the way they are."

The Goat Man laughed. "You have fire. Good. My master so likes fire."

Abeni tugged on Nyomi's arm. It was time! The porcupine girl responded with an explosion of pink mist, and Abeni found herself floating in a familiar place that smelled heavily of flowers. Nyomi claimed that the closer they were to where they needed to go, the surer her jump would be. Hopefully, this was enough. Suddenly Abeni was on solid ground again—or slightly so, she realized, as her foot slipped, almost taking her over a ledge.

Nyomi grabbed hold of her arm, pulling her back. Regaining her balance, Abeni looked down to find the floor of the pit far below. They were standing on the earthen lap of the statue of the Witch Priest, as planned. And beside them was what they sought.

The giant bloodstone sat embedded, nestled between earthen fingers that appeared to hold it. The size of a boulder, it shimmered like dark red glass and was cut smooth all along its sides. This close the throbbing of the thing was strong, pounding like a living heart. The many voices that came from it could be heard plainly—children calling into the night. They were lost, they said, and couldn't find their way home.

Their cries filled Abeni with sadness. And something else was welling up inside her. Anger. An intense fury at all of this needless suffering. She was going to end it—now!

Turning, she lifted her staff and waved it from side to side. It was a signal, and it was met with a fierce roar. A panther the color of night sprang into view. It leaped down the earthen walls of the pit, skidding as it descended, scattering rocks and dirt as it went. When the panther reached the ground, it took off in a burst of speed, getting faster as it went. The first monster that turned to meet it was knocked from his feet as the big cat landed atop it and then bounded for a second. In moments the pit was in chaos as the panther ran through it and the monsters gave chase.

Abeni watched. Damju and Songu had been the first distraction. Zaneeya was the second. All to buy time. Taking her staff, she dug it into the earthen lap of the statue, just beneath the giant bloodstone. Sliding it in deep, she pulled down on the length of wood as hard as she could, grunting at the effort. She had seen men in her village do this to lift heavy stones. Only she wasn't as big as any of them.

"Nyomi! Help!" The porcupine girl hurriedly moved to join her. Together the two pulled down, rocking the staff back and forth to get it beneath the great bloodstone. Slowly, the thing began to lift away.

Abeni ground her teeth, pulling harder. "Almost there!" she wheezed, watching as the bloodstone lifted higher and tilted. It was heavier than it looked but they had managed to shift it nearly onto its side. Abeni's hopes rose. This was working!

"I think that's enough," she panted. "Now, together!" The two girls braced their backs against the giant stone and began to push. It moved, inching towards the ledge. Abeni wished they had Zaneeya's added strength. But the panther girl was doing her part of the plan. And they would have to do.

"Just a bit more!" She planted her feet, pushing as hard as she could. She wasn't sure how much longer they could keep this up. Just then, the giant bloodstone teetered on the ledge. There was a moment where it seemed to hover, before it finally fell.

Abeni held her breath as she watched it drop away. She had remembered the mound of rocks beneath the statue. Damju's mother said the bloodstone was harder than they thought. Dashing it against those rocks seemed like their best chance at getting it to break. The Goat Man twisted his head to look up, eyes widening behind his mask as he saw the giant crimson stone heading for him. He leapt from the mound just as it came crashing down. The sound caught the ear of everyone in the pit, and they turned as one to watch the bloodstone shatter.

At least, that's what Abeni had hoped.

The giant bloodstone struck the rocks and rolled onto its side—but it didn't break.

The Goat Man stood to the side as the great stone settled. Then his gaze turned upward. When his eyes landed on the two girls, he pointed a clawed hand and cried out in rage. The monsters in the pit followed his lead, roaring up at them. Several bounded atop the rocks and began scrambling along the base of the statue, making their way up.

"Abeni, we have to go!" Nyomi shouted. "Abeni!"

Abeni barely heard the porcupine girl. Her eyes remained fixed on the giant bloodstone—still not believing it hadn't broken. All their planning had been for nothing. A strong shake from Nyomi brought her back, and she found herself staring down at a horde of angry monsters.

"Let's go," she said, hating herself for saying the words.

She clasped the porcupine girl's hand, and in a blink they were floating in the pink mist again. Solid ground returned beneath their feet and she found herself looking at Damju and Songu.

"I didn't hear it break!" the girl said, her face distressed.

"No," Abeni answered painfully. They had failed.

Fresh roars alerted them that the monsters had seen their arrival. With a squeal Nyomi grabbed hold of each and they were floating once more. Abeni prepared herself to land somewhere out of the pit, wrestling to not let her disappointment overcome her. How would they possibly free Asha now? Or the missing children? Or her friends?

Her thoughts were cut short as something encircled her waist. Before she could look down, she was yanked back—hard. Nyomi cried out, and instead of floating they were suddenly falling, the swirling pink mist disappearing. The night welcomed them back and the ground came up in a rush.

Abeni felt a jolt of pain as she landed and tumbled. She managed to lift her head, dazed and trying to figure out what had happened. They were still in the pit. They had never left. She looked down to find a dark rope circling not just her but the others. Before she could shout a warning, monsters surrounded them, snarling and pointing sharp weapons. She raised her staff, but clawed hands easily snatched it away. One monster lifted her from her feet. Another lifted up Damju and Songu. But Nyomi was left tied. Struggling was useless. Their captors were just too strong. The four were carried to the base of the mound of rocks where the Goat Man waited, and deposited at his feet.

An angry growling came from somewhere behind. Abeni turned to find several monsters dragging a panther bound up in rope—like the one that held Nyomi. In a blur the panther shifted into a defiant but haggard Zaneeya. The girl was thrown down beside them, her orange eyes staring up scornfully.

"So," the Goat Man rumbled. "My mysterious visitors of the night return." He moved closer, crouching to inspect them. A clawed hand gripped the ropes that still bound the two spirits, pulling at it harshly.

"Nyomi!" Abeni shouted. "Get out of here! Jump away!"

The porcupine girl whimpered. "I can't. I don't feel so well."

"I don't either," Zaneeya panted.

The Goat Man laughed, staring down at Abeni from behind his horrid mask.

"Go?" he rumbled. "My master has given me the magic to trap meddlesome spirits." His hand tugged again at the ropes that bound Nyomi and Zaneeya. "Last night you caught me unaware. This time, I was ready."

Abeni stared in dismay. The ropes must have been magic. They were all trapped.

"And Songu." He shook his head. "I expected better." He looked to the giant crimson bloodstone that remained unbroken behind him. "Did you intend to steal from me?" He tilted his head in thought. "No, not steal. You sought to destroy it!"

He stared in surprise for a moment—then burst into bellowing laughter. "Who put you up to this? Four little girls couldn't have devised such a plan. The villagers? Do those cowards now call on children to protect them?"

Abeni didn't answer, instead looking to Nyomi and Zaneeya. The two grew weaker by the moment. The porcupine girl's skin took on a sickly hue, and the panther girl was drawing rattling breaths. That rope was killing them!

"Let my friends go!" she pleaded. "The bloodstone doesn't work on them. You can have . . . You can have me!"

The Goat Man eyed her coolly and then rumbled in laughter.

"I can have you all. And you are in no place to make bargains, girl."

He beckoned one of the monsters forward—who handed over a necklace with a dull-colored stone. Abeni shrank away as the Goat Man moved to place it over her head. But the other monsters held her still, forcing her neck to bend.

"Do not fight it," he said, securing the necklace. "Look at you, so small and weak. I was small and weak once. Don't you tire of it?" He put a clawed hand to her chin, lifting it so their gazes met. "I see pain in your eyes. Someone has done you a great wrong. Wouldn't you like the power to seek your vengeance?"

Abeni glared at him in resentment. He had no idea what pain she carried. And how much of it was his fault. Seeing her face, he laughed again. "There's anger there too. Good. My master so loves anger."

Lifting a knife, he brought it to her shoulder and nicked the skin. She cried out as he drew blood and smeared it on the stone about her neck.

"Why are you doing this?" she asked through clenched teeth.

"Because I can," he said. "Because I'm strong enough now to seek my own vengeance." He turned to look up at the iron horn. "And when I complete my great instrument, I will send the music across the land to take more children. Do you know how I came by the inspiration? The spirit who once ruled this valley, when I slew her, she sent out a final cry—so powerful it entered the dreams of children far, far away. I have been unable to walk dreams so easily. But I thought, what if I could send my song out, a great distance, so that many children might hear." Abeni knew that beneath that awful mask he was grinning. "I will create an army of children turned monsters. An army that their own parents will dare not fight. Together we will march beneath the banner of our master and set the world on fire!"

He gripped the blood-covered stone about Abeni's neck and squeezed. Smoke hissed from his closed fist and he chanted things in a tongue not even she could understand. White hot flames erupted from between his clawed fingers as his body trembled and he finally went quiet, letting go.

Abeni looked down to see the dull-colored stone had changed. It was now a dark red. Like blood. And it pulsed in time to the beating of her heart. As she gazed inside it, she saw a single living flame burning bright. Like the fire in the eyes of the storm women. Like in the eyes of the Goat Man and the monsters about her. Unable to look away, she stared at it entranced until she was falling, spinning towards it, into darkness.

Abeni lifted her head back up. The flame in the bloodstone was now in her eyes and it burned fierce. Her skin was hot—like she was on fire! She screamed and the part of her that was Abeni melted away in that heat. Her body began to change, her arms and legs growing longer and muscled. The brown of her skin faded away, replaced by a hard grayish tone. Curving blades of long ivory bone broke her flesh to run down her forearms with ends so sharp they gleamed. What was once a scream turned into a roar as the fire no longer burned but filled her with a thrilling power.

Rough monstrous hands wrapped crimson cloths around her new body, fastened together by bits of jagged metal. She pushed them away, rising to her feet to gaze out and inhale the night. Her senses were alive, more than ever before. She basked in the sight of her new brothers and sisters and the commander who stood before her, crowned in goat horns. Behind them towered the image of their terrible master, his fiery face burning bright—a fire that now burned in them all. Around her she could hear the wish song, beautiful and strong in her ears.

Her gaze fell to two spirits that lay at her feet. She snarled at the sight of them, her lips curling back to reveal sharp curving teeth.

"Behold you now," her commander praised, coming to stand before her. He clapped his hands and one of her sisters walked forward, bearing a mask of iron adorned with carved snakes.

"For you," her commander said. "The pain you carry is deep. I think you will be of great use." She tilted her head as the mask was placed over her face, leaving only her eyes and chin visible. "You will be my Viper, striking down any in my path."

She gazed up at him, and from behind the mask grinned widely. Viper. She would come to like that name.

CHAPTER TWENTY

ABENI'S SONG

The girl who was no longer a girl stood among the Children of Night, now one of them. Her commander stood beside her in his mask of goat horns. He had gifted her a mask of serpents along with a new name. Viper!

"See your enemies." Her commander gestured to the two spirits that lay tied at her feet. One was a girl like a porcupine. She stared up with large frightened black eyes. Another, like a cat, glared at her behind an orange gaze and bared teeth. She bared her own teeth back.

"These two cannot receive the blessings of the bloodstones," her commander said. "They are spirits and must be cleansed from the land. This is what our master demands of us, for his gifts." Reaching to his back he pulled out a sword of dark iron. Its flat blade was surrounded with barbs of sharp teeth. He offered it to her. "Show us that you are worthy of his gifts."

Viper took the weapon from him, gripping the hilt. Holding it made the fire inside her rise higher. She would enjoy this. As she lifted the blade, her commander and the others stepped back, eagerly awaiting her swing.

Then, from nowhere, there was singing.

Viper turned angrily to find who would dare intrude on her task. They would suffer! Her eyes found a small girl. No—a spirit. Locked in a cage of iron. Her song was piercing for one so small, cutting through the night like a knife, competing even with the wish song that played always in her ears. She could not help but listen. The song was about a girl . . .

"Quiet!" her commander snarled. "I am to hold you to give over to my master. But I will end you tonight if I must!"

The small spirit stopped singing and set a pair of dark piercing eyes on her commander. "It's time for *you* to end, Goat Man. You've caused enough trouble."

Her commander's eyes rounded at such insolence. Viper too was struck. Filthy spirit! How dare she speak so! "And what will you do, little songbird?" her commander mocked.

The small spirit, however, didn't seem afraid. She just shook her head. "I know how the villagers hurt you, how they made you feel small and weak. When the Witch Priest offered this bad magic, you took it. You thought stealing the children and turning them against their families would make you strong. But it hasn't. You're still small. You're still weak."

Viper couldn't understand. What was this spirit talking about? But behind her master's mask of goat horns his eyes appeared to waver—as if struck to his very core. Then they turned firm again, and burned.

"You know nothing about me!" he shouted in a snarl. "Nothing!" He waved a hand and the bars of the iron cage fell away to clatter on the rocks below. "Viper! End this little one first!"

Viper turned and moved forward with her blade, eager to obey. She was angry at this small spirit. It felt like an anger she had held on to for a long time. She lifted her sword as that anger fed the fire inside her. But before she could strike, those piercing eyes looked up. They weren't angry. Not even fearful. They only looked sad.

"I warned you not to get lost in the dark," the small spirit said. "Find your way back. Listen to your song." Then, as before, she began to sing.

Her commander bellowed laughter. "Is this what my master's enemies send against him—weak spirits with feeble magic? Do you not see that his song is greater?"

Viper wanted to agree. She wanted to cut down this little spirit who angered her so much! But instead, she found she was listening to the song. The girl the spirit sang of had a mother and father and brother. It was her birthday that day—when their village had been destroyed. Everyone had been taken. Everything had been lost. The girl thought she'd been left alone. But she found new friends, who were lost as well.

As Viper listened, a voice called faintly. It was the same girl from the song. She was trapped, locked away in a dark place. She cried out, trying to be heard, pleading to be let free. She was far away, but also somehow very close.

Viper shifted her eyes to a great red bloodstone lying among the rocks. It was like the one about her neck, but so much bigger. The girl's voice was coming from there—along with many others, all lost in darkness. She looked down to herself and frowned. Something was wrong. This body no longer seemed right. These weren't her legs. These weren't her arms. A clawed hand went to her face and touched a mask of iron instead. None of this was her!

"Viper!" her commander ordered. "Slay the small one now!"

She looked to him. Viper? That wasn't her name. Her name was . . .

Abeni shuddered as she came back to herself. What had happened? Where had she gone? She turned to find the Goat Man glaring, his mouth moving and snarling orders. Down at her feet, Nyomi and Zaneeya lay bound. And sitting in a broken cage before her was Asha, eyes closed, singing loudly. Then it all came back, like light filling a dark space. She looked down at her body in horror. She was a monster now, like the rest of them. In her mind, the words of the scrying pot took on their final ominous meaning.

Beware the Children of Night. They become hidden in darkness. To free them you must seek them. But in finding them, you risk losing yourself.

"What are you waiting for?"

She looked up. It was the Goat Man, barking in her ears. "Destroy them!" he ordered, the rage in his voice emanating from behind that frightening mask.

In her broken cage, Asha had stopped singing. She looked at Abeni now, smiling.

"You found the way out, little rain bringer," the girl said. "You know what you have to do now."

Abeni nodded slowly. Yes, she had found her way out of the darkness. And she knew precisely what to do. An image of her mother came then, holding a blade before her, eyes glinting steel, bravely facing off against a storm woman. The memory made Abeni smile. She could be like her mother. She could be just as strong.

Lifting her sword, she swung. Not down at her friends, but back at the Goat Man beside her. The blade struck him fully in the face, cracking the horned mask, and he staggered back at the unexpected blow. Using the sword like her staff she remembered one of the first forms Obi had taught her. *Farmer Harvests the Field* sent the broad side of the blade against the backs of his legs, sweeping him from his feet. He roared in outrage as he went down hard. And then she was moving!

The other monsters stood by, momentarily stunned. But they soon charged after her. Still, she had a head start. With a terrific leap, she bounded up the mound of rock, knocking a monster in her path down as she went. Behind her she could hear the Goat Man screaming orders to his army that now surged as one towards her. They were all too late.

With all her new strength she swung the iron blade, striking the giant bloodstone. The force of her blow sent fractures racing across its surface, so many that they became impossible to count. The trapped spirits within pushed out at this chance at freedom. She swung her blade again to help them. Then once more. As the sword struck the bloodstone for a third time there was a great blinding burst of light as the trapped spirits shattered their prison into endless shards.

The blast sent Abeni flying. She fell from the mound of rocks, landing on the ground below. Around her she could hear a howling she knew came from the Goat Man. Then everything went quiet.

Blinking her eyes open, Abeni found Asha kneeling over her. She tried to sit up, but the mask on her head felt suddenly heavy.

Lifting her hands to pull it off, she only then noticed they were her own again—brown, not gray, with fingernails instead of claws, and returned to normal size. Throwing off the mask, she felt at her face and smiled in relief. She felt awful and her head hurt terribly. But she was herself again.

"Do you realize that since I've met you," she said to the small spirit wearily, "I've been turned into something unnatural three times?"

Asha cupped Abeni's cheeks in her small hands. "Let's make sure it doesn't happen again. I like this face." She turned to look about. "I hope everyone else likes their faces too."

Abeni managed to sit up and followed her gaze. Across the pit the monsters were changing. Some knelt as their bodies convulsed or trembled, growing smaller. Others had transformed fully, and stared around in shock, as if waking from some long nightmare. Looking down to her chest she found the small bloodstone. It was a dull rock once more, cold and lifeless. She tore it from her neck and tossed it away.

"Kambo! Dawda!" It was Damju. The girl shouted into the night in every direction. Voices soon cried back, and she turned towards them. Two older boys who looked much like her ran up, and the three were suddenly embracing and crying. All around there were other tearful reunions, as siblings and playmates hugged and greeted each other. At the sight of them, Abeni suddenly remembered her friends.

Jumping up, she scrambled over to where Zaneeya and Nyomi still lay tied and began undoing the ropes. Some other children who saw her frantic moves dropped to help. In short moments the two spirits were free. They struggled to sit, shaking their heads and looking around.

"Glad to have you back," Zaneeya said hoarsely.

"Glad to be back," Abeni said, relieved. She reached over and hugged her tight. The panther girl went stiff at first but loosened and weakly hugged back. She reached to do the same to Nyomi but minding the quills just kissed the girl's furry cheeks.

"A-a-a-beni? Is that you?"

The voice sent her still—like someone had grabbed at her heart and tugged.

She turned slowly around, not even daring to breathe. Two girls stood behind her. One was short and staring at her dazedly. The other was looking everywhere at once, like someone trying to figure out if she was in a dream. At the sight of them Abeni didn't know whether to laugh or shout or cry. As she ran forward to wrap up both in a terrific hug, she decided to do all three. Fomi. This was Fomi! Her best friend! She shouted the girl's name over and over again, fearful that if she stopped the moment would no longer be real. The taller girl was Sowoke. Silly, stupid Sowoke. She shouted her name too. She had never wanted to hold on to anyone more. She'd found the stolen children of her village. She'd found them!

"Abeni," Fomi managed. "I don't think I can breathe!"

"Oh!" Abeni let go but kept her hands on them. They were real! They were here! "Where is this?" Fomi asked. She looked around, confused. "What's happening?"

Abeni sighed. "Oh, Fomi, there's so much to tell. Do you not remember?"

Fomi frowned, opening her mouth silently. It was Sowoke who answered.

"I remember." The girl's voice was a thin whisper. But the gaze she locked on Abeni was full of meaning. "I remember . . . everything."

A terrible look came across Fomi's face then, and she began to shake. Abeni reached back out to her friend, but Sowoke wrapped an arm about the shorter girl, holding her as she trembled. Not knowing what to say, Abeni remembered the others and quickly called them over. "I would like you to meet my . . . friends. New friends. Nyomi. Zaneeya. And this is Asha."

Fomi's eyes widened at the sight of Nyomi and Zaneeya—who had stayed in their spirit forms. Sowoke took them in stride but blinked at Asha. "Have we met?"

The little girl grinned. Abeni was wondering how to explain that when someone cried out.

Everyone turned and began walking to a figure that lay curled in a ball at the base of the mound of rocks. A man, Abeni could see. He was short, his thin body covered in thick furs much too big for him and his head hidden behind an overly large mask of goat horns—cracked from where she'd struck it. Abeni bent down to grab hold of the mask and pulled it off. Beneath, was a surprisingly plain face. Older and bearded, but not frightful or menacing at all.

"Goat Man," Asha said with disapproval. "You've been very bad."

"You're not a monster at all," Abeni murmured in surprise. "You're just a man."

"No," Sowoke said, her voice tight. "He's very much a monster."

He glared up at them bitterly, snarling.

"I was almost a god! You took it from me! You took it!"

More children had come over, and now stared down at the man.

"Do you know him?" Abeni asked.

A boy nodded. "His name is Brima. He herds our goats."

"He's from your village?" Zaneeya asked. "One of your own did this?"

"I was never one of them!" Brima spat. "I was no one to them. They treated me like nothing. They laughed at me and put me to doing children's work, herding their goats! But my master made me strong! And I took all their children away!" He laughed scornfully.

Abeni had no idea what to make of this man—so different from what she expected. Before any more could be said a sudden rumbling came. All eyes turned to look to the massive statue of the Witch Priest. Its head no longer burned with flames and the entire structure trembled and shook. Whatever power had held it together seemed to have vanished with the giant bloodstone.

As they watched, the masked head began to creak and wobble. Everyone scrambled back as it broke off from the statue and tumbled away. It came crashing down on the rocks below, burying the standard with the single flame. The smoldering iron mask fell off and rolled just before them—almost crushing a yelping Brima. Abeni grimaced at the sight of the thing; it was easily taller than any of them. She wondered if one day the real Witch Priest would fall so easily.

"We should get out of here!" Nyomi exclaimed.

Abeni agreed. Everything about them was collapsing. She pointed to the rickety ladders where other children were already making their climb out of the pit.

"What of the great horn?" Zaneeya asked. At her words, the giant headless statue began crumbling. Rock and dirt came crashing down on the iron contraption, burying it and breaking off the flaring head that tumbled down with a clang upon the rocks below.

"That will do it, then." The panther girl nodded.

They turned to go but there was a shout.

"Wait!" It was Brima. The man was trying to disentangle from his giant goatskin furs and fumbling after them. "You won't leave me here, will you? You can't!" Before they could answer someone else spoke.

"We'll take care of him." They turned to find Damju's brothers with some other older children nearby, holding a lengthy rope at the ready. Seeing their faces, the once terrifying Goat Man shrank back and whimpered.

CHAPTER TWENTY-ONE

HOMECOMING

The return of the children was a noisy one. They arrived just after sunrise, singing as they passed through the stone wall of the village of Kono. People stumbled out of homes, come to see the unexpected voices. At first, they stood not believing their eyes. But as familiar faces called out names there were shouts of joy. Men and women clutched children, crying and exclaiming at their return.

A group of older children dragged along a bound Brima, who huffed and struggled to keep up. The villagers looked on confused, recognizing him but not understanding why he was bound. When the children related the tale of who he had been and what he had done, there was shock. Angry shouts erupted, and Brima wailed as he was pummeled by fists and kicks. That might have been the end of him, but the man who was like a chief intervened. He ordered Brima taken away to await a later judgment. The villagers grudgingly listened, and the onetime goat herder was led off.

When the returning children told of what Abeni and her friends had done to free them, the anger of the villagers turned to thankful jubilation. Abeni endured endless hugs and kisses. Both Zaneeya and Nyomi had remained in spirit form, seeing little need to keep up the charade since the children had seen their true faces. Now people stopped and fell to their knees, giving thanks and praising the return of the spirits. Both girls looked on uncomfortably. It was certainly a change from their last visit.

The day fast turned into a celebration. The villagers brought out what food they had and decorated where they could. Brima—the

Goat Man—had insisted by the Witch Priest's orders that all masks and costumes related to the spirits be burned. But some villagers had secreted the items away, and now pulled them from hiding. Drums were retrieved from where they had been concealed. Soon music filled the air of the once dead village, giving it a semblance of life again.

Abeni sat and watched. This wasn't her home. And Harvest Festival was much more elegant. But it was still the closest she'd been to it in a long time. She turned to look at Fomi, who sat eating while watching the festivities. Sowoke was there too. So were Adwe and his brother Danwe—those stork legs a welcome sight. There were others, all children she'd grown up with. She looked over their familiar faces, quietly putting a name to each.

There were some missing faces. Maybe a dozen. One was Ekwolo. His absence left a sharp disappointment. It would have been nice to see him again. Danwe said the Goat Man sometimes sent children elsewhere. He brought other children here too, from different villages. Like her friends, these outsiders sat in their small knots, looking bewildered—fright still on their faces. It was hard to think on who they had been, *what* they had been turned into. The scene made Abeni's eyes tighten. She was glad the villagers hadn't had their way with Brima. Because she still had questions. And one way or another, he was going to give her answers.

"I can't believe that's the old woman—the witch," Fomi said. Abeni followed her friend's gaze to find Asha. The girl was jumping and dancing with some masked villagers, locs flying wildly, squealing with laughter.

"She's not a witch or an old woman really," Abeni reminded. "She's—"

"A spirit." Fomi finished, her face wrinkling. "Could you tell us that again?"

"Yes," Sowoke put in. "I could stand to hear it again. And what you learned about our village . . . ?"

That last part brought a hush. Abeni looked about to see the other children staring at her expectantly. She had tried her best to explain on the way back from the pit—of all that she'd done and seen. But it had come out in a big ramble. And it was probably too much to take in at once. Maybe she needed to try another way.

"Would you mind very much," she asked, "if I sang it to you?"

Both Fomi and Sowoke eyed her curiously, but nodded.

Abeni didn't start her song from the very beginning of her village. That would take too long. Instead, she began on the day it had ended. The storm women. The Goat Man. She sang of how the old woman had saved her. Of a witch's house, with its endless rooms and enchanted garden. She sang of returning to their ruined village, of ghost ships and the Witch Priest's war. She told them of talking pots and sparring with a straw man. Of shadow things and an old woman who was not *really* an old woman— and who became a little girl who was not *really* a little girl. Of meeting a vanishing porcupine spirit and a panther girl in a trap. Of bush babies, mimic salamanders, talking doors, and arriving at the village of Kono. She even made up some new verses, about fighting the Goat Man and ending his terror. When she finished, her old friends stared wide-eyed.

"Abeni!" Fomi gasped. "You've had a lot of adventures!"

"Like a hero in the stories!" Danwe whispered. His brother nodded, slack-jawed.

Abeni flushed. "It's not all that much, really. You had your own adventures."

Sowoke rolled her eyes. "You're friends with spirits. You carry around a magic bag with magic stones. We just got turned into monsters. Hardly an adventure."

Abeni flushed further, fumbling for an apology. But Sowoke's face softened, in a way she never remembered seeing before. "You came after us. You didn't have to. But you did. You *saved* us. As far as I'm concerned, that makes you a hero." With a lurch, the girl unexpectedly wrapped arms about Abeni. "Thank you!" she whispered. "Thank you, thank you, thank you." Fomi joined her. So did Danwe and Adwe. Abeni watched as all the children of their village formed a circle about her. They held tight to one another, and she gripped them back just as fierce. It was a long time before anyone thought to let go.

◎ ◎ ◎

"And do you remember when the Chief Elder and the old man who keeps time almost had a fight?" Fomi asked, grinning. "The timekeeper got up on one leg, holding a stick over his head, and was making this sound like a bird—*Whoop! Whoop!*"

Abeni clutched her sides, laughing as Fomi told the story. Everyone was laughing. Sowoke laughed so hard water dribbled out of her nose. They'd spent the past few hours at this. Telling stories of their village. It had started out somber, recalling fond memories. Then somewhere along the way, they'd begun to tell these kinds of stories—that made them smile and laugh. Now they were all trying to think up the funniest ones possible. Danwe and Adwe had told a few. Abeni too. Even Sowoke. But no one could touch Fomi. She always had the best stories—and even acted them out. Right now, she hopped up and down on one leg, flapping her arms and making whooping sounds.

"Stop! Stop!" Danwe cried until he wheezed. "I can't take anymore!"

"Yes, please!" Sowoke pleaded, giggling as she wiped water from her nose.

Fomi sat down, cackling at the mayhem she'd caused. She did love telling a good story. Slowly, the self-satisfied smile on her face faded and her eyes turned serious.

"Do you think we'll ever see them again?" she asked.

The laughter died, as everyone went quiet. Abeni saw the despair on each face, and it tore at her. Even their jokes couldn't hide that for long. She decided to speak up.

"Yes, of course we will."

Every head turned to her.

"How can you be so sure?" Fomi asked in a low voice.

Those despairing faces all fixed onto Abeni now, looking desperate for an answer. She almost shrank away from the need in those eyes but drew herself up to respond.

"We found each other," she said. "If we can do that, we can find them all too."

"But you said they were taken away," Danwe said. "To the . . . ghost ships."

He whispered the last words, but everyone still shuddered. That part of her song had chilled them the most.

Abeni nodded solemnly. "We'll just have to find those ships. It won't be easy, but—"

"We?" Sowoke interrupted. She had one eyebrow raised.

"Well, yes. I figured now that we're all together, we'd go after them." She sat up, getting excited. She'd been giving this a lot of thought. "Maybe we can break up into groups and search in different directions. The villagers here know of other villages. We could visit all of them. Somebody's bound to have heard some news. That way . . ."

Abeni trailed off as she realized everyone had gone quiet. They were just looking at her, and exchanging anxious glances.

"What's wrong?" she asked.

There was more silence. Finally, Sowoke spoke.

"You mean for us to go chasing after *ghost ships*. To go after storm women and this . . . Witch Priest."

Abeni looked to her, puzzled. "What else would we do?"

"What else?" Sowoke asked. She snorted. "How about going back home? To our village?"

Abeni shook her head. "I told you . . . it's gone."

Sowoke shook her head back. "No, you said the houses were half burned. Not gone."

"It's *empty*, Sowoke. There's no one there. It's like a place of ghosts."

The girl's face tightened. "We'll be there."

Abeni took a breath. They didn't seem to understand. She tried another way.

"Someone will have to repair the houses," she said, looking not just to Sowoke but the others. "Someone will have to plan and then harvest. Someone will have to hunt. You'd need to do all the things grown-ups did. How are children supposed to run an entire village?"

Sowoke barked a laugh. "Listen to you! You want to go hunt down storm women and wraiths that steal away people in the middle of a war—but rebuilding a village is too hard?"

Abeni opened her mouth to protest. It wasn't like that. But someone else spoke.

"I know how to fix things." It was Adwe. "Danwe too. We could mend houses."

"I know how to plant seeds," a girl offered. "And when to harvest crops."

"I know how to spin cloth!" a boy spoke up. "Does anyone know how to stitch?"

Soon everyone was saying all the things they could do. Abeni listened in confusion as they each put up their skills. They were truly serious about this? She wasn't expecting the last voice.

"I can fish." Fomi spoke the words while staring at the ground, not meeting Abeni's shocked face.

"Fomi," she said gently. "You hate fishing."

"Yeah." The girl kept her eyes to the ground. "But I can do it."

"See there?" Sowoke said triumphantly.

Abeni shook her head. "But our families are out there. Someone has to save them."

Sowoke sat down, taking her hand, the fierceness in her voice gone. "I wish I could go out there and find them. I wish I had whatever drives you. But the rest of us don't have any magic powers. We don't have spirits for friends. We're not looking for adventures. We just want to go home." She drew a breath. "I think . . . that's what my parents would have wanted me to do."

Abeni looked around to see the other children, all nodding. This talk of going back home was the only thing that broke their despair. She looked to Fomi, but her friend still wouldn't meet her gaze. Sowoke's grip tightened. "We would like it very much if you came with us, Abeni. You don't have to go out there, hunting after monsters and ghosts. You can come home too."

Abeni stared at the girl, unable to answer. In her head, the offer echoed.

You can come home too.

ᯤ ᯤ ᯤ

It was late in the day when the celebrating in the village of Kono finally died down. Abeni sat near a fire, lost in her own thoughts. Fomi and Sowoke were some ways off, their heads together, talking. It was an odd thing to see. Back home, the two couldn't stand each other. She and Fomi had been the ones who spoke quietly together. But now . . . A twinge of jealousy shot through her, but she didn't know what to do with it, so she stuffed it away. Too much had happened between them all for that.

Here and there across the village small groups gathered to talk. Some were families reunited with sons and daughters. Others spoke with children who mingled and shared stories. Asha had come over some time ago to plop into Abeni's lap. Now she lay curled up, humming some new song she'd learned.

"I wanted to thank you," Abeni told the little girl.

Asha stopped her humming. "For what?"

"For saving me," Abeni replied. "If it wasn't for you, I might have become completely lost to the Goat Man's magic."

Asha smiled. "I knew you'd know your song."

She had. And it was what saved her. But she needed to say something else. "You said before that I was mad at you. I think you were right. I told myself I wasn't. But somewhere deep down, I blamed you for what happened to my village. And I blamed you for not saving them. I was mad that I had to take care of you when there was no one to take care of me. The Goat Man used that anger. He would have made me hurt you."

Asha looked up at her, those dark eyes curious. "Are you still mad?"

Abeni shook her head. "You tried to keep my village safe. You kept me safe. You even made a whole song to remember them because it was your village too. You might have lived alone out in the forest. But you were a part of us. You lost as much as I did. I'm sorry I didn't see that before." She looked out across the village. "What happened to *our* village was like what happened to this one. The one to blame in the end is this Witch Priest. He and his war are the reason for all this suffering. Someone should stop him."

"Yes," Asha agreed, and put her arms around Abeni's waist. "Someone should."

The two sat quiet for a while before Zaneeya and Nyomi found their way over and sat down. Their faces were haggard, weary of the attention of the villagers. Damju and her mother followed. So did Fomi and Sowoke, returning from whatever they were talking about. Together they all watched the sun go down, a great orange ball descending into the horizon. It was good to know that there would be no wish song tonight or ever again.

It was later, as they sat talking, that Abeni noticed someone sitting alone, his knees drawn up to his chin and eyes fixed on the ground. Squinting through the dark to make him out more clearly, her eyebrows rose.

"Songu!" The boy turned from where he sat to look at her, but did not come over, instead looking back down. Frowning at his behavior, she turned to Damju's mother. "What's wrong with him?"

Damju's mother, who had happily been relating a story about an overly clever hare, became quiet suddenly, the smile fleeing her face. "Darkness follows that one," she said, making a sign they'd seen other villagers use to ward against evil.

Abeni looked at her in confusion, and then to Songu. Darkness? But they had saved him, like all the other children. His parents should have been overjoyed. But now that she thought on it, she hadn't seen Songu for much of the day. In fact, she couldn't remember seeing him with any of his family.

"Why is he alone? Where are his mother and father?"

Damju's mother didn't answer, looking away and going quiet once more. Abeni turned to Damju questioningly.

"Abeni," the girl said delicately. "Mama told me of what the village suffered, at the hands of the children Brima turned into monsters. It was awful. Some of it, I can't even believe."

"Where are Songu's mother and father, Damju?" Abeni demanded, not liking the sound of this. A pained look crossed the girl's face, and she shook her head. Abeni looked to Fomi and Sowoke. But both girls were quiet—their eyes fixed on the fire.

"They're gone," Damju's mother answered finally.

"Gone?" Abeni asked. "You mean they left the village?"

Damju's mother sighed heavily. "Not everyone accepted the Goat Man's—Brima's—rule. In the beginning, some defied him. And he would order his monsters—our children—to teach us cruel lessons. Many were hurt terribly. Those who angered him the most were bound in chains and sold away like goats." Her eyes went to Songu, staring hard. "That one, Mosquito, was charged with taking away those to be sold. He carried off wives from their husbands, and grandfathers from their families—heedless of the cries of those left behind. When it came time to take away his own parents, he put the chains around their necks without flinching, even as they wept calling out his name." She shook her head, as if reliving the memories anew.

A sick feeling came to Abeni's stomach. "Where were the people of your village sold off to?" she asked.

"We do not truly know," Damju's mother answered. "Brima only boasted that it would be a place of no return—a far and distant land ruled by wraiths . . ."

Abeni let out a shuddering breath, squeezing her eyes tight. "Ghost ships," she whispered. "Your people were taken to ghost ships." Her eyes opened again and went back to where Songu sat. She had wanted to know more about the ghost ships that had stolen away her family. But she had not expected to learn about them like this.

"You can't know the things we saw," someone said in a low

voice. Abeni turned to see it was Sowoke. The girl's eyes glistened with tears that would not fall. "The things the Goat Man made us do."

Abeni stared at her friend, and then out on the darkened village. Now she saw things she'd neglected before. Some children sobbed uncontrollably as their families held them. In a corner a boy cradled the bony arm of a grandfather missing a hand. A mother whispered reassuringly to a girl who poked a stick into the fire, staring blankly. Despite the sounds of celebration, this was a village filled with scars.

Looking back to Songu, Abeni felt a deep sadness. "What will happen to him?"

Damju's mother shook her head. "His remaining family will not have him. Most here scorn him or fear him. To many, he is still Mosquito."

"But it wasn't his fault," Abeni countered. "He wasn't . . . him."

"That may be true. But the child who does such things . . . to his own parents." The woman shook her head again. "Many say he's cursed and should be sent away."

"Sent away?" Abeni recoiled, unable to hide the anger in her voice. "Where? This village is all the family he has left!"

"Mosquito will have little here," Damju's mother replied.

Abeni glared at the woman, then looked back to Songu. She couldn't begin to imagine what he must be going through. And to have to do so alone . . . she knew what that was like.

"We must seem cruel to you," Damju's mother said. "But what Mosquito did—"

"His name is Songu!" Abeni cut in.

The older woman didn't chastise her for her manners. Instead, she sighed. "I can't tell you how to feel. I only ask you not to judge us too harshly. We have been through more than you can know." With that, she rose and left. Damju gave them an apologetic look before following. Abeni watched them both go, unable to settle her anger.

"It's not right," she insisted.

"None of what happened to us was right," Fomi said tiredly. She and Sowoke hugged each other tighter.

Zaneeya walked over, putting a hand on Abeni's shoulder. "The wounds of these mortals are deep," she said. "They will not easily heal."

"But it wasn't his fault," Abeni protested. "Why can't they see that?"

"The same reason he can't, I suppose," Nyomi said, nodding towards Songu.

They all looked over to him, and his loneliness reached out across the distance.

◎ ◎ ◎

Most people had gone to sleep when Abeni made her way to the small house in the back of the village. She left Asha with Damju's mother, who had offered a place to sleep to Fomi and Sowoke as well. The villagers had taken in all the children, finding somewhere for them to rest for the night. All except Songu, who they left outside. Abeni had made a point to get him food, and a blanket. But the sight of him curled up there alone on the ground infuriated her. It was that same anger she held on to as she stood looking at the small house, knowing who sat inside.

"Ready?" she asked.

Nyomi nodded beside her. There were men guarding the small house. Abeni doubted they would let her in, especially at this hour. But she had other means. There was an explosion of pink and the smell of flowers. She was floating for just an instant before her feet settled on firm ground. Blinking past the mist of Nyomi's jump, her eyes adjusted to the dark room, fixing on its only occupant. She nudged at him with a foot.

"Wake up," she said roughly.

Brima shot up, moving to sit. He squinted, then rounded his eyes at Abeni.

"How did you get—"

"I have questions," she cut in. "And you're going to answer them."

He looked at her, then at Nyomi. Perhaps it was the sight of two children. Or the nervous look on Nyomi's face. But his spine appeared to stiffen.

"You're not supposed to be here," he said. "Maybe I'll call out and . . ."

He trailed off, eyes rounding again as a midnight-black panther trotted out from the shadows. Zaneeya stopped inches from his face, baring sharp teeth as a low rumble sounded in her throat. Brima's trembling hands, still bound by rope, went up protectively.

"You're not calling anyone," Abeni said, sitting down. "You're going to answer my questions, before she gets hungry." Zaneeya growled again, orange eyes flickering. The man quailed.

"What do you want to know?" Brima stammered.

Abeni sighed inwardly. *So many things.*

"Tell me how you met . . . the Witch Priest," she said.

He frowned. "Me? I have never faced . . . the great lord."

"Don't lie to me!" Abeni said hotly. "He gave you your powers!" Zaneeya growled, echoing her mood.

Brima shrank away. "I'm telling the truth! I only met his servant! A thing of shadow!"

Abeni felt her skin pimple with cold. A thing of shadow. "Tell me everything," she demanded.

Brima did. There were lots of stammerings and fearful glances to Zaneeya, but he spoke. He told of tending goats one night, alone outside the village. Of seeing a shadow with wings move across the sky—a shadow that dropped to the ground and took the shape of a tall man. Of the way it spoke to him, many voices at once. How it seemed to know him, his life and history, of his hurt and how he was treated. And it had promised him great power if he did its master's bidding.

". . . so, I did," he finished. "Just like it asked. I became strong. Someone to be feared!"

He said the last part proudly, and Abeni had the urge to ask Zaneeya to growl.

"Why did it want you to take the children?" she asked. "To make them monsters?"

He nodded. "The shadow thing said a spirit lived here. Taking the children away would break it. Turning them to monsters would kill it."

"You wanted to kill a spirit?" Nyomi asked, hurt and shock in her voice.

Brima shrugged, indifferent. "What have any of you ever done for me?"

"Everything is about you, isn't it," Abeni said. She really disliked this man.

He twisted to regard her, scowling. "You don't know anything about me. Or my life." Before she could reply, he went on. "They bought me, you know. The people of this village. I was sold by a family I barely remember, to pay off a debt. And sold more times than I can remember. Until I came to this village. I was just a boy then. They promised a family would take me in, make me a son. But instead, I was sent from house to house, to be scorned, laughed at, to work. They called me useless and put me out to herding goats. Taught their children to mock me. Told them I was no one." A burning lit his eyes and it wasn't the Witch Priest's power. It was an anger, long-held and simmering. "The shadow thing knew all of this. And when it made its offer, I didn't hesitate to say YES!"

Abeni stared at the man, trying to sort through the knot of feelings in her head. The life Brima described sounded horrible. No one should be treated that way. But what he had done in return seemed worse. How could that be excused?

It was Nyomi who spoke.

"I'm sorry you were hurt," she told him. There was a gentle sincerity in her voice. "That should not have happened."

Brima looked to the porcupine girl in surprise, as if no one had ever said such a thing to him before. Something in his face slackened, and the light in his eyes dimmed slightly.

"But that doesn't mean," Nyomi continued, "you have the right to hurt others."

His face drew tight, the burning light returning. "I took my vengeance! And I would do so again!"

Abeni found herself feeling something she hadn't expected, not for this man. Pity. She couldn't help but wonder, if this village had treated him differently, could all of this have been avoided? Could all this hurt and suffering not have happened, if one little boy had been treated better? When she spoke again, her words were no longer voiced as threats.

"Why did you come to my village that day? So far away?"

Brima shrugged. "I did as I was told. I went where I was ordered. The great lord bade me to bring him more children to make monsters. To build him an army. I did not question his reasoning."

Abeni thought she knew the answer. Asha. The Witch Priest had sent his army to snatch away the people she protected to ghost ships and take the children for monsters. Perhaps he thought that loss might destroy her as it had the spirit of this valley.

"Is the shadow thing the one that told you of ghost ships?"

Brima gave her a curious look. "You know of the ghost ships?"

"I know that you sent people there. Tell me about them."

"All I ever heard of ghost ships is that the great lord barters the living to the wraiths who sail them," he said. "I was never told more than that."

"You had your monsters take people to them," she said, frustrated. "You must know something!"

Brima laughed. "I never saw a ghost ship with my own eyes. I do not even know where they are. My monsters took the villagers to other servants of the Witch Priest. And they took them to others. And so on. Those I sold away will pass through many hands before ever arriving at a ghost ship." He leaned forward. "Do you have an idea how many serve the great lord? Can you begin to comprehend the lands my master now holds under his sway? The reach of his power?"

Abeni felt her hopes dashed and tried not to shudder at the gleam in his eyes. But there was more he could tell her.

"Some of the children you took, you sent them away from here. Where?"

"To the great lord," he answered, sitting back. "Sent to deliver his gems."

"He kept them?"

He shrugged again, as if not caring. "So I assumed."

Poor Ekwolo, Abeni thought. Was that where he'd gone?

"I was to build an army," Brima went on. "So what was it to lose a few stock?"

Stock? Stock! Abeni jumped up, pushing past Zaneeya to get into his face—and he reared back.

"They're my friends!" she yelled. "Not your goats!"

Nyomi's hand on her back calmed her trembling. And outside they could hear the guards' shouts. She'd been too loud. Her eyes pinned Brima where he sat, and when she spoke again all the threat and hardness had returned to her voice.

"Tell me now where you sent the other children. And be quick."

Brima nodded. "That's more like it. No need to play nice. You're no better than me. But I don't know where they went. Someplace . . . west, I think."

Now Abeni really was angry. "That's all you can tell me? Someplace west?"

His eyes looked her over. "It doesn't matter, does it? Surely, the great lord will be seeking you."

Abeni stiffened. "What do you mean?"

"That small spirit you travel with. Different than these two." He nodded to Nyomi and Zaneeya. "I could see it when I was still powerful. I could feel it."

"What does that have to do with anything?" Abeni asked.

Brima leaned forward, his gaze eager. "What I see, the great lord sees! What I feel, he feels! At least, when I still held his blessing. He will know what has happened here." He broke into a toothy grin. "Very soon, you and your spirit friends will be hunted. And there is no hiding, not from him."

Abeni's jaw tightened, even as the pit of her stomach fell away.

◎ ◎ ◎

It was a sun-filled morning on which Abeni chose to leave the village of Kono. They had stayed three more days, enough time to rest and prepare. The villagers offered what little food and water they could. Perhaps it wasn't fair, but she couldn't help still feeling anger towards these people. The hardest part wasn't facing them, however. It was facing her friends.

"You don't have to do this," Sowoke said, watching as Abeni disappeared gourds of water into her magic bag. "The others look up to you. We could use you back home."

Abeni looked to the taller girl, who stood with arms crossed—haughty as ever. Whatever else had changed in the time they had been apart, that hadn't. "I have someplace else to be, Sowoke." She put on a smile. "Besides, you're doing just fine."

Sowoke had quickly taken control of the children of their village, preparing them for the long trek back. They were doing their own packing and would be ready to set out in a few more days. Some of the grown-ups of the village volunteered to go along—not that they needed the protection. Abeni's eyes went to the knife at Sowoke's waist, a gift from a local blacksmith. The girl was good with it—surprisingly good. Knives like this were being made for the others. Abeni suspected that all the children who had been monsters would show uncanny skill in handling them—as if their hands carried memories their minds sought to forget. Their ordeal hadn't just left them with scars. She honestly didn't know if that was a good or bad thing.

"You're really doing this?" Sowoke asked. "Heading off someplace west?"

Abeni nodded. She had told them what she'd gotten out of Brima. Well, partly. She told them the miserable man had given some vague directions. She left out the Witch Priest hunting them. That was too much for anyone.

"It's not much to go on," she admitted. "But I set out to find everyone stolen from our village. I'm glad I found so many of you. Some of our friends are still out there though. Our families are still out there. I'm going to bring them back."

Sowoke shook her head, muttering indignantly, "Going after storm women and ghost ships. Someplace west." She turned to Fomi. "Will you talk some sense to her? Maybe you can do better than me. I have to go make sure Adwe and Danwe are telling the blacksmith to stick to knives, and not having swords made that none of us can lift. Boys can be silly."

Fomi, who had stood by quietly, watched Sowoke stalk off. She turned back to Abeni. The two looked at each other for a long while, then burst out laughing.

"I think she's herself again!" Abeni said. "How long can you stand that?"

Fomi snorted. "Sowoke is going to be Sowoke. But she means well. If she gets too bad, I can still find some itching root to set her right!"

"Or fish guts!" Abeni added.

They laughed again and for a moment it felt like old times— like the day of Harvest Festival. So much had happened between then. The laughter stopped and a quiet descended. The two stared at each other awkwardly for a moment. Abeni could hardly believe it. When had they ever not known what to say to each other?

Before she could make her mouth work, Fomi took her hand. "I'm not going to ask you to come with us." She released a long breath. "I know that once you have your mind set, no one's changing it."

Abeni squeezed her hand in thanks. "I wish you could come with me," she said.

Fomi shook her head. "I'll stick to fishing, thanks."

"But you hate fishing!"

Fomi made a face. "I do. And cleaning them! Blech! But I miss home more."

Home, Abeni thought. That was why she knew she couldn't go with them. Not after what Brima said. If the Witch Priest was hunting them, she wasn't going to draw him to her village—not a second time. She pulled her friend into a fierce hug. "I'm going to miss you—again. But at least I'll know you're safe."

"Go have your adventures," Fomi whispered. "Find our families if you can. But you come back to us, Abeni. You make sure you come back home!"

Abeni nodded, hoping it was a promise she could keep. They hugged for a long time. When they finally broke apart, it was with lots of sniffles and wiping tears from cheeks. After Fomi left, she was still filling the magic bag when Damju's mother appeared.

"I wanted to wish you a safe journey," the woman said in greeting.

Abeni nodded her thanks, not saying much more.

"You will be happy to know we're going to refill the pit," Damju's mother told her. "We want to bury all memory of what happened there, even the bright stones."

"But you won't bury the memory of what Songu did," Abeni snapped, unable to help herself. She'd managed to get the villagers to find an empty house for him. But none of them visited him. It was like they were trying to pretend he wasn't there.

Damju's mother looked stung, and Abeni blushed with embarrassment.

"I'm sorry, auntie. That was rude."

"I've seen the kindness you offer him," the woman said. "It made me remember who he was before. I've talked to others, trying to get them to see. But they're afraid. And still hurt. I might persuade them to let him stay, but I can't promise more."

Abeni frowned at that. She was thankful, but what would happen to Songu if he stayed? Would this be his life—ignored by everyone, forced to live as an outcast? Hadn't he suffered enough? She wondered if this was what they had done to Brima. What if

Songu grew angry and twisted the same way, and became a monster like him? No. She wouldn't let that happen. In fact, she'd already come up with a plan.

"Come with me, please," she said. Dropping her things, she walked across the village to the house where they'd left Songu. A few eyes turned to watch them, but looked away at seeing their destination. The boy was already outside, sitting with his head on his knees. When she reached him, he stared up blankly. Restoring his spirit had not brought back his voice. That wound was deeper. She knelt to talk to him.

"You don't have to stay here," she said. "I know what it's like to be alone. You don't want that. I've talked to my friends—Fomi and Sowoke. They'll take you with them. You can live in my old village. It's in a forest. I think you'd like it."

His gaze followed her gesture to where Sowoke, Fomi, and the other children of her village were gathered. He stared at them for a long while, then shook his head.

Abeni sighed. "So, you want to stay?"

His eyes wandered from her to the village, as if he was looking at something that was no longer familiar. He shook his head a second time.

Abeni frowned. "I don't understand what—"

His gaze lifted until it met hers—and did not look away.

"Oh," she whispered, and understood.

When she walked back to finish packing, the others were waiting.

"What was that about?" Zaneeya asked, raising an eyebrow.

"Songu wants to come with us," Abeni answered. "I told him it would be dangerous, but I don't think he cares. So, I said yes." She braced for a challenge. But the panther girl only rolled her eyes.

"Surprised it took you that long," she murmured. "We'll soon have a caravan."

"I like him," Nyomi put in. "He's a good listener. Never once interrupts a story."

Abeni opened her mouth to remind the porcupine girl that

the boy didn't talk, but decided against it. Instead, she turned to Asha, who sat engrossed in wriggling her toes. The girl looked up and beamed. "Songu!" she exclaimed, throwing her arms up happily. Abeni supposed that was an endorsement.

It was late morning when they finally set out. Abeni hugged all of her friends. Saying goodbye to Fomi was the hardest, and both their faces were wet again by the end. She hadn't expected the same from Sowoke, who shifted between fussing at her like a big sister and sobbing, telling her to be safe. The entire village of Kono showed up to see them go. Abeni scanned the crowd as she said her farewells, searching for Songu. For a moment, she thought the boy wasn't coming. Then he appeared, walking right up to her. She put a hand on his shoulder and smiled.

"Songu!" Both turned to find Damju rushing in their direction, her mother leading. She carried something clutched to her chest. The girl had given Abeni endless pouches of herbs and powders, with meticulous instructions on how to use each. But this looked different. Reaching them, she held it out—a small flute of dark wood, covered in intricate designs. "You used to play this. I thought you might want it again."

The boy looked to the flute blankly. Then something in his eyes came alive in recognition. Taking the instrument, he held it in his hand, running his fingers across its length as if conjuring up a lost memory. Slowly, he placed it to his lips and blew. The first sound was weak, almost timid. But it grew clear as he became more certain.

Abeni's eyebrows rose at the music that came from the flute. It was slow and sorrowful, but beautiful in its own way. The whole village stopped to listen, going quiet. When he finished, Songu took the instrument from his lips and looked at it in surprise. Then, gazing at Abeni, he did something she hadn't seen him do before—he smiled.

"I told you he was good," Damju said. She flung her arms around him in a tight hug. "Take care, Songu! All of you take care."

They all hugged Damju in turn before walking for the last

time past the stone walls of the village. Abeni kept looking back at all those familiar faces she was leaving behind, until she couldn't see them anymore. They strode out into the valley they'd first entered—what now seemed ages ago—and after a long while came to a stop.

"Does anyone know where we're going?" Zaneeya questioned.

Everyone looked to Asha. The small girl had gone to her knees and was examining something closely. It was a bright green shoot of grass that peeked up from the dry ground. Abeni knelt down with her.

"Asha, what does this mean?"

The girl smiled. "My sister. She's returning."

"It's very small," Nyomi commented, her black eyes squinting.

Asha nodded. "Yes. She will need help." Wriggling fingers into the cracked earth, the small spirit closed her eyes, inhaling deeply before sounding a low hum. It echoed through the valley, and the very air seemed to vibrate. As they watched, bits of green pushed up from once lifeless soil. Fresh vines sprouted flowers that opened into a multitude of colors. Leaves sprang up on the branches of shrunken trees. When Asha finished, she opened her eyes to look out on what she had made. It was not the only change.

"Asha!" Abeni exclaimed. As the girl worked her magic, her locs had undergone their own transformation, slowly turning from black to ivory—like the old woman's. "Are you alright?"

The little girl nodded. "My sister needed my magic. She'll be better now."

Abeni stroked the white tendrils. "Did you have to give so much?"

"Yes. I told you, my sister is very, very big." She stood up, extending her arms wide. Abeni stood with her and looked out. New life showed everywhere between the dried brown stalks as far as she could see. It would take some time for everything to be green again. But the valley *was* coming back to life. Then, taking in the small girl's wide arms, she looked again. *Really* looked. And when she saw it, she gasped. The valley had a form to it. The way it rose and fell and was shaped: when you looked just right it looked like a woman who lay on her side—curled up around the small village of Kono. Along a rocky ridge, Abeni traced a wide hip. Turning where she stood in a circle, she followed a long torso and up to a shoulder, where the outline of a round earthen face was nestled. Fresh shoots of grass covered closed eyelids and bold lips that pressed together in a faint smile. It was breathtaking!

"Can you talk to her?" Abeni asked, gawking at the enormous spirit.

"A little," Asha said. "Only she's still very weak. Even with my magic, it will be a while before she's strong again. She says she's sorry, but she can't take care of us. Not like she is now." Her small face turned grave. "She warns that my brother will be coming for me."

Zaneeya growled, and Nyomi whimpered. Asha had kept her word about no longer holding secrets. She'd told the two everything—who she was and why the Witch Priest hunted her. Both had listened in awe. Zaneeya asked repeatedly if Asha was certain, unable to believe the Witch Priest was a spirit and not a wicked mortal. Nyomi had Asha tell it not once but three times. Even though she squeaked in fright, it was too good a story to pass up.

"What do we do, then?" Abeni asked.

"My sister says there are spirits who are fighting him," Asha said. "Not as old as us, but strong. We have to go to them. They can protect us." She paused. "But they're far away."

Abeni sighed. Of course they were. She turned it over in her head. The choice seemed obvious. "Asha has to get to these other spirits before the Witch Priest finds her," she told the others. "I'm her guardian. So, I'm going to get her there. I'm also thinking theses spirits might be able to help me find my family. It'll probably be dangerous. Who am I kidding? Of course, it'll be dangerous. If you don't want to come, I understand. You have your own families to find. I only ask that you take Songu. Get him to another mortal village where—"

She was cut off as the boy walked up and grabbed Asha's hand, his face defiant.

"Songu," Abeni said. "You don't know the danger we—"

He shook his head, touching his chest and pointing at her. She sighed. He had said he would come with her. He wasn't going to be left behind. Besides, he had his own reasons for finding the ghost ships.

"I suppose I should go along as well," Zaneeya remarked.

That caught Abeni by surprise. "But what about finding your sisters? Your mother? Have you given up on that?"

"No more than you've given up on finding the rest of your friends, or these ghost ships," the panther girl said. She gave Asha a meaningful look. "I meant what I spoke before of spirits keeping the balance of the world. This Witch Priest works to upset that. I'm not letting him claim this little spirit for his plans." Her face broke into a crooked grin. "Besides, who'll pull the lot of you out of any trouble?"

"I don't want to be by myself again!" Nyomi blurted. "It's scary out there!"

"Nyomi," Abeni said gently. "With the Witch Priest after us, it may be scarier."

The porcupine girl shivered but said: "Better to be scared together than alone."

Zaneeya rolled her eyes. But Abeni smiled. Nyomi was right. Whatever they were going to face, she'd rather have her friends there. The new friends she'd made along the way. She turned to Asha, who pointed, of all places, someplace west. The little girl sped off, pulling Songu along. Abeni followed with the others. As they took their first steps on this new journey, she began to sing her song, knowing that it was not quite finished yet.

ACKNOWLEDGMENTS

Abeni's Song is the story I've been wanting to write my entire life. And it wouldn't have been possible without the inspiration, help, and guidance of so many people. I'd like to thank everyone who read this story in its earliest phases and provided feedback—from friends and family to Fizzgig to my old writing group in Washington, DC. Please know that *all* of your suggestions and input helped make this book better!

Thank you to my agent, Seth Fishman, who encouraged me to pick up this story after I'd set it aside. You saw the worth in this! To my editor at Starscape, Ali Fisher, thanks for all the notes and brainstorming talks that helped shape and revise this book. Your input was invaluable! Much thanks to the entire team at Tor, including Dianna Vega, Lesley Worrell, Rafal Gibek, Jessica Katz, and Jim Kapp—you all worked hard to get this over the finish line. To my publicist, Saraciea Fennell, and to Anthony Parisi in marketing, thank you for helping me get word of this book out there. Y'all are the best! Angus Johnson, you've been copy editing my stuff at Tor since way back, and you are a wizard at your craft! A special shout-out to Suyi Davies Okungbowa, who is not only an amazingly talented writer but was gracious enough to give me some language lessons. And much props goes to artist Michael Machira Mwangi, for that beautiful cover—you helped bring Abeni and her world to life!

Thanks to my mom, who took my sister and me to the library every week when we were younger, allowing us to get lost in Narnia, tesseract with Meg, and travel Earthsea. Thanks to all those librarians for making those spaces brim with magic. Yaay librarians! I especially want to big-up all the storytellers in my life who taught me how to spin a good yarn and keep my audience riveted. And, of course, thanks to my wonderful partner, best friend, and wife, Danielle, for all the encouragement and love.

Last, to all of you who are reading this book, thank you for taking the time to journey with me and Abeni into this world. I hope you enjoyed it and are ready for more!